SUCCUBUS takes
MANHATTAN

D0711914

Also by Nina Harper

SUCCUBUS IN THE CITY

Books published by The Random House Publishing Group
are available at quantity discounts on bulk purchases for
premium, educational, fund-raising, and special sales use.
For details, please call 1-800-733-3000.

SUCCUBUS
takes
MANHATTAN

NINA HARPER

BALLANTINE BOOKS • NEW YORK

A Del Rey Books Mass Market Original

Copyright © 2008 by Bill Fawcett & Associates

Published in the United States by Del Rey Books, an imprint of The Random House Publishing Group, a division of Random House, Inc., New York.

DEL REY is a registered trademark and the Del Rey colophon is a trademark of Random House, Inc.

ISBN 978-0-345-49507-5

Printed in the United States of America

www.delreybooks.com

OPM   9   8   7   6   5   4   3   2   1

For MRF, on the occasion of (soon to be) ten years

Acknowledgments

No writer manages to create a book alone. Many wonderful people have helped me with their knowledge and concern, their support and their unstinting advice—this book never could have been written without them!

Thanks are due to Sheeri Cabral for making an introduction, Cecilia Tan, Vandana Singh, and Sarah Smith for writer geeking on the finer points, and Karen Marcovici for shelter and research assistance.

A very special thank you to Aaron Macks for Akkadian. I have never met Aaron except by e-mail, and he has answered endless questions very quickly with amazing patience. Any mistakes are clearly my own.

chapter
ONE

Venice is my favorite city to visit in the world. I love living in New York, but when I've been scared and hurt and need to hide and heal, Venice is where I want to go. The constant presence of the water calms me, and many of my happiest memories were made here. After the second love of my life dumped me unceremoniously on a Sunday morning, my best girlfriends bought me a first-class ticket to Venice.

Even better, they called my boss and arranged a week off, even though I had only recently returned from a long weekend in Aruba. Fortunately, I had been on top of things at work, where I am the accessories editor at a fashion magazine.

No, not *that* magazine. I am the accessories editor for *Trend*, a magazine that real women all over the world rely on to find clothes and looks that those of us who are not Paris Hilton can afford and wear. But I had already put together my Accessories pages for the next two months. I had my special feature on shawls in with a writer and at the fashion houses who would provide samples so I could take the week off and not worry about deadlines.

I was looking in the window of a jewelry shop on the Rialto Bridge when my Treo rang. It was the middle of the night in Venice, but it was late afternoon in New York. Fortunately, the shops on the Rialto are open late and hordes of tourists keep the narrow streets around the great stone bridge vibrant and safe.

The caller was Danielle, the shoe editor at work. "Lily, when are you coming back?" she wailed.

"What's the problem?" I asked. Danielle is my best friend at work, and since she does shoes and I do accessories, we're natural allies. She's French and has great respect for the brokenhearted, and she strongly encouraged me to leave New York and try to find some pleasure elsewhere in the world.

"Lawrence Carroll is making me crazy," she sobbed. "You must talk to him. He is insane. Please, Lily, I tell myself over and over that I must not kill him, that I look dreadful in orange and a jumpsuit wouldn't suit me at all."

"What's the problem, Danielle? What specific nutcase thing has he done this time?" I had to keep her focused on the single event or else I would never get to the bottom of this. And much as I did not want to talk to Lawrence Carroll, or remember his existence, I owed Danielle in a major way for covering for me.

"He is arranging a feature on the white shirt for fall, the one that he has talked about ever since he arrived," she said, half sobbing. I knew the feature. We all knew in great detail far more than we ever wanted to know about Lawrence Carroll and white shirts for fall. "He is crazy," Danielle whispered. "He has taken every belt in the building and laid them all out across the corridors and he's screaming the whole time. And no one can walk anywhere. If we try to pick up a belt he screams to put it down and that no one can touch any of them and that they're all ugly and that it's all our fault that he can't find the belts he wants. I think Mary Elizabeth will push him out the window soon. I wish to assist her."

"Can you put him on?" I asked.

"I do not know," Danielle whispered. "He is insane. He may stab me, I think. I suggested a very nice pair of Donna Karan boots and he waved a letter opener in my face and said I was his enemy. Because I am French and he is British and we never stopped fighting over Agincourt and he doesn't know if he hates us or Americans more. The interns have locked themselves in the ladies' room, including Robbie. If you cannot talk to him we will have to call the police and have the hostage rescue team come in."

I thought that might be overstating the case, but maybe not. Lawrence Carroll came to us from *that* magazine's London office, and prima donna didn't even begin to describe him. Which was weird, because his old colleagues in London said he was a great guy, easy to work with, and supportive of the team. Maybe they'd just wanted to be rid of him.

"Okay, I'll do what I can. Is he in his office?" I asked.

"Yes. Oh, thank you, Lily, you are the only one he will listen to. Especially about the belts. Once we have chosen the belts, then he will understand the shoes. He will agree. The interns will unlock the toilet and the rest of us will be able to pee."

Being French, Danielle has no inhibitions talking about bodily functions. This often upsets the interns even more than a fashion editor going slightly psychotic, but I was used to it.

"I'll try to talk to him, Danielle. Just give me a minute, okay?"

I was standing on a bridge leaning on a wide marble ledge, no longer occupied by the display of delicate gold earrings. I took the stairs down to the street and chose one of the several bars because I really wanted to sit down. My very elegant pink D&G stilettos looked wonderful but my toes felt like they were on fire and the rest of my feet were identifying with the Christian saints. The ones who are regularly shown with implements of excruciating martyrdom. If I am ever depicted with the instrument of my torment, it will be a gloriously beautiful designer shoe with a four-and-a-half-inch heel and narrow straps.

My feet were ready to go on strike, I was on vacation, and now I had to talk to a drama queen fashion editor having a hissy fit. I needed a drink as well as a chair and a quiet corner.

I sat, ordered Campari and soda and an ice cream before I hit the address book in the Treo. It was barely after lunch in New York. I waited for my drink and eased my feet out of my shoes gently, not taking them off entirely but lifting just a bit so that the pressure of the straps eased.

The phone rang in New York while an attractive waiter in an ankle-length apron served my drink with a flourish. "Hello?" Lawrence said, his voice full of suspicion.

"Hello, Lawrence," I said as cheerfully as I could manage. "Danielle told me there was some issue about belts for the white shirt shoot."

"Issue? There's no issue, there's bloody world war three going on in here! I cannot find One. Single. Belt. That gives the right look, the right message. And you are on the other side of the pond and doing no fucking good to anyone."

I sighed. "Of course, Lawrence. You had talked to me about the feature before I left, and I pulled the belts for it. There are a few nice pieces by Coach and a Kate Spade that will be just right for jeans, and a darling Kenzo for the edgier look. They're all in my office in a box labeled Lawrence on the top shelf over my computer."

"How did you know what I wanted?" Lawrence asked, paranoia dripping through all five thousand miles of the connection.

"You told me when we first discussed the feature in February," I reminded him. "So I pulled the belts then."

"Why did you do that?" Lawrence asked.

"Because that is my job," I said slowly, enunciating every word.

There was a pause that might have been transmission or might have been Lawrence's brain engaging. "I am going now to look for this box. I'll look in it. If there's a problem I'll call you, and I expect there to be a problem. There is not one single bloody belt in this entire benighted country that will make the statement I want."

I caught the waiter's eye and pointed to my nearly empty glass. I was definitely going to need more alcohol to get through a Lawrence debacle. "Go and look. And if you see things you like, call me back, right away, okay? Because it's the middle of the night here and I'm going to go to sleep soon."

He hung up without a good-bye. I called Danielle and told her the potentially good news. She had some reservations but reported Lawrence walking down the hall and entering my office. No explosion followed.

* * *

If I could deliver Lawrence I would. It would be a blessing to all of New York and probably London as well, though his old office said he was a great guy. Best guess is that they lied. And I wouldn't even mind covering up the consequences; unlike my coworkers, I know how to clean a crime scene and I would have no guilt whatsoever in making sure Lawrence arrived on Satan's doorstep ASAP.

Except he was the only kind of man I couldn't seduce and eliminate. Lawrence was gay.

I truly regretted that incubi and succubi do not get along. The split had been old when I'd been recruited. Anyone reasonable would think that we'd have a lot in common and would benefit in sharing. I certainly thought so, and I wasn't the only succubus who held that opinion. And if there were a number of succubi who agreed, there would have to be incubi on the other side who thought that an alliance would be better than current hostilities. Because if I could talk to an incubus then Lawrence would get what he so deeply deserves, and sooner rather than later. I'd so completely vote for sooner.

I sipped my second drink and contemplated a post to MagicMirror about incubi and succubi. The more I thought about it, the better the idea seemed.

The Treo cut short my rumination. It was Lawrence, sounding suspicious. "The belts were there. You're right, they are the ones I want. Especially the Kate Spade. But you should know I don't trust you, Lily. No one should be able to pick out just what I want before I've even seen them. Are you sure you're really American? No one in this atrocious excuse for a country has any sense of style."

"I'm glad you like my selections, Lawrence. Always a pleasure." And I hung up.

Danielle text messaged a discreet thank-you and I acknowledged and turned the Treo off before I threw it back into my bag.

The second drink made me mellow. I wondered if anyone had posted anything interesting on MagicMirror while I'd been away. I couldn't access the demon blog from any computer but my own, or one set up for the Underworld. I no longer had the contacts in Venice, and while I could have made some I was here to get away. Away from my real life and especially away from Nathan.

The first love of my life, Niccolo, had been found floating under one of the ubiquitous arched bridges right here in Venice. He had been murdered and no one had ever found out why. Maybe it was an opera rivalry, or maybe politics involving his patron, the Count. Though that had happened back in 1727, it felt very new.

I had not fallen in love again until last month, when I'd met Nathan Coleman. He had black hair and brilliant blue eyes and a love of ancient history. After almost three hundred years I had begun to trust a man, enjoy his company.

I thought things were good between us. Things had been good between us—until Nathan dumped me. Because I am a succubus. Because I showed him Hell to prove it, introduced him to Mephistopheles and Satan and showed him the souls in torment. He loved me, I was certain of that, but he'd freaked. He couldn't handle my immortality, and he couldn't handle the fact that I damn men to Hell for eternity.

I couldn't entirely blame him.

Still, in three thousand years I had only fallen in love twice.

I wasn't enjoying the café anymore, so I paid my bill and walked back to my hotel. My feet had rested enough not to protest the heels and the straps. Looking beautiful had again trumped comfort, and it wasn't that far to Apostoli.

My hotel, the Giorgione, didn't have the opulence or levels of service I used to enjoy at the Danieli, but it was quiet and the staff were genuinely hospitable and warm. My room was quite pleasant in the overdecorated and ridiculously gilded manner of the city. The double bed, covered in green brocade, ruled in splendor behind two golden twisted pillars. I felt sorry for myself again, seeing that bed and knowing that no one would share it with me. I did not want to bring back prey, not to my temporary little lair. No, I wanted Nathan.

For all that he'd left me and run, I missed him. I wanted him. And I was furious at him for not being able to accept the realities of my life. I'd accepted them for three thousand years. The least he could do was make an effort.

The anger at Lawrence merged with fury at Nathan's betrayal and I sat enthroned in the center of my green brocade bed and seethed.

Which was not a very satisfying activity.

I was too awake to go to sleep and too angry to do anything fun or useful. I'd already hunted once and wasn't up for going out again. So I pulled on my Citizen jeans and my extralarge No Rest for the Wicked tee shirt and went down to the hotel computer room. It was late enough that the computer was free and no one was play-

ing pool or cards. I signed in to Worlds of Warcraft and
blew things up for a few hours, which made me feel
much better. By the time the sun rose I was ready to call
it a night.

When I woke up in Venice, I had not been able to forget history (my own and its own) and misery (all mine),
and so the only reasonable thing was to go shopping.

Shopping in Venice is as picturesque and inconvenient
as anything else in this city, with no wheeled vehicles
and hundreds of bridges, all with steps. It isn't easy to
get a water taxi. They don't cruise like taxis in New
York. Gondolas, which had once been used for actual
transportation, are now tourist commodities. The gon-
doliers all have their regular routes and little chats like
the people who drive horse-drawn carriages around
Central Park. They won't take you to, say, Barneys.

Down in the shopping district around San Marco I
bought two Prada jackets, several pairs of Versace slacks
that hadn't shown up in New York, and a pile of
Valentino shoes, blouses and skirts. I hauled the packages down to the vaporetto stand and took the Number
One public boat up the Grand Canal.

On the boat I saw a face that I was certain I'd seen in
Versace, or maybe outside La Perla. Not a particularly
remarkable man, not a face I would have noticed except
that he bore a strong resemblance to Vincent, my doorman back home. The Number One is the most used vaporetto in the city, I told myself. It is big, a water bus
with multiple stops. Probably just a coincidence. But I
nervously shredded the ribbon handle of the shopping
bag all the same.

It was not far to Ca' d'Oro, just behind the second

bend in the canal. Ca' d'Oro is one of the most beautiful of the Grand Canal palaces, smaller than some but decorated in the vaguely Eastern and very ornate style that has become the hallmark of Venetian design.

I got off the boat as quickly as possible and walked across the Campo Apostoli to my hotel. If he followed me I should be able to spot him in the open square, but I wanted a running start. Apostoli is open but there is a café, a restaurant, and a church, to say nothing of the tobacco shop on the corner. Plenty of places to hide. I cut through the restaurant tables set out on the cobblestones with their green and white checked cloths and walked close to the building until I hit the gelateria half a block up. Not the best gelateria in Venice, but I could duck inside rather than buy my ice cream from the window. As I ordered and the strawberry ice cream was scooped into a cone, I watched out the large glass door.

He was there, casually perusing the menu at the restaurant where I had tried to disappear. I pressed my back against the wall, trying to watch him while he couldn't see me. The server had to call me twice to get my ice cream, and I took the cone and resumed my post inside the door.

This could have just been his stop, I thought. He could just be hungry. But when he looked around the square, took a few minutes to read the café menu (which was very short) and then crossed the campo to inspect scarves set out on a rack in front of a shop, I couldn't believe it was coincidence.

"Is there a problem, miss?" the petite woman behind the counter asked in Venetian dialect.

I wanted to say no, but I couldn't manage to speak until I'd taken a few deep breaths. "I think that man followed me when I got off the vaporetto," I said in the same dialect. When Admin changed my identity and gave me American English they had not removed my Italian. I speak it fluently and the Venetian dialect also, which is not really Italian and is unintelligible to anyone not raised Venetian.

The woman came out from behind the counter and looked where I was pointing. She snorted. "Here," she said, and showed me out the back of the shop into an alley. I circled from the opposite direction and entered the hotel from the side entrance instead of the front. If the man waited for me to emerge in the square he was going to wait a long time, but that didn't stop my heart from pounding.

I threw the new bags into the closet and they landed on top of several other shopping bags with elite logos. All I had done for days was hunt and shop and be angry. And when I was angry I hunted and made random men pay for my heartbreak. Which, in my opinion, was perfectly reasonable.

Now I was afraid and confused. How could anyone know I was in Venice? Who would possibly know I was here? They couldn't have followed me, not the men who had hunted us back in Brooklyn. Only my closest friends knew where I was.

I thought about changing my clothes, going out and hunting down the man who had followed me. Hunting him and delivering his soul to Satan. The part of me that was furious with Nathan, the part of me that had been hurt and frightened so many times by the Knight Defenders, who had tried to eliminate all the demons in New York, was all for it. But I didn't really want to hunt. I didn't want to get that close, that intimate, with an enemy who was trying to destroy me.

I waited, tense, for a call from the hotel desk. I expected my shadow to come looking for me, but after an hour and a half the call never came. Maybe he hadn't known where I was staying. The hotel is discreet and down several blocks from the campo; you would have to know it was there. Perhaps he didn't know.

Perhaps I was just overwrought and stressed, and still too miserable about my breakup with Nathan to make much sense. Maybe the man just had been some random person who'd gotten off the boat, maybe he had been lingering because he was meeting someone in Apostoli. Maybe the events of the past month had made me more paranoid than reasonable.

I took a hot bath to calm down, then dressed in new Italian clothes. I pulled my auburn hair into a tight chignon, so if anyone happened to be looking for a Titian-tressed succubus, they wouldn't notice me. I looked perfectly and properly Venetian. It was a little late for dinner, but there would be places open. And I was certain that this time I wasn't followed.

Still, it was time for me to go home.

chapter
TWO

I arrived home at seven in the evening, after a reasonable flight and a horrific cab ride that included all of the Long Island rush hour. Vincent, my doorman, welcomed me with a flourish and took immediate charge of my bags. Home. I was tired and jet lagged, though the time disassociation hadn't really caught up with me yet. It was just very late and I wanted to take a hot bath and go to bed.

They had fed us very well in first class on Lufthansa. I had drunk my way across the ocean: excellent wines, vodka served with the caviar, and ice wine with dessert. I had indulged in all of it, along with a salmon dinner almost good enough to be served in a restaurant. I remember when travel, even for the wealthy, had been arduous. When the only way to get from one place to another had been a horse or a cart or carriage and even the best inns had assumed shared beds, to say nothing of shared facilities.

I staggered into my apartment, Vincent behind me with my bags. All I wanted to do was kick off my shoes and figure out whether I was awake enough for a hot bath before bed.

What I got was Mephistopheles.

He was wearing a bespoke Savile Row suit in conservative charcoal and was sitting in my Eames chair reading *Bon Appétit* magazine. Not that he cooks, but it was their yearly restaurant issue.

"Listen to this," he enthused as I collapsed on the sofa. " 'The chef has combined a deft hand with the traditional preparations of Provence and the ingredients of their own organic farm in upstate New York, and has an imagination rarely found.' I must go there."

"Meph, if you've come here to read me restaurant reviews, I'm going to scream," I said wearily. Meph might be my friend and Satan's first lieutenant, but he had never shown up in my living room before. Usually we scheduled an appointment and he had made reservations at one of his favorite restaurants. And since Meph was a gourmet of the first order, his picks were worth whatever he wanted from me. Which, truth to tell, was rarely anything more than the current buzz about a newer, trendier restaurant or an idea for a birthday present for Satan.

His showing up in my apartment like this was unprecedented, and I was worried.

"I'm just this minute back from Europe and I have work tomorrow and you didn't even call. Or leave e-mail. I checked my e-mail and my voice mail on the Treo in the cab. There was plenty of time."

Meph looks like a CEO, which in some ways is precisely what he is. The CEO of Hell. Satan is the sole stockholder, but Meph runs most of the daily operation. "Telephones and e-mail are not secure," he said. "I've placed a silence on this apartment for the time we are both here, but it will dissolve when I leave. I don't want to leave any possible trail."

My eyes got wide. This was bigger than I had anticipated. "Okay," I said. "But maybe I should have some coffee. I'm horribly jet-lagged."

"Of course," he said. And waved his hand and an extralarge Kenyan appeared in my hand, steaming with just the right amount of sugar and hot milk, with a sprinkle of nutmeg on the top. Meph is a class act all the way.

"You remember the slight problem you had with some fanatics recently? I believe they called themselves the Knight Defenders?" he asked.

I nodded. I wouldn't have called it a slight problem. They had pursued me and my friends, tried to kill us, and, for all I knew, had followed me to Venice.

"They haven't managed to resolve their leadership issue and regroup, have they?" I asked, worried. They had made my life pretty unpleasant for the past few months. They were also the reason I'd met Nathan. He'd been trying to hunt down their leader, who had happened to have my name and contact info in his files.

"I do not know," Meph told me. "That is not the question at the moment. As I recall, you were concerned that they were getting their information from a source inside Hell."

"That was one possibility we thought about," I agreed, and then took a long sip of my coffee. "But we couldn't think anyone could be disloyal to Satan."

"You are too loyal yourself, Lily," he said. "Certainly that is possible. But I remember at the time you were also concerned that it might be some junior demon who was trying to get Satan's attention or eliminate you in order to move up. Now, I have no reason to suspect anyone, but it has come to my attention it might be me someone wishes to replace."

I took a sharp breath and drank some more coffee. "Tell me more," I said. "I'm tired, and I might not be up to speed right now, but I want to know what's going on."

He got up and looked out my window. "There is one other thing," he added. He hesitated. "Please do not tell Satan I've been here, or that I've talked about this. I don't want to upset Her."

That was an understatement. No one wanted to upset Satan. Even Upstairs they tried to avoid it. A grumpy Satan could make lots of lives amazingly unpleasant. I'd seen Her in a bad mood a few times in my very long demonic existence and I'd have to say, although She is my dear friend and my close mentor, that even I avoid Her at those times. If She can terrify Her own Chosen, I didn't want to think about what She could do to the rest of the world.

On the other hand, I was loyal, first and always, to Satan. If Mephistopheles was going to tell me something in confidence that could hurt Her, or that I thought She needed to know, I would violate his confidence in a heartbeat.

"I can't promise unless I know what this is about," I said carefully. "I'm one of Her Chosen, and if I think there is something She needs to know, I will tell Her."

Mephistopheles blinked. "Of course. I can talk to you, I chose to talk to you, because I trust your loyalty absolutely, Lily. The problem is, outside of you and a few of Her other Chosen, I can't trust anyone. But I don't want to go to Satan immediately with simple gossip—I could risk hurting a loyal demon. And truthfully, I need your help. Is there any way you can talk to Marduk? You are Babylonian, after all, and I thought he had some fondness for you. Which would be quite silly, given that there are much better reasons than your long-gone nationality to find you an excellent companion and pillar of Hell."

I wanted to roll my eyes. Meph sometimes took it over the top, but then he was a gentleman of the old school. The very old school.

"I can probably get in to see him," I offered. "What do you need? Can it be something casual, like at a party? Or do you need me to actually go to him and have a formal conversation?"

"Oh, informal would be much better," Mephistopheles said immediately. "I just want you to sound him out a bit."

"About what?" I hated being blunt, but I wasn't ready to commit myself until I knew what this was all about.

"Really, I would like to know what he says to you, if he's trying to sound you out," Meph answered.

"You think he might be plotting something?"

Mephistopheles shrugged. "You know there has always been bad blood between us. A rivalry of sorts, though I never thought it was a problem. I just always thought he was more conservative and afraid of change. And that could be the truth; I would not want to harm his reputation if it's just Marduk trying to pretend we all live back in the time of the Roman Republic."

I giggled. "The Empire is more like him. Marduk really can't deal with democracy."

Meph actually smiled. "You're right. Make it under Tiberius. Tiberius was his kind of emperor. But don't start anything, Lily. What makes me suspicious of Marduk may only be a quirk of his own personality and he could be an ally."

"Or he could be an enemy," I said softly.

"No, not an enemy," Meph countered. "A rival. Maybe. But it could be someone else. Keep an open mind."

I nodded. "Will do."

"When can you see him?"

"I'll have to look at my calendar. I'm too tired right now and I don't have a clue as to what's up in the social life of Hell. I haven't been on MagicMirror for a week."

Mephistopheles shrugged. "Nothing interesting on my friends' list," he said firmly.

Fortunately, I knew him well enough to realize he meant that no one had posted any foodporn. At least not from any restaurant he had yet to try.

"Give me a few days and I'll find something," I promised, yawning. "But I'm not worth much now and I'm fading fast. The coffee helped but . . ."

"Of course," Mephistopheles said. Then he took my hand and kissed it with a flourish before he disappeared in a haze of sulfur stink that did not dissipate until I opened the window. In early March, which felt like January this cold winter.

I didn't care. At that point, nothing but sleep mattered. So I closed the door, left my bags and shoes in the middle of the floor, and shed Italian couture down the hallway to my bed.

I got up at a ridiculous hour the next morning, well before the sun or any of my friends or coworkers would be up. My body was still on Italian time. If I were the type, I would go to the gym for the six a.m. step class. I'm not that type.

I wanted to go back to sleep. I wasn't well rested, but I was definitely too wide awake to stay in bed.

Thank the military-industrial complex for the Internet. It's always open and I didn't have to bother getting dressed to get online and catch up on what my friends (and enemies, and those in between) have been doing.

MagicMirror, the demon version of MySpace, can only be accessed from a computer with credentials from Hell. Which means it remains secure from prying human eyes.

Gloriana had written a long screed about how she found human cursing demeaning to demons. Normally I would have just scrolled by but I did find it funny that she was so upset humans considered "damn you" and "go to Hell" to be nasty. After all, for them it is. For demons, that kind of language was meaningless. "Go to Hell" came out sounding like "Go to California," only personally I way preferred Hell. More interesting people, no cars, no pollution.

Okay, the real problem with California for me is—this was very hard to admit. I am not one of those Luddite demons who couldn't use e-mail and even hate the telephone. I knew demons who didn't have a microwave or a DVD player because they couldn't figure out how to use them. I had a dishwasher and a microwave and a computer and a DVD set up and was very seriously thinking about TiVo. But I had never learned to drive a car.

I came to New York in 1893, and before that I lived in Paris. I'd never needed to drive and as a New Yorker part of my identity involved not having a driver's license. Like many Manhattanites, I have a nondriver's ID.

While I mused over the driving thing, I scrolled through

a number of posts on food and travel and problems with humans without paying attention. There had been so much traffic when I'd been gone that I didn't really have the time to read every entry carefully—or even not very carefully.

So I nearly missed Hatuman's invitation.

Hatuman is one of the old ones, and rarely uses the computer. Probably one of his minor minions had actually posted for him, but there it was, a private party at the Waldorf-Astoria next weekend.

I sighed. The Waldorf. Like they couldn't have found an older, stuffier venue. But then, the old-school demons preferred sedate, conservative places where the only dancing would be the waltz, and even that was a little new wave for them. Probably five hundred demons were invited, and I was going to just ignore the invitation until I thought again.

Hatuman was fairly friendly with Marduk, and this was an event where I could see the old Babylonian god socially. Being Babylonian myself, talking to Marduk casually at the party would only be good manners, required even. This was too good an opportunity to do exactly what Mephistopheles wanted me to do.

I just hated giving up a Saturday night for a boring party where no one would wear anything interesting and there wouldn't be any younger demons to flirt with me.

I studied the invitation again. Should I bring a date?

But there wasn't anyone I could bring. Nathan had dumped me. Nathan, who I bet would be brilliant in that crowd, was out of my life. He could talk to Marduk in his very strangely accented Akkadian and ask all kinds of personal and embarrassing questions and Marduk wouldn't even notice.

It was six thirty in the morning and my alarm wasn't due to go off for fifteen minutes and I was already furious. Though I did remind myself that my body thought it was just past noon and maybe I needed lunch, and I was tired in that dragging, too-awake way that was this century's special travel curse.

Maybe I could drag one of my girlfriends along.

I sent an e-mail to all of them, to Desire and Eros and Sybil, asking if anyone could manage to go to Hatuman's shindig with me. I hit Send with a sense of resignation. I certainly wouldn't want to go to Hatuman's party if I didn't need to talk to Marduk. I'd rather stay home and wash my hair.

And then the alarm rang, interrupting my self-pity session. I turned it off and put myself under the shower and resolved to start the day as if nothing had ever happened. As if I had just woken up out of a good restful sleep and looked forward to my day as an editor at one of America's most popular magazines.

Yeah, right. Go me.

chapter
THREE

The first morning back at work turned out to be wonderful. I walked into our office and people I barely knew stopped to thank me. The whole ambience reminded me of a movie premiere or a procession entering the Ishtar Gate and proceeding down the avenue, cheered by the people and showered with flowers by those lucky enough to get up on a roof.

I could almost hear people thinking "Hail, O Vanquisher of Lawrence Carroll." And there was the man himself, looking sour but grudgingly thanking me for saving his shoot, as he put it.

Danielle and two of the fashion editors treated me to lunch at Butter where we ordered two bottles of wine on top of cocktails and got completely drunk. But no one was going to challenge our productivity that afternoon, Danielle assured me. "If you had not appeased him, no one would have been able to work for days and we would have lost all the interns. They were so afraid, the little ones. And I cannot say that I blame them."

We giggled in the cab uptown, and then Danielle pulled me into her office. "What do you think of these?" she asked, showing me a selection of Jimmy Choo, Manolo Blahnik and Christian Louboutin boots. We both clucked over them all, and Danielle pointed out her favorites and showed me the ones she thought suited me.

"And the very best is that we can keep these," she whispered drunkenly. "After they are used in my articles, and in the fashion shoots, we do not need to return them the way we usually do. And these"—she swept her hand indicating four pairs of stilettos on her conference table—"these are your size. So I think that, in order to make room for the next collection, you must take them away."

At the end of the day I got even better news. I went to check my e-mail before I went home and all the girls said they had already been planning on Hatuman's party and had expected that I would be there. Everyone was going to be there. So it had been the perfect first day back when I got into the taxi to go home.

Vincent met me as he held the door for me. "Lily, Azoked is waiting in your apartment."

All the happiness of the past few hours dissolved instantly.

"Why did you let her in?" I cried.

"I got her Florentines and Ben & Jerry's because I thought you needed your reserves if you even had anything left after being away. Though it would serve her right to have it freezer burned," he said.

Spoken like a true demon, I thought. *And a true friend.*

There was no help for it. I couldn't make Azoked go away without seeing her. I tried to breathe deeply in the elevator. I counted to ten, and then fifty, as the elevator deposited me at my floor and I walked down the hallway to my door. Breathe. Deeply.

I had thwarted Lawrence Carroll. I had been Satan's

friend for several hundred years. I had survived Nathan Coleman dumping me. I could survive half an hour with a Bastform Akashic Librarian. Without committing murder. I hoped.

I opened the door to find Azoked sitting on my sofa with her feet up, eating Cherry Garcia out of the carton. Even I do not put my feet on the upholstery, at least not unless I was freshly washed. Then she put her used spoon on my coffee table and looked up.

"You are late," she said, as if I were her secretary and had arrived at work two hours late and hung over.

I refused to dignify her attitude with a reply. Instead, I made rather a show of saying nothing to her while I took off my shoes and unpacked my bag. I made certain to show off the new shoes that had been packed down with stacks of proof sheets.

She seemed to take no notice of my rudeness, but licked her whiskers and her fingers (which were surprisingly human looking, for her face mostly resembled a Siamese cat. A very large cat in a sky blue silk robe and glasses hanging from a matching macramé cord around her neck). Something about the steel gray coloring and the glasses made her appear the perfect blend of feline and strict head librarian. Not the nice librarian who suggested really good books and set aside the latest Janet Evanovich, but the nasty head of department who shushed you as soon as you even thought above a whisper.

"I thought the case of the Knight Defenders was on hold for the time being," I said. "Have they found a new leader so quickly?"

"They have not," Azoked answered, not looking up from her grooming. "But I have not come on Satan's business. I have come as your friend." Friend? Since when had Azoked ever been anything but a thorn in my side? For any of us? My actual friends, who had met her only briefly in Aruba, thought I must secretly belong Upstairs just for dealing with her.

She had been some use when we were being attacked, and even then it was hardly worth dealing with her. But—a friend? Not in this universe.

"Do you know who was following me in Venice?" I asked immediately. "Was it the Knight Defenders, or was it just some random thing?"

She shook her head. "I have seen nothing in the *Record* about the Knight Defenders. If you were followed, perhaps it was your succubus pheromones."

I didn't think so, but I remained silent. Azoked didn't have the one piece of information I cared about, at least that she could give me. She couldn't tell me anything about demonkind, and that was where Meph's enemy lay.

"I have some information that may be of use to you," she continued, as if she thought my behavior perfectly normal. "About your boyfriend. He is planning to come to Hatuman's party, it appears. How very odd indeed. I do not know whether he is searching for you, or if he has reasons of his own for attending."

I shook my head. "Impossible. He can't deal with me being a succubus. That's why he isn't my boyfriend anymore."

Azoked shrugged. "I only know what I read in the *Akashic*. I thought you would want to know, to be prepared."

"Thank you," I said. "Is that all?"

She licked her fingers delicately. "You could offer to

take me out to Balthazar. You could invite me to join your brunch at Public."

"Not even Satan joins our brunch," I told her. Which is true, but Satan would have been most welcome at any time. She was just too busy, especially on Sunday mornings, and we were thrilled on the very few occasions She could snatch a few minutes and grace us with Her company.

"Well, you could take me out to dinner tonight. I will accept that as a deposit on what you owe me for my assistance."

"I did not request your help," I said, pronouncing each word carefully. "I do not owe you. You have never shown any interest in being a social friend."

Her eyes narrowed and she hissed.

"Unless you can tell me who in Hell is gunning for Mephistopheles," I amended, knowing full well that she couldn't find any information on Hellspawn. The *Akashic Record* is the Book of Life. Immortals leave no traces in the Book, no resonance in the threads of Fate for a Librarian to trace. Only the living, the mortal, are recorded in the Book of Life.

And everything about them is recorded. What they think, what they consider, what they discard, as well as what they actually do. Which is why Librarians were so highly skilled. They didn't simply look up information—though I'd seen Azoked use Google.

"If I find this, you will include me in your brunches forever," she pronounced.

"Forget it," I told her. "It's a Hell matter anyway. No mortals involved anymore. Sorry."

She hissed again.

I shrugged.

"You will regret this," she shot at me before dematerializing in a haze of blue smoke, faintly scented with crumbling parchment and stale chalk.

Awful, awful, doubly awful. I wanted my friends. I definitely did not want to go to a party where Nathan would be present. How did Nathan get invited to Hatuman's anyway? I thought it was Hellspawn-only, no humans need apply. Even then, I was only going because Marduk would be there and I needed to talk to him for Meph.

Life felt pretty sucky just then, so I did what any reasonably smart, hip New York woman would do. I called my best friends.

chapter
FOUR

If I'd looked at my e-mail, I wouldn't have been so shocked. I could have prepared, could have decided on my story or whether or not I would pick up my phone. But I didn't look at the e-mail, figuring that there would be time while I puttered around my apartment and got dressed to meet Desi. So when the phone rang I thought it was Des running late, or at worst a telemarketer.

I didn't expect Nathan, not in a thousand years.

"Lily, I'm really sorry to disturb you," he started off.

"I thought you didn't want to talk to me anymore," I blurted out.

Silence hissed on the line.

"No, Lily. I think about you all the time. I wish we were still together. I keep trying to wrap my head around . . . what you showed me. I keep wondering if I could ignore it somehow, or maybe I'd get used to it. Or maybe it's not so bad. But that's not why I called."

"So you can't get around it," my voice must have sounded bleak. Maybe as bleak as his.

"I'm trying. But I called you about our old friend Craig Branford. Who has resurfaced as Richard Bowen, in Huntington, Long Island. Which is where he was from, if you'll remember," he started out.

"I don't know why you couldn't just send me this in

e-mail," I said softly. Just hearing his voice, so very close on the phone, brought back the stabbing misery I thought had abated.

"I did," he said, and his voice was tight. "But I think he's planning to move against you again, possibly very soon. Maybe as early as sometime this week, though I'm not sure."

"That's not much information," I told him. "How do you know? I thought that case was closed anyway. You weren't getting any money for it."

There was a moment where I could almost hear him deciding how much to tell me. There was something going on here, I was sure. Invisible threads woven around me, Nathan and Meph and this weirdo fanatic. I just couldn't figure it out.

"We've got another contract to trace his movements and contact the client if he does or says anything that would make us suspect that he is planning to move again. The client in this instance suggested that I call and warn you. I don't think he wants you involved."

"Who is this client?" It no longer sounded like a jealous wife.

Nathan shook his head. "I'm not at liberty to say. Just let me reiterate that this client does not want you involved."

"And you?" I asked, the words out of my mouth before I realized that I'd spoken.

"I . . . Lily, I've been trying to just get on with my life. I can't. I think about you all the time, and then I think about, well, you know, and I'm sliced up all over again. I didn't know whether I was thrilled to have a reason to call you again or whether I am just being stupid. I want to talk to you every day, and then that image comes back and . . . I'm confused."

"Thank you for warning me," I said coldly. "Do you have any more specific information as to what he might try this time? Or should I just be paranoid? And do you know anything about him or any of his minions traveling to Venice?"

Okay, I admit, I was being mean. But I was hurting too much to be more careful.

"Venice?" he asked. "I can look into it, but the records I have now don't show any European connections."

I heard him swallow on the line. "Look, I think he may be trying to find you. Especially watch out at Public, okay? He knows that place, knows that you and your friends have brunch there on Sundays. He might be planning something there. I don't know precisely what he's up to but he's getting information from some very good source, because he was talking about you dating some Dutch guy, and he's interested in the guy, too. Saw him in Aruba or something."

So now all was clear. Nathan knew that I'd had a fling in Aruba. Well, he'd dumped me. I was a free agent and if I wanted to date anyone, he had nothing to say about that.

"And how is this relevant?" I demanded.

Nathan sighed. "I think that Branford might be trying to get both of you. I know he wanted you and then appeared to lose interest. Now he's back trying to harm you again, and he's somehow focused on this guy in Aruba, too. You didn't tell me about the guy in Aruba."

Oh, so that was what it was about now. Nathan was jealous, looking for some reason to justify himself. And

I thought about Danielle's good advice and decided that he didn't need to know anything about what I'd done in Aruba. We weren't dating and it was none of his business. "Yes, I talked with a few guys in Aruba. I had drinks with one. I danced at the resort club. I told you all of that," I reminded him. "And yes, I'm ready to date again. Which is no crime. I'm not your girlfriend. Your choice."

"I'm sorry," he said, and he did sound truly contrite. "I didn't mean to snap. Just that I'm following Branford and I've managed to listen to a lot of his cell phone calls and he's a nasty character. And he's mentioned you several times and said that you'd gotten out of his grip by luck, but he knows better now."

I digested this information. "Do you know where he's getting his information?" I asked. This was exactly what Meph needed to know. Branford was clearly being primed and aimed by whoever was gunning for us. "And his money? For someone with no income who just went all over the Caribbean, he pops up in the weirdest places."

"I'm working on that," Nathan snapped. "Why are you interested? But I think it's clear he's got some backing with some deep pockets. He's rented another office, by the way, in Park Slope."

"Not cheap," I said. Which was an understatement. Park Slope was a chic and expensive neighborhood in Brooklyn.

"I've been following that but so far I don't have enough hard evidence. I don't know who's backing him or who's giving him his information. For all I know, it's one of you. I'm working on the account traces now."

"Could—would you tell me when you find out?" I asked contritely.

"I'm sorry, that's for our employer in the case. He's paying for the information."

"But I could get hurt again," I protested. I understood perfectly well that his client had first call, and I wondered again who his client was. I almost asked, but I thought that would be pushing too far. I wondered if it could be Meph, but dismissed the notion. Just wandering in to some random detective agency and asking them to follow the small fry? That was not his style.

"Lily? Okay, Lily, if I have any idea it could involve you, I'll tell you. Why do you think I called tonight? I just heard that he would be looking out for you, maybe tonight or tomorrow. Where were you planning to go tonight?"

Suddenly I got paranoid. Suspicious. If I told Nathan and this Branford guy showed up, would that mean that he'd known before or that Nathan had told him? "A sushi bar," I said carefully.

"Good. Because from his conversation he's planning to find you at Public. So you should be safe enough somewhere else. But don't tell anyone else."

"Thank you," I whispered. And then he hung up.

So I was fifteen minutes late to the sushi bar where Desi and I were meeting. She had already ordered sake when I walked in. One look at my face and she got up and hugged me before we sat back down and I ordered for us.

We were on our third order of sake before I told her about Nathan's call, and about being followed in Venice. And about Azoked showing up in my apartment and telling me that Nathan was going to be at Hatuman's.

"Don't worry about it," she said. "Wear the tan de la Renta dress. You'll be the most smashing demon in the place. And we'll have fun at the party, really. Besides, I don't think Nathan is really going to be there. I think Azoked is a nasty little pussy."

We were both drunk enough to find that funny. Spending time with Desi was just what I needed.

chapter
FIVE

The cleaners screwed up. My dress wasn't ready even though they'd had plenty of time. Time to change cleaners, but that wouldn't help me for the party.

Hatuman's parties were always spectacular. He might be a demon stuck somewhere in the Stone Age, but it had been a Stone Age where throwing a good party was admired. Which was why all the important members of the Hierarchy would show. He wasn't trendy, didn't have a clue about the newest elegant boutique hotels or the hottest chefs in New York. So he booked the Waldorf-Astoria and put on a six-course dinner with a string quartet playing waltzes in the ballroom and a gambling setup worthy of Harrah's.

After much angst and six costume changes, I had finally settled on a short green Dior dress with bronze Christian Louboutin's. Because I was vulnerable and an aggrieved party, my friends showed up at my place to coordinate before we arrived en masse. Eros added a few strokes of eye shadow in glitter moss and insisted that I use her dark vixen lipstick. Sybil fluffed my hair, which I had left loose in my natural long, heavy, dark auburn waves. Even Vincent made admiring noises and insisted that I turn and model at least twice.

And then no one could find any more excuses to wait,

so we went down and took two cabs over to the Waldorf.

Most demons look reasonably mortal, and even those who don't can fake it for an evening. Tonight's crowd glittered with more genuine bling than any six guys with blankets down on St. Mark's. But while they wore a fortune in jewels and the clothes were made of beautiful fabrics, the whole appeared oddly mismatched. Demons who had little reason to deal with modern Earth wore whatever their last idea of party clothes had been, and the result approached a Renaissance fair on crack. Demons wore frock coats with kilts, sixteenth-century kimonos, and ball gowns that would have been appropriate in Versailles.

No one, I was certain, would look at me once, let alone twice, wearing a perfectly modern dress that had been featured in at least two photo spreads. Hard to feel uninteresting in Dior, but then I wouldn't have been caught dead in the Worth number from 1902 that drifted by. As I recall, I rather disliked that dress in 1902 and it hadn't improved with age. Neither had the demon in it.

"Tahidra," I greeted her, smiling stiffly. Really, with that grayish complexion she should not wear plum and silvery green. But then Tahidra had never had much of an eye for what looked good on her.

She paused, studied me for a moment, clearly confused. "Lily," I reminded her. "Last time you saw me was at Ludivico's Saturnalia, I think."

"Oh, yes, excuse me. Always a pleasure," she murmured before moving on. Okay, so she didn't remember me. At first I felt hurt and then I remembered that she had been down in the bowels of Hell doing paperwork while I'd been working as Satan's Chosen. I could afford a moment of pity.

We swept through the party and even though we looked great (as opposed to outlandish) we didn't see any sign of Nathan. Or Azoked either, come to think of it.

The *Akashic Record* is never wrong and it never lies. But that doesn't mean that the reporting Librarian might not take a few liberties, I thought. I fumed at Azoked. I'd been nervous about this party every time I thought about it. I'd gotten the icy cramps in my stomach and the vague nausea that came from a combination of fury and nasty anticipation.

"He's definitely not here," Vincent said, his eyes roving the room like a Secret Service agent. "I've done two sweeps and have put a quiet word out with some friends. He's not on the guest list, in fact, and it seems that we're the only ones who know him at all. Do you feel better?"

"Yeah," I said, although that was only half the truth. Yes, I felt half relieved to know that I wouldn't have to see him, think about him, be hurt by him. And I felt half miserable because I had wanted to see him. If he had come to a demon party that would have meant he was learning to cope.

"But Lily, it's good he's not here, right? He was awful to you," Sybil reminded me.

"Yeah," I agreed, lying. He hadn't been awful to me. He'd been wonderful, genuine, interesting, smart, romantic. He just had a problem with me being an immortal demon succubus, and I could see how that would bother a normal guy.

"You don't sound convinced," Sybil said.

I bolted for the ladies' room before I embarrassed myself.

The ladies' room at the Waldorf is the nice kind, with a sofa and a basket of real cloth hand towels and lots of tiny toiletries in case a guest needed some hand cream or a toothbrush or a tampon.

I sat on the cushy upholstered sofa and tried to breathe deeply and relax. Gentle arms held me and patted me. I hadn't heard Desi and Sybil follow me in. "Oh, Lily," Desi said, and I looked up and found myself between two of my best friends.

"I got your dress wet," I said, looking at a dark splotch on Desi's shoulder.

"It's okay," she assured me. Then a knock came at the door. Sybil left and returned with a huge mojito.

"I thought you could use this," Sybil said. "Vincent got it for you."

I took the glass gratefully and drank it down, the cool sweet liquid calming my throat if not my heart.

"Where's Eros?" I asked.

"I think she's trying to get hold of Satan," Desi said. "She was worried about you. I think she wants Satan to damn Nathan or something revengeful like that. Or Eros would do it herself. She's furious at him."

And Eros is a demigoddess. She had never been human, and she was far more powerful than the rest of us put together. When she chose to be, which wasn't often. Eros may be the most strikingly radical-looking of the four of us, and the coldest emotionally to nondemonkind, but she's also a loyal friend. And very traditional. Which means that she is perfectly capable of hunting down Nathan and torturing him to death and then damning him forever for hurting me.

I have the best friends.

"I don't want Satan to find me here in the ladies'," I gasped. "Do I look like a raccoon?"

Vincent knocked again. Another mojito appeared and the empty glass was whisked away.

I drank. I didn't know what special magic Vincent had used, but the drinks were extra strong. I got a bit giggly. Nathan seemed somewhat less important.

This was a party, a party for demons and I was beautiful and single and I could turn the head of every male in the place. Why should I be sitting in the ladies' with mascara running down my face?

I washed up. Sybil and Desi were digging through the makeup in their bags so that I could repair mine. "No, that blush absolutely will not look good on her," I heard my friends say as they examined their combined collection.

"I can't find Satan, but I will still make sure that this mortal pays for his transgressions." Eros had arrived and was angry enough to pass for a vengeance demon. Her lips were drawn tight and her hands balled into fists, and her voice sounded like a snake hissing before a strike.

" 'S okay," I told her. "I'm drunk. Do you have any black mascara?"

Desi is the only one whose blush looked at all right on me, but I had my own lipstick and Eros came through with the mascara.

"Come on, let's go out and have a good time," Sybil urged me. "You look fantastic."

Nathan was not at the party and wasn't going to be at the party. Ever. But there were demons I could talk to and besides, I was drunk enough that I had almost forgotten the entire reason I'd come. I had to talk to Marduk for Meph. If I hadn't promised I would have been out hunting or watching DVDs of the *Gilmore Girls*.

I'd promised. And so I went back into the fray, determined to find Marduk and learn whether he had been plotting against Mephistopheles. Which was not going to be entirely easy. Marduk might be a traditionalist, but he was not a fool. And he and I didn't have much of a relationship, despite our shared roots. We didn't run in the same circles, didn't go to the same parties, didn't have the same friends. He would hardly trust me with his treason, if he were involved in treason. I would have to be careful.

First I had to go through the polite noises with a number of demons I hadn't seen in ages. Had to repeat what I'd been doing for the past decade or two, tell everyone how pleased I was to have come and no, I hadn't been avoiding or snubbing anyone. I'd just been busy, they knew how it was . . .

I worked my way around the first room and then the second. And then I saw Marduk.

Marduk had been a god in Babylon, at times even the head of the pantheon, and he never forgot it. Neither did anyone around him. He was seven feet tall, which was not unduly large in a gathering of demons, but towering enough that he stood out in the room. He had a carefully curled and trimmed beard, and his hair rippled down past his shoulders in a perfect pyramid. He reminded me of my father, who had worn precisely this style three thousand years ago when he had been king. It had been quite the thing back then, but Marduk had never changed. Even his robes were cut to the ancient patterns and looked like they had been made out of the same scratchy fabrics.

I drifted closer to him, until I was at the edge of the circle where he held forth, and I remembered why I'd avoided him for the past fifty years, and for a hundred and fifty before that.

Marduk is always at the center of an adoring clique. He can't stand to be alone, or to listen to anyone else. He is always talking as his sycophants circle around, applauding his stories, asking questions, showing unending interest in whatever caught his fancy.

When I approached he was telling a story about some Greek scientist who had figured out that all of Babylonian astronomy had come directly from Marduk, and how this Greek had begun a cult to him in Athens. I'd heard the story before and besides, I found his arrogance tiring.

Did Meph know what he had been asking?

Yes, he had to know. He was Mephistopheles, and he knew how completely self-involved the older ex-gods all were. Even Eros has momentary flashes. Marduk's only concession to modernity was that he acknowledged Satan as the chief god of Hell.

I maneuvered so that I would be in his line of sight. He squinted at me as if he didn't quite remember who I was. "Lilith?" he asked.

I bowed at the waist. Not the full obeisance required by a godhead, but we were at a party. And the fact of modern Hell was that, as one of Satan's Chosen, I outranked him. But I was politic enough to play along with his vanity, especially since there was no other way to get what I (or Mephistopheles) wanted. "Indeed, Lord, it is good of you to remember your servant," I said in Akkadian. It didn't sound quite so smarmy in my mother tongue; they were just ordinary phrases that didn't mean anything more than polite greeting.

"You have been absent from my court for a very long time," he observed.

I bowed again. (Marduk liked the bowing and it cost me nothing. So long as I didn't have to go down on my knees on the carpet, I was fine with buttering him up.) "I have been required to serve," I said, my eyes on the oversized flowers woven into the rug just in front of his feet.

"Ah, yes." He sighed. "But I do not forget the daughter of the royal house, albeit a minor daughter of a concubine, not a wife, of my devoted worshipper."

There was only one royal house Marduk acknowledged, which worked very much to my advantage. Marduk would not forget my regal heritage.

"I crave a moment of your time, Lord." I made my voice as humble as I could. "If you would be so good to grant it to me."

He took my elbow and steered me toward the balcony, where we had a bit of privacy. "Why would you request audience of me?" he asked formally.

"I have heard that you might have use for me," I told him. "I have heard that you are to be restored to your former glory under Satan, and that you might find a use for a handmaiden who speaks your mother tongue and knows the rituals of the old world."

"Then Satan has released you from your vows?" he asked, with some surprise. "You are Her Chosen handmaiden."

"That is true always, Lord," I agreed. "I had heard that you required assistance to render Her the best."

Marduk sighed. "My little Lilith, it does you credit that you come to me. Both your loyalty to Satan and your loyalty to your Babylonian roots. And while I know that you did study accounts when you were a Priestess, I really need someone who is an expert in double-entry bookkeeping."

Marduk's official position in the Hierarchy was the head of the Budget and Finance Department of Hell. Looking for accountants was well within the scope of his normal duties.

I bowed my head again. "I am sorry. I heard that you might need more generalized assistance."

He seemed confused for a minute or two, and then his features relaxed. "Oh, indeed. You must have heard that Tahidra is transferring to HR." He waved his hand. "You would be utterly wasted in Budget and Finance, my dear. Let alone as the HR officer of the department. Now, if you could get that lovely greed demon Sybil to leave the Upperworld and join us, she is a financial genius. She, possibly, could get us through this spate of overspending. But your loveliness would only be wasted, and I think you would be unhappy doing the work of our department."

"Overspending?" I asked. Satan cares deeply about budget. Her pockets are deep and She believes that all Her minions should live well, but She does not approve of bad management.

Marduk sighed again. I spotted a waiter circulating with a tray of gin and tonics and nabbed two. I handed one to Marduk. "You look like you could use a drink," I said, handing it to him.

He poured it down his throat in a single swallow.

I took his empty glass and traded it for my full one.

That he began to sip, not delicately but at least he didn't chug the whole thing.

He rubbed his eyes and looked at me, and for the first time I noticed that he looked vulnerable and tired.

"I have a problem, Lilith," he said. *It must be the drink,* I thought. "There is money missing from our reserves."

"Missing?" I asked. I didn't know what this was about but something told me that it was important.

He nodded slowly. "No one knows yet. I have auditors looking. I have only just discovered this. But there are only a few demons who have the authorization to draw from the Treasury, so it must be one of a very small number. But for what? Satan would approve any legitimate expenditure. For personal finances? The higher ranks of Hell are all well-heeled. No one needs to steal. And who would have the nerve to steal from Satan?"

I agreed that that seemed unlikely. Satan is the best boss and the best friend ever, but She does not forgive transgression. And stealing from Her Treasury would be unpardonable. Anyone, even the highest demon, caught with a hand in the till would be cast into the lowest pits of torment for eternity.

Marduk looked pale and drawn, and he had finished the second drink already. "I must find out who is doing this, Lilith," he said, using my old name. "Satan has not demanded an accounting recently, but She will. And if I do not find the thief before She does, then I will be held accountable."

No wonder Marduk was scared. I looked around for the waiter with the drinks, but he had disappeared. If I were Marduk I would need a lot more than alcohol to keep me sane.

"I appreciate your offer, Lilith," he said, his words thick. I suspected that those two gin and tonics were far from his first drinks of the evening. "But you see, I need someone who is a brilliant auditor. I may look up one of our business residents. Do you think Ken Lay would be able to trace the problem? If I offered a reduction of his sentence to a less horrific pit of torment?"

For the first time ever I actually felt pity for Marduk. Old-fashioned and stuffy he might be, but he was in trouble. It sounded like no fault of his own, but Satan would surely hold him responsible for the missing funds. No one would want to be Marduk now.

"Ken Lay is a great idea," I said, partly because it was better than anything else I could come up with and partly to reassure him. "If you like, I will try to target some more financial and banking types. Once I deliver them, you can recruit them. Would that be helpful?"

Marduk patted me on the shoulder. "Thank you, Lilith. That is a kind and thoughtful offer, and will be useful too. Yes, indeed, if you can target prey with financial acumen, that will be helpful to me. I knew it would be good to talk to you. You do your father and your House credit."

I bowed my head deeply, and he put his hand on my curls in blessing. For a moment he was a god again, and I was a princess of the royal house of Babylon.

And then I had a brilliant idea. "I do know an accountant who might be able to help," I said hesitantly. "He's a ceremonial magician, so he's used to demonkind. And it might be useful to have one under our thumb rather than the other way around. But could I just give a reference without a delivery?"

Marduk looked at me curiously. "I have accountants. Is this one as good as Ken Lay?"

I shrugged. "I don't know, truth to tell. But he is an accountant and if it's useful . . ."

Marduk studied me. "I will think on it," he said. And then another waiter passed by with a tray of what appeared to be whiskey sours, and Marduk followed after.

Poor guy, he certainly needed the drinks.

chapter
SIX

I'd learned plenty for Mephistopheles, probably more than he'd imagined I would. Certainly I had learned more than I'd expected. While it looked like the plot was deeper than the group of fanatics who had attacked me and my friends last month, I was relieved to think that Marduk was not to blame. For all he was an old-fashioned stuffed shirt, he was a fellow Babylonian.

And he hadn't been a bad god, either. He'd been responsible and responsive to his worshippers and had regularly delivered aid and miracles.

And he was being set up to take the fall for someone else in the Hierarchy. This sounded more and more like a power grab at the level of the high lieutenants, which meant that no junior sex demon was taking out her jealousy on us. On the whole, I didn't know if that was better or worse.

Worse, probably. A junior sex demon I could best without thinking of it. Someone on Marduk's level would be much more difficult. And someone on Marduk's level who had managed to steal from the Treasury without Marduk knowing it was threatening indeed. This demon could do far more damage than any three disgruntled sex demons.

I was thinking so hard about what I'd learned from

Marduk that I barely realized that I was at a party. I wanted to sit down with Mephistopheles right away and go over the problem. He, no doubt, would have some insights. Especially since it was probably he who was the ultimate victim.

Or maybe not. Marduk, not Meph, had been set up to take the fall. What if the purpose of this whole plot was to discredit and eliminate Marduk, not Meph?

Could Meph even be behind it? No, I couldn't believe that. Meph, as CEO of Hell, was certainly capable of such an action, but what would it benefit him? He and Marduk might be rivals, but I had the impression that Meph was just as happy to have Marduk in Budget. He'd called it a boring department more than once, and considered it to be no more than support for his own Operations.

I was musing over these possibilities so deeply that when someone called my name I jumped.

"Lily? Is that you, Lily?" The voice was full of pleasure and excitement, the accent was familiar and entirely unexpected. The speaker was a handsome blond man with brilliant blue eyes and a great tan, dressed in Helmut Lang. The very accountant I had thought of for Marduk had just materialized in front of me.

Marten? What was Marten doing here? He didn't belong here. He had just been a brief fling in Aruba. How had he managed to get to New York? To this party? I was in shock, and after three thousand years I had thought I was impervious. But I had never, ever, in my wildest imagination thought that I would see Marten again. I gaped at him silently.

"You didn't tell me that you were in New York," I finally mumbled, because I had to say something.

"This was, hmm, not exactly a planned trip. I was asked to come only yesterday. This is my first experience of your fair city. I have not been cold in two years now, and it is very surprising."

Azoked had done this before. She'd misled me. She had warned me, yes, but it wasn't Nathan she had meant. It was Marten. Who had never been my boyfriend. He had just been a guy who'd picked me up in Aruba and had been a good enough lover that I'd let him live. But the deal was that I left Aruba and it was over. He hadn't been any more interested in a real relationship than I had been. I'd been in love with Nathan then.

I was still in love with Nathan.

But Nathan had dumped me.

And here was Marten. Hmmmm . . .

"How long are you in town?" I asked.

"I will be here until Tuesday," he said. "And I came to this party hoping to see you."

"You could have sent e-mail."

He shrugged. "You did not give me your address, or even your last name. This is easier."

Yes. Easier. Because since we were both here, we knew we were both associated with the Underworld.

"I am surprised," I admitted. "I had not thought you were demonkind."

"I am not," he said, and shrugged. "But you are. And I, I have dealings with many demons. I am, what would you say, *amicus demoni?*"

"Really?" I asked. One thing to be a ceremonial magician. But to identify as a demon friend was something very different indeed. Unless it was his English. Or Latin. Or something.

"But since we are both here, and I will be in town until Tuesday, perhaps you and I could get together?" His grin was close to irresistible. "Perhaps you could steer me to a good place to eat? Or to have fun? You must know the very best of these places."

"Sure," I said, pleased at the prospect. "Where are you staying?"

"A very interesting boutique hotel—Hotel Gansevoort? It is very new, I think. I love the Dutch name."

I managed to bite my tongue before I asked how an accountant could afford one of the hippest hotels in New York. "That hotel has one of the best restaurants in New York, and one of the trendiest clubs."

"Then we must go there. I insist! Tomorrow night?" Marten was quite enthusiastic.

"Well, maybe dinner," I agreed. "It's a work night for me, though. I've got to be at meetings on Monday morning and we've got editorial on Tuesday."

Marten raised an eyebrow. "You are a succubus. Surely you do not need to work. Doesn't Satan take care of you in the finest style?"

I shrugged. "Yes, well, I'd get bored if I didn't work. And besides, I'm the accessories editor at an important fashion magazine."

"And since you are so much the leader of fashion in any event, best to use the media," Marten agreed. "It is generous of you to share your expertise with the world." His tone was not even a little bit sarcastic.

"So as long as you don't mind making it an early night, I could spend some time in the evening. And I could tell you some places to go, if you're interested. What kinds of things do you like to do?"

Funny, I'd spent three days in Aruba with this man.

We'd gone to bat caves and clubs and had fabulous sex. I knew what he did for work, and that he'd been born and grew up in Rotterdam and had only moved to Aruba two years ago. And that was all I knew about him.

Except, of course, that he was a ceremonial magician.

And that I had an odd idea to plant him in Marduk's department.

"Well, I do plan to go to Weiser's and The Magikal Childe," he said. "And possibly the Masonic Lodge in New York—I believe that it is quite magnificent."

"Is that the one on Twenty-third and Sixth?" I asked, knowing full well it had to be. "There's a very good restaurant near there, very popular, with excellent cocktails."

He nodded and his lovely blond hair fell into his eyes. "Then it is settled. I cannot tell you how happy I am to see you, Lily. I have thought of you so often since you left."

"It's nice to see you, too, Marten," I said. Nathan had broken my heart, and the ego boost of having another handsome, charming gentleman (who wanted to see me more than once) was a kind of solace. I smiled at him and held out my hand. He gathered me into his arms.

As we swept around the room, turning to the music, I was happy. Really honestly just happy. I forgot everything except the music and the dancing, the glittering lights and parade of beautiful clothes—and the handsome, accomplished man who held me in his arms.

I felt pretty again, and lighthearted, so long as the music played and we danced. Sybil and Vincent were on the dance floor as well. So was Eros—with Beliel. I knew they were friends but when they danced they looked like a couple, and Eros hadn't said anything about Beliel that would lead us to believe he was anything more than just a friend.

And then Marten steered me expertly to the edge of the dance floor and slowed down the whirling so that we finally came to a halt by the tables and chairs. "My lovely, lovely Lily," he murmured into my ear. "I would love to stay with you all the time I am here. I would love to whisk you off to my hotel right now and never let you go. But alas, there are things that I must do. I must make a meeting tonight and will not be available until tomorrow afternoon. But after that, I am all yours."

He bowed in the courtly manner I had not seen in two hundred years, and I wondered whether he actually was a demon after all. Most ceremonial magicians were old and sour and didn't go out dancing or have fun. Their rituals took forever and often called for all kinds of disciplines (which often included celibacy) and constant attention.

Marten wasn't like them at all.

"Do you skate?" he asked me, breaking into my thoughts.

"Skate?"

"Ice skating. That is one thing I have missed since I have moved to Aruba. Do you skate?"

"I never have. I'm willing to try it, but you'll have to promise to teach me, or at least hold me up so I don't fall," I told him. "I grew up in Babylon. We didn't have much in the way of ice rinks."

The one thing I could never, ever tell Nathan I could say to Marten perfectly casually.

"Well, then, it is well past time to rectify this," he said, grinning. "But now I must go. I see my host and I have promised to spend some time with him and his friends tonight."

I nodded, but didn't quite understand why. I thought that generally ceremonial magicians tried to control demons, to bind us to do their bidding. They very rarely did anything for us. So why was Marten meeting with a demon? Did he have a bargain with one? That had happened before: Faust had bargained with Meph and Meph had won.

But it wasn't Meph that Marten went to meet. He stood in a knot near the screens with Greish and Ezamian, both of whom ranked on a level just below the lieutenants of Hell. Hatuman, our host, joined them and the four of them engaged in what appeared to be a serious, if short, conversation. Then the four of them left.

Why would Hatuman leave the party? He was the host.

But then I noticed that the party had thinned out considerably. Marduk was gone. So were my girlfriends. I wondered if they'd all gone home with someone. I'd find out at brunch, no doubt. They wouldn't have interrupted me with Marten to say good night.

As I stood there I saw most of the demons in evening dress drift toward the door. Most of the beings walking through the party space now wore Waldorf uniforms and were gathering up stray cups and canapés.

It was time for me to go. I joined the line at the door. Hatuman was there saying good night to his guests. There was no sign of Marten or the two demons who had accompanied him.

I paid my respects to my host and thanked him sincerely for a delightful evening. Then I found a cab and went home and lay in bed half awake until dawn.

*   *   *

The alarm went off at eleven, jolting me out of a bad dream. I had managed maybe five hours of sleep and I felt awful. A long hot shower helped, though not enough.

My face looked ragged when I finally got the mirror cleared enough to attempt makeup. It was one of those days when I was grateful for foundation and blush and Visine. These miracles take a little time, though, so once I was fit to face the day there was no time for coffee.

No help for it. I flew out of the elevator and through the lobby, not noticing which doorman was on duty. When he whistled me a taxi and held the door for me to get in, I did notice that it wasn't Vincent. I wondered if Vincent had gone home with Sybil last night.

I'd certainly lost track of the party.

I arrived at Public precisely at noon. None of my friends were there.

I fumed. I was furious. I was on time and I hadn't even had my coffee and I'd had a bad dream and I was tired. And I was there first. I had never ever in my life arrived anywhere first.

They were supposed to be here already. They should have put us on the list. I wanted to know what had happened that I had missed. And it was cold.

I went inside to the hostess stand, a modernist statement in poured concrete that only made the rich mahogany and antique brass of the entrance area more elegant. There was the usual crush and at least six names on the list before us. I lied and said we were all here so the hostess would add us to the queue, and was conflicted when she said that it would be at least a twenty-minute wait.

Desi and Eros came in a cab together, about five minutes after the hostess had given me a suspicious look. Sybil arrived last, her face glowing with something other than the chill.

But just as she opened her mouth, the hostess announced "Lily, party of four," and so we had to drop all hope of information until we were seated (at our second-favorite waiter's station) and had our menus. Then Sybil, being either shy or actually hungry, refused to say a word until we had all carefully studied the menu, which hadn't changed from last week or the week before, and even if it had I was still ordering the banana-stuffed French toast.

Ryan came over to take our order. Since he'd served us about a hundred times, he just checked in with each of us. "Lily, the banana-stuffed French toast today? Coffee and a Bellini?" I didn't have to say anything, I just nodded. One of these days I might surprise him and order something different. One of these days I might move to Long Island, too.

"So?" Eros asked as soon as Ryan disappeared.

Sybil blushed but the three of us stared her down. "I'm not the only one who had an interesting evening," she protested. "What about you? You spent half the night with Beliel."

Eros rolled her eyes. "What about Lily? What about her Aruba fling showing up like that?"

Sybil's eyes became very large and dark with worry. "What if that happened to me? If one of my Aruba flings showed up at the party and I was there with Vincent . . ."

Eros waved her hand. "It won't happen. You had actual flings. Even if they did show up in New York, they wouldn't have been at that party."

"But Lily's was," Sybil protested. "Is he a demon?"

"He's not a demon," I told them. "He's a ceremonial magician, or so Azoked said. And I really don't know what he wants or why he's here, but he seems to be hanging out with Hatuman, which could be dangerous."

"Do you have a date with him?" Desi demanded.

I hung my head in shame. "But that's only because I promised Meph that I'd look into what's going on politically," I protested.

Desi patted my shoulder, since she was sitting next to me. "It's okay. You can admit to having a date. He's very attractive and he was wearing Helmut Lang. And besides, you need a little fun and pampering now."

"And there's no reason to be ashamed," Eros added. "If you want to go out and have a good time and forget the creep who treated you badly, that's the best thing you could do. I, for one, am all for it. If I'd thought of it, I'd have sent him a ticket myself."

"I'm seeing him," I admitted. "But he's only here until Tuesday. And what about Sybil? What's up with Vincent?"

But we were thrown into silence again as Ryan arrived with a busboy and four huge, steaming plates. Waffles and French toast swimming in syrup, fruit stuffings, chopped walnuts sprinkled on top. And our Bellinis, which always make life and embarrassment easier to endure.

Not only did we not talk in front of the waiters, but we were too engrossed in our food to waste a moment on chat. Brunch at Public is delicious and while gluttony is a guilty pleasure, it is a pleasure indeed; for a mortal sin, it's fairly low-level. Pride, lust, and greed are the power trifecta in Hell, and sins like gluttony and vanity are at the bottom of the list. Sloth and wrath are in the middle, respectable enough for a demon to admit to the specialization, but they're never going to catapult anyone into the higher ranks.

Though, truth to tell, with the rising rates of obesity in the world, the gluttony demons are starting to organize and demand some respect. We had always discounted them as losers who couldn't manage a real sin, and here they were slowly taking over the world and causing more death and misery and despair than the big three. Quite a shake-up in the boardroom. Perhaps Meph will be able to come out of the closet as a fan of gluttony any day now.

Or not.

"Okay, Sybil, spill," I said when I had finished half my Bellini. I gestured to Ryan to get us all another round. I thought Syb might need it.

"Really, there's nothing to tell," Sybil said to her plate. "Vincent and I are dating now. The only thing different is that it's official, that's all. He's still a doorman at Lily's building, he's still working on his Level Three qualifying courses, and plans to take Level Four as soon as he passes the exams for Three. That's it. No big announcements."

"Yet," Desi said, her eyes gleaming.

Sybil shook her head and her soft honey-blond waves fluttered around her shoulders. "Not yet. Not now, anyway. We're just going to see how it goes. Where it goes. He hasn't been a demon very long, but if he doesn't make at least upper tier in a year or so we may have to rethink this. I think he's still traditional enough that it would be very hard for him to be an entry-level demon and doorman while I'm one of Satan's Chosen."

"To say nothing about being one of the great stars of Wall Street," Eros observed dryly.

"That too," Sybil agreed with remarkable candor. For Sybil, at least. "Honestly, it would be an issue for me if all he could manage was being a doorman and a low-level enforcer. The disparity could be a relationship problem."

We all nodded in glum agreement. Maybe, being immortal and so very old, we weren't quite able to shake the idea that a guy should be at least a little taller and every bit as successful as we are. The problem here is obvious, and it has nothing to do with height.

Maybe it's not all old-fashioned assumptions about a man making the money and having the status. In fact, I remember times and places where that wasn't true. My status as the daughter of the king would have increased the status of any family I married into.

No, while there are issues of status and money and compatibility, there is also the fact that we don't want to be used. I don't ever want to wonder if a man is dating me for my money or my proximity to Satan.

Well, that wouldn't be a problem with Nathan, I thought grimly. As soon as he found out that I was a succubus he had fled. Run. Totally came apart at the seams. He wasn't using me for my contacts, that was for sure.

"Your Aruba guy, what's his name?" Desi asked.

"Marten."

"Right, Marten. Well, Marten could be using you because you're a demon," Desi reminded me sharply.

"While he's great in bed, I don't think that sex is his greatest desire."

"He's very good at it," I defended him. "Besides, what would he be using me for?"

Desi shook her head. "Power? Don't all ceremonial magicians want power over demons? And what about your ichor?"

"You think he'd be dating me to bleed me?" I was aghast. Yes, ceremonial magicians used ichor in certain of their workings, but it had never occurred to me that Marten might—no, I wasn't even going to think it.

"But how come we're talking about me again?" I asked. I turned to Sybil. "What about you and Vincent? So you're now officially dating. Did he take you to his place last night?"

"Oh, no," Sybil looked offended. "Certainly he didn't. He came to my place. He only has a tiny place in a sketchy neighborhood."

"You took him to your place . . ." Desi tried to pick up the thread. "And?"

"He liked the new wallpaper," Sybil said stoutly.

And she wouldn't say any more. We all knew, and since Sybil was not a sex demon, sometimes she got a little prudish if we asked about her intimate life.

Thinking about Sybil, I had managed to forget that my friends were also curious about me. Or rather, about my plans for and with Marten.

"So is he a ceremonial magician?" Eros asked.

I shrugged. "I don't know for sure myself. Azoked said he was, but we all know that she can be misleading. He hasn't asked me for anything yet."

"Except sex," Desi pointed out.

"Except sex," I agreed. "But if he knew at the time what I was, then he's either brave or stupid."

"Or arrogant," Eros suggested.

"Or he just knows he's a very good lover," Desi defended him. "Some of them put real effort into it and are proud of their results. It's like any art form, really."

I shrugged. "I don't know. I'm seeing him tonight, and maybe tomorrow night. Maybe I'll find out. Maybe I'll just have fun. Mostly I'm thinking about having fun."

Sybil nodded vigorously. "You should definitely have fun with him. If he wants anything, well, you can find out what it is. If he knows what you are, he knows that you can't give him riches or position or anything."

I giggled. "No, but you could certainly give him riches. If he asks for that, I'll recommend you as his financial adviser. And give me the name of that fund you're managing again?"

Sybil rolled her eyes. "You know, Lily, you own several thousand shares of that fund. Don't you ever read the prospectus?"

My food was all gone. I scooped up stray syrup on my fork. It was time for dessert. Sybil might be embarrassed by blatant sex talk, but I was a little embarrassed myself. I didn't know the name of the funds or the stocks I owned. I threw all those little pamphlets they sent around into recycling without opening them.

"So, what are you going to do with Marten tonight?" Desi asked.

I looked at her pointedly and Sybil blushed, but Desi is not so easily embarrassed. "Oh, I don't mean that. I mean, where are you going to dinner?"

It was past two and I'd finished dessert. It was time to go. We'd paid our bill, left a more than generous tip, and were just settling wallets back into purses and making sure that favorite lipsticks were in place when I caught a movement out of the corner of my eye.

I turned and recognized Craig Branford just inside the door.

I froze. He was looking at me, at the four of us, and his face was screwed up in a terrible scowl. Nathan had warned me.

Desi went white, and she's not the timid one. Sybil looked like she was about to dive under the tablecloth. Me, I stared him in the face.

"Well, hello, Mr. Branford. Fancy seeing you here in Public," I said rather loudly. "Would you like to join us?"

chapter
SEVEN

"Why would I want anything to do with you, hand-maidens of Hell?" he hissed.

"Well, you've been pursuing us for over a month now. I thought it was time we at least stopped pretending that we didn't know you've been trying to do something to us. So I thought that maybe we could talk it over like reasonable people," I said. "I did try once already and thought we'd come to an agreement."

Sybil and Desi had disappeared as I spoke, but Eros sat stone-still, a hint of amusement in her eyes.

Branford's eyes were so wide that I thought he had been drawn by the guy who does *South Park*.

Suddenly I had the urge to giggle. He appeared as terrified as Sybil had before she fled, as if he believed that Eros and I would annihilate him on contact. Which was completely convoluted, since he was the one who'd tried to kill us with holy water–infused letters. I'd gotten mine first and had third-degree burns over my palms. If Satan hadn't come and healed me on the spot I would still be in the burn unit at Columbia Presbyterian. Fortunately, She had gotten word to the others before they had ripped open those thick, creamy envelopes that had looked just like wedding invitations.

"You could sit down and order a cup of coffee," I reiterated. "That would probably be better than standing there with your mouth open."

"I do not take refreshment with demons," he said stiffly.

I shook my head slowly. "You know, I don't know where you got this idea or why you've got it in for us. But after busting up our friend's date and then talking nonsense to my date in Aruba, I think you've got some explaining to do. Not to mention those weird cryptic notes you sent. You're stalking us." I didn't mention the holy water. Only a demon would have known there was holy water on those notes, and right now my defense was running toward the fact that none of us had suffered any harm he could see. And that Marten had laughed in his face in Aruba.

"You are Hellspawn and it is our mission to rid the world of the likes of you. Go back to your master Satan."

I don't know what possessed me. Maybe I just lost it. Maybe I was sick of being stalked, and of hiding. But mostly I think I just got a raging case of the what-the-hells. "I don't know what's wrong with you. Do you believe that there really are such things as demons walking around the streets of New York? And that I'm a demon? I'm a fashion editor. Some people might think that I'm pretty rotten, I'll admit that. Several of my ex-boyfriends would agree with you, and at least two designers whose bags I refused to show on the Accessories page. But trust me, the bags were horrible."

He turned pale. He might be a weak, puny mortal, but we couldn't overlook him completely; whoever was feeding him the information about us, what we were and where we were, was the real demon we were after.

And even that demon was likely in the service of someone else. Whoever had been stealing from Marduk's Treasury.

"You're lying," Branford said, clearly upset. "I know what you are."

Eros rolled her eyes. "Do you have any evidence?" she asked quite reasonably. "Or do you just accost random women in restaurants?"

"You are of the devil," Branford sputtered.

Eros laughed heartily. "Oh, don't you just wish. Your actions over the past month and a half would constitute stalking, and I think a judge wouldn't think twice about issuing a restraining order. Demons aren't real, and I would heartily recommend that you get yourself into therapy before you get into any more trouble."

Then she turned to me. "Come on, Lily. Let's get out of here."

She rose and slid into her coat. I followed her out onto Elizabeth Street, and up the few feet to Houston where she flagged down a cab.

"There," she said. "That should take care of him."

"It was brilliant, Eros." I had to admire what she'd done. "But I wanted to talk to him. I wanted to find out who was giving him the information. Because someone had to have told him who we are and where we go and where we live. He had all of our addresses. And there was someone following me in Venice. I think."

Eros shrugged under her pink and orange fake fur. "It doesn't matter if he's gone. And I think you're just being paranoid about being followed. He's just some little creep, that's all."

I didn't say anything, but I was angry. It did matter. She might have scared off Branford, but whoever had been feeding him information wouldn't stop. And at least we knew about Branford, knew who he was and that he was dangerous.

Downside of having a demigoddess for a friend. I couldn't really blame Eros for being who she was. Nor had she been privy to my talks with Meph and Marduk; she had no reason to think Branford was anything more than an annoyance, a fanatic who had somehow decided we were his nemeses. She didn't know how big it really was.

The cab dropped me at home and then went on with Eros. I had only a few hours until I had to get ready for my date with Marten, and I wanted to look killer. After being jilted by the first guy I'd fallen for in three hundred years, I needed to shore up my self-esteem.

But first, Meph. I needed something faster and more personal than e-mail. I called his cell.

Yeah, Hell is wired, and Meph's phone works any-where—on Earth or elsewhere. Only about ten people or so have that number. He picked up on the second ring.

"Lily, I've been waiting to hear from you," he said without preamble.

"I've got a lot for you and my phone isn't secure. Is there someplace safe that we could meet face-to-face?" I asked.

"Do you have my sigil?"

I didn't, at least not one that hadn't been published in about a million books.

"You've got photo capability on your cell, don't you?" he asked. "I've got a picture on mine and I'll send it to you. Work the sigil and you'll be here, and this here should be secure."

"Okay," I agreed. "It'll take me a couple of minutes."

"The sooner the better," he said, and hung up.

The sigil displayed on the tiny phone screen was new to me. Meph must have changed his locks since the last time I'd had to do this.

I hate porting by sigil. It's uncomfortable and messy. I went into my bathroom because I needed a mirror, and the bathroom would be easier to clean up after than my bedroom. Besides, the bathroom is where I kept the lancets.

Once upon a not very long time ago I had to use a knife or a straight razor to nick myself. Ichor is essential to the process. Now I can buy lancets by the fifty count at the local Duane Reade.

Before the ichor came the setup. I got out the brazier and laid out the lancet, the cell phone, the chalice, and the salt before I dragged the step stool out of the kitchen and into the hallway.

The top of the hall closet is full of the magical equipment I don't use very often. Once upon a time I would have had this all much closer to hand, but since the Internet and the cell phone had become commonplace among Hellspawn, I didn't need to do ritual to communicate anymore.

I could ask Marten tonight. That would be amusing dinner date conversation.

No. I had to return my attention to getting to Meph. I had already compounded an incense for porting to the highest regions of Hell, and of course it was on the bottom of the big paper bag of incenses. After a good ten minutes of rummaging, I found the packet in a Ziploc baggie with Meph's name in Magic Marker on the side. The only other thing I needed was salt. That came in a dark blue Morton's carton on top of the fridge.

When I had everything organized, I lit the vanilla-scented candle that lived near the brazier, hit the light, and focused my thoughts. I scattered salt in a circle around me that included the sink and mirror, touching the tiled wall on each side. Then I started the self-igniting charcoal over the candle flame. I lit the incense and presented the brazier to the four cardinal points, thoroughly stinking up the bathroom, the towels, and my hair. Only when the entire area had been psychically cleansed and prepared did I pull the plastic cap off the lancet and stab the end of my first finger.

Then, as the ichor started to well up in the cut, I followed the lines of the sigil on the phone screen, and reproduced the drawing on my bathroom mirror.

A sigil is a map and a word and Names of Power all at the same time. Some are linked to entities, others to places, and a very few to organizational centers. When I was satisfied that the sigil was drawn correctly, I began to chant the Names of Power associated with Meph and the area of Hell I needed to enter. The vibration in the chanting activated the ichor sigil in the mirror and it began to shimmer.

I repeated the chant again, louder, watching as the lines of the figure went from flicker to steady glow. A third repetition and a final censing of the image with the smoke made the lines and symbols before me blaze like neon, and the color of this brilliant sign suffused the small circle I had drawn.

Smoke from the incense obscured the bathtub and toilet. The sigil became more real than I was, and I saw my hands as ghostly shadows in the smoke. It was time. I called on Mephistopheles in his secret Names of Power and reached out to the small circle that indicated the starting point of the map.

I felt my being sucked into the bars of light. The sensation was like being propelled through all the strokes of the sigil, each in order. The movement was rapid but on some level it felt like it took forever.

And then I was in Hell. In a tiny jewel box of a room appointed in the Venetian manner, gold and deep red and sky blue all combined into a dizzying Baroque array. A great gilded wing chair upholstered in pink and blue and gold brocade sat facing a delicately curved settee in a different brocade of similar hues. A Murano chandelier glittered overhead in four falls of dolphins and dragons that reflected and enhanced the warm golden candlelight. Two delicate side chairs completed the seating and the rest of the space was filled with tables made from inlaid marble and wooden marquetry.

I knew Mephistopheles would appear on the wing chair, but try as I might to concentrate, I could not see him arrive. I was watching an empty space for a few minutes, and then Meph was there, sitting as if he had been there waiting for me, his Brioni suit a matched chalk-striped medium gray that brought out the subtle silver at his temples. Mephistopheles makes a very good-looking man.

"Lily, thank you for joining me," he said graciously as he passed his hand over the table. A platter of fruit and cheese and paté appeared in the center, and three Venetian wineglasses and a decanter of red joined it somewhat closer to Meph. "I know this is less convenient than sending me e-mail or telling me over the phone, but you were concerned about our privacy."

I nodded, in complete agreement.

"I am sorry not to engage in small talk, but perhaps under the circumstances it would be best if you simply told me as much as you know, as clearly as you can."

So I told him. I told him about talking to Marduk and the problems in the Treasury and Budget. And I told him how frightened Marduk was. I also told him about Craig Branford showing up at Public today of all days.

Meph sat absolutely still. I had no idea of what he was thinking; he could have been a simulacrum for all the reaction he showed.

He waited until I was done with my recitation, and paused for a moment after to pour wine.

"Interesting," he said. "So Marduk may even be approachable as an ally."

I nodded vigorously. "I think so. I think he is more concerned with where the money is going and who is stealing from Satan than with his own status at the moment."

If Satan discovered the theft before Marduk had caught the culprit and replaced the funds, Marduk would have less status in Hell than a newbie demon doorman. Marduk was fighting for his survival, which for a former god and head of a pantheon must be horrible.

I smelled the familiar incense, almost identical to what I had lit in my bathroom, and Mephistopheles poured a third glass of sherry. "Our newest confederate," he said.

The smoke glimmered, and when it cleared Marten stood in front of the spindly chairs. In a long deep-gray robe and iron lamin, with a silver ribbon tied around his forehead, he looked haggard, and older than he'd seemed on Aruba. His face was set and grim and he shook Meph's hand before taking a seat.

Only then did Marten notice me, and his eyes grew wide for a moment before a slow knowing smile acknowledged me.

Well, that answered a lot of questions.

Suddenly I was conscious of the fact that I was not particularly well dressed for the occasion. Marten was dressed in robes that probably reflected some astrological event and sphere of existence, Meph was in Brioni, and I was in jeans.

"I believe you are already acquainted," Mephistopheles said in his best imitation of a Regency gentleman. "Still—Lily, Marten, as you know, is a ceremonial magician. Part of his agreement with me includes a bit of investigation in the same matter as I have asked you about. Marten, I know you are aware that Lily is a succubus and one that I am proud to claim as an ally. You may not be aware that she is also one of Satan's Chosen companions, and so is assisting me in this matter as Satan's Own Handmaiden."

Marten stood and bowed to me formally. I just waved my hand. "Oh, sit down," I said to him. "I'm still going to dress nicer for tonight."

He sat.

"Please let us know what you have discovered," Meph said to him. "Lily has just given me evidence that Marduk is probably not the traitor we're looking for, but is being set up himself."

Marten nodded slowly. "Yes, that would make sense. Hatuman mentioned several times that Marduk might be replaced. I found that especially interesting as there were no rumors, no gossip, about why Satan might be displeased with him."

I shrugged. "Marduk can be a stick in the mud, but he's loyal. And he's happy doing a job that no one else wants. He's not important enough in the Hierarchy himself," I mused, but Meph held up his hand and nodded toward Marten.

"Please continue."

Marten addressed his next remark to me. "I don't believe that Hatuman has anything to do with this. He's more interested in passing gossip than actual politics. Honestly, I believe that Hatuman is too lazy to take initiative against Mephistopheles. Or, to be more accurate, that he has achieved his ambition. He throws the most popular parties in Hell."

"Not much of an ambition," Mephistopheles huffed.

"Now who's being a prig?" I eyed him pointedly. "He had a goal and he's attained it. Everyone wants invitations to Hatuman's parties. Sometimes even Satan will make an appearance. And he's a great source of information."

"For anyone," Mephistopheles sighed heavily. "If this is all true. If we are not falling for some concealment." He turned back to Marten. "Is there anything more?"

"A great deal, none of it important, or even meaningful . . . on the surface. Beliel was not approachable last night." At that, Marten looked at me with an eyebrow raised. I shrugged. Eros had deflected all questions at brunch and that had made me suspicious.

"More interesting," Marten resumed his briefing, "no one else from Security was there either. Now why would all of Security stay away? Even Beliel's incubi were notably absent. Hatuman felt snubbed."

Meph filled the three goblets with wine. I sipped with pleasure. I had never drunk a Spanish Reserva before, and this was a lovely '81 that was perfect with the salty Gouda Robusto on the tray.

"I had an idea while I was talking to Marduk," I said slowly, not sure this was the right time. I hadn't had any time to develop the concept, but with both of them in the room it seemed too opportune to pass up. "He said he needs an accountant, someone who might be able to find out who's stealing. And I told him I knew one." I looked pointedly at Marten. "He said he would be interested in talking to someone. I realize I don't know what you actually do. For all I know you specialize in Dutch taxes and this would be ridiculous. But if you could look at Marduk's books, maybe you could find out more about what's going on."

Meph's eyes widened and he looked at me, and then Marten, and then he smiled. "Lily, you are a genius. This is brilliant. Marten's expertise is precisely in the areas that Marduk needs."

"For a fee," Marten interrupted. "For my full consulting fee plus expenses and extra for rush and confidentiality."

"But you're not going to keep it confidential," I protested. "You're going to tell Mephistopheles."

Marten's eyes became cold, and I could see that he was a little more dangerous than I had suspected back in Aruba. "I will not tell Satan, unless Marduk himself is the one behind it."

"I don't want him hurt," I said to Meph. "These people are dangerous."

The cold smile never left Marten's face. "I can handle them, I think."

"I know they're dangerous, Lily," Mephistopheles interrupted. "They are threatening the base of the power structure and they have to be getting inside information. Which is why we have to take every possible opportunity to get rid of the source of information as quickly as we can." Satan's most trusted deputy came over to me and took my hands in his, palms up. "We cannot risk you," he said softly. "The Knight Defenders came far too close last time. We have got to find the demon who has been giving them information before those fanatics can try anything again. I suspect that the increased activity of groups like Branford's has been encouraged by someone in Hell. Someone is giving them information and money."

I stared at my palms. They had been burned deeply, roasted, by a note written on elegant bond that had been impregnated with holy water. My flesh had scalded and turned black and smelled like a backyard grill on the Fourth of July. Thanks to Satan they were perfect. Not a mark or scar marred my skin, no sign that someone had tried to destroy me.

But Marten was still talking and I'd missed a bit of what he'd said.

"There have been far more successful attacks on demons in the past decade than in the several hundred years before," Marten was finishing up. "As a ceremonial magician, the numbers of demons are important to me, to all of us. The decrease is problematic, and I think there has been an actual campaign to eliminate numbers."

"You care because you bind demons," I said.

He shrugged. "I'd prefer to say that we make mutually beneficial agreements," he said mildly.

"The bottom line is that there has been a radical drop-off in demon concentration on Earth," Mephistopheles mused. Trust Meph to pay attention to the important stuff first. "A radical drop-off that coincides with a pattern of attacks. For ten years there have been more and more attacks of the kind that you have been subject to, Lily. But most demons are not as strong as you, and most don't have direct access to Satan. So a few were eliminated. Younger, unimportant demons. We never noticed, really. We didn't see a pattern."

"Like people don't notice if the homeless go missing and are being killed," I mused.

"Exactly," Marten said. "Their one biggest mistake so far has been targeting Lily and her friends. They must not have realized that these are Satan's Chosen."

"Or they're going for bigger game now," I added. "Or even, they no longer care whether Satan is on to them or not. But that would be an unbelievable level of pride."

Mephistopheles smiled thinly. Pride is the premier sin. On the right demon it sat well.

"We need to analyze the patterns of attacks over the past ten years at least," I declared. "There has got to be something here. The more we dig, the worse this gets. I mean, I thought this was some fringe group of nuts, and now we're looking at a major depopulation of demons, and maybe threats to Hell itself."

Marten nodded. "Ceremonialists have been talking about how hard it is to even locate demons anymore. There are areas in the world where it's very hard to find the demonic orders. Only the top ceremonialists have the strength to pull demons from farther away, which means we are less effective and that younger cere-monialists give up."

Mephistopheles took the disk out of the laptop. "I'll keep this," he said, slipping it back into its cover and onto one of the fussy side tables. "I have already con-tacted the research department and I expect that I'll have some raw figures soon enough. I'll have someone on the analysis immediately and get back to you both. This has been very useful."

"Wait a sec, Meph," I said as he started the conclud-ing tracing of sigils. "What about my idea to have Marten work for Marduk?"

Mephistopheles nodded. "We will add an addendum to our contract, naturally."

"You know what my price is for this. I received your e-mail on that." Marten waved his hand at the laptop on the coffee table. "This will be direct work, and under Marduk. And will require a fair bit of specialized knowl-edge."

"That required a fair bit of specialized software," Meph said, nodding at the demographic display. Meph looked at the ceiling for a moment and then sighed. "You know I cannot guarantee what you want. I am willing to make concessions on your current contract, but the other matter has to be approved by Satan Her-self."

Marten spread his hands and sighed. "That is a prob-lem. Because it is really the only thing I want. But in the meantime, I will agree to another five hundred years with all the usuals," he said. "Health, eternal youth, wealth, position, my choice of assignments, and access to at least two reassignments from Admin. And your solemn oath that you will pursue the other."

I whistled. Hard bargain indeed, and I didn't even know what the other he wanted was. Very few concessions had to be approved by Satan Herself. Marten rose in my estimation—we appreciate good bargaining in Hell.

"In return for working for Marduk to trace the missing funds," Meph clarified. Marten nodded his agreement. Meph waved his hand, and a large leather-bound folio appeared next to the laptop bound with straps and silver buckles. Nice. If that was his contract, Marten rated very high in Hell. Meph opened the document case and the first sheet was clearly the newly inscribed addendum, calligraphed in a twelfth-century hand in Demonic Latin. I tried to peer over their shoulders to read the agreement, but they were shielding it with their bodies as they checked it together.

"Agreed," Marten said after he had finished reading over the document. Meph handed him what looked like a Montblanc and a small horn-handled knife. Marten incised the tip of a finger and touched the pen to the blood before he signed.

"Thank you Lily, that was a brilliant idea," Meph complimented me. "And I'll leave it to you to introduce him to Marduk, of course."

"Of course," I agreed.

"Then if we are finished, I suggest we get started." Meph closed the proceedings firmly, and took up tracing the sigil dismissing us precisely where he had left off.

And then the entire room, all the busy brocades, the Murano chandelier, the ormolu-mounted marble clock, the inlaid tables, all of it dissolved into static, only the buzzing went just below my skin and made me feel rotten.

I tried to cover my ears but it was no use. I wanted to scream.

When I came to, I was in the salt circle I'd drawn in the bath. My body was still rigid, looking in the mirror where the sigil had gone a dead powder white. I waited for a moment to regain my equilibrium before I ran one finger over the emblem. The dead sigil crumbled and dissolved at the touch like the lightest dusting of ash.

I breathed deeply, broke the circle, and took out the Dustbuster. Then I started a very hot bath with a soothing, pink bath bomb.

After all, I still had a date.

chapter
EIGHT

I lay back in the sparkly water and tried to clear my mind. Marten was the last person I'd expected at that meeting. Of course I hadn't expected to see Marten ever again, and certainly not in New York. Above all, not at a demon party. So why not at a meeting with Mephistopheles?

Meph likes ceremonial magicians. Faust and all that. I should have realized.

I should have been happy, anticipating the evening, thinking about what to wear. But seeing Marten with Meph had been too disconcerting for me to relax. Even the lovely scent of the bath bomb and the sparkles in the water couldn't ease my mind. And since I was supposed to have a date with said magician in just a few hours, I couldn't just clear my mind and concentrate on what I needed to do immediately.

So I did the next best thing. I spent the time getting dressed to the max.

I laid the rich teal Donna Karan dress on my bed and threw on an oversized tee and then spent forty minutes on my makeup.

After I finished I pulled off the tee and put on my newest La Perla bra, panties, and matching garter belt in soft gold and lavender. Then a layer of Chanel No. 19. And then the Donna Karan and my boots.

It was time to leave. I grabbed my bright green fake fur coat and went downstairs, where another doorman hailed my cab. *Must be Vincent's night off*, I thought. So I wasn't the only one with a date.

Marten was waiting for me in the hotel lobby. He rose as soon as he saw me and steered me expertly to the restaurant. He, too, had changed; his ritual robes and accoutrements would be just a little out of place in this ultrachic space, but his Armani leather jacket with a fine-gauge-knit silk sweater were just perfect.

In fact, viewed quite objectively, Marten looked completely yummy. I wished I hadn't seen him with Meph this afternoon, wished that I wasn't off balance and wondering whether this was a date or just a meeting at a nicer venue.

"Lily, you look magnificent," Marten whispered in my ear as he took my coat to hand to the host.

Our table was ready and we were seated immediately. I missed spending time at the most beautiful bar in New York, though I supposed we could go there later. And the menu did demand immediate attention.

"I was surprised to see you this afternoon," I said as soon as we ordered every small plate on the menu. I wanted to get it out immediately, wanted to know if I was just bait for him. Okay, I felt a little wary after Nathan. That, and finding out that Marten had known all along what I was. That he had searched me out in Aruba, that it had been about him being a magician and finding a succubus, not about liking me for me.

Marten at least had the good manners to look embarrassed. "I didn't know you'd be joining us. I thought that I was working with Meph alone."

"Meph's good like that. Everyone thinks they're the only one he's partnering with. Learned it from Satan, I believe. She's amazing."

Marten nodded. "The thing is, Lily, I would really prefer if we didn't talk about business tonight. I would actually prefer if we weren't both involved in Mephistopheles' troubles at all. I would prefer things as they were in Aruba, just you and me, spending time together because we like each other."

"Well, I am going to have to introduce you to Marduk. I suppose we should schedule that now," I said in my most businesslike manner.

Marten took my hands. "We will have to decide that at some point, yes. But not tonight. Tonight I want it to be just us, just about us being together again."

I wasn't buying it. "In Aruba, you targeted me because you knew what I was," I said flatly. "I don't know what you wanted from me or why you did that, but now that I know, I don't have any romantic illusions."

Marten shook his head. "I am sorry you got the wrong impression. Yes, I knew what you were when I met you. But . . . I wasn't looking for a demon succubus then. And if I really want a demon I know how to do a summoning."

"I expect so," I agreed coldly. "That's what magicians do, isn't it?"

"Yes, it is," he admitted. "But if you think about it, that also means that if I had simply wanted you for your demonic powers or your ichor, I wouldn't have dated you the entire time you were in town. And I wouldn't have bothered to go to Hatuman's party."

That pricked my paranoia. "No?" I asked. "I thought you were there on Meph's behalf, same as me." I admit that the disappointment made it into my voice and I sounded like the plain girl in a high school movie.

"I would not have gone to the party if I had not hoped to see you," Marten said, his eyes holding mine steadily. "There were other things I could do, have done, for Mephistopheles. And I have been rewarded for them."

"And I was your reward for this one." I didn't bother to make it a question.

"No, Lily. Mephistopheles has no power over you. You know that. You are Satan's Chosen, Her handmaiden companion. No one can force you against your desire. I just wanted an opportunity to appeal to that desire, that is all."

He seemed sincere, but I didn't really trust him. Yes, it was true, even Mephistopheles, who commanded most of the denizens of Hell, could not compel me.

Still, that was a long way from a date.

I tried to pay attention to my dinner. The foie gras with soy caramen and mustard-brushed tuna was exquisite, skewers of Kobe filet and quail with five dipping sauces was a treat for the palate. We ordered loads of sushi and half a duck barbequed in plum sauce. The food was a riot, delicious and sassy and only three-quarters Japanese.

Right now I couldn't keep my mind on my food, on the atmosphere, even on the fact I was on a date.

Maybe Marten liked me, but I couldn't let myself believe that. He was a mortal and mortals didn't date demons. Not when they knew what we were. Not when they had their own agendas with Hell.

I was going home. Alone. I wanted to just break down

and cry, to feel horrible about Nathan and wish that I could trust Marten and think of when I was happy (only a few weeks ago) when I was falling in love with Nathan and having spectacular sex with Marten and thought that he just liked me. And everything then had been good and now it wasn't.

Thinking that things were as bad as they could get, I got up to go to the ladies'. I stood up and walked past a few tables and there I saw too-familiar black hair pulled back into a ponytail, a sculptured nose, and bright blue eyes that met mine from several feet away.

I wobbled and my stomach tied itself into knots. Nathan. And he was with a woman, a blonde dressed in Prada tweed, elegant and fashionable.

I tried to dart, to run, but four-and-a-half-inch stilettos are not made for fast getaways. I had almost made it to the ladies' room door when Nathan came up behind me.

"Don't," I said. "Just don't. Go back to your date. Leave me alone."

I tried to shove through the door into the sanctuary of the restroom, but he held my shoulder. "Please, Lily, talk to me," he whispered, and his voice was ragged and thick. I could almost believe that he was fighting tears as badly as I was. "At least tell me you're okay."

"Let me go," I said, though the words fought hard to get through. I knew what I had to do but the sound of his voice, the electrical feeling of his hand on my skin ripped my composure to shreds.

"I . . . God, Lily, why can't you be the woman I met? Why do you have to be this—thing?"

The pain in his voice was real, was undeniable. And it tore me straight through to the core. "I am not a thing,"

I managed to choke out before I bolted into the sanctuary where he couldn't follow.

Oh, dear Satan, I felt like I was being ripped apart. I had not known hurt could be so horrible, that rejection could hurt as much as death.

And Marten was waiting at our table, expecting to have a perfectly normal date with me.

Right now I just wanted Marten gone. I wanted to rip up the blonde's Coach bag, throw her Jimmy Choos across the room, and drag Nathan back to sanity, which was to say, back to his place with me.

None of that was going to happen. Nathan had chosen. I could not change his mind. If it could be changed, I had no idea how.

I got out of the stall and went to the line of sinks and studied myself in the mirror and pulled on my mojo. It was there, wrong astrological alignments and all, but it lay just beneath the surface. I concentrated on the immortal succubus, Satan's Chosen, the total "It" girl.

"I am beautiful and sexy, no man can resist me," I whispered to myself over and over like a mantra.

Except for Nathan. The thought came immediately, and I wanted to cry.

NoNoNo, that wasn't happening. I concentrated on remaining calm. No Nathan.

I am a succubus. No one can resist me.

The words reverberated in my mind.

The mojo rose. I could feel it shimmering just under my skin, my entire body bathed in the radiance of power. It glowed inside me, subtly illuminating my face, my complexion, my hair. Power was in me, was me.

Marten? Nathan? They were mortals. They were not

my kind. I felt numb, above them, not part of their world at all. Nor were they part of mine.

The reflection in the mirror affirmed the change. The makeup was still Laura Nars, but my face glowed with the aura of magic. My eyes sparkled, inhumanly green, and my hair was electric and wild. I was of the elements, pure and free, and I looked like a million bucks.

So I walked out of the ladies' room and tried very hard not to look where Nathan had been sitting. I walked back to our table, where Marten took one look at me and smiled blandly.

"They brought the dessert menu," he said, handing it to me.

A flicker of arrogance touched the power. Marten should be speechless and trembling, not talking as if this were a normal date.

On the other hand, dessert. I wondered what kind of chocolate they had.

I felt good again, in command. I was succubus Lily and I was both charmed and very curious about the man before me. He treated me like a date, but he was up to something. There was something he wanted and it wasn't just to help Mephistopheles out of the kindness of his heart.

Our desserts arrived. Somehow I just wasn't in the mood for trendy Japanese-inspired dessert. I wanted something rich and heavy and chocolate, full of calories and comfort. Something that would take my mind off the not-date and the question facing me, nibbling on sake-infused kiwi.

How to find out what Marten wanted? That was the question. He was not going to ask, at least not me, at least not yet.

Marten paid the tab, and I linked my arm through his as we walked toward the club. The line outside was around the block, all the beautiful New Yorkers in their finest D&G, Helmut Lang, Christian Dior, their strappiest Manolos and Jimmy Choos, all waiting for those arbiters of taste at the door to open the velvet rope and let them in.

I pitied them. Since we had dined in the restaurant, we could take the private elevator to the rooftop club with its justly famous 360 views, innovative drinks, and company of the most chic and trendy denizens of the Big Apple. This was not a place for tourists or weekenders, this was the hard core of the New York club scene in their finest.

Marten had been a standout in the resort on Aruba that somehow seemed frozen in an era of big hair and glitter balls. Here in the best of the best, the hottest club in the coolest city, he held his own. The surfer-boy body and tan looked perfect in his Armani, and his eyes sparkled the purest aquamarine. The music was much better than in Aruba, and we danced. It was too loud to talk anyway. He held me against his body and I felt the warmth and desire in him, rising to meet my mojo.

"Shall we go to your room?" I purred.

He assented. I smiled. Part one of the plan.

A simple and straightforward plan. A plan that I thought would work, in part because it was so direct. The one possible complication had already been swept away. Go to his place. Have amazing sex. (Keep him alive if he was true to form and I enjoyed him, and deliver him if he didn't give me an orgasm first.) Then, when he was asleep (or dead) search his room for clues as to what he was up to. He had clearly brought magical articles with him, at least enough to make the meet with Meph. There had to be written instructions and rituals; he couldn't have memorized everything.

One thing I did know about ceremonial magicians is that they are all about complexity. They don't get simple. They love their rituals long, with lots of symbols and articles and very strict protocol. He had to have brought his instructions along with all the accoutrements, and there had to be a clue in there about what he was after.

I hoped.

And if not, I had good reason to believe that at least I would have stellar sex.

His room was on a high floor far from the elevator, and it was larger than I had anticipated. Oversized marble bathroom and ultramodern fixtures and a tub the size of Rhode Island. The bed could have hosted a seventeenth-century Venetian orgy with room to spare.

I wondered if Marten had sprung for this luxury.

Or was Meph picking up the tab out of petty cash?

Marten dropped his leather jacket on the floor and pulled me into a slow, warm embrace. "So, so beautiful," he murmured as he traced the line of my cheek with his finger. "So difficult to decide. I wanted you all to myself all night, alone in my room, not to have to share you with the whole club. They do not deserve you. But to be seen, in public, with the most beautiful woman in New York, can you forgive me that I wanted to show you off? I wanted to see every man in the room so very jealous of me. All of them would have given years of their lives to be in my place for an hour."

I laughed, low and husky. He was only speaking the truth, understated, at that. Thousands of men had given their lives for less than an hour with me. The mojo that had sustained me since I'd raised it came through and wiped my mind clear of regret. I was pure power, a force of nature.

Marten took one step back and looked at me, and his answering smile was full of challenge. "I see I am to be your slave tonight," he said softly. "And if I do not serve your pleasure I will not see morning."

I shrugged and turned my back. "You can always leave," I reminded him.

"I can't leave," he said. "You know that. Your magic works on me as much as on any man."

He stepped away from me and when he caught my eye sank gracefully to his knees, head bowed and eyes subdued. A Renaissance courtier or priest could not have been more elegant in submission and his polished pose made me pause. Head bowed forward, the back of his neck was deliciously exposed, as if for an executioner.

I stepped out of my Manolos. He held out his hands and I pulled the desk chair around so that I could sit facing him. He did not move until I had seated myself in comfort and placed one delicately abused sole in his waiting palm.

Thumbs firm against the tender metatarsals, he stroked and massaged until I sighed with relief. Through my hose I could feel his ministrations but not his actual skin. I leaned back into the seat, closed my eyes and gave myself up to bliss.

The touch changed, became hot and moist. I opened my eyes and saw his lips moving over my arch, up to my ankle, where he licked my stockings as if they were made of cotton candy. Do not react, I told myself, but it was impossible to ignore the deep attraction of his deeply vulnerable act.

There is something delicious about being caressed through nylons. The garment is so very thin, almost not there at all, and yet is so very much a barrier. His fingers kneaded my calves, working the muscles bunched by dancing in stilettos so that they relaxed and released. His touch was demanding, intimate, and yet adoring.

I had forgotten the joys of worship. In modern egalitarian America, with modern arrogant men, I had forgotten the delicious pleasure of demanding a man's service, his submission. As a princess, even the most minor female member of the royal family, I had regularly enjoyed the attentions of attendants and slaves who had treated me with this level of deference.

I knew it was just a sex game. I knew that Marten was proud enough to be a demon—which was why this act of submission was so very sexy.

And I wanted it. Suddenly I knew that I was going to take what I wanted for myself. Not for Satan, not for Meph, not for anyone else. I was going to demand my pleasure for myself alone and . . .

I smiled slowly as I relished the thought.

Marten had already begun on my other foot. Oh, of all the reasons to wear heels, this was the best. To be pampered, to be massaged, and to feel the slow relief that made wearing those beautiful implements of torture all worthwhile.

His lips were back on my ankle, kissing slowly up my leg. I bent over and took a handful of hair in my hand and jerked his face up to me, his neck extended. "You serve me tonight," I said. "You are mine and you serve me."

Fear crossed his face, and a touch of defiance, but both gave way to desire. Cocky Marten, master of demons, wanted to be my boy toy and I wanted him right there. So long since I'd indulged in a boy toy for a night, and I deserved it. "Do you understand?" I asked, my voice soft.

"Yes," he said as I gripped his hair.

"Yes what?" I replied.

He blinked. "Yes, Lily?"

I shook my head.

"Yes, ma'am," he tried, and I let his head go.

"Better," I told him. I lay my legs over his shoulders (mm, such nice broad shoulders) and let him glimpse my lavender and gold lace panties.

He took the hint admirably and massaged slowly up my thighs, kissing lightly where his fingers had been, slowly approaching my own desire.

I leaned back, resolved that I had only to enjoy the evening, to enjoy him. I didn't have to do anything for him, nothing that I didn't want to do. I wanted to be worshipped, for him to realize his great good fortune and thank me in the way I could most appreciate.

He understood. His mouth moved up my thighs, warm and soft at the tops of my stockings, and then he breathed gently on my mons. I writhed just a little as he took his sweet time, barely touching my panties to build my anticipation.

Oh, the revenge of the boy toy on his knees. I could not protest his careful attention as he reached under my dress and caressed me lightly above the line of my panties. Then he stroked over the fine lace, teasing, approaching and then darting back to my leg, my belly, my lace.

"That's very nice, but don't make me wait too long or I'll be angry," I commanded.

As if my order had freed him, he removed my panties (which had been worn properly, over the garter belt for easy access) and sought the center of my pleasure with his tongue. I lay back and gave myself up to the sweet sensation, his demanding, untiring mouth creating waves of delight that shuddered through my body and crashed before I crested higher.

More, more, I couldn't wait, couldn't stop. Delicious heaviness centered at my core, promising sweet release soon, so very soon.

Reading my sighs and shudders, Marten stepped up his pace. Maybe there was arrogance in his ministrations, maybe he reveled with pride in how my hips thrust and I moaned, demanding more, but he gave me what I needed more than breath in that moment. Gave me more sensation, harder, faster, until I cried out and my body succumbed to desire.

I came, and came more, and wanted him inside me. There was only so far I could go without him, and yet the demon in me wanted to deny him. To have my orgasm and refuse him his seemed only justice for all the men who had had their pleasure with me and left me uninspired and, frankly, bored.

The tension of decision grew with new waves of desire, until Marten picked me up and lay me on the bed.

"May I?" he asked.

Asking was what I needed, not his denial but his acknowledgment that tonight was for me. He asked and gave me the opportunity to withhold, and so there was no longer any need to refuse him. And I wanted him so, to be filled up with him, replete.

"Yes," I said. And there was a moment of cool air while he left me and then hot skin next to mine. He entered me slowly, careful to show that he was serving my need and not sating his own. I wrapped my legs around his waist and pulled him into me harder. "Give me," I commanded. And he obeyed.

Rapture. Joy and rapture as only a succubus can know or give, I met his pent-up need with my own.

I howled and came and melted into a climax that went on and crested and did not abate but built immediately again. On and on, glory on top of need, I screamed out my satisfaction. And only then, only when I told him I was ready, did he join me.

And when he withdrew and wrapped the condom in a tissue, he thanked me. And then he curled up next to me and cuddled me until he fell deeply asleep.

chapter
NINE

I lay next to him and smelled his sunwashed skin, and wiggled my toes. Marten, like all men, had managed to fall asleep. I enjoyed the sensation, listening to his deep breathing. It isn't often that I get the chance to experience that after-sex languid sleep with someone. And Hotel Gansevoort has lovely linens, soft and superfine that feel every bit as good on my bare skin as my own Frettes.

Then, after the novelty of soft indulgence had worn off, I remembered my plan. Which had worked brilliantly. I felt like one of Charlie's Angels, only more cool because I didn't need any gadgetry to help me out. (I tried not to think about the part where I don't have any martial arts training.) I slid out of the bed without disturbing Marten's rhythmic breath and started to snoop.

I opened his suitcase and found it empty. The closet was full of clothes, all hung properly and spaced so that they wouldn't crease. All designer, all lovely. The gray ceremonial gown I had seen him wear in the meeting was nowhere in sight.

How did an accountant on Aruba acquire this wardrobe, I wondered. There weren't even many places to buy this kind of clothing on that island, at least so far as

Margit would tell me. She always went to London or Paris to shop.

I went through the drawers incorporated into the closet, full of socks and shirts and sweaters. No magical implements, no robes, no books.

There had to be books somewhere, and a computer. Or something.

I went back to the room. My eyes had adjusted to the dark and I opened the curtains slightly. Enough moonlight filtered through the glass that I could make out the desk, the piles of clothing we'd dropped on the floor, the telephone and the little hotel pad and pen on the bedside table.

Marten's computer sat on the desk. I opened it and turned it on and cursed softly. I'd forgotten how much I hated Windows. I'd heard XP was better, but he was running 2000 and it was miserably slow.

First off, I knew I'd need some kind of cover prepared in case he woke up and found me with his computer, so I opened Explorer and brought up Zappos. If he asked I could always say that I couldn't sleep and was just looking at shoes. In fact, I found Zappos.com high up in his history. Which answered part of how he found great shoes on his tiny island.

Then I opened another window and clicked on a familiar icon that looked like it should be MagicMirror. If he actually had credentials on the site that would explain a lot. And would demand a lot of other, more difficult explanations. I could understand him having some of the software. I knew that certain departments made software for the Initiated among the mortals, and it seemed that Marten ranked there. But if he could actually connect . . .

It was slow. I didn't know if it was just searching aimlessly or if the machine was just slow. And then, haltingly, the familiar welcome page came up with the animated graphic fire motif. He was on.

I was going to have to ask for some answers on that one.

Unless— I wondered.

And then I was very lucky, because he'd stayed logged into his account, which meant that his access to MagicMirror was wide open to me. I had thought he was smarter than that. My respect for him took a nosedive, and then I reminded myself that he lived on Aruba, with a low crime rate and one demon. He probably didn't think about passwording his private data—Aruba was a lot more secure than New York. At least I hoped it was a cultural difference and not an indication of unfathomable stupidity.

The window took me directly to his profile page, complete with picture. Meph was on his friends list, along with Marduk and Hatuman and a few other demons of my acquaintance. Margit wasn't on his list—so at least he didn't know about her. Or maybe he did and chose to make himself less visible to the local Hierarchy. I made a mental note of his user name.

He had found me, too, and had added me to his hot list to read, but not as a friend. Which meant that I wouldn't know that he was reading my public postings.

How long had he read my journal? Suddenly I was paranoid. Had he been stalking me? Had he been reading for a while before we left the States? Or had he only found it after I'd left?

I went to read his journal, and since I was reading with his sign-in I had access to all of his locked and private posts. I went back to before I arrived on Aruba. I wanted to see if he'd been tracking me beforehand, and if he wrote anything about meeting me.

The days leading up to my trip were boring and then blank. He posted about surfing and weather conditions and once about a French restaurant that was supposed to be the best new place in Aruba. Idly, I wondered if he had met Meph through foodporn. Nothing about his supposed job.

Ah, there it was. "Met quite a lovely lady last night. One of us, I'm certain, but even if she were just the typical tourist she would be compelling. Alas, the life of the solitary magician is not conducive to serious relationships."

Hmmm, I wondered. Did magicians all give up actual relationships for their magic, or was this just Marten pitying himself? Though he never seemed to be the type for self-pity, and he must be aware that the only reason he didn't have a serious girlfriend was that he didn't want one. A man with his looks, charm, dancing ability, wardrobe and, well, bedside manner, shall we say, could have any woman he wanted. So he must not have wanted, not beyond a series of flings.

I read further in his journal. "I am so sorry she is leaving. Always before I have felt that a short acquaintance and fun was what I wanted. And yet, this one intrigues me more than I had anticipated. I had expected beautiful, but not so intelligent, accomplished, and stylish. And sophisticated. No wonder Meph thinks so highly of her! Well, then, perhaps it would not be impossible to visit New York after all . . . Hmmm . . ."

Well, that was nice to know. At least he wasn't entirely using me for my demonic contacts and position with Satan—he had found something about me alone to be intriguing. And maybe he really had used the party and all because he wanted to be here to see me.

I smiled a bit and gave myself about five seconds to feel pleased. Then I went on. While I'd answered one question, I'd found another. The more I looked at his MagicMirror, the more I was certain that he wasn't an accountant. Not like the guy I go to for my taxes, at least. And even if he were, he certainly wasn't supporting himself on that salary.

I went through his MagicMirror, but there wasn't anything terribly useful. Clearly he had learned not to put anything online that you wouldn't want your mother to see. Even in such a locked and protected place as MagicMirror.

So I closed the browser and took a look at his documents folder.

And there was everything I wanted to know about Marten and what he was doing, how big a fund he had accumulated from Mephistopheles, everything. I'm certain of that.

And it was all written in Dutch.

I swore under my breath. How completely ridiculous, insane! What kind of modern metrosexual was he, to keep his records in a language I couldn't read? The nerve of him.

And I bet, just like Nathan, he believed he was safe because no one could read what he'd written. Only in this case, thinking about me, he'd be right. I'd never learned Dutch and my German wasn't particularly good. I'd spent time in Berlin in the 1920s, of course—the cabaret scene there was unlike anything in the world before or since. But there had been plenty of foreigners and no one cared if my German sounded like it had been learned in an Italian high school. Admin had not installed the language so it was not hidden deep in my brain structure. No, what little I'd had (and it had only covered directions, menus, and tourist necessities) had deteriorated as badly as if I'd been fully human and hadn't used a language in eighty years. It was gone.

German isn't Dutch anyway, and I couldn't make out anything in the documents labeled Ritual and Mephistopheles and Program. Why had he labeled them in English but written them in Dutch? (Okay, he wrote them in Dutch because that was his native language, but why had he labeled everything in English? Just to make me crazy? I wouldn't put it past him.)

Barely containing my frustration, I closed My Documents and went to look at the programs under Start. And I found Quicken.

And there I found out that his income was somewhere around two hundred eighty thousand Euros a year. Even for an accountant that would be very high.

I heard a groan from the bed and quickly brought Zappos.com back up. Then I looked over to check but Marten appeared to be asleep. Still, I figured I didn't have much time and that I was pushing it as it was. The only thing left to try was his e-mail.

And here, like on MagicMirror, he had put his user ID and password on permanent Remember Me.

And I hit paydirt.

Really, people ought to not leave things like this in their e-mail. But . . . people very rarely do what they ought to do. And I'd already seen Marten's notions of computer security.

The From line was Mephistopheles' private e-mail. If

I hadn't known that address I might have passed it by—
Meph is careful and keeps his private address known
only to his intimates. Which already told me plenty
about Marten. The Subject line read "Your Soul." I had
to at least glance at that.

Dear Marten,

*You have sent me an intriguing proposition. Let me
remind you of our earlier agreement, that you would
be provided with funds, a background and status in
the place of your choice, and the services of one
demon (Level 2, fifteen hours a week) along with vigorous health and youth for the full span of your natural life plus five hundred years. At which time, in
payment for the above advantages, your soul and full
body of knowledge was forfeit to Satan. I have two
copies of the traditional agreement, signed in blood,
in our files. The third copy was for your own records.*

*Now you have proposed that, should you be able to
help me in my current difficulties, you be allowed to
reclaim your soul without losing your privileges. This
is a highly unusual arrangement and I am not certain
it is covered in the original contract. There is also, you
understand, the matter that the executor of your original contract is Satan Herself. While in this matter you
would be helping me personally in my service to Her,
you would not be directly in Her chain of command.
She may well choose to keep to the original agreement
and void any further amendments that I, as Her servant, might make. So I do not have the authority to
grant your request immediately.*

*However, as you have ascertained, this matter is of
the utmost importance, not only to me but to Satan*

and the Hierarchy as a whole. If you are able to render substantial assistance, there is precedent for Satan being willing to grant you a boon. She is most generous and has always honored Her word, especially when acknowledging someone doing Her great and useful service.

If you are quite serious about voiding the terms of your prior agreement, this would be the best way to go about doing so. I will promise nothing, but I do advise you that Satan becomes quite annoyed by humans who renege on the terms of their agreements. If you put Her in the position of offering you a favor, you will have avoided a potentially difficult negotiation, and one that you might not be able to win no matter what your skills and who your allies.

If you choose to continue on this course and offer your assistance on these terms, I will accept most gladly.

Sincerely,
Mephistopheles

So. Now I understood a lot more about Marten. He'd made a bargain with one of the Hierarchy to sell his soul in exchange for a rather hefty set of benefits, and now he wanted his soul back as well. I had to remember not to whistle through my teeth. He had to be a good negotiator to have gotten so many concessions. That, or he was a more powerful magician than I had heard about in a very long time.

I closed out the program and turned the computer off. I'd found enough.

Without the light from the screen the hotel room was covered in layers of shadow. I could easily imagine things lurking in the corners and behind the curtains. I stared into the dark recesses of the room, my mind far away.

On the bed I saw bright gold hair, shimmering in the stray starlight.

Marten was more complex than I had anticipated, even despite his lack of computer security. A strong enough magician to wrest money and power and the services of a demon along with the normal perks of soul selling, he must have caught one of the higher-ups in his salt triangle. Or whatever it is they use these days.

And coming forward to ask Mephistopheles to void his contract in return for help that he hadn't even rendered yet—that took a lot of arrogance.

But then, we like pride in Hell.

The fact that Meph sounded like he thought it was a good idea for Marten to try meant that Marten had to have enough power to back up his grandiose plans. That said a lot, too. Meph is not easy to impress.

Not that the e-mail looked impressed, but I know enough about Meph and the way things work to know that normally he would have strongly discouraged a mortal with a contract from doing anything to change the terms. Not only is that standard policy, it is also wise. Almost nothing irks Satan as much as a human trying to get out of a contract with Her, especially when She honors all the provisions that Her underlings negotiate. Annoying Satan is not a good idea. Not for anyone, not for higher-ups in the Hierarchy, not for Her Chosen friends, and especially not for mortals who are enjoying their end of the bargain.

It takes great service and loyalty for Satan to grant a boon. Okay, if some mortal could uncover who had stolen major funds, who was gunning for Her lieutenants and had targeted Her Chosen, She would probably be moved to be very generous. But it was a very long shot.

So who was Marten, I wondered? He wasn't immortal, but he could be approaching centuries, he could be quite old. There had been a number of famous magicians in the past century or two. I wondered. But none of them had been Dutch . . .

I took my clothes into the bathroom and put them on. Using the bedside pad, I wrote Marten a quick note saying that I had to be at work early in the morning and didn't want to disturb him, but that we were still on for the evening and left my cell number.

I wasn't sure I wanted to date Marten (though I wasn't sure that I didn't want to date him, either), but I was dead certain that I needed to see him. Now that I knew vaguely where he stood, I at least knew the questions to ask.

chapter
TEN

Work. I wasn't lying, I had a lot to do and I was dead exhausted. A date, no sleep, great sex, sounds like the right life for a demon to me. Only the getting up, getting dressed, and actually doing any work was not easy under those circumstances.

"Lily, your eyes are puffy," Danielle said when I dragged into the office at ten with two grande double-shot mochachinos that I bought on the theory that the double boost of caffeine and sugar would get me through the morning. What was left of it.

"Yes, I know," I said and shrugged. "It happens."

She gave me a long penetrating stare and then smiled. "Oh, indeed. Well, that is good, I expect."

Then she disappeared behind the closed door to shoe-land and I was in my office. Which had, since I'd left on Friday, filled up with parcels that someone had thrown all over my sofa and coffee table.

I sighed and started unwrapping belts, beaded earrings, and bags. Lots of bags. I sat down, cradled my head in my arms on my desk and tried to ignore the universe.

Unfortunately, the universe seems to know when it's being blown off and doesn't like it much. The phone rang. I wasn't going to pick up, but I didn't want anyone thinking I was taking a second sick day.

"Where have you been?" a familiar voice started without even a greeting. "Do you know how bad Sybil is? Why didn't you pick up your phone this morning?"

It was Eros, and I had no idea what she was talking about. "What do you mean?" I asked. "We saw Sybil yesterday at brunch and everything was fine."

"Vincent disappeared this morning," Eros informed me. "He was supposed to go to Syb's right after his shift ended last night and he never showed up. He isn't answering his cell phone, and she needed to check with you to see if you'd seen him or heard from him, and you weren't answering."

"Wait, wait," I said, and dug through my purse.

It was off. I hadn't left it off, I was certain. I tried to turn it on and there was the culprit: low battery. I'd been so distracted I hadn't thought about recharging the thing.

"Look, Eros, I haven't been home and forgetting to charge my phone is not a hanging offense. I've had some extra work, okay? And a date. How was I to know that Vincent would go and disappear and Sybil would need me? How about you fill me in and I'll call Sybil," I suggested.

"Sybil is over here now, where she's been since seven thirty this morning when Vincent didn't show. We went by your place and there was no trace of you or him," Eros informed me. "We were afraid you'd both disappeared."

Did they think we'd run off together? I wanted to laugh but that would only make Sybil and Eros more upset. It isn't like Eros spent every night at home.

"Put Sybil on, okay?" I asked.

"Hi, Lily," Sybil said, sniffling. "I just wanted to know when was the last time you talked to Vincent, or saw him. You didn't see him this morning or late last night, did you?"

And then I remembered that I hadn't seen him when I'd left the night before. I hadn't thought anything of it at the time—Vincent works a regular shift rotation and sometimes he had time off, so it didn't alarm me when he wasn't there. "I didn't know he was supposed to work last night," I admitted sadly. "If I'd realized he was supposed to be on I could have alerted you then."

I felt awful. And afraid. Demons, especially talented, capable demons like Vincent don't just disappear.

"I want to find him," Sybil said.

"Of course," I agreed. "Of course you do. But he's probably fine. I want you to admit that, that he's probably just fine."

Sybil broke into tears again. "I don't know that he's probably fine. I keep thinking of him burning in holy water or being held in a salt triangle and being tormented and commanded by some ceremonial magician."

"The only ceremonial magician I've met in a hundred years is on our side," I said reassuringly. "And if Vincent had run into him, the two of them would be more likely to be in trouble for their bar tab than anything else."

"Stop making fun of her," Eros yelled into the mouthpiece. She must have grabbed the phone from Sybil, who I could hear sniffling in the background. "You are—what's happened to you, Lily? You know Sybil isn't up to your humor at a time like this."

Sybil is the most fragile of the four of us and we all know it. For centuries, Desi, Eros, and I had all conspired to take care of her. Keeping Sybil from being hurt yet again was our sacred duty as her friends, and our duty to each other as well.

"Find him," Eros ordered me. "You. Now. Find Vincent and make things okay for Sybil. Or I will curse you. I am still a demigoddess, and you still have the roots of a mortal."

Oh, give me a break. I was mortal three thousand years ago, and while I was never as powerful as Eros, I am not entirely without strength. Besides which, Satan has favored me on several occasions. Even among Her Companions, Satan has shown me particular affection.

Besides, where did Eros get off giving me orders? If she were so much more powerful she should just find Vincent herself. Eros pretended to always be so cool and above it all, but she was overreacting as badly as Sybil. I knew that, and I knew that Eros always put on an imperious front to cover up for feeling afraid.

"Give me Sybil again," I sighed. Talking to Eros was useless until she calmed down.

"What?" Sybil asked through her sobs.

"Has Eros tried to find Vincent?" I asked.

"Won't work," Sybil whispered.

"Speak up," I said. "I can't hear you. And why wouldn't it work? Why do you think that I could do it if Eros can't?"

"He likes you," Sybil confessed.

"Oh."

I had no idea that Vincent hadn't liked Eros. I also didn't know what his liking me had to do with me possibly being able to find him.

"But how do you expect me to find him if you and Eros can't?" I was definitely confused.

"You know a detective," Sybil said as if it were the most obvious thing in the world. "And he told you about Branford showing up again, so maybe he knows where the guy is. Maybe he's seen Vincent. Could you call Nathan?"

Now it all made sense.

Call Nathan. He'd called me, to warn me. It would be reasonable, natural even, for me to call him about Vincent's disappearance. That's what private detectives did all the time, right, find people? And he was the only private detective any of us knew. Oh, sure, there must be a few million in service to Satan, but we didn't know any of them personally. And they might not understand all the issues with Branford, what he had done and what he was trying to do.

Nathan was an obvious choice.

My mind went blank. It should be so simple. And this is just what I had wanted, a sincere and legitimate reason to talk to him.

I said my good-byes to Sybil, and hit speed dial for his cell phone.

He picked up on the first ring. "Lily, are you okay?" Concern warmed his voice and I knew he still cared.

"I'm fine," I reassured him quickly. "It's not me, it's Sybil. Well, Vincent, the doorman at my building, is missing. And he's been dating Sybil and she's afraid that Branford caught him. Or something else bad happened to him. So can you find him? As a detective, I mean. We can pay."

"Let's take this one step at a time. Do you have any reason to believe that he's been targeted by Branford? What's his relationship to Sybil? Start from the top."

I calmed down, at least enough to talk. "Vincent is a

demon. He's very junior, but he's doing well and has a lot of promise. And he's been dating Sybil. I always have a demon doorman who runs errands and sometimes helps cleaning up after my deliveries."

"Wait a sec," he interrupted. "Do other succubi have demon servants? Or only you?"

I thought for a moment. "I don't know," I admitted. "But Vincent is hardly my servant. He's more like my keeper sometimes." I heard his sharp intake of breath and I recanted. "Okay, not really like a keeper. But he does keep an eye on me, pass messages, help clean up and so on. It's a low-ranked position, but Vincent is better than almost anyone in his class. Meph is impressed with him and he's going to rise in the Hierarchy. We think he's headed to at least a deputy chief."

"So he's a talented young demon on the rise," Nathan said, very matter-of-factly. I wish he had been so professionally calm when I told him about what kind of demon I was. But he hadn't believed in demons then.

"Exactly," I agreed. "And he's been dating Sybil. Which we think is a little inappropriate because Syb is one of Her Companions and Vincent is just a junior newbie with a lot of promise. But they've just started dating officially and now he's missing. He said he was going over to Sybil's when he got off duty this morning, and he never arrived. And I don't remember seeing him last night when I left, either, so it could be that he never even made it in to work."

"When does his shift end? When did Sybil expect him?" Nathan was all business now.

"I think he gets off at seven in the morning. And Sybil said she started to worry at seven thirty."

"Hmmm," Nathan said, and I could see him rolling

the pen between his long fingers as he gazed out the window, thinking. "And Sybil's place is?"

"Only five minutes away by cab. I can walk it in heels in fifteen minutes. So half an hour including time for him to pick up coffee and finish signing out or whatever they do," I said wearily. "So can you do it? Can you find him?"

"I can try," Nathan said briskly. "I should also talk to Sybil, and she or you or whomever needs to sign a contract and give us a deposit. And there are more details I should get and a picture, also, if you have one. When can you come in? Or I can go over there, no problem."

"What day?" I asked. It was hard enough for me to talk to him on the phone. The thought of seeing him in person was terrifying. Excruciating. I had to remind myself that there was no hope. Still, deep inside me I believed that if I got to see him, if only he thought and listened, he would reconsider.

"Today," he replied firmly. "The sooner the better. The faster I can pick up his trail the more likely I am to find him."

"Before anything bad happens," I whispered.

"We don't know that anything bad is going to happen," Nathan said crisply, and I could tell that he had made this little speech loads of times. "It's only been a few hours, and there could be a perfectly good explanation. He could have decided to stop home and shower, he could have decided to go shopping and gotten distracted, he could have run into an old friend. We don't know. I want to talk to both of you as soon as possible. Just let me know when and where and I'll meet you."

"I've got to call Sybil to figure it out," I said lamely. "Thank you." And then I hung up.

I was going to see Nathan today. I didn't know whether I was elated or miserable. I had a date with Marten that evening, Sybil was crying, and Vincent was missing. And me—I was exhausted and confused and wanted more than anything to take a long bath and a longer nap and have the entire world go away.

Instead, I called Sybil back and we agreed to rendezvous over at her place in two hours, which I could call lunch. She had pictures and information there.

"But one thing, Syb," I said before hanging up. "It sounded like Eros was upset with me this morning. Or was she just worried about Vincent and I'm being paranoid?" I knew I had to be politic in asking Sybil; she was terribly frightened, and with good reason, and I didn't want to make things worse.

Fortunately, I think the question distracted her. "I don't think it was you at all," she said after a moment of consideration. "She had wanted to call Beliel right away, before you, and I said that I wanted to talk to you first. I don't think you noticed, but she spent a lot of Hatuman's party with Beliel. And I wanted Nathan, not one of Beliel's Security demons, looking into things. I know Eros is friendly with Beliel, but that whole department makes me twitchy."

"Me too," I agreed, thinking about this new information. Could Eros be dating Beliel? That thought was entirely weird but it niggled and wouldn't leave my brain. Something to look into later, maybe, but a low priority now.

Instead, I called Nathan back, gave him the address, and checked my shoot log. If I was going to disappear for a long lunch with a private detective and a distraught friend, I'd better be caught up on work.

I opened my features book and started to look through at what shoots were scheduled and where an editor had requested bags. While I am thoroughly modern and fully computerized, I keep this record in a spiral-bound notebook. That way I can sketch and color in ideas to have a more accurate image of what the feature is about.

The Fendi was definitely going in the holiday issue and there were a couple from Coach that were just right for Helene's October spread on plaid skirts. I giggled with glee as the new line fit almost effortlessly into the upcoming issues, practically placing themselves. I pulled out my boxes and labeled each of them by shoot and editor and started filling them with bags.

Of course, jewelry and scarves and other possible accessories (glasses? belts? gloves?) would all be added as I found just the right things for the clothes to be featured. The best part of the process was showing their hand-picked accessories to the editors when they came to show me the clothes. They thought I was psychic because I could so accurately predict what would work best for a particular spread.

Well, okay, I'd been setting fashion for three thousand years, give or take a decade or so. There have been eras when the fashions were just awful. The eighties, for example. Big hair and ankle socks with heels. Who thought of that? Sheesh!

I was so focused on the task, so consumed by the new pieces and the smell of leather that I lost all track of time. So I jumped, shocked, when my office door banged open and a six-foot-two man in exquisite Lagerfeld barged in like a tornado.

"Lily, Lily, save me from this madhouse," Lawrence

yelled, his fingers clutching compulsively at his hair, dis-arranging his two-hundred-dollar cut and blow-dry from M. Louis. "You are the only sane, reasonable person in this hellhole. These others are insensitive, evil, cutthroat demons out to murder me and dump my mangled body into the East River."

I blinked. "I don't think they do that anymore. Especially not with all the work that's gone into cleaning up the river."

Lawrence looked like he was going to explode again, so I shifted a few boxes to the floor and motioned for him to sit on the sofa. He looked at the spot as if it might be contaminated, steeled himself and perched on my elegant reproduction eighteenth-century French brocade. I glanced at my mantel clock and figured I had half an hour before I had to leave.

"What's the problem?" I asked.

"What's not the problem?" he spewed. "The gross incompetence? The fact that no one can get me the photographer I want on the same day the model I want is available? The fact that the model's agency objected to the outdoor shoot? Where can I start?"

Classic Lawrence. "Well, do you need any accessories? I can't do anything about models' schedules or shooting permits in the park, but if you need a really nice bag I can take care of it. How were the belts for the white shirt shoot, by the way?"

He gritted his teeth. "They were perfect. I still don't know how you knew . . ."

I smiled perkily. "You told me what you wanted. I've got the inventory of belts. It was no big deal. So . . . do you want a bag?"

"No," he said, pouting.

"Well, do you want some jewelry? Or glasses? I just got in a shipment of new Versace frames, they're very interesting. Very Euro."

"Oh, that's how you categorize us? Euro? That's so—Americans are so provincial." His accent was stronger, but I didn't know if I was supposed to take that as more Euro or that the British were something different from effete continentals.

I just stared at him in big-eyed innocence. In three thousand years, a girl can learn to impersonate a lot of innocence. "I was talking about how great the glasses are." I paused for a moment to let it sink in. "What do you want? I can't help you if you don't tell me what you want."

"I want Sonia available on the same day as Jackson Keefe."

Okay. Fine. What precisely did he want me to do about that? I'm the accessories editor. I don't book models. Sometimes I choose photographers, but except for my very few features (like my shawls and wraps special, where I already had a commitment from the selfsame Keefe) I have nothing to do with scheduling. Mostly I do my accessories page every month and support the fashion division.

I shrugged. "I don't know how I can help you with that," I said softly. "Really. I do accessories. You know that."

His eyes narrowed and turned sly. "And you've got Keefe on the roster to do your shawl shoot. On a day that I'd already booked for Sonia."

Uh-oh. I could see where this was going and it was very bad.

"But that's a cover story," I said softly. "Accessories

gets a cover story maybe once every other year if we're lucky. And I booked Keefe a month ago."

Lawrence glared. "Fashion is more important than accessories. My feature on emerging British designers is more important than shawls." Somehow he managed to spit the word "shawls" as if it were a curse.

"When is your feature scheduled?" I asked quite reasonably. My shawl story was set to run in November, and if he was after that I could possibly negotiate.

Lawrence waved his hand in the air. "No definite date yet."

Oh. That had to mean that it hadn't been approved yet. A thought quivered in the back of my head.

Carefully, deliberately, I kept my face and voice perfectly innocent. "Did Amanda just approve the feature? Because I don't remember it at the editorial meeting, but I was out of the country for a while . . ."

Lawrence stood up, all six foot two of him towering over me, and glared down his nose. "You will sign over your booking to me," he ordered in exactly the same tone my father the King might have used.

I smiled at him. "I'll be happy to do that," I told him. "When Amanda confirms your cover article and the date."

"You do not say no to me!" he yelled, moving menacingly close. "You do not contradict me. You do exactly as I say and you do it right now."

I am not a princess of Babylon for nothing. I stood up and stared him down. "I report to Amanda, the same as you." I kept my voice soft and even, but the threat underneath was clear. "And you'd better think twice before you start ordering your colleagues around as if we were your personal servants. No, Lawrence, we do not have to do what you tell us to just because you want something. Your article isn't approved yet. I don't think you've even proposed it yet. You want to go in with a complete setup to make it harder for Amanda to turn you down, but trust me, she doesn't like being manipulated that way. I'd recommend that you propose the article through proper channels and schedule your model and photographer through the right office. Now, please leave."

Lawrence bellowed. When I wouldn't drop my gaze, he picked up one of the boxes I'd so carefully set up and hurled it across the room. Then another, and another. Bags flew, cardboard broke. I ducked behind my chair as a Gucci bag weighted with hardware flew at my head.

Large bangle bracelets bounced off the chair and broke, leaving pieces of jagged metal and plastic in the carpet. Lawrence bellowed again and emptied a box of assorted gloves and scarves for the outerwear issue over my ficus and kicked the plant.

Then he spotted my spiral-bound notebook lying in the middle of my desk. In his rage he picked it up and tried to tear the entire thing across. When it wouldn't tear, he began ripping pages out and tearing them and throwing them like confetti around the room.

I picked up the chair and held it in front of me.

It's made of Lucite, both light and see-through so it worked just like police riot shields. As he yelled and stampeded I turned it around so the legs pointed toward him. "Get. Out. Of. My. Office. Now." I said as I drove him toward the door with the chair.

My office was a shambles, bags and costume jewelry scattered across the floor. Lawrence cast around but couldn't find any more ammunition.

"I will have you fired," he threatened.

"I don't think so," I replied, nudging him the last few inches.

There was nowhere else for him to go. With a roar of rage, he left. I locked the door after him and surveyed the wreck of my office, and sank to the carpet in shock.

I don't know how long I sat on the floor. The phone rang insistently and finally I couldn't ignore it any longer. At least he hadn't trashed my desk. The phone sat where it always did, untouched. I pulled a tissue from the glass box on the windowsill, blew my nose, and picked up the phone.

"Did you forget our meeting with Nathan?" Sybil asked, her voice full of confusion.

And that was all it took to break through my haze. "Oh my goodness, Sybil, I'm so sorry. But my colleague barged in here and tried to take my photographer and trashed my office and threatened me!"

"Oh, dear Satan, are you okay? Can you come over now?" she asked.

"Yes," I said, horrified that I'd spaced on the time, and opened the door.

I started to pick up the boxes, wondering how long it would take me to re-create all the selections I'd finished up. They were all carefully recorded in my spiral notebook, the pages of which were torn and scattered among the other detritus.

"Wait." Danielle stood in the door watching me. "Don't pick anything up yet. Do you have a camera? We should take pictures."

My eyes widened at this suggestion. "This is assault," she said. "Physical aggression. Destruction of property.

Harassment in the workplace is a major issue at any corporation these days."

"I need to go home and I need to do something about this," I said, waving my arms at the mess.

Danielle shook her head. "Not now," she said. "Not just yet. Just go home."

I caught a cab and hit Sybil's building two minutes after one. I went upstairs to find that Nathan was already seated on the sofa with a thick portfolio open on the coffee table.

Sybil was barefoot, her eyes neon red and her hair carelessly pulled into a ponytail. She wore a pair of Citizen jeans and a Donna Karan cashmere sweater as if they were old sweats. She tried to smile at me but she was too close to tears.

I flung my arms around her, not noticing the last streaks of her mascara on my shoulder. "I'm so scared," she said as she hugged me and cried again.

"We'll take care of this," I said gently. "You've been talking to Nathan. He told me that Vincent was probably fine."

"Yes," she said. "Probably." And then the waterworks started again.

I wondered where Eros was. She'd probably gone on to her office now that she'd taken care of Sybil and scolded me and got Nathan working on the case. I wanted to ask, but that probably wouldn't be a very good idea under the circumstances.

Nathan got up and came over to me. He looked as if he were about to shake my hand and then stopped, confused, because it was appropriate and weird and wrong all at the same time. We stood there awkwardly for a minute until I sat on one of the silk-upholstered slipper chairs.

Nathan sat down and resettled his papers on his lap, looking for all the world like a salesman or an accountant. "Let me go over this," he said, all business. "Do we know that Vincent left his place of work at seven? Did anyone see him go that you know of? I'll go down and ask the day man myself, but when did you actually have contact with him last?"

"I talked to him around four in the afternoon," said Sybil. "And he said he'd come straight over after he finished at seven."

"We know that he knew about Branford and was dedicated to keeping both of you safe, but do you know if he actually saw Branford? Did he plan to try to investigate on his own? Or did he plan to stay in place to protect both of you? And are there any other obligations he might have had, anyone else who might wish him harm, anyone whom he might want to work with? You've indicated that he is quite ambitious. Could he have gone off on his own to try to impress someone? You? Mephistopheles?"

Nathan's voice remained entirely even. Sybil poured coffee and tried to answer, and I tried to help her. But we didn't know any more than I had told him over the phone. No, Vincent had said that he was staying at work. And while Vince may well have wanted to go off on his own and be a hero—both for Sybil and his future in Hell—he was also disciplined and careful about his priorities.

Sybil and I just looked at each other and shook our heads.

"What were the circumstances of his death?" Nathan asked, nonplussed.

I shrugged. "I think he was killed in an accident. A car accident," Sybil said, waving her hands helplessly. "I'm sure there were some enemies, he was qualified to become a demon, after all. But nothing big. And he wasn't from the city, though I think he'd been familiar with it before he died. I mean, I think he might have come into town for some of the clubs before, but he was never on the Upper East Side. He used to tell me about it. I was teaching him about shopping and what kinds of clothes he should wear, as someone shooting for CEO."

Nathan's eyebrows went up. "He was shooting for CEO?"

Sybil winced. Nathan was hopelessly naive about Hell. "No," she said. "But you should always dress for the role ahead of the one you want. It impresses people. Especially our people. Satan is a stickler for style, especially in Her inner circle. The more powerful and important demons are always physically beautiful and exquisitely dressed."

"Is Vincent beautiful?" Nathan asked.

"Not quite yet," I told him. "Vincent is definitely attractive as humans go, but upper-level demons usually pay Admin for improvement jobs. It's expensive, but worth it."

He studied me. "Have you had an . . . improvement job?"

Suddenly I was seeing the ex-boyfriend, the unpleasant part of the ex, too. I rolled my eyes and said nothing.

At least Nathan had the grace to look embarrassed. "So you expect that at some point in the future, Vincent will change his appearance as a career move. Do you think he could have done that already, or be in the process?" he asked, avoiding my eyes.

Sybil shook her head. "He couldn't afford it. We'd talked about when he would have saved enough in favors and gotten enough power on his own to pay Admin. Their rates for this are pretty steep and he wasn't there yet. He'd only been a demon for a few months! And for that he's come very far. And he would have told me if he were ready to do anything like that. He would have consulted me, discussed exactly what he wanted done or should have done. I have more experience and I know Satan and I know he wanted to please Her. And now—" Sybil burst into tears again.

Nathan nodded and made a notation in his book. "Has he ever missed or been late for an appointment before? Do you have his current address? Was he reliable at work?"

Sybil nodded vigorously. "He's never late. He's good at work, I know. The other guys think he's amazing, especially for such a young guy. And his address—wait a minute, let me write it down for you." I glanced over and saw it was way uptown on the West Side. That would give him an unpleasant commute to my building. "Are you going to go search his apartment?" Sybil asked, almost as an afterthought.

"I may," Nathan said carefully.

Sybil bit her lip. "I'll come with you. He gave me a key."

I sat up a little straighter. I hadn't known they'd been that serious.

"Did he have the key to your place as well?" Nathan asked, all business.

"Yes," Sybil said. "It was reasonable. He was always doing nice little things for me."

"So he had your key," Nathan repeated. Then he turned to me. "And he had access to your apartment as well."

I shrugged. "He's our doorman, what good would he be if he couldn't let in the plumber or hang up the dry cleaning? But I don't think he would have it on him, I think they have a set of master keys in the office."

Nathan made notes and asked more questions about Vincent's habits and his job. I was a little embarrassed that Sybil knew a lot more about my building security than I did.

"You've called his apartment as well as his cell?" Nathan asked after it seemed like he'd exhausted all the avenues of inquiry.

"He doesn't have a landline," Sybil said. "He just uses his cell as his main phone."

He seemed to consider a matter before he spoke. "Normally, I don't like having clients along when I'm investigating, but since you have a key to his apartment I'm not sure there would be a problem if you came along."

"And me," I included myself immediately. Nathan looked like he was going to protest, but I stood up and put on my coat. "I'm going with Sybil. I'm not letting her deal with this by herself." The fact that he would be there was immaterial. A close woman friend, that was one thing. Your friend's ex? Not much better than useless.

chapter
ELEVEN

So we all crammed into a taxi to Washington Heights, right up under the George Washington Bridge—the west One-Sixties and on. Washington Heights is what real estate agents call a "transitional" neighborhood. Until very recently, it was working class and poor and ethnic, mainly immigrants who didn't have family established in better neighborhoods. I remembered when it was Jewish and Italian and Greek and then Hispanic. Bodegas—where you can buy pork rinds and saints' candles and other occult paraphernalia mixed in with the Campbell's soup and ramen noodles and toilet paper—still dot the street corners. The complexion of the area is in the process of changing again, this time from poor and immigrant to young and hip and hopeful.

Overhead the bridge traffic rumbles nonstop and the streets are in deep shadow from the tangle of overpasses and the bus station that perches atop giant pylons. Sybil led us to a run-down building next to one of the bridge access entrances. The place looked like a relic from the near past, the first floor and stairwell covered with graffiti, mainly in green and silver, probably gang tags. The linoleum on the stairs was worn through to the subflooring and I could hear TV voices shouting in Spanish.

Vincent lived on the third floor. Sybil fitted two keys

into two locks, one of them of the police bar variety favored in iffy areas. The door itself was solid metal, made to withstand serious attack.

We entered through the kitchen, which was aggressively clean and unfathomably large. I looked to explore the cabinets under a huge slab of countertop, but couldn't find the doors. "It's a bathtub," Sybil said softly, and then I saw that the Formica slab was just a loose, heavy piece which could be removed. And, as Sybil said, it was a bathtub, old and scarred enamel scoured impeccably clean.

The kitchen led directly to another room in the railroad car arrangement. This middle room appeared to be a study and living room. A large TV sat against the wall and a small desk was tucked into a corner. I watched Nathan go through the desk methodically, sifting the bills and noting the books. I noted the books, too, all of the new demon coursework through the first four years. Vincent was definitely ambitious. Most demons didn't qualify past the first year or so of study. Most preferred the other employment opportunities to the long years of apprenticeship and all the exams to rise in the ranks of Hell.

Nathan moved around with confidence, making notes, looking, wiping a finger over the remotes to see how long they'd been unused. I was impressed with the way he searched: patient, organized, in command in an unfamiliar environment.

Sybil had already moved into the bedroom. I was shocked to see the bed was made. Fine linens, six-hundred-thread-count sheets and a duvet cover in sage green looked vaguely familiar. Oh, right, Syb's from before she'd redecorated. They had seemed feminine mixed with her florals, but here the simple lines and solid colors looked tailored, disciplined, and masculine. A framed picture of Sybil stood on the left side of the pine dresser, symmetrically balanced with a photo of an older, dark-haired woman on the right.

"His mother," Sybil said when she noticed me looking. "That was his biggest regret about being a demon, that he couldn't come back and take care of her."

Other than the photos, the bedroom seemed strangely impersonal. The bed was freshly made, the clothes uniformly folded and organized in the dresser, the closet hung with all the shirts arranged by color and facing in the same direction.

Sybil stood in the middle of the room shaking her head. "It's wrong," she said, and wrung her hands. "It's just . . . wrong."

Nathan was next to her immediately. "What's wrong?"

Sybil looked around as if she were trapped. "Vincent is neat, he keeps the place well," she stared slowly. "But . . . he's not this anal. Not usually. And there's only one uniform hanging in the closet, and he has three."

"Well, he was wearing one for work," I said. "And the third could be at the cleaners."

"Then he didn't come home to change," Nathan said crisply and made more notes. "Let's go through room by room, Sybil, and you tell me what's wrong."

She looked around the bedroom again. "The uniforms. Everything is too neat in the closet. I think someone else must have gone through it." She turned and looked at the bed. "There's no book on the end table."

"He kept books in here?" I was surprised. I hadn't pegged Vince as an intellectual.

She nodded. "His current course work, and notebooks.

He wrote out his notes by hand. He was working on *The Hierarchy and Sin* series."

We went back to the living room and this time Sybil looked over the bookcase by the desk. "And look here, none of the books from that series is here, either." She looked around and appeared confused for a moment. "Something else is missing."

Nathan nodded. "Electronics. We can assume he had his phone on him, but there's no computer."

Sybil nodded thoughtfully. "Right. I don't see his computer. Or his iPod, or his camera. None of them."

"You know he had the iPod and the camera?" I didn't think he'd earned that much.

Sybil turned red. "I loaned him my old ones I didn't need anymore."

"Are we done?" I asked, but I should have known better. Nathan went to examine the bathroom, only to find that there wasn't one. There was a tiny water closet next to the kitchen.

"There's only the tub and sink in the kitchen," Sybil said. She opened a cabinet next to the sink and, sure enough, it had a cheap mirror hung on the inside and the lowest shelf held a toothbrush, toothpaste, shaving cream, deodorant, and shampoo.

"Lily, would you look at this?" Nathan's voice sounded a bit strained and low, close to my shoulder.

I turned to face him and was overwhelmed with his presence enveloping me. We were alone and the smell of his cologne (Versace L'Homme—thank goodness, something decent) and cashmere, the broad shoulder so tempting to lean on, the impulse to simply melt into him was nearly irresistible. Suddenly his arms were around me and he held me so tight and it felt so good. His face was just over mine. "Lily, Lily," he whispered and all of a sudden we were kissing.

His mouth devoured me. Why had we been apart? Why had we broken up? There was only this feeling of return between us, the knowledge that we both belonged here, together, with each other.

He knew it, he had to feel it quivering like a frightened thing between us.

Then he broke the kiss gently and stepped back. One single step. Not so much away from me but to show me something.

"Look at this," he said, and he pointed to the trash bin which he had pulled out from under the sink.

"I'd rather not," I replied, smiling. "It's trash."

Nathan nodded. "Exactly. Do you have any idea how much information is in the trash? Archaeologists love trash middens. And here we are, and . . . look. Just look."

I took a deep breath and looked into the plastic-lined canister. There was a toothpaste box, coffee grounds and filters, and a few pieces of paper that looked like grocery receipts and movie stubs.

Nathan reached down to the papers, and that was when I noticed that he had put on latex gloves. I was impressed; I never would have thought of that. But it enabled him to reach into the garbage and grab the papers. I didn't see why they would be interesting. Nathan, though, wasn't bothering with the movie tickets. Instead he had laid out the receipts on the counter, facedown, and that was when I saw the writing.

Single words, as if they were personal reminders. They didn't make any sense to me. "Get Sybil," Nathan said to me.

I found my friend still fondling the remotes with a be-mused expression. "The other things should be here," she said. "He was methodical, he kept all the remotes and the iPod and camera together. Everything in one place, he always said. And I always joked that this apartment was so small that there was only one place."

I put my arms around her and let her cry quietly for a minute before I told her that Nathan needed her in the kitchen. Then I steered her gently around the beanbag chair and the table.

Nathan wasted no time. "Please, Sybil, we need your help. Take a look at this. Don't touch it, just look. Is that Vincent's handwriting?"

She shook her head No.

"Are you sure?" he asked again.

"I'm sure," she said.

"Even I'm sure," I added. I'd seen Vincent's writing any number of times, on work orders and messages and notes detailing what a plumber or electrician had done while I was out. Vincent printed everything in neat, boxy letters that looked like he'd been trained to write on blueprints or something like that. The words here were scribbled cursive only vaguely intelligible, where Vincent's writing was more legible than half the fonts on my computer.

Nathan looked at them and hummed. Then he turned them over to the receipt side. I was confused. What could a grocery receipt tell him? Well, one was from Duane Reade. Nathan looked at that and then opened the cupboard where we'd discovered Vincent's tooth-brush.

"What information can you get from a pharmacy receipt?" I asked, curious.

Nathan smiled. "Look at this. First of all, this Duane Reade is in Brooklyn, see the address down here? Now look—there's a shampoo purchase here."

"Yes, so?" I asked.

Sybil's eyes opened very wide. "Not the same shampoo as in the cabinet. The one on the receipt is Suave—look here. And Vincent uses L'Oréal."

"So this isn't his handwriting and it isn't his receipt," I repeated slowly, understanding the implications. "And so if there are addresses on the other receipts we have some idea of where he's being held!"

"Not so fast," Nathan said softly as he studied and made notes to himself. "We don't know that he's kidnapped or in trouble. So far as we know at the moment, he could be gone entirely voluntarily, although that looks less likely. What we do know is that there was someone here who was not Vincent. We know that this person shopped someplace that was not in this neighborhood."

"We know that person used cheap shampoo," Sybil added.

"A common brand," Nathan agreed. "Those are the hardest to trace. Anyway, we know that someone else was here and possibly cleaned up after himself, and maybe took the electronics."

"A thief?" Sybil asked.

Nathan shook his head. "A thief wouldn't have left the place so neat. I'd bet serious money that whoever was here wiped down the surfaces so there won't be prints. No, the electronics that were taken were things that could have useful information. I wonder . . ." He looked out the window blankly, his mind somewhere else.

"What?" Sybil was agitated and worried. And I didn't blame her.

"I wonder if he was waylaid so that someone else could come up here and search. But for what? For keys? For his computer?"

The computer was obvious. "You're sure he didn't bring it to work?" Nathan asked.

"No, never," Sybil insisted. "It was a Dell laptop, a big one. Fifteen inches, I think, too big for me to haul around. Mostly he just used it here, and for MagicMirror, of course. But it's definitely gone. It's too big to hide easily and it always sat on his desk or the bedside table."

Nathan gathered up the receipts from the counter and looked in all the other trash cans in the place to make sure there wasn't anything else interesting in them. Then he put the slips of paper into an envelope and labeled it, and then put it into a plastic baggie in his notebook. I was impressed; he was acting just like a detective on the cop shows. He peeled off the latex gloves and dropped them into the kitchen garbage and asked Sybil to close up. "I don't want any of us to leave prints, but Sybil has been here and her prints would be expected," he explained as we exited.

"I want to get this into the office and check it for prints, though I doubt they left any. Whoever was there looks very professional," he added.

"What do we do?" Sybil asked.

Nathan turned and faced her, and took both her hands in his. He was so kind with her, so grave and determined. "We will find him. I'm in a big agency and we do this all the time. What you do is wait. Try to go about your normal routine. I know that'll be hard, but try anyway. Go to your office, go home, see friends, go to your usual places. If this is a kidnapping they will most likely contact you."

"Do you think it is a kidnapping?" Sybil asked softly.

Nathan stared into her eyes and smiled slightly. "I can't tell yet, but right now the indications are against it. I think they wanted Vincent's computer and files, and got him out of the way for a while. I don't think they intended to kill him or even hurt him, or they wouldn't have left the apartment so neat and clean. That wouldn't make sense. They don't want him to know that it's been searched and things are missing, not immediately. And they cleaned their prints. They expect him to come back here."

"You really think so?" Hope was struggling feebly in Sybil's eyes.

"I'm just pointing out the evidence," Nathan said firmly, and I wanted to throw my arms around him and kiss him again. Once for myself and once for how wonderful he was being to Sybil, addressing her concerns and calming her with facts, but not making empty promises.

But it still bothered me. "Why?" I asked. "Why would anyone search Vincent's apartment? Why would anyone kidnap him? What would they want?"

"Money?" Sybil suggested. "I do have money. I don't know what else. Unless they just hate demons."

"But if they just hate demons, why Vincent?" I pondered. "Because he's associated with us? Why not one of us? And what would they want, anyway? It doesn't make any sense to me."

Nathan shook his head. "We don't know for certain that Vincent has been kidnapped. We don't know what happened, yet, and it's my job to try to find out. Why

don't you both go home for a bit? Lily, could you go
with Sybil? You both need lunch. I'll bet you haven't
eaten anything all day, have you?" This last was said to
Sybil again, and she shook her head.

"Then go on. See if there is anything else you can
think of. There may be some information when you get
there. I'm going to take this to my office. We'll be in
touch." With that last he looked directly at me. I wanted
to throw my arms around him and tell him not to go, to
come with us, with me. To stay with me tonight, forever.

And then he was down the staircase before I could say
anything. By the time Sybil and I had made it to the
front door he was closing a car door behind him.

"We'll have to call a car service," Sybil said. She had
a number on speed dial, which made me wonder how
often she came this far uptown with Vincent.

Sybil insisted that she would be fine, and that I should
go home and get some rest; and so I dropped her at her
apartment and went home. Alone.

chapter
TWELVE

A short nap and a hot bath later, I had just climbed into the realm of survivable. I'd lit three aromatherapy candles, one for calm, one for relaxation, and one for stress release. This was possibly a mistake as the scents blended into a jumbled mishmash rather than a pleasing potpourri. Still, I managed not to think about Vincent or Lawrence or work or even Meph and his problems. I let my mind drift over my wardrobe instead. After all, I still had a date tonight.

Then my cell phone shattered my fragile cocoon.

I debated not picking it up. The whole thing hurt too much, as if I were sore from a ski accident and achy all over, and any pressure, any interruption only made the dull throbbing erupt into acute agony.

The phone did not stop, and so, knowing that this was a stupid move, I answered it.

"Lily, you were brilliant," Danielle said over a strangely echoey connection. "Lawrence, he stormed out of the office screaming. He ran into the street, he didn't even take his coat."

"Don't tell me he got run over," I said, terrified that I'd killed the guy—without ensuring his eternal torment first.

"We are not so lucky," Danielle answered. "But he is

gone for today, and who knows how long he will stay gone. He was in a rage. He pounded on Amanda's door and demanded that she fire you immediately."

"And?" I asked. Lawrence might be powerful enough to make such demands and even get Amanda to listen to him, but she didn't make editor in chief by being an idiot.

"She told him to stuff it. Just like that," Danielle chortled. "She said she was tired of his infantile displays. I quote exactly. She said those very words. That is when he left."

"Danielle, you're an angel," I told her, crossing my fingers. Not that Danielle is not the best coworker in the world, but "angel" isn't exactly a compliment where I'm from. "What do you think will happen?"

"I do not know," she said airily. "It does not matter. You have won. Amanda supported you and told Lawrence that he was infantile. Which he is. I think the meeting tomorrow will be very interesting. But . . . I still do not understand what the problem was. What made him so very angry with you?"

Ahhhh, now I understood why she was calling. I was shocked that she hadn't been able to hear every word even though the door was closed. And I wondered if she'd called out of her own curiosity or if some of the others had put her up to it.

"You know, everyone has looked at your office," Danielle told me after I'd finished my recitation. "It looks like Iraq, like someone fought a war in there. All those lovely purses, all over the floor."

I almost sniffled. "Don't let anyone take anything. Tomorrow I'll have to redo what I did today. There are some really nice bags for a bunch of the upcoming shoots. If nothing's damaged, a lot of the folk in fashion are going to be very happy."

"You will have much support," Danielle assured me solemnly. "What are you doing now? When you left for lunch we thought you needed to go home and drink and take a lot of Valium."

"I had a bath and I'm going to have to go get dressed. I have a date tonight."

"Oh, no," Danielle exclaimed. "How can you have a date after such a terrible day? Tonight you should wear only your slippers and eat foie gras and chocolate and not have to be amusing or look elegant."

I laughed. "Really, Danielle, I'm a bit shaky but I think a date is just the thing to take my mind off the whole Lawrence debacle." Not to mention Vincent.

She joined me in laughter. "Well, then, we shall see you tomorrow at editorial meeting?"

"If I'm not in before the meeting do you think anyone would mind?"

"Lily, if you manage to make it to meeting tomorrow at all you will be our heroine. Already everyone thinks that you deserve at least a full day of sick leave and extra hazard pay." Danielle said this very seriously, which always made her accent more pronounced.

"That's the best reason in the world for me to show up. So I guess I'll see you tomorrow."

When I got off the phone I felt much better. Definitely worth dripping down the hallway to get the call, I decided. Suddenly I felt free of the crushing misery of Lawrence's tantrum and ready to go out with Marten.

I was just thinking it was time to leave when the intercom buzzed. An unfamiliar doorman came on the line and announced that Marten was here and should he send him up?

I was disoriented and a bit confused. I'd thought I was meeting Marten at his hotel. I hadn't expected him to come up to me. "I'll meet him in the lobby," I said, and grabbed my coat and bag.

The lobby of my building is not as grand as Eros's, but it is warm and comfortable. Two large overstuffed club sofas face each other on the polished marble tile floor in front of an oversized fireplace. Usually fires are lit from December through February, but this month was cold enough that a fire was roaring on the hearth. I was glad that Marten had the opportunity to sit in comfort. He sat as close to the fire as he could get and was staring into it, and he didn't see me arrive.

"Marten, I'd thought I was going downtown to pick you up. I hadn't expected you to come here," I said as I approached.

Marten shrugged. "Yes, I know I was taking a chance, but it did seem the more polite thing to do. You don't mind?"

I shook my head.

"You didn't want me to come up," he said. He made it a simple statement of fact, without accusation or edge.

"I had a bad day at work and the place is a mess. I didn't want you to see dirty dishes and lingerie draped all over," I said lightly.

He smiled, and his eyes crinkled pleasantly at the corners and warmed. "I am sorry, I should have thought," he said. "Of course you could not be expected to want a visitor on a workday. Where did you want to eat? Un-like my own city, which is more like a small town compared to this, there are so many choices that I could not decide."

"I made a reservation at Pastis," I told him. Thank the Internet for Opentable.com—and some pull in Hell to get a table at one of the hottest places in the city at the last minute. Meph must want something from Marten very badly to give us his reservation, because it was Meph who offered. I would have been fine taking my chances on the line at Cafeteria.

We got into a taxi and piled several large shopping bags into the trunk. I waited until we were settled and the cabbie confirmed where we were going before I popped the question. "Why did you come pick me up? We could have missed each other."

"But we didn't," Marten said. "I was in the neighborhood anyway and I wanted to see where you lived. It's very nice."

"In the neighborhood?" I was suspicious.

"Barneys." Well, okay, he did have the evidence. Those shopping bags. There wasn't anything like Barneys in Orangestad.

But Barneys was twenty blocks downtown. Not in the neighborhood at all, not by my reckoning.

Marten reached over and took my hand across the cab's backseat. "I am so happy that you have some time to see me this evening. You had a bad day at work—will you tell me about it?"

Maybe I was just in a suspicious mood, but I wasn't buying the terribly nice-guy act. He was covering something up. I was intrigued, but I wasn't going to pass by an opportunity to tell him about Lawrence and his temper tantrums and how he terrorized the entire office. I didn't tell him about Vincent, though. Not quite yet.

And Marten listened. All the way downtown from the 60s (since it took that long to have the earlier part of the conversation) he paid attention, asked appropriate questions, appeared to actually process what I was saying. By the time we got out at Pastis, he had said very little besides "Why is that?" and "He did what?"

We were seated much faster than I had ever been at Pastis. I don't know whether it was because it was a Monday night, which is traditionally slow, or whether there was a special tick next to Meph's reservation. In any case, we were shown to a quiet table far from the door and the waiter's station, handed menus and left alone.

We took a break in the conversation to think about food. Pastis is the sister restaurant to Balthazar, but their menus are somewhat different. After some consideration I decided on the homemade mushroom ravioli because I was definitely in need of comfort food.

After we ordered, Marten asked again about Lawrence. "Are you certain he isn't in the Hierarchy? He sounds like he could be demonic."

I shook my head. "Not a chance, unfortunately."

"Unfortunately?"

I rolled my eyes at my date. "If Lawrence were a demon, unless he's at Meph's level I would outrank him. He'd think twice before blowing up at one of Satan's Chosen. And he really wouldn't try to make me give up my reserved photographer for a project that he hasn't even gotten okayed yet. Besides, if he were a demon, I expect that I would have learned somewhere."

"Have you looked for him on MagicMirror?" Marten asked.

I raised an eyebrow. "You know about MagicMirror?

I didn't think humans knew. I thought it was Hell-space," I said to cover up for the fact that I'd gone into his MagicMirror account.

"Hellspace does not necessarily mean demon-only access," Marten corrected me.

"I didn't know that. I thought it was demons only," I said slowly. "You know I'm a succubus. What else do you know about me?"

"Nothing," Marten answered, and for some reason I believed him. Maybe it was the way he looked at me, as if all the masks and pretenses were gone. Or maybe he just had a very good act. "I know what Meph told me, that is all. I thought you might be a succubus when I saw you at the resort, but only because you are so beautiful in a way that is not quite human. You have an aura that feels like sex and Hell, but I can't describe it more completely. I knew that it was dangerous for me to have sex with you, but that just made you more attractive. I didn't know that you were one of Satan's Chosen until this minute when you told me so."

"Meph didn't tell you?" I think I squeaked.

Marten shook his head. "He told me that you were important and that if I hurt you he would see to my torment himself. He made me feel as if I were fifteen years old and meeting the father of my date. A very stern father who says that he has seen the movie that we are going to see and that he will quiz my young date upon her arrival home to be sure that is where we went and to promise me that he will be waiting up."

"And I thought the Dutch were so liberal."

Marten laughed. Really laughed with his eyes crinkled up and his face red, a laughter that pierced the tension and fear that I'd wrapped around myself. So I laughed with him and we laughed until we couldn't breathe, even though I didn't know what was so funny.

"Yes, we are liberal," Marten said when he finally caught his breath. "We are like New Yorkers, really. We are very liberal with what we believe people ought to have permission to do. That does not mean that we will do it, though. There is a very big difference. And so we are famous for the red-light district and the smoking cafés in Amsterdam, but most of the people there would not go to them themselves. It is all good for tourists who bring in money, and we go about our business."

"That does sound like New Yorkers," I muttered.

Marten grinned at that, a disconcertingly innocent grin. "You all forget that of all the places in the New World, New York was Dutch for a hundred years. It's here, in the culture. Sometimes I can feel it, see a little shadow or trace of something I recognize."

Just then our server arrived with our food. I wasn't starving anymore, I'd forgotten in the moment of release that I had been hungry. But the food smelled good and my body remembered that I never had bothered with lunch. So I left the subject to attack my plate and I was glad to see Marten do the same.

After the first wave of hunger had been overcome, Marten lay his fork on the table and leaned toward me. "Lily, I know very little about you, but what I know I like very much. I was surprised that Meph invited you to our meeting on Sunday, but it was a good thing for me. It meant that I could relax, that you knew what I was the way I know what you are, and we could go on without pretending. I will tell you something. Yes, you are right, I do not have long or serious relationships with women. Not because I would not like to have a real girlfriend, not because I cannot care for someone, but because I am afraid of my secrets. What if I date a nice woman and she discovers what I am? Will she leave me? Will I always have to hide? How can a person have an honest relationship if they have to hide something so important? It is easier not to have a relationship at all than to take that risk."

Did I dare trust him?

I wanted to trust him. What he said made sense, and having been rejected so recently for the same thing, I knew the issue was real. If Nathan was going to love me, then I wanted him to love me, who I really was. I didn't want to hide all the time. I could understand why Marten didn't want to hide either.

"So tell me about your secret. I've never met a ceremonial magician before, at least not socially," I said as I reconsidered. Could I actually become interested in Marten as more than just a holiday fling?

"I discovered ceremonial magic when I was fourteen years old," he began. "There was something in a newspaper about Aleister Crowley, describing him as the most evil man who had ever lived, and what fourteen-year-old boy can resist that? So I went to the public library and I found books. Crowley, Dion Fortune, Mathers, and the Golden Dawn. Yeats. I read them voraciously. I wanted to be a magician. There was a group of the OTO, Crowley's order, in Rotterdam. It was just a small group who met twice a month in someone's living room in a suburb. We recited passages from the *Book of the Law* and I learned a few basic rituals.

"It should have been wonderful, but it was not. I learned a little, but the older members of the lodge were more obsessed with the politics of the OTO than with actually doing any ritual. You must understand, the politics of the modern magicians are more arcane than what we wish to learn. We spent more time talking about why we were the real heirs of Crowley's order than we spent talking about magic."

I rolled my eyes. "That sounds like a waste of time."

"It is," he agreed. "But we often have to put up with unpleasantness to actually get to the root of the things we seek. There are so many false trails, so many tricks, so many ways the real truth is hidden. It is like that for you as well, I think."

It seemed silly to me. "Why don't you just make a pact with Satan?" I asked innocently. "I did. And here I am with everything a magician could want." I eyed him coldly. "Is that why you flirted with me and seduced me in Aruba?"

Maybe Marten was going to answer, but the waiter showed up with the dessert menus and preempted him. I wondered whether that was an act of magic in itself.

We considered the desserts, pondered the eternal question of crème brûlée or molten chocolate cake and decided to order both.

Marten was more animated, more directed, more sincere than I had ever seen him before. His eyes were shining and he wanted to tell me more, wanted to talk on and on about his strange obsession.

That fascinated me. He had been all polish and style in Aruba, at the party, even in the meeting with Meph. Even in bed. But here talking about his quest for magic, his passion showed through the camouflage of uberhip Eurotrash.

"I cannot tell you, Lily, how great a pleasure it is to talk about such things. In Rotterdam I could not talk at all outside of my circle, and they . . . they disappointed me. They were not the magicians I had dreamed of. They taught me, that is true, and I learned the basics of ritual, of astrology and gematria, of the uses of Tarot. But they were limited. Even their faith was limited. They did some magic just to prove to themselves that magic worked."

Excited by his love for magic and his pleasure that he could share it with me, Marten became more engaging and amusing than I had thought possible. His eyes sparkled the way Nathan's had when he talked about the ancient world.

"But you see, Lily, there are no women I have dated who I can talk about this with. Never. So I had given up, so many times given up."

"Aren't there women magicians?" I asked. After all, I had been trained to be a High Priestess and had been as adept as any of the men I'd known in the Temples of Babylon.

He sighed and shook his head. "There are, but few. In the old days, the Golden Dawn was the great innovator because they counted women the equal of men. In many of the orders, women are seen as the passive vessel for a man. The feminine power is important, but too many magicians think that women are to be used, not to be treated as partners in the working."

"That's ridiculous," I said flatly. If I had been able to take that stupidity seriously I would have been furious, but as it was all I could think was that no wonder almost no magicians ever achieved anything.

"I agree it is ridiculous," Marten said, and something in his face made me think that he was telling the truth. "And I had always hoped to find a Sister in one of the orders who would be my partner in a great working. But there were too few women, and most of those who would be worthy partners were too suspicious of men. And I cannot blame them, not after what I have seen."

"That's so sad." The words came out of my mouth before I could stop them. "But why did you move to Aruba? I would think that you'd be even more isolated there."

"If I am alone and cannot talk about those things that move me the most, at least in Aruba I'm in the sun and it is always warm and I can go to the beach every day. And, there are some learned people on the island. One rabbi, who holds a study luncheon at the bagel shop in Orangestad, has helped me with my Hebrew, and there is a priest who has taught me much Latin and even some Greek. And there is a community, a very small community but not such a contentious one. That, too, is worth something."

"This community, how much do they know about you?" I asked. I was pretty sure that he was far ahead of them, if he had managed to get demon services and a fortune from Satan. To say nothing of lifelong youth. Again I wondered how old he actually was.

Marten shrugged. "They are well meaning and they have respect for me. And do not question too closely."

We had been so involved in the conversation that I had barely noticed when the desserts arrived. Dessert! And I hadn't even paid attention.

But Marten appeared glad of the distraction and plunged his fork into his chocolate cake as if it would yield buried treasure. Which, being molten cake with a chocolate syrup center, it did.

"So why were you telling me all this?" I asked as I licked crème brûlée off the tines of my fork.

He laid down his fork, as if this were to be an important revelation. "In part, I think, because I can. Because you are a succubus, you know about magic and power, and you already knew what I was." Then he took another bite of cake and thought for a moment while he savored the richness of the molten filling. "I think, also, I have told you because I wanted you to know, Lily. I like you. Not just because you are beautiful. I only date beautiful women. But you are intelligent and interesting and know about the unseen. And you make jokes and love good food—you are Lily, you are just you. And it is all of you I like. And, I want you to like me. Not just the clothes and the tan, but that I am a person too."

Something changed inside me. Something twisted and knotted up and the world was a different place. Oh, we were still in Pastis, but my crème brûlée was only half finished and I didn't even care.

I looked at Marten, really looked. Yes, his fashion sense was impeccable, yes, his body should be up for *Cosmo*'s men-without-their-shirts page, and yes, his accent was charming. But inside the cutout of the "perfect cute guy" there was something deeper, something more interesting. He had a passion and fulfillment in life, he had chosen a difficult path and had become a master. To wrest the concessions he had won from Satan he had to be a master.

Passion and mastery in a man are sexier than broad shoulders and soulful eyes.

Dinner was done and the check arrived just quickly enough to prove there were people waiting, but just past the point when we would feel rushed. Marten withdrew his credit card and raised a hand when I took out my wallet. "No, you are my guest," he said.

And, being a woman of the world and an earlier time, I returned my wallet to my purse.

"Shall we walk?" he asked. So walk we did, chatting. For about twelve blocks with the wind frigid off the river full in our faces.

"It is cool out here," he noted, and blew into his ungloved hands. "Would you like a coffee?"

While I wasn't interested in coffee, I understood that he would welcome the opportunity to warm up. So I nodded with what passed for enthusiasm as he led me to the nearest Starbucks. Luck held and there were two armchairs available.

For a while we just sipped our lattes in companionable silence.

"You're a magician," I said softly. "Isn't there anything you can do to find out who's attacking Meph? Can't you do some spell or something?"

Marten winced. "I thought you would know better. Spells are for gamers and fantasy books. In the kind of magic I do there are no spells. There are rituals that may create an environment to make something happen, but there is no recipe like so much eye of newt and stir three times and voilà!: a reliable result. This is not chemistry, not cooking."

"Don't be angry because I don't know anything about it," I protested. The incipient deeper feelings I thought I might have for Marten made me uncomfortable. "I'm a succubus; I don't do magic."

He shook his head. "You do it all the time. We all do. Crowley defined magic as a deliberate act of will to

change the objective environment to conform with sub-
jective desires."

I sighed and drained the last of my latte. "That would
include turning on a light."

"Precisely," he agreed.

"So I don't understand what isn't a spell and what it
is you do," I complained. He wasn't being at all clear,
and while I knew ceremonialists had a reputation for
being cryptic, this was ridiculous.

He leaned back into the wing chair. "I cannot make a
charm or a spell, do this and that will happen. That is a
fantasy. There are two ways to work with this particular
kind of magic. The first is the old tradition, to force a
demon to do it for you. You, my dear Lily, are magic.
The right demon can accomplish whatever a magician
desires."

"Hmmm," I said, but I could see it quite clearly. I'd
avoided those traps for aeons, but I knew demons who
hadn't. "And the other way?"

"The other way is to manipulate energy," Marten
went on. "We live in a sea of energy all the time," he
continued. "And we are part of it, we interact with it.
We manipulate it without thinking. What we think,
what we imagine, what we focus upon, is and becomes
more real. The focus, the image is like a mold. And if we
pour enough energy into it we can fill this mold and
bake it and what comes out will conform to the mold we
have created. We are always making these molds and
pressing energy into them. What is different for the magician is that we are trained to make better molds."

"Doesn't sound so different from scientists." I tried to
needle him. But he grinned. "Precisely. We were the first
scientists of the world."

"Science isn't magic now," I noted.

"It is very much still magic," he said, smiling. "It is magic that everyone can do. Once upon a time it was great magic and power to be able to read and write, to add and subtract. Today we have general literacy, but that does not make the skill less powerful. It only means there is far more power in the world."

Partly I wanted to tell him that he was crazy, but I knew the magic of literacy. When I first learned to read and write as a young royal Priestess three thousand years ago, it was truly a magical power. To have such access to memories, to the knowledge of those who were dead, to communicate over time and distance, that had been great power. Nor was it less because it was no longer secret.

"So you're saying that you can't do anything for Meph? For me? You know that I was injured recently? Satan healed me, but they tried to destroy me and my friends."

His eyes widened and he took my hand. "I did not know you had been injured. What happened?"

So I told him about the witch hunters who had sent holy water–infused letters through the mail to me and my friends. About how it looked like a wedding invitation and so I opened it and it had burst into flames in my hands and the fire clung like napalm. How Vincent had come up and called Satan, and how She had sent word to the rest of Her Chosen. And then how She Herself had healed my hands. How She had taken my blackened, charred hands between Her own and how I had become whole again.

He took my hands as She had, turned and examined them. There were no scars, no trace of the violence that had been done. "You are much beloved of your Mistress," he said softly.

"Master," I corrected. "She is feminine to those She loves, and a scourge to all the rest. Well, at least that's the way we think of it."

Marten laughed at that. "You know what I'd really like to do with you?" he asked softly.

"What?" I expected some kind of kinky sex or maybe something just racy.

"I'd like to wake up with you and eat a proper Dutch breakfast with ham and cheese and real Dutch bread and hot chocolate in bed and then go shopping in New York."

"When do you leave?"

He shrugged. "I have a flight tomorrow, but I can probably rebook later."

I smiled slowly. "I'm sure you can rebook. I have to go to the office tomorrow. It's Tuesday. But if you can stay a few more days . . ."

"I can stay," he said. "I will stay." We went back to his hotel and he arranged to extend his stay, and then we went upstairs and snuggled while we watched *Batman Begins* on Pay-Per-View.

By the time the movie ended I was yawning. I tried to cover it up because of course we would have sex, but Marten surprised me again. "You are tired," he said. "And you must go to work tomorrow. So I will send you home now and we will meet again for dinner tomorrow. And perhaps you can take part of Wednesday so you can stay over and I'll order breakfast from room service and we'll shop. How does that sound?"

Could I arrange it with work? Suddenly I was grateful to Lawrence. He was a complete jerk with arrested development, but no one would question me taking a day off when he had just run half the office off in terror.

So Marten poured me into a taxi and gave the driver my address, and even money for the fare. Putting me in that cab, being more concerned about how I felt than about his getting the sex I would have given him, endeared him to me like nothing else. On the long ride uptown I was giddy and felt like singing. Marten had made me feel glorious.

Somewhere in the back of my mind I knew that intense flying feeling meant I was falling in love, but I ignored it.

chapter
THIRTEEN

The next morning I awoke well rested and ready to attack the Lawrence problem. First, I donned battle dress. I wore a simple chocolate Jil Sander suit that said I meant business, with a sleek Ralph Lauren messenger bag without any of this year's must-have hardware. Hardware was fun and today I was anything but fun. Today I was the avenging angel of Hell on a mission.

I arrived at the office at eight thirty, which was the earliest I had managed in nearly two years. Only the assistants and interns were in, and the hallways were quiet. I slipped into my office and surveyed the damage.

It was as nasty as I remembered, with purses tossed around as if they'd been caught in a hurricane. My boxes, all organized with names of editors and shoots written on the fronts, were torn and crumpled. But worst of all, my notebook had been shredded and flung around the office like confetti. All my notes, all my careful descriptions of upcoming shoots were destroyed.

I took out my phone and started taking pictures. Everyone might have trooped through yesterday, but they might not remember the full extent of the damage, how abused and forlorn all those lovely bags looked. The disrespected Fendi, the demoralized Coach, the oppressed Gucci, such beautiful purses, any one of which any woman would be thrilled to own, all of them treated like so much trash. By my colleague.

I set the purses on the sofa, gauging the extent of harm. Most could still be used, though a few might need a daub of shoe polish to cover a painful scuff. The lovely little Fendi had fared the worst. Several beads had been ripped from the complex design and the silk had been snagged in several places. I laid it on my desk to bring to the meeting as evidence.

When that was done, I tried to untangle some of the remnants of my notebook. I did find a few pages whole, or at least with most of my scribbles intact, but the rest were hopeless.

The office door was thick and the walls well insulated. Deep carpet covered the floor, not only of my office but of the hallway and every other office on the floor, with the exception of Amanda's Brazilian cherry with a custom Tibetan hand-knotted carpet. Even surrounded by quiet, I could hear that the area was no longer deserted. Wisps of conversation, an echo of laughter, a random knock on the wall all told me that the place was coming to life.

A timid knock sounded on my door. I wasn't in the mood for company. "Go away," I yelled.

The handle moved gently and Danielle stepped in. "Oh, Lily, I thought I'd come by and see if you wanted any help in cleaning up. Or a hazelnut latte." I noticed the cup in her hand.

She handed me the coffee and I handed her the violated blue Fendi bag. Danielle held it carefully, as if afraid to inflict more damage. "A travesty," she whispered to the purse. "You shall be avenged. And we will see Lawrence in Hell."

I blinked, and then remembered that for Danielle that was merely a figure of speech, not a concrete reality.

But really, I wanted Lawrence in Hell. Not anywhere where I could see him, of course, but stuck in some backwater of torment. If there were any reason to try to heal the rift between the succubi and incubi, now was that time. And I was ready to take the risk because I could not bear the thought of Lawrence ending up anywhere other than eternal damnation.

"Now come." Danielle pulled a little box of eye makeup remover wipes out of her huge Kate Spade tote that could double as luggage. "We've got twenty minutes before the meeting. Just think, these are the last twenty minutes that Lawrence will be here to torment us. Because Amanda will not tolerate this kind of random destruction. Especially not of samples. Some things are sacred. Now blow your nose and use the Visine, and tell me where you keep your makeup bag."

"Bottom drawer, left," I said. We all keep full makeup kits at work, along with several pairs of shoes, hose, and as many hair accessories as we could pack into one desk drawer. And Visine. It is a fashion magazine, after all. We are expected to fulfill the image, to dress and look every day the way we tell women they ought to look for work.

Danielle went through my bag, chose the heavier foundation and concealer to hide the red blotches, picked out a warm cocoa eye shadow and matching pencil and lay them all with military precision on the desk. She even placed the cotton balls next to the foundation and the brushes right in front. "No blush," she said. "Your color is already high, you don't want to emphasize it."

I looked in the mirror. I looked pale without any blush. Pale and angry and vengeful, and I hoped threatening, in my very tailored clothes. My eyes were so green they nearly glowed. I hoped the effect was good enough to worry Lawrence.

"Excellent," Danielle approved. "You look like some ghost come back from the dead for vengeance."

"I don't want to look dead. I just want my office back and my work put back together." I touched the beaded blue bag lightly.

"Come, let us go now and take good positions at the table."

She was right. The meeting didn't start for ten minutes, which meant that no one would arrive for fifteen and Lawrence for twenty. As predicted, the conference room was empty. Danielle set her tote almost at the far end and indicated that I should take the foot of the table, immediately opposite where Amanda would sit. She was the only one who had a reserved place; the rest of us jostled where we could.

"You don't think I should sit next to her so that she can see the Fendi?" I asked.

Danielle shook her head. "She needs to see you, dead-on. And when you pass the Fendi to her, every other person at this table will have to examine it. Besides, the end of the table is almost as powerful as the head. And it will mean that Lawrence won't sit here."

I wondered where she had gotten so much information about authority in the workplace. Had she taken some kind of adult ed class? But she was right, we had often left the foot of the table for Lawrence, mostly because it was closest to the door and he often arrived late.

I had my laptop out and my exhibits arranged when

others began to arrive. Amanda came in precisely at ten past, threw her clipboard on the bare glass and glared at us all. "I have heard about some, difficulties, yesterday. Let me say that I will not tolerate any kind of disruption that jeopardizes the production timetable. Is that clear?"

Danielle and I looked at each other. Lawrence had not yet arrived. Who was Amanda talking to, then?

"Well, now, then let's get directly to business. Articles for the July issue are already in process and we're shooting our September features. Let's go over the rest of the fall before we start ideas for January."

And with that, the meeting continued like every other meeting we had. I didn't have an opening to talk about what had happened yesterday. Surely Amanda knew that Lawrence had been responsible for the disaster.

The disaster chose that moment to enter. He stood over me and glared. "You're sitting in my seat."

"I wasn't aware that seats were assigned," I answered smoothly, glad that my voice did not show how badly I was shaking inside.

"You know that is my seat. Well, Lily, you are merely the accessories editor. You can be replaced."

"Stop it," Amanda ordered us both coldly. "Lawrence, there is a seat up here. Take it. We are in the middle of discussing the evening gown spread for the December issue. If either of you continues to behave like this is a day care center, I will ask you to leave."

I nodded mutely, horrified. While Amanda was not directly taking Lawrence's side, she was certainly not censuring him for having destroyed my office. Danielle patted my thigh under the table and caught my eye. She shook her head imperceptibly, as if she had known what I was thinking.

Ian was at a loss as to where to do the shoot for his December evening wear spread. This was always one of the most important spreads in the most important issue of the entire year, and it was a mark of Amanda's trust in Ian that he had been given the job. He was nervous and uncertain, and kept glancing at Lawrence as if His Snottiness should have been favored with the evening wear piece.

"And so I thought it would be great to do the dresses outdoors, with snow. Very evocative, with all that white to frame them. But I'm not sure of the location, though if anyone has any ideas . . ."

Lawrence leaned back in his chair, his arms folded across his chest as if he were daring Ian to come up with a decent idea. "If Ian can't manage a location that will properly set the most important feature of the year, perhaps he isn't up to the job."

And all of a sudden words started tumbling out of my mouth. "I know of this stonecutter's yard on Elizabeth Street," I said. "There are all kinds of white stone pieces, statues, funeral pieces, closer together than a cemetery, but very haunting and pale. And interesting. And there are big iron gates and such, so it could look like a formal party with the boundaries of inside and outside confused. Magical realist for a magical kind of New Year's."

Ian gaped at me. Lawrence glowered. And Amanda smiled. "That might do," she said, musing.

"Is there some time I could see it?" Ian asked, halfway between excited and disbelieving.

"Sure," I said. "Probably anytime you like. I'm not sure of the number but it's on Elizabeth Street, just around the corner from Houston." I wrote down what information I could recall and passed it over to Ian. I was sorry I'd never bothered to note the name of the place across the street from Public, and I wasn't about to mention the restaurant.

Amanda looked pleased with me. Lawrence was furious, which made the entire effort worthwhile. I'd worked with Ian for several years, and he really was quite a good editor, creative and interesting, and supportive of the rest of the staff.

"If that is all, then." Amanda began to wrap up, when Danielle waved her hand.

"Amanda, we had an incident on the floor yesterday. Lily's office is a complete ruin and several of the samples have been so badly damaged that we will have trouble returning them to the designers." She waved a hand at me and I mutely passed the Fendi up the table.

"And Lily is making a scene because she doesn't have the accessories I need for my shoot," Rebecca spoke up. "Her office looks like it was ransacked. I don't know why she can't keep her office in anything like decent condition and do her job."

"Mr. Carroll and I had a disagreement about booking Mr. Keefe for the cover shoot for the November issue," I said, trying to keep my voice steady.

"What did you want Keefe to shoot?" Amanda turned to Lawrence.

"This," he said, and tossed a set of photos into the middle of the glass expanse.

The clothes were beautiful, brilliant, very different from what we were used to with Italian and British and American design. These younger designers were clearly influenced by Issey Miyake and by Japanese art and textile.

"We have never given proper consideration to Japanese fashion, and now there are several interesting people working in India, too. When India and Bollywood have become such an inspiration to fashion in the West, we should start to look at the new fusion in Tokyo and Bombay."

The idea had caught Amanda's attention. Danielle's mouth was open with shock, and after a minute I realized mine was as well.

"Hmmm," Amanda said. "This has merit. But you won't need a photographer for a while yet and the shawls feature is a cover story. Lawrence, come into my office and we'll nail down the details here."

"Excuse me," I said, standing. "My office is still a disaster, the work I've done for the past two months is thrown all over the floor and I do not deserve the derision of my colleagues for someone else's lack of control."

I was fuming. At that point I didn't care what happened. I turned my back and left the meeting before Amanda dismissed us. I was beyond furious, cold and controlled and completely focused on the disaster. If I got fired, I would be free of Lawrence and at the moment that was my main concern.

I went back to my office to try to re-create the work. At least new boxes from the mail room had arrived during the meeting, so I set about labeling them with Magic Markers. Then, my notebook destroyed, I had to go into the sketchy computer files and see if I could reconstruct the various assignments from different departments and what accessories they would need. Paying attention only to the needs of the editors meant that I didn't have to think about Vincent being missing, or Meph's rival, and being followed in Venice, and Nathan and Marten. Accessories were a lot easier.

I was in the middle of untangling a necklace from two earrings that were not related when Danielle arrived with two Dove bars and handed one to me.

"Is there anything I can help with?" she offered. And she meant it. Danielle would have happily spent the afternoon trying to piece together scraps of my notebook if it would have really helped me. When I hate all humans and think they should all be delivered, I could think of Danielle. If she weren't mortal she would be my friend.

That was stupid, I realized. She was my friend. Just like Eros and Desi and Sybil, Danielle listened to me and supported me and was always there when I needed her. There were parts of my life she didn't understand. I'd never told her about being a succubus, and I didn't think she'd believe it.

On the other hand, Eros and Desi and Sybil didn't really understand my work life. Oh, they all worked. Even Eros, the demigoddess, had a day gig as the creative director of an advertising firm. But they didn't know what the magazine was like, what the demands were. They all thought that what I did was fun all day long, that I got to play with pretty bags and scarves and see the latest fashions before they were ever shown on the runway.

So Danielle was the friend who understood my life at work, about Lawrence and getting a feature article that was going to be a cover story.

I was surprised to realize that Danielle was a real friend. Even more surprised to think that I felt a little queasy at the notion, as if I were betraying my dearest buddies in Hell. I felt vaguely as if I were being disloyal to Satan Herself.

Only I wasn't, I knew that. Having a mortal friend wasn't frowned upon. Sybil had certainly had plenty of mortal friends when she lived as a wife.

If Danielle were a true friend, then I could tell her about Marten and Nathan. She might even have some good ideas. They were both mortals, after all, and so was she. She might have insights I'd forgotten.

So, in the middle of refilling my boxes, I turned to her and dropped the Magic Markers on my desk. "Danielle, there's something I want to ask you about. About men."

Danielle nodded solemnly and sat on the sofa, in the same spot where Lawrence had exploded. But Danielle's neat figure perched at the edge of the upholstery was reassuring. "I have a date tonight with this guy I met in Aruba. He came up here for some, well, some business. And I found out that he didn't tell me the whole truth in Aruba but I'm having a good time with him."

"And Nathan?" she asked.

It was my turn to shrug, though I couldn't pack that movement with all the nuances of meaning that Danielle could manage. "He dumped me. I told him some of the truth about my past, it upset him."

Danielle shook her head. "Lily, why did you do this stupid thing? Even if you love a man, you cannot tell him everything. You must leave some mystery. And they do not want to know so much, really. They say they want to know, but they only want to know their fantasies." She nibbled gently from her ice cream bar. "American women are sometimes so silly. You want things that do not exist. There is no need for your lover to know everything about you. I thought you were more sophisticated, Lily. You lived in Italy, I thought you knew these things. I thought you said you fell in love with an Italian. Did you tell him everything?"

"Yes," I answered.

"Hmmm," she said, and pondered. "Italian men are more accepting than Americans. And they take things less seriously. I still would not tell any man, Italian or French or American, anything that I did not think they truly needed to know."

"I thought he needed to know," I said, honestly confused.

"But you are still in love with Nathan, yes? He did not do a thing that hurt you, did he? He did not stop loving you, only that he was upset by a thing in your past. Is this the truth?"

I nodded.

"Then this person from Aruba, he is maybe not so serious. He feels serious because you need someone to think about who is not Nathan. But I think that your heart is not so easily engaged."

I turned her words over in my mind. She was right about parts of it, about Nathan. But that didn't tell me anything about Marten. Was I really falling for him or was I just using him to get over Nathan? I'd dated so rarely that the idea of dating one man to forget another seemed strange.

"Could I fall in love twice? So quickly?" I asked.

"This is dating, not love," Danielle said. "This Marten cannot be serious. He is from Aruba, which is far away. He is handsome and treats you well, yes? So he will take your mind from Nathan while you heal, but then he will be gone and your confidence will be restored to you. And you will be able to find someone else suitable."

"You don't think Marten is suitable?" I asked. I thought he was terribly suitable. At least he knew I was a succubus and he was fine with it. He saw me as someone to care for, someone vulnerable, even if I am a fiend from Hell.

Danielle shook her head as if I were a slightly slow child. "He lives thousands of miles away. Suitable is someone in New York."

"He could move," I offered lamely.

"That is just fantasy," Danielle corrected me. "And really, Lily, if he were your real boyfriend you probably would not like him so much. Right now you are hurting. Right now you could use an attractive man to court you, to take you to nice places, to pamper you. And this is what you like. You do not have time to know him."

Then she stood up and smiled at me. "I will be happy to listen to you at any time, but right now I have some work to do. Elizabeth needs more sandals."

"More swimsuits?" I inquired.

Danielle shook her head. "Vacation wear, not beach. For going to dinner after the beach. It will be a nice article, white dresses, sheer fabrics, lace. But they need shoes."

Then I remembered that I had had a box for Elizabeth. The necklace I had untangled belonged in it. And a Kate Spade clutch and two rings. I found them all, dumped them into one of the smaller boxes, and wrote Elizabeth's name on it.

Then the phone rang and Desi asked if I would like to go for a drink. After the past forty-eight hours I think I deserved more than one.

chapter
FOURTEEN

Des met me at the small neighborhood bar around the corner from my office. Not our usual kind of place; it reeked of old boys' network. At least the drinks, while neither innovative nor trendy, were strong. Desi was already seated in front of a half-empty glass when I arrived. She got up and hugged me before I went up to the bar to order, and then sank into the lush leather club chair next to her.

"I hope you weren't too busy," she started, "but no one else is telling me what's going on. Sybil is sobbing and said something about Vincent being kidnapped and Eros is closeted with Beliel planning revenge and none of it makes any sense. Do you have any idea what's happening, Lily, or have our friends gone nuts?"

I sipped my vodka and cranberry and sighed. "I can't believe they didn't tell you. I'm sorry I didn't but on top of the Vincent crisis I'm having an incident at work. The short version is that Vincent is missing. He never showed up at Sybil's and we don't know what happened. So I've hired Nathan to try to find him. We don't know where he is but we don't know he's kidnapped—we haven't gotten a note or a ransom demand or anything."

"You don't think he's run away or something?" she asked, horrified.

I shook my head. "We can't go to the police about it, and there is the small matter that he is legally dead. But no, I think something bad happened. I think it has to do with Branford. After I was followed in Venice—how did he know I was there? Who does he know in Venice? And then he showed up at Public. No, I think there's something going on. Maybe Vincent went off to try to capture Branford. Or something. And got hurt. Because otherwise I can't think of why they would go after him. It doesn't make any sense to me. And working with Nathan is hard. I don't want to think about any of it."

"Of course you don't," Desi said and patted my hand. Then she gestured to the barman for fresh drinks. "Dealing with Nathan at all is way above and beyond. Especially after what he did to you. Poor Lily. Do you want to get back together with him?"

I nodded. "Of course I do. But he won't, he hates what I am even if he loves me. Dealing with him to try to find Vincent makes it all worse. And that's not all." I told her about Lawrence and my office and about seeing Marten. "I have another date tonight." Looking at my new drink I tapped the table lightly. "And, given that, this should probably be my last drink for the afternoon. I don't want to be tipsy when I meet Marten. Des, I think I'm falling for him."

Her soft round eyes got even wider. "Really? As in really falling in love with him? You hardly know him. I think it's a little . . . sudden."

"Me too," I agreed. "But I keep having these feelings about him. Especially when he's so nice to me and put me in a cab when I was tired and didn't have sex with me. I always think men only want sex from me, but he really seemed to care more about me. But what about you? You've been so quiet since Aruba. What happened to you at Hatuman's party? Did you meet anyone nice?"

Desi shrugged. "Since Steve, I do my job. Both at work and as a demon. But I'm just going through the motions. My heart isn't in anything anymore. I feel like I'm sleepwalking through everything. I just left the party. I wasn't having any fun."

I hugged her. I was certain being hurt and betrayed had made her emotionally withdrawn. The same had happened to me in the distant past. "It'll get better," I told her. Then I hesitated before I asked the next question. "What about Eros and Beliel? Do you think they're together? Or just friends? She seems to be spending a lot of time with him lately."

Desi nodded sagely. "Yes, I'd wondered that myself. She was practically his arm candy at Hatuman's. You were with Marten, Sybil was with Vincent, Eros was with Beliel, and I was all alone."

I hugged her again. "Given the choice between Beliel and alone, I'd choose alone," I told her as she whimpered on my shoulder. At least that got a giggle. "Do you have any idea of what Eros sees in him?"

"He's attractive in a kind of military way," Desi said. "And he's important and powerful. You know, people have been speculating about you and Meph recently, too. Just to give you some perspective."

I was astonished. "But you know I'm not dating Meph," I protested. "Not even a little bit."

"Exactly. Eros hasn't said anything to us, and if she were really dating someone I think she'd tell us. But they do seem to have become more friendly lately." Then she looked at her phone. "Oh my goodness, it's almost six," she exclaimed, jumping up (at least as much as anyone with two very strong drinks in her could manage). "What time is your date? You need to get home and get ready."

So I was late again getting ready. I stepped into a steaming shower and lathered up with my latest acquisitions from Lush, and thought about what Desi had told me. I wondered what was going on with Eros and Beliel. Because if I were honest, Beliel frightened me. He was always perfectly correct, but there was something about his manner that made me feel as if he disapproved of me. Maybe he disapproved of everyone. Maybe that was what Eros found interesting about him.

By the time I got a cab and fought the traffic downtown, I was twenty minutes late. Fortunately, Marten was reading in the hotel lobby. His eyes widened as he saw me in my jeans, but he didn't seem terribly disappointed.

"I had this idea," I said breathily. "Why don't we go somewhere more . . . traditionally New York, if you know what I mean. We haven't eaten in Chinatown, or Little Italy or Curry Row. We could even go skating at Rockefeller Center, if you like."

Marten grinned. "But you said you don't skate."

I laughed and some of the tension that had been tight in my chest broke. "You're right, I don't skate. I've tried twice and couldn't manage to keep my feet under me. I think I crawled off the ice. But—maybe you could teach me."

"What makes you think I can skate?" Marten asked, all innocence. "I am from Aruba, remember."

"Ha! The Dutch are famous skaters. Lots of Olympic

medals in speed skating. I watch the Olympics," I told him.

We went upstairs. He was going to change, but once his clothes were off it seemed so much more reasonable to, well, take advantage of that situation. And then we had to shower, and this time he dressed in tight-fitting jeans that showed off just how athletic he was (which was, very. Yum). And an Armani sweater.

We went to Chinatown, to Wo Hop downstairs where there was always a line and the waiters were always rude and the linoleum had been worn and cracked for as long as I could remember. And the roast duck chow fun was full of crisp bits of duck and big enough for two.

We ate. We giggled at the rude waiters and the streaky glasses of tea, and talked like we were normal nonmagical people. I told him about Lawrence and my horror at work; he told me about how he'd ended up in Aruba and how he had gone to university and worked as an accountant back in Rotterdam.

We finished our dinner, paid the ridiculously low bill, and then walked out into Chinatown, which was loud and bright and busy even on a weeknight. So many people crowded the streets that it was hard to navigate. Windows displayed glazed or raw ducks, fish tanks, vegetables that I didn't recognize. Some stores had racks of silk kimonos, Chinese shoes, little plastic toys, and paper fans on the sidewalk. People talked loudly in English, Chinese, Spanish, Greek, Italian, and the food smells were just like the languages: demanding, competing, enticing, and confusing.

We turned off the tumult of Mott Street and wound through some darker, less populated streets until we came to the Chinatown Gate. In the dark, it was impressive, painted in red and green and gold. At least four theaters displayed posters from current kung fu films. Beautiful women in diaphanous silks wielded swords and long pikes, men in Mao caps clashed with men in sleek Hong Kong–tailored suits.

Marten and I held hands under the trees. We wandered aimlessly through the neon and posters, taking in the ambience. This was not a New York I frequented, and every time I came down here I wondered why it had been so long. We should have gone for dim sum, I thought, to those cavernous palaces where skinny women wheeled carts full of delicious little plates that I couldn't identify.

"Dessert?" I asked.

Marten agreed, so we turned back to the lights and crowd of Mott Street and held hands as we navigated the press. Two blocks up the brilliance and noise suddenly disappeared, and it was darker and quiet. No one wandered these streets.

"If I were paranoid, I would think that you had brought me here to be robbed," Marten said, and his voice held just a hint of apprehension.

I laughed. "Once upon a time that would have been a very real possibility. Especially in this neighborhood. Only that was over a hundred years ago and we're both scarier than anyone who would find us here."

"No Mafia?" he inquired. "I saw *The Godfather* at least three times."

"Oh, no, they're all respectable businessmen now," I informed him solemnly.

Then we turned onto Canal and our destination was in sight. Ferrara, purveyors of amazing Italian pastries for generations, had not changed since the last time I'd wandered into Little Italy during a saint's feast. Then the avenue had been packed with people and there had been a line for Ferrara's cannoli, which are the best in New York and possibly the best outside of Italy. Better than some I've had in Italy, too.

The restaurant is long and narrow with dark stone tables and brass trim. By ten in the evening the dessert case was picked over. Marten chose an éclair and I ordered three cannoli. We took our desserts and coffees to one of the dark reddish brown marble tables and, after sampling, Marten agreed with me that the cannoli were definitely better than anything else and perhaps we should get three or four more.

"Is this a popular place for demons?" Marten asked interestedly.

I glanced around. "No," I told him. "This is really old New York. That's why I wanted to come down here."

"You remember when it was trendy?" he asked.

I shrugged. "It was never really trendy. Why do you ask?"

He looked at me and the pretenses of normalcy dropped. "I have sent Meph a secure e-mail, and I have copied the evidence and secreted it. Do you remember the man in Aruba who warned me that you were a succubus? And I told him that I had slept with you and lived, so he must be mistaken?"

I nodded, wanting to say his name but biting it back.

"He is here. I have seen him in the lobby of my hotel. He . . . watches me. I think that maybe he has figured out that I am not innocent of Hell. I think he is following me, but I do not know if he hopes that I will lead him to you, or to Meph. Or to someone else entirely."

"Maybe it's you he's after," I offered, in part because

I believed that wasn't true. No, Craig Branford was after me and mine. And he was being directed by Mephistopheles' enemy. I was certain that was true, just as I was certain that Vincent's disappearance was part of the larger pattern.

"Was he in the lobby when I met you?" I asked, suddenly paranoid.

Marten smiled. "No. I had seen him earlier and just before we were to meet I went on a short brisk walk and confused him in several places. I believe that I lost him in an art gallery, but it might have been the hot dog stand before that. I saw nothing of him when I returned, or I would have called you and asked you to meet me elsewhere."

Suddenly light dawned. "Is he the reason you came to pick me up yesterday instead of waiting for me to meet you downtown? But he knows where I live. He could have staked the place out!"

"He knows you're on to him, Lily," Marten said. "I don't think he'd risk showing up at your place again."

If only I could deliver Branford I could keep us all safe. But if I delivered him, I couldn't find out who had been feeding him information all along. Not really a good plan. The demon in charge would just find another human to use and everything would go on as before.

"I don't want to go back to your hotel," I said.

Martin nodded and touched my hair lightly. "We don't have to go back there. Shall we go to your apartment?"

I shook my head. "Branford knows where I live. I'm afraid. I don't feel safe anymore, not even in my own home."

I hated feeling weak in front of Marten, but while he

had heard of what had happened he hadn't been the one to suffer the burns. I had bad memories of that man. Satan had healed my flesh without a mark, but She hadn't erased the knowledge of being burned, of being in more pain than I had ever experienced in my life. I shook with the memory and the fear.

"It's okay," he said, rubbing my back. "I know what we should do. We will go to a hotel, some old grande dame of a hotel. The Pierre. The Ritz Carlton. The Plaza. The Waldorf-Astoria. Somewhere where no one would ever expect us to go. I will leave my things and we will disappear and let the Enforcers trace this man while we hide in luxury."

"I don't have my things," I said.

"Nor do I," Marten agreed. "We will buy new things. For one night. We shall have an adventure and pretend to be tourists. And really, I am not pretending. I have never been here before. I should like to go to Weiser's . . ."

I sniffled and blew my nose into the paper napkin with the elegant F of Ferrara's stamped in mustard gold.

"Weiser's shop closed years ago" I said, sullen. Sometimes being surrounded by men who all think they're James Bond makes me crazy. They all have plots and plans and think they can outwit the bad guys (while keeping their designer sportswear spiffy) and play spies.

"Then tomorrow we will go to the Empire State Building and Barneys," he said firmly.

"You've already been to Barneys," I pointed out, not mollified.

"We'll see what Security comes up with tonight. Or that PI of yours, who appears to have some other interest in the case. We can figure out tomorrow tomorrow, but for now I will assume that it will be safe to return to my hotel and your apartment and everything will be fine. Resolved."

"And then you'll get on a plane and leave," I finished the thought.

He studied my face as if he were trying to decide something. I could see the conflict in him but I wasn't even sure that I wanted to know what he was thinking. Nothing was easy anymore. I wanted it to be easy again. Hunting, clean and simple, serve Satan and womankind, weed out the jerks and hang with my girlfriends and not feel this way inside.

Not feel confused, wanting and not wanting and not knowing what I wanted. I wanted Marten to stay, to live in New York. I wanted him to be my boyfriend. But I also wanted Nathan back. Was it possible to get Nathan back? What happened if Nathan decided to get back with me and Marten had stayed in New York? Would he hate me? Would they both hate me?

My head was spinning with possibilities, each of which was weirder than the last. And some of which were definitely appealing.

"Come on, let's go shopping," Marten said as he stood up and collected our plates.

It was after ten, but New York is the city that never sleeps. Some of the shops in SoHo and the East Village are open until midnight, and the street vendors are there unless the police shoo them away. There are the all-night convenience stores with their brilliant bins of flowers and fruit displayed outside like old-fashioned market carts, but with necessary items like toothpaste and aspirin on shelves next to the Pepperidge Farm cookies and the Campbell's gravy.

First we collected the necessities, a razor for Marten

and toothbrushes and toothpaste and floss, little plastic combs and a tiny mirror for me. Then we went in search of clothes, and without the better shops open I was forced to abandon my usual brands.

We scoured the stores up and down Eighth Street and St. Mark's that were still open. In a weird way it was kind of fun. I could see the appeal of James Bond. In less than an hour we had managed to acquire what we would need for one night. "Where shall we go?" Marten asked, smiling broadly. He was enjoying this entirely too much. I disapproved. This was serious self-protection, not a lark.

I thought about it. Where? Nothing too special, not the Plaza or the Sherry-Netherland. Something huge and less personal. A Sheraton, perhaps, or a Marriott, which were well outside my usual preferences.

We decided on the Courtyard by Marriott on the East Side in the 40s.

"Are you worried about any of your things?" I asked Marten as we stood at the check-in desk in the creamy marble lobby.

"You mean like my computer?" he asked. "No. I don't think so. There are things on there I would not like someone like this person to see, but I have some confidence that he cannot get into those files. And in any case, he could not trace us here. No one can trace us here; we didn't know we would be here ourselves until fifteen minutes ago."

"And we still might not be," I mumbled sourly. The clerk was still fussing with something at the computer and hadn't paid attention to us yet. For all I knew they wouldn't have a vacancy.

Then the uniformed clerk noticed us and lit up with a

kilowatt of fake smile. We were checked in to room 1427 and asked (entirely too cheerily) if we needed help with our baggage. Normally, of course, I would have said yes. I always need help with my bags. I do not carry luggage anywhere, not if there is a bellman or porter somewhere in a neighboring country.

But Marten airily said, "No, I can manage," and then fought with the cheap handle on our hastily purchased wheeled case. Eventually he manhandled it into the elevator and I hit the button for the fourteenth floor.

We got out, got to the door, and had to try both of our keys at least twice before the door decided to open.

This was not turning out to be as much fun as we had anticipated. I didn't want to stay in this place. I wanted to go home, to my apartment, to my familiar bed with my Frette sheets and my Lush soaps and a doorman downstairs watching out for me. I followed Marten and the bag into the room—and found it occupied.

"How in Hell did you . . . ?" I sputtered.

Azoked was curled up in the easy chair eating Ben & Jerry's Fudge Brownie out of the pint container. A room service tray bearing evidence of a full meal sat pushed to one side.

"Oh, you are not in the Library," Azoked said as she licked the back of her spoon. "But he is. I didn't even know that you would be coming here, but his residency was registered in the Akashic much earlier, so I knew I would be able to trace you. And you're late, by the way. I had to skip the dinner I had hoped for at The Palm and wait for you instead."

I studied the tray. "Looks like you tried half the entrées on the room service menu," I said, furious.

"I didn't know what I would like," the Librarian in

her blue robe told me as if this were the most reasonable motive in the world.

Marten stood stock-still and gesticulated deliberately. After a few firm sweeps of his right hand I could see that he was drawing sigils in the air, I suppose to confine Azoked to some segment of the room or something. Or maybe to banish her. I knew there were lots of rituals for getting rid of demons and maybe Marten could make her disappear for good, an act of ceremonial magic I would enthusiastically applaud.

"Stop," Azoked yelled. Then she turned to me. "Tell him to stop! I have important information and he is treating me like an enemy!" Her voice rose sharply as if someone had tweaked her tail.

"It's okay, Marten," I said. "She's one of ours. She's the Librarian that Satan has assigned to the problem."

"Librarian?" Marten asked suspiciously, his hands frozen in midair.

"From the Akashic Library," Azoked said. "And my rank is a full Librarian and you had better stop trying to get rid of me."

"Really, it's okay," I sighed. It wasn't okay. Azoked managed to make my life miserable every time she appeared, but she wasn't the enemy and she wasn't going to do either of us harm. Well, unless you counted high blood pressure and homicidal urges. "She's not going to hurt us. And she might have information."

Marten, who had been staring wide-eyed ever since he heard what Azoked did, bowed low. To Azoked. I was horrified.

And Azoked just lapped it up, smiled and started grooming flecks of ice cream off her whiskers.

"Azoked is a Bastform demon," I said to Marten.

"But she's mostly a Librarian, so you can just treat her like me or anyone else in the Hierarchy. Except that she loves ice cream."

"Bastform," he whispered, as if he had never seen one before. And perhaps he hadn't. They aren't common, not anymore, so even Marten's magical training might not have covered them.

"Do you know what the Akashic is?" Marten turned to me, his eyes glowing. "It's the Holy Grail, the Book of Life and the Book of Knowledge all together. It is the dream of every magician to enter there, just once. I never knew there were Librarians."

"It had better not be the Holy Grail," I said curtly. "Or else I would go up in smoke even worse than the holy water incident that I would really prefer to forget. Or doesn't anyone else here appreciate that?"

Marten just shook his head, but did not take his eyes from Azoked. "Access to the *Akashic Record* is one of the most difficult feats of magic," he told us.

"Even better than turning lead to gold?" Azoked led him on.

Marten nodded.

I was getting a little tired of the mutual admiration society.

"What did you want to tell us, Azoked?" I asked, trying to keep it businesslike.

The Bastform demon smiled and hissed. "He can bow to me again," she said. "I liked that. Why don't you do that?"

Because I'm one of Satan's Chosen, I thought, but I wasn't about to say that to Azoked. Well, I was about to, but thought better of it. It didn't cost me anything for Marten to bow if he wanted to.

Marten bowed again. Azoked giggled. I wanted to throttle her, so I sat on the bed and strangled a pillow instead.

"Okay, greetings over," I announced. "What's up?"

Azoked settled herself back into the easy chair and returned to her Ben & Jerry's. "I believe that you are searching for the same human that we have been trailing for over a month now. He is very hard to trace in the Akashic, even though he is fully human and his record should be clear. I have determined that there has been demonic tampering in the *Record* on his behalf."

I shrugged. "And this means?"

Azoked shook her head. "This means that whoever is sponsoring him both is a very powerful demon and has access to the Library. Which rules out a great many possibilities and includes several that you may not have considered. There are very few demons who can access the Library, let alone follow a single trace and obscure it."

"Could someone from Upstairs do that?" I asked. After all, Branford thought he was working for Heaven, though I couldn't imagine what stake Upstairs would have in a power struggle for Satan's deputy.

Azoked considered the question for what seemed to be a ridiculously long time. "I do not know," she finally admitted, her voice reflecting amazement that there was a question about the Akashic that she couldn't answer. "I shall inquire. But we can leave that speculation until I have actual information. What is important here is that someone powerful has been obscuring Branford's threads in the *Record,* that is what you need to know. And I do know that there are demons who are capable of this manipulation: Mephistopheles, Marduk, Ashtoreth, Daigon, Beelzebub, Beliel, Lilith, Salome, Azrok and Merab, to name a few. But then one must ask why. With his records obscured we can be sure that he is involved in something much more serious, something sponsored by one of the most powerful demons."

"You say to name a few. What others?" Marten asked. I turned to him and saw that he had started to write the list.

Azoked sighed. "Oh, that's about it, I think. I don't know about Upstairs, that's not my department. Much as I think it's not likely, I will check on that question, though. More because I am interested to know the answer."

Marten read back the list to us. "Is Hatuman capable?" he asked. "Coyote? Coatlique?"

Azoked turned her cat gaze to him and licked her fingers deliberately. "I do not believe they are capable. It is always possible that some demon has developed a skill that they do not register with us. We cannot tell who will have ability in the Akashic—it chooses its own Librarians and partners. We only know those who have been able to move like this before."

I nodded seriously as Marten scribbled.

"Now, if you would care to order me another of those fish dinners, I will report to my superiors that I have not been ill-treated," she said as if this were a reasonable request. In fact, I had become so used to Azoked's off-the-wall requirements that I thought it might be—at least for Azoked.

"But you just had a dinner," Marten said. "And Lily and I need some time to relax."

Azoked arched on eyebrow. "Oh? That's what you call it? Relaxing?"

"That's none of your business, Azoked," I took the initiative. "Marten and I have had a very stressful, tiring evening. You know that Branford is tailing me again. My doorman was kidnapped. You probably want to stay far from me unless you want to be around for the next attack. How about going down to Ono—they have wonderful fish. And put it on Marten's room."

"That will take a cab ride."

I handed her two twenties. Honestly!

But Azoked had taken the money and asked for Marten's room number and left in the time that it took me to fume.

"I have never met a demon so cheap," I hissed after I checked the hallway and found it empty. Figured. I would bet that Azoked used magic to get downtown and pocketed my money just because she could.

"Isn't greed a major sin?" Marten asked, interested.

I thought for a moment, distracted from my distress. "It is, of course. But being chintzy is not the same as greed. Real greed is huge and noble, that is all about collecting as much of anything as one can. Money, stocks, real estate, stuff. But Azoked isn't greedy, except for certain kinds of food. It's more like she wants to chisel funds, get a free ride, get something for nothing as often as possible. And for what? She does this all the time. Stupid things, like ice cream and the trip to Aruba."

"She was in Aruba?" Marten asked, interested. "You met with her there?"

I nodded. "She wasn't supposed to be there. It was supposed to be all vacation, just fun. The four of us were off duty that weekend, and we did visit the one resident succubus and go out for dinner, but that was purely social. And in the middle of that, Azoked showed up to tell us that Branford was on the island. And for that, she got three nights in the Royal Sonesta, per diem, and travel. Although I'm sure she got upgrades the whole way. We all always do."

"So she arrived after you did, and left around the same time?" Marten seemed too concerned with Azoked. As if she were anything other than a nuisance. I wondered again how much Satan was paying for her contract. Anything was probably way too much.

"Have you considered her?" he asked.

"Don't be ridiculous, she's one of us," I said, waving his concerns away. "Satan Herself holds the contract."

"And this Librarian couldn't be ambitious?" he asked very reasonably.

I thought about it for a minute. "I don't think the Akashic Records Division follows our ranking and promotion plans," I said. "They're under Admin and mix Upstairs and Hell, and I'm pretty sure that Upstairs has a different HR organization. So interfering with us wouldn't change anything for Azoked, and so why would she bother?" I thought about that a little longer, chewed on the idea. But the more I considered it the less sense it made. "Also, she has given us valuable information, and has warned of Branford's attacks. And she gave us the names of the demons who could have been hiding his record."

Marten sat down in the easy chair that Azoked had abandoned and pushed aside the rolling tray with distaste. "I don't know, it just seems too convenient. And she is so . . ."

"Horrible," I supplied with a smile. "Believe me, there is no one I would rather deliver over to Meph than Azoked. I would love to see her tortured for a thousand years. No one deserves it more just on general principle. But . . ."

"But you do not think she is our informant."

I nodded. "Exactly. And if she can help us find whoever is after us, then putting up with her is probably worth the misery."

Marten came over and put his arms around me. It was all just too much. I was just an honest, working succubus, trying to do her bit in the world for her Master, and trying to have a little fun on the side. And now I was being hunted and attacked.

Now I understood why Sybil had PTSD, having been hunted before, and by men with the law behind them.

Marten held me and patted my back. He said nothing, just stayed there as I felt overwhelmed. Waves of fear broke over me, through me, as I clung to his body. I didn't think about how beautiful he was, or how good in bed. All I knew was that he was there and safe and hadn't tried to get rid of me when I wasn't fun anymore.

I let him take care of me. He called room service and they sent up several pots of tea, crème brûlée, a plate of very pretty cookies, a piece of cheesecake, and a beautiful slice of devil's food. He fixed the tea without asking, sugar and lemon, no milk, and handed it to me. Then he passed over the chocolate. "Seratonin precursor," he said as he gave me the plate.

"And devil's food," I said, trying to smile. "Particularly nutritious, just what I need."

He nodded solemnly. "Good," he said, and then he watched me eat. I got through all the cake, the cheesecake, and half the crème brûlée before he offered to help with the other half.

"How are you doing?" he asked when I licked the last taste of crème brûlée off my finger.

"Better," I said. "Thank you."

"It's late," he said. "And it's been a very stressful day. I think we should both just go to sleep and get adequate rest. Things will be better in the morning. I even think you should have a nice hot bath. It will help you relax."

The idea of a hot bath appealed. A high-end luxury hotel has amenities like Jacuzzi tubs large enough for two, marble tile, and lavender bath salts sitting on the ledge. Unfortunately, the Courtyard is not that class of luxury. But the tub was old, which meant at least deep enough for immersion, and there was a tiny bottle of shower gel. I ran the water hot and sank into the steam. Bliss. Mindless comfort, so long as I didn't think. Just pay attention to the scent of the gel on my skin, the languor brought on by water, by the need to release after the tensions of the day and then the evening. Just release and be quiet.

By the time my fingers were red and wrinkled I was in a calmer frame of mind. The towels here were at least thick and thirsty and I wrapped one around my body before leaving the hazy heat of the bath.

Marten had turned down the bed and I climbed in, grateful. He had opened out one of the sofas into a bed and was reading.

"You're not sleeping here?" I asked, and patted the mattress beside me. It was a king, after all.

He smiled. "I think tonight we should just sleep," he said. "I didn't want to disturb you."

"You won't. If you would like to . . ." I thought for a moment. "I think I would feel safer if you were here."

"Thank you," he answered, and folded up the sofa

again. He dropped his clothes all over the floor and slipped between the sheets on the far side of the enormous bed. I wiggled toward him and he held me.

We fell asleep and that was all.

For the first and only time in three thousand years, I slept with a man without sex. Without even the thought or promise of sex. And it was good and comforting and I did feel safer for feeling the brush of his hand in the night.

We had sex when we woke just before eleven. Marten was right; I did feel a whole lot better in the morning.

chapter
FIFTEEN

Morning sex, mmmmm. I didn't remember that I had ever gotten to wake up to sex first thing, which is somehow more intimate and comforting after spending the night with someone. I don't know why that would be, but Marten not only satisfied me but took his time about it, too. And I appreciated the extra languor of his movements, the fact he clearly was there for my support and comfort and wasn't being driven by his own torment.

I showered and put on the new clothes, and remembered why I hated cheap things. They didn't look too bad, but the fabrics were stiff and chafed my skin, and some of the seaming was less than perfect.

"A good thing we were going shopping anyway," Marten said brightly.

While he took a shower I called Mephistopheles and left voice mail.

Then Marten dressed in his emergency clothes and grimaced as much as I had done. We went out for breakfast, a big traditional diner combo with eggs and bacon and sausage and English muffins and coffee, and then oversized blueberry muffins because they looked so good. And more coffee and more after that, the bottomless cup which, for once, I hadn't needed. I'd slept very soundly with Marten in the bed, knowing that Branford would never find us.

There is something particularly delicious about playing hooky from work. It's not like a planned and scheduled vacation—even my trips to Aruba and Venice, while rather last-minute, were scheduled with the office. But to just take a day in the city to sleep in, shop, spend time with a new lover, there is a particular decadence in the extra sleep, the freedom on the streets knowing that your coworkers are all at the office dealing with people like Lawrence, thinking you're at home in bed with the sniffles.

We went into new territory for me—the men's departments.

I had never shopped with a man. I had never shopped for a man. At least not for three hundred years, before the advent of department stores and ready-to-wear fashion. I had never noticed the men's sections of stores. I had never looked there. The magazine is for women and we don't discuss menswear, not even in a passing article on how to get your boyfriend to dress better. I could spot a man wearing decent clothing across the street, but I had never thought about trying to buy any.

I got an education fast. Barneys, the mecca of the fashionable woman, doesn't do nearly so well by their potential male customers. Armani, on the other hand, has a full shop dedicated only to men, and I'd never turned the other way in Prada and seen what was available for the guys. Hmmmm.

Marten turned. Marten wanted it all.

And Marten looks wonderful in clothes, wears them like American men just can't manage, chic and sophisticated and assured. It didn't hurt that, the Dutch being the tallest people in the world, on average, Marten at six-three didn't stand or move as if he were aware of being tall. Six-three, blond hair precision-cut just a little shaggy in the front to fall over his brilliant blue eyes, surfer-dude tan on an athlete's body, and a little sparkle of mischief, Marten was completely desirable. I thought he was delicious, and fun, and watching him shop was an education.

But what would he say about "occupation?" "Ceremonial magician, works with Mephistopheles and is one of the few to bargain with Satan for the services of a minor demon along with all the other usual inducements." I didn't think that would fly.

He might shop like a girlfriend but he spent like a Venetian nobleman. He didn't appear to care about how much anything cost. If he wanted it, it went into the pile and he signed the credit card slips without even glancing at the total. He had everything shipped so we wouldn't have to carry the packages.

Even if I had been bored by the men's clothing, Marten was so attentive that I felt petted and adored. Just being with him made me happy. Meeting his snarky smile behind the back of some officious clerk, making faces at merchandise that just wasn't up to its label was simple fun. We laughed and stuck out our tongues and I felt wicked and giggly. He struck exaggerated runway poses when he got out of the dressing room and I clapped or booed and horrified several respectable silver-haired gentlemen in elegant gray suits with yellow tape measures dangling around their necks. His sense of humor was acid and offbeat, his taste was impeccable and he looked like a movie star. The hunky kind that women worship. How had I ever ended up with this paragon?

Oh, right, he was also a magician and lived in Aruba and was commitment-phobic. Well, every fairy tale has a drawback or two.

"I forgot, we have not even stopped for lunch," he said as the clerk rang up yet another pile of purchases. "I am sorry, this has been so selfish of me. But we ate such a large breakfast so late I was not hungry and now I am famished. No wonder you look so tired. Where shall we eat?"

Balthazar, being conveniently around the corner, was the obvious choice. And it had been weeks since I'd had fennel ravioli and I was starving.

"You know, if I did not hear everyone here speaking English, I would swear we were in Paris," Marten said. I took that as approval.

Fennel ravioli, duck confit, onion soup and, of course, crème brûlée revived me.

"And now we should do something that is entirely what you want to do," Marten said. "I have bought enough clothing that I will not have to shop again until I return to New York, I think. And it is easier in Aruba. I do not need to worry about what to wear in the cold or the warm—it is always warm." He swept the empty plates aside and leaned forward on his elbows. "You would be happy in Aruba, Lily," he said, gazing into my eyes. "No, it is not New York, but there is excellent hunting with the cruise ships and tourists, and we could always take side trips to Curaçao and other islands. I know you have sister succubi in the Caribbean, even one in Orangestad, I think you told me. There is hunting and warm beaches all year round and we are finally getting high quality restaurants and shops."

"My job—" I started to say, but he waved his hand.

"You do not need the money," he said, and this was true. "But perhaps this is too early. Perhaps I can come back to New York and we can spend more time together. Perhaps you will come to Aruba again, maybe for a little longer on this visit, and I will show you the real Aruba, not simply the tourist sites."

I was startled, and it must have shown on my face.

"I would like to get to know you better," Marten said simply. "I know you are a succubus and I am a magician, so we understand each other, at least in part. But I like you, Lily, the person who is you inside the succubus. I would like the chance for us to build something, perhaps, if we are suited."

I drew my breath in sharply. "This is a little sudden," I said haltingly. "I never expected to see you after I left Aruba. And then you were here in New York. And so we spent time together but I never thought it was anything other than a fling. Maybe between friends, but there's too much distance . . ."

He shrugged. "Perhaps. But you are immortal and I am . . . promised an exceptionally long life. Neither of us is native to the place where we live, and neither of us is dependent on a job or family to survive. We are both mobile, at least to some extent. I have a working group in the islands—I often go to Martinique and St. Maarten and Jamaica. I think you would find that while Aruba is small, the Caribbean as a whole offers a large variety of amusements for a sophisticated woman."

"I, ummm, Marten, I need to think about this," I stammered. I had never considered the Caribbean anything but a place for New Yorkers to escape to during winter.

But I suddenly realized that I very badly didn't want

Marten to go. I snaked my hand over the piles of starched linens and took his hand. He smiled and raised my fingers to his lips. My sadness in remembering that he would get on an airplane the next morning was far more profound than I had thought possible.

"I'm sad about leaving tomorrow, but there are things I need to do at home," he said softly.

"I'm sad you're leaving too," I confessed sincerely. "I wish you could stay longer."

"So do I," Marten agreed. "But let's not spend our last evening on this trip being sad. Because really we should celebrate that this is not our last evening together. This is the beginning of our long-distance dating, at least until we know where we will go. What is today's date? This will be our anniversary, and next year we shall celebrate it in style. Promise me that next year we will have a wonderful dinner and stay in an extravagant hotel on this date! You name the city and we shall meet there."

"I promise," I said, slightly giggly. "Maybe Paris. Maybe London. We'll have to think about it."

"Just one more part to the promise," Marten said, and he looked very serious. I worried about what he was going to demand now. "Not Rotterdam. I don't want us ever to go to Rotterdam."

"Okay," I agreed quickly, but inside my curiosity was aroused. Not the city of his birth? He didn't want to show me where he grew up, introduce me to his old school friends? I wondered about that. But then, there was a whole year to go and a lot could happen in a year. A lot could happen in a month. A month ago I had been happily in love with Nathan and thought that Marten was a casual island fling and that I was being pursued by some crazy guy who was very dangerous.

Well, some things hadn't changed.

I staggered into work before ten with circles under my eyes that could double as helicopter landing targets.

Marten had awakened me early, gently, with his mouth teasing me to desire. I'd come once already before I was fully awake and able to demand more vigorous amusement. I was so ready I could hardly stand the moments that he spent licking my nipples and fondling my breasts. "Now," I hissed into his ear.

And when he paused for a condom I pulled him back. "We both know," I gasped. "Safe. Succubi can't get diseases. Or pregnant."

He entered me slowly, savoring the sensation, and I succumbed to his pleasure. He swept me away, alternating between driving need and restraint to make it all last as long as possible. Which was impossibly long by human standards.

I tried to provoke him. I nibbled his neck and licked inside his ear and luxuriated with the power of him contained. Contained by me, needing me.

Yes, I was used to being desired, being the ultimate fantasy. But Marten's desire was more complex. He wanted my desire, my pleasure, as much as his own. I could see it, feel it in his rhythm, in the delicacy of his touch. My joy was as important to him as his own, and that overwhelmed me.

Why is it so rare for a man to care about how a woman feels? Once he knows he can have sex with her, most men seem to assume their partner's desire without doing anything to ignite it.

It was hard to let him go. When he pulled his clothes back on, preparing to pick up his bags at the Hotel Gansevoort and then take a cab to the airport, I offered to come along, but he shook his head. "This is better," he said, kissing me as we stood on the red carpet that led to the street. "I will remember you here, happy, and we will not have the sad ride sitting together quiet because neither of us wants to speak. I will send you e-mail. You will send me e-mail. We will meet again soon."

There was no question in his tone; he spoke as if his pronouncements were absolute.

A lot can happen. No one knows that better than I.

I went back to my apartment and threw the newly bought cheap clothes into the back of the closet. A long shower removed the feel of them from my skin before I dressed in something more appropriate, something decent, lined in cloud-soft silk, well cut and made with care. A Dolce & Gabbana tweed jacket, a pair of black Prada slacks, and a wonderful sea green Versace blouse in silk so soft I could believe that I was in the uniform of Upstairs. A pair of last year's Jimmy Choos, classic black and elegant, finished the outfit. I looked strong, powerful, creative.

And I had circles around my eyes that looked like they'd been drawn in greasepaint, my hair was flat and sticking out the wrong way, and my skin was sallow. I looked like I'd never slept and was much the worse for wear. Well, I was supposed to have been sick yesterday. I'd pass.

chapter
SIXTEEN

It wasn't such a bad afternoon, all things considered. The cleaning crew had removed the last traces of Lawrence's tantrum. Smoothing out the crumpled pages of my savaged notebook, I found that I could re-create most of the work in the new, elegant, large-format journal I'd picked up earlier in the week. I liked the new book. The heft of the paper, the flecks of flower petals and silk fibers appealed to my aesthetic.

As I added pages of notes, sketches, and clips from photo shoots I found that I had relaxed. No thoughts about doormen or demons or magicians or gorgeous ex-boyfriends intruded. I was in my element, and the work was meditative. It was six thirty before I knew it, and then it was time to go home.

Sybil was waiting for me in the lobby of my building, pacing up and down in front of the reception desk. She kept raking her fingers through her hair, and her soft blond curls were ragged.

"Where were you? I've been waiting since six, don't you finish at five? Weren't you supposed to be here an hour ago? Where's Nathan? What's he doing?" she shot at me before I could even say hello or get my mail.

"Let's talk upstairs," I said, and laid a gentle hand on her arm, which seemed to settle her a bit. I got my mail, which consisted mostly of offers for more credit cards and pleas from a slew of charitable organizations. I dumped them all into the incinerator before I got to the elevator.

Upstairs, Sybil dropped her coat on the floor and pulled me over to the sofa. "I'm sorry, Lily, but I'm just so scared. Vincent is in danger," she sputtered between choked sobs. "Look at this." She handed me a printout of an e-mail.

Vincent is with us, it began. *If you want to see him again, you will meet us at midnight at the Carousel in Central Park. You are to bring Lilith Al-Hazar to us in exchange for Vincent. She will not be harmed if you turn her over to us. Vincent is unharmed and if you follow our directions he will remain so. It is in your hands.*

"Did you call Nathan?" I asked her. "When did you get this? Have you told him yet?"

She shook her head. "He's your boyfriend, he's not going to trade you for anyone," she said timidly.

I sighed. "He's not my boyfriend, he's my ex-boyfriend. He dumped me, remember. But he's also our PI and you're supposed to call him first. When did you get this?"

"Somewhere around four. I was trying to do some work from home, and I checked my e-mail, and there it was. So I came over here hoping that you'd be home from work. Look at this stupid typeface! Does that give us a clue? It looks juvenile."

"Did you call Eros or Desi?" I asked.

Sybil shook her head. "I think I was hoping this would all be a joke and I'd be here and Vincent would come on duty and tell me that he'd spaced out or had an emergency with a buddy in New Jersey or something."

"We have to call Nathan," I said evenly. "If you won't,

I will. He'll be angry that you didn't tell him immediately."

"Do I have to call?" Sybil said.

"It might be better coming from you, but if you can't, I will," I reassured her.

She pulled out her cell phone, hit two digits and was connected; she had Nathan on speed dial. "Nathan? Sybil here. I've gotten some communication from the kidnappers. No, I'm at Lily's. Could you meet us here?"

I wandered into the kitchen. There were three Ben & Jerry's cartons in the freezer, none of them full. And there was no Vincent to send out for more. I scooped what I had (Chunky Monkey, Cherry Garcia and Chocolate Brownie) into two bowls, and gave the one with the largest serving of Chocolate Brownie to Sybil. I assumed she needed the extra calming effects.

"What are we going to do?" she asked over and over as she ate the ice cream. I didn't know. I was afraid, but I had absolutely no intention of turning myself over to kidnappers to save her boyfriend. This was getting out of hand. Vincent is my doorman. He's supposed to provide security for me, not the other way around.

"I think we should call Eros and Desi," I suggested finally, after the last of the ice cream was gone and the bowls were deposited in the kitchen sink. "If they can get here before Nathan, then we won't have to bring them up to speed."

Sybil nodded blankly. I made the calls, and Desi, ever thoughtful, volunteered to bring Chinese takeout for dinner.

The three arrived at the same time. The Chinese food smelled good. Desi set it out on the coffee table while Nathan studied the note.

"May I see the original e-mail?" Nathan asked.

Sybil sat down mutely at my computer and called up her e-mail. The entire apartment smelled of Orange Beef and Shrimp Lo Mein and I was hungry. Nathan and Sybil were busy at the computer so I served myself a healthy plateful and sat around with my friends and speculated.

"It's them," Eros said with certainty. "Branford and his crew. He must have reorged and he's got some heavy backing. How could they have nabbed Vincent? He's a demon, and Branford is mortal."

"I think you're assuming too quickly," Desi contradicted her. "I mean, I think it's clear that there's someone in the Hierarchy who is making trouble for Meph and for Marduk. Branford is one of his tools, but there could be others."

Eros gaped at Desi. Usually it's Eros who is the strategic thinker and Desi who is the doomsayer. I was so stymied that I had another Peking ravioli.

"That's entirely wrong," Eros said. "I talked to Beliel, and he is the head of Security and he knows something about these things. He believes that the Burning Men are an aberrant splinter group, possibly with ceremonial magical training. They certainly know a lot about magic for a pack of fanatics."

And why Vincent? I wondered. What did the demon in charge want? We were being destabilized, and suddenly I wondered about others in the First Rank of Hell. Damn. I was going to have to ask Azoked, and I hated that.

"Can I use my e-mail?" I asked, interrupting Nathan and Sybil at the computer. They moved toward the food without stopping their conversation. I took over and sent Azoked an e-mail, marked urgent, through priority channels. If she got it in time, she might actually be of some use.

After I sent off the e-mail I couldn't resist taking a quick look on MagicMirror. Demons have just started using tags on entries, but I just played around and queried "trouble" and "enemies" and "attack" just to see if there was anyone else who had experienced similar problems. It didn't take long to confirm that there had been an unusual number of posts on attacks, muggings, burglaries, and a general atmosphere of fear among demonkind. I knew that I didn't have the time or the access to find a real pattern in the attacks—surely there were many more that weren't reported on MM. It would be embarrassing for a minion of Hell to report being attacked.

"You don't have any Shrimp with Cashew Nuts," a loud, catlike voice announced. "That is my favorite. If you are going to request me on an urgent basis, and I must drop the important research I am doing immediately, the very least you could do is have my favorite dish."

"I thought you said Crispy Orange Beef was your favorite," I said, remembering another night with Azoked and takeout.

"There's Shrimp Lo Mein, you can pick out the noodles," Eros said in that tough voice that permits no argument. "We're demons, not mind readers." Eros shot me a look that made clear that she didn't know what I was doing and wasn't all that pleased with Azoked's arrival.

"Thank you for coming so quickly," I said to the Librarian. "I'll even call out for a delivery if you don't like the Shrimp Lo Mein."

"I prefer fish. Maybe some sashimi?"

"It's a critical situation," I interrupted. "A young demon is in danger, and we've been attacked fairly regularly in the past few months. Something is going on."

Azoked licked orange sauce off her paws. "I have told you, we do not have Akashic records on demonkind. Only the living leave records."

"But you have other records," I said. "I know that Admin reports attack activity on us as well as Upstairs and you've got the archives. I want to know if there's a pattern. Are there really more attacks on demons, or is it just us? Is it happening all over the world? Only in New York? Only in a few cities? Is there anything the demons attacked appear to have in common? We need to see if this is part of a larger conspiracy or if we are particular targets."

"And what do I get for doing this?" Azoked asked.

"Well, it is your job, and Satan did contract for your services," I began, but Eros cut me off.

"You get to serve Satan, which is reward enough. And you may be able to help Mephistopheles, and if you do he'll be grateful."

Azoked looked interested. "Mephistopheles is known to be very generous when he is grateful," she purred. "Can you guarantee that?"

Eros's pale skin glowed an unearthly color and suddenly it was obvious she had never been of humankind. "No one can guarantee Mephistopheles' gratitude," she countered, her voice commanding and cold.

"Except Mephistopheles," said Satan's Second in Command himself, appearing in a whiff of sulfur next to the window. "I will guarantee that I will be very grateful indeed."

"I didn't get enough food," Desi said in the background. "Maybe we can order a second round?"

My living room was getting rather crowded and overly hot. Nathan was blinking at the new arrivals. Today Mephistopheles appeared different, more threatening, more powerful. More protective if you are me and Meph wants to protect you.

"I'm going to call in an order," Desi said too brightly. "What do people want? We've got one Shrimp with Cashews. How about more Peking ravioli and some Mu Shu Chicken?"

"Um, fine," Nathan gulped.

"How's the Hunan Pork?" Meph asked.

"Not bad," Eros said. "But not as hot as you might like it."

"I'll take an order of Firey Twins, then," Meph said, and returned his attention to Azoked.

"I see precisely what Lily is asking for, and I applaud her for thinking of the larger picture and calling you in on the case. So, Azoked of the Akashic Library, I am asking you myself to undertake this project. It could prove vital in the history of Hell, of the entire Hierarchy. And we shall all be most grateful."

Azoked got up and nodded to Mephistopheles. "Indeed, I shall be happy to do this research. This is the kind of analysis that a Librarian lives for, that does not come so often to those of us who labor among the records. And, of course, it will be my honor to serve Mephistopheles."

My mouth was open so wide that my jaw nearly hit

the coffee table. Azoked certainly knew the polite phrases of the older aristocracy, that was for sure.

Then, even more amazingly, Azoked bowed to Meph and disappeared. Back to the Akashic, I assumed, to start on her new project. But she hadn't even waited to see if we'd ordered her sashimi. Which we hadn't.

"Well, the answer to the kidnapper's request is simple enough," Meph said as he cast a glance over the debris of our demolished takeout. He must have been hungry. "We take a minor demon, enchant her to look like Lily, and then make the switch. When we do the enchantment we add a marker we can trace in the magic, so we can find where they take her. Then we attack the lot of them on their own territory where they think they are safe. . ."

"Except for the demon you enchant," Nathan protested. "What happens to her? She could be tortured, or even killed, and you don't care."

Eros rolled her eyes, but Meph met him head-on. "No. The demon will be a volunteer, and she is immortal. She can't be killed. She may suffer a few moments of pain, yes, but she will be serving me and, more important, Satan. She will have my favor and will be well situated to advance. It is a very small price for the potential benefits. I expect that we'll have a fair number of volunteers."

"Absolutely not," Nathan protested. "Even if it weren't unethical, we don't negotiate with kidnappers. Ever. We have no guarantee that they actually have Vincent, and if they do we can't trust that they'll actually trade him back. We need to track them down, and we should be doing that now."

"But it's a good plan," I said. I think I was pleading. Then Nathan turned his eyes on me and his look was cold. "Yes," he said. "You're one of them. Ethics in Hell, what was I thinking? Of course you'll let someone else take the fall for you while you go off scot-free and you don't even care. You know, Lily, until this minute I had almost forgotten what you are."

No. Oh no. He wasn't going to blame me for that. That was his problem. I was about to lash into him when Meph held up his hands.

"Nathan, why don't you pursue your avenues of inquiry?" Meph said diplomatically. "I can certainly get a volunteer and we can be ready to go in case we need to. We have four hours. If you can't find any leads in that time, we can go with my plan. Unless you have a better one?"

"Lily, where are you in this? Are you going to help Mephistopheles or are you going to try to track down the kidnappers with me?" Nathan pleaded.

He was clearly confused. Meph's plan was excellent, and would work. And would gain the volunteer a career in Hell that she couldn't have dreamed of otherwise. Thousands of lesser demons compete every day to come to the attention of the higher circles.

"You think a little bit of physical pain is unethical," I said to him in a low voice. I didn't really want all these witnesses to our argument. "But you can torment me, you can throw me out of your life without a second thought and that's just fine. Because I'm a demon so my feelings don't count. At least our volunteer will know what she's getting into and will get some serious benefits in return for her few hours of misery. Me? I've been miserable for a month and you think you're Mr. Nice Guy."

I turned my back and flounced across the room. I

didn't want to hear his answer, didn't want to see his face. I was too furious to even think.

Fortunately, the intercom rang just then as a doorman announced the arrival of the second wave of food. I went to the door and Meph met me as the delivery man arrived. Meph pulled out his wallet, which I found strange. I already had cash in hand. Meph slowly returned his wallet to his jacket pocket as I paid for the large bag.

As I cleared away the empty cartons and opened the new steaming ones on the table, I heard Nathan move to the door. "I'll be in touch," he said. And then I heard the door close behind him.

Even though my apartment was jammed with people I felt cold and horribly alone. I think a tear rolled down my cheek.

"You're getting the Peking ravioli soggy," Eros said.

I didn't care.

It was Desi who came up to me, Desi who led me from the food table to the sofa and sat me down and handed me my own Kleenex. It was Desi who told me to blow my nose and Desi who fed me a Benadryl and a big dish of Shrimp with Cashews.

"You've been so brave and caring," she said as she petted my hair. "You've put Vincent's safety ahead of your hurt at seeing Nathan now, to have to work with him and even feed him in your own apartment. You've been so good to all of us, to Sybil, to everyone, and no one has said anything to you at all. So I'm going to say it. You're the best friend ever."

And then Eros and Sybil joined Desi hugging me while Meph disappeared into the bedroom.

"I'm sorry," Sybil said. "I've been so scared and worried about Vincent that I didn't ever tell you how much I admire you being willing to deal with Nathan at all. I'm really sorry about this whole mess and about dragging you into it."

What can I say? My friends are the greatest.

I was heartbroken and so was Sybil; we didn't talk much. Meph broke the silence when he came back into the room.

"I have a volunteer," he announced.

chapter
SEVENTEEN

Her name was Raven (how unoriginal) and she was scrawny, too young, and scared-looking. She also looked determined.

"I've been a demon for seven months," she said. "And yeah, of course I want to advance. I'm not stupid. But I also know Vincent from class—we were in orientation group together and we've been study partners, so I'm doing this for him, too."

Sybil eyed her suspiciously. "Are you in love with him?" she practically hissed.

Raven laughed, and her laughter was clear and resonant and merry, and made me like her at least a little better. "Not even a little bit," she said straight to Syb. "He's too mainstream for me. Nah, I go for skinny long-haired guys with ink and facial piercings who wear nail polish and read Rilke. Preferably in the original. But Vincent is a good study partner. He doesn't distract me and he's smart and, even though you might not figure it out from the way I look, so am I. We're buddies, that's all."

I could feel Sybil tremble next to me. "Come on," I whispered. "She's flat-chested and she bites her nails. And look at her clothes. No, Vincent appreciates class and beauty and elegance. You've got no competition, Syb. Relax."

"That outfit came from some mall shop on Long Island," Eros agreed. "Not Vincent's style at all."

Raven giggled. "Yeah, I'd agree that I'm not his style. He's not mine." She studied Sybil carefully. "You're his girlfriend, the famous greed demon?" the little baby demon demanded.

Sybil nodded.

"Well, if you want to know, he talks about you all the time. About how beautiful and elegant and smart and talented you are. He's been pushing the coursework really hard because he wants to impress you, doesn't think he has a shot until he makes a mark in the Hierarchy. He keeps saying things like, 'She's Satan's Chosen, how could I be in her league?' And I'm the one who has to keep reminding him that everyone started someplace and you couldn't have started out as Satan's Chosen. But it gives me hope for my own future, so it's really exciting for me to meet you."

"And so you're hoping to catch his attention by volunteering. He should be grateful to you," Sybil said.

The girl deflated. I tried to imagine her when she was human, probably from some suburb, a little too smart, a little too weird for her family and school, always passed over and pushed aside. Her hair was dyed black with blue and violet streaks, shaved underneath but stringy and spiked on top. For some reason the facial piercings were actually cute on her, one emphasizing her lower lip, and the other in her cheek. Where a dimple would have been if she'd had dimples. If she ever smiled.

The look she gave Sybil was suddenly shockingly mature and measured. "No," she said, and it was clear she was serious. "I'm doing it because I have ambitions too. I want to be one of Satan's Chosen. I might never have thought of it if Vincent hadn't told me about all of you. Here he was in my orientation group and dating one of Satan's personal friends! And positioned to serve another. It made me think about what I want to accomplish— and this is a great opportunity."

Sybil nodded solemnly. "Yes, I understand," she said, and I think we all did.

The girl might have chewed-up nails and too much smudged eyeliner, might look a little too much like a junkie or a Neil Gaiman fangirl, but there was something under that ridiculously dyed hair that I could respect. Raven had a spark, determination, ambition, things that we've seen too rarely in Hell of late. Give her a thousand years and a better wardrobe and she could be one of our friends.

"You do know that it's highly likely you will be physically hurt, possibly badly?" Eros said. Leave it to Eros to make sure that the girl knew the worst right up front.

Raven nodded firmly. "That was in the description." Then she pulled up her sleeves and we saw the scars. She'd been a cutter in life, and I'd bet a suicide as well.

Not all suicides end up in Hell, not anymore. Once upon a time, killing oneself was considered the greatest sin, the rejection of His greatest gift of life. Today Upstairs is full of psychologists and theorists who are ready to say that humans who kill themselves are mentally unstable and therefore not responsible for their actions. Anyone who manages to get too far on that road but repents, even a little bit, is immediately saved. Even the ones who merely feel a little sad for the life they are rejecting are grandfathered in as "repentant" and don't end up in Hell.

No, it takes a deliberate act without any second thoughts. I wondered what Raven had done.

"Now, if we can douse the electricity and get Lily to stand next to Raven . . ." Meph directed. As I took my place beside the ragged-looking girl, I did notice that we were both the same height. And close to the same weight, although hers was not distributed as strategically as mine. This close, and by candlelight, I realized that under the clown makeup and the pallor of death her skin was not bad at all and her eyes would be rather pretty without all the thick black liner. Gray eyes—that wouldn't be too hard to glamour to my green.

Her hair was another matter, though. Spiky and straight and possibly overdue for a wash, it could not be more different from mine. Good thing that it was a demon of Meph's status and expertise who was doing the glamouring. He could pull it off. I didn't know if I could have done it.

I wondered if Marten could.

Candles burned. My friends stood in a semicircle around us, candles in hand. Raven and I stood together as Meph muttered words in Greek, Aramaic, and Hell Latin.

I felt dizzy and just a touch motionsick. I swayed and put out a hand and laid it on Raven's shoulder. And I felt something pour from me to her, a liquid element of essential magical identity that in a human would have been drops of soul, and she shimmered and glowed.

And changed.

First her gray eyes became green, and then the shape of them shifted, and then each of her features followed.

It was like seeing an image morph in Photoshop, fabulous and impossible. Her body filled out in the right places but her clothes still looked like they fit—because this was illusion. Her body really was no different than it had been before we started. Neither was her face, but it would take more than a mortal a very long time to figure that out.

Finally her hair started to curl and lighten. Meph passed his hands over her hair several times, and with each pass copper-colored sparks fell onto and into her lifeless tresses. And, bit by bit, they came to resemble mine.

Meph raised his hands, muttered more pseudo-Latin, and then clapped three times. At each clap, one of my friends doused her candle, until we were standing in the dark.

"It is done," Mephistopheles intoned, and it was done indeed.

"Now," Meph said, turning the lights back on, "you'll have to loan her an outfit and get her put together."

As I could see. There she was, me, but her face was still covered in way too much Urban Decay and her clothes—it was better not to think too much about her clothes.

"Why don't you take a shower and wash off the makeup, and I'll figure out something for you to wear?" I asked her too brightly. She shrugged as if it didn't matter to her and went into the bathroom.

"Clean towels on the top shelf," I called after her, worried that I would have to disinfect the place. Then I firmly reminded myself that some of my prey were skuzzier and that Raven, for all her grooming needing some improvement, was doing us a great service.

That didn't help when it came to thinking about what clothes of mine she could borrow. I couldn't part with my favorite Seven for all Mankind jeans. I really didn't want to loan her any of my La Perla lingerie. I don't believe in sharing underwear, so if I loaned it, it was hers.

Okay, think, I told myself as I dug through my drawers.

"I'll replace anything you give her," Sybil said at my side. I hadn't noticed Syb enter the bedroom.

"No, please, it's the least I can do," I muttered as I pulled out panties, bras, merry widows, garter belts, and stockings. My favorite new lavender and gold were there, the lovely reembroidered Chantilly lace in sea green, the four sets of pink and pearl, each a different combination and lace accent. There was the delicate powder blue and cream, the sky blue with satin ribbons, the cute retro polka dots, turquoise on lime.

And then I remembered. In the hamper, the things that I'd bought on Eighth Street when Marten and I had been hiding. Mint green, but without the subtlety of finer lingerie, scratchy polyester lace that was too stiff to mold to a body's curves, this I wouldn't mind getting rid of. I smiled grimly. "Thank you, Syb, but I think these'll do. No trouble."

"You're going to give her unwashed underwear?" Sybil was truly shocked. She was a senior demon in Hell, but the thought of giving a skanky girl like Raven lingerie that I had worn for only a few hours horrified her. I sighed. "Okay, I'll rinse them out in the kitchen sink and run them through the dryer. Good enough?"

Sybil nodded mutely, her sensibilities salvaged.

The three-year-old Calvin Kleins were no longer the

most fashionable, I thought. I could part with them. I threw them on the bed and then considered the top. It had to be something that would really look like what I would wear, but that I wouldn't mind giving up.

I started pulling things out of the closet, out of the dresser, throwing all of them on my poor, overstrained duvet. Not the green D&G camisole, not the Versace voile floral blouses, not a Prada anything. I found a very old Betsey Johnson that I hadn't worn in at least five years, with little pink rosettes and ribbons through dense black stretchy lace. I thought Raven might like that, and she could keep it. It had short, slightly puffed cap sleeves, so she would definitely need another layer, but I thought that little ribbons and rosettes were too last year. There was a Betsey Johnson faux fur shrug that I'd bought to go with it that I had forgotten about completely.

I draped the outfit on my boudoir chair, and sighed at the mess around me. "Do you want some help getting that all put away?" Sybil asked.

I nodded wordlessly and she began to fold and arrange gently, organizing my tops. Sybil hung things in the closet, all facing the same direction, all of a color group, and separated into long and short sleeves. I was fascinated. I would have said something, but just then Raven padded in, wrapped in a towel and dripping on my Persian silk carpet. "Dry your hair," I ordered her. "The blow dryer is in the cabinet under the window. Bend over, turn your head upside down, and use the diffuser."

The young demon rolled her (my?) eyes at me. "Whatever," she said, and left wet footprints on her way back to the bathroom.

Was this the way mothers feel about teenagers? They're messy, they're entitled, they don't have any sense of the cost of things, and don't think about what other people are putting out or doing for them. I was glad I'd never had any children of my own if this is what it was like to live with them.

Syb kept glancing at her watch. Raven took over twenty minutes to dry her hair and I was terrified that she was playing with my makeup, and that she'd paint up her/my face to look like some Siouxsie wannabe. Fortunately, when she returned her hair was nearly dry and her face was still bare.

I handed over the clothes, expecting her to be pleased and even excited by the better quality. She held up the Betsey Johnson. "Pink ribbons? Little roses? Are you kidding? Yuck."

"That happens to be a Betsey Johnson, who designs extremely trendy clothes for younger women and who was one of the movers in the London Mod scene," I recited for her edification.

"Yeah, about a million years ago," Raven groused. "The little roses are still gross. And this underwear? You really wear this? It's the color of monkey puke."

"Yes, I really wore that," I snapped, exasperated. The girl might be useful and a willing volunteer, but I wanted to take her head off. "And the rest of it. And if your fashion sense is more early Madonna, that's your business. Tonight you're supposed to be me, and these are my clothes."

"I hate Madonna," she wailed. "Madonna is so, like, not cool."

It was my turn to say "Whatever," though I expect that my intonation wasn't quite as utterly world-weary as a nineteen-year-old's could be. "Just put them on. And don't do any makeup."

The girl stuck her tongue out before she took the clothes and departed. I was so aghast that I was unable to move or speak or even think for minutes.

It was Desi's giggle that brought me back. "You should see yourself," she said, standing in the doorway. "I don't think I've ever seen you so . . . stunned, Lily. You look like you've just been slapped."

Then it was Sybil's turn to laugh lightly. "Oh, much worse than that. Raven doesn't like Lily's clothes."

"The little philistine," Desi said, her tone completely heartfelt.

"I heard that," the little philistine yelled from the bathroom. I heard the door slam, and she entered the room.

"Makeup," Desi said. "And shoes. What size do you wear?" This last was directed to Raven.

"Nine," the girl answered, and I groaned. I wear size five and was thought to have large feet when I was alive. Though it comes in handy now because a lot of samples are sent in less-salable, very small sizes, so I often luck out.

No such luck for Raven. I didn't have a pair that would come close. "This is going to be a problem," I muttered. "Anyone else here wear a nine?"

Eros did. We all looked at her, but she said nothing. I couldn't blame her—she was wearing the cutest pair of Christian Louboutins, from the spring line that had just been released a week ago.

"Meph," Desi yelled. And Mephistopheles knocked discreetly on the door.

"Come on in," I said, but he merely nudged the door a few inches. "Really, it's okay," I reassured him, but he resolutely stood his ground. Meph does not think it appropriate to enter a woman's boudoir unless he is about to seduce her. (Well, that's the way he would put it.)

"Raven won't fit into Lily's shoes," Desi explained. "And she can't go barefoot."

"And you can't find shoes that will fit?" he asked, a little horrified. Meph does not want to know anything about women's clothes, except how to take them off. He certainly didn't want to be dragged shopping. Not that that was an option at that hour of the evening.

"Can you throw a glamour on her shoes?" Desi asked sweetly, pointing to Raven. "Make them look like these?" She held up a pair of my favorite Manolos, the ones with the pink trim on the black straps. They would be exactly what I would choose with that outfit, come to think of it.

Meph shook his head slowly. "If she were wearing sandals, or something close, I might be able to do it. But she's got those heavy flat boots the kids wear these days. I can't enchant them to look like anything but heavy boots."

He seemed sad. Raven shrugged. "Why don't I just wear my boots then? It isn't like anyone will be looking at my shoes."

"Anyone who knows Lily knows she would never, ever, in a million years, wear Docs," Sybil said.

"They don't know Lily that well, though," Eros pointed out. "They think they know something about us, but Marten confused them in Aruba. They have some information but it's incomplete."

"They know about Public," I corrected her.

"Public is, well, public," Eros continued without missing a beat. "They know things that can be observed, things that they can find out through conventional means. Some things we know they have inside information about, but mostly they're going on mortal investigation."

"My shoes are not exactly a secret," I groused.

Eros shrugged. "I doubt they've got your Barneys bill. Maybe Meph can do something to smarten up the Docs? Put a few pink flowers on them, or make them appear more like Betsey Johnson's? She *has* done some heavy boots with a punk look."

I wasn't sure that Meph could pull it off without at least a picture, and the boots Eros was thinking of were a couple of years out of date.

"I could possibly do some pink flowers on the boots," Mephistopheles said dubiously. "If you'd sketch out what you mean. I'm not sure I have any idea how they ought to look."

That wouldn't be hard. Big daisies, throwbacks to the seventies, pink and yellow. Not that I would wear anything like that, but at least they would look like something.

"No," Raven protested. "No pink. No flowers on my boots. I'm doing this all your way, but enough is enough."

"It's only illusion," Eros explained reasonably. "The whole thing will dissolve in a few hours anyway."

"No," Raven said again. She softened. "Please? I'm

wearing the clothes, we'll do the makeup your way, but please don't make me wear boots with big daisies."

How did she know they were daisies? Had she actually remembered the style we were trying to re-create? If she could identify designer boots she might not be completely hopeless after all.

Something about the girl intrigued me. So many contradictions, all unresolved. Brains and ambition with a clichéd (and unattractive) look, willing to sacrifice, to be hurt, but not to have an illusion cast on her boots.

"Satan wears Chanel," Desi said as if she were revealing a secret. "And Dior and Lanvin. Definitely classic French fashion."

"Ladies, we're running out of time," Meph announced, clearly uncomfortable with the subject matter and where the conversation had ended up. "I suggest that we permit Raven her preferences in footwear, do her makeup, and start over to the park. We have only forty-five minutes."

"We'll never manage her nails," Eros groused. "So the nails and the shoes will be definitely not Lily."

"It's dark and late and they'd have to notice. They'd have to know and we have no reason to think they will," Sybil said, and she sounded like a leader, like the kind of powerful, definite person who would turn your quarter of a million into a fortune. "We should just finish up with the makeup and get on with it or we'll be late, like Meph said."

Desi and I took Raven into the bathroom and initiated her into the mysteries of Real Grown-up Makeup. A soft Estée Lauder blush, Lancôme eyebrow filler, and some shaping and arching to the brows themselves (she squirmed and protested while we tweezed, the whole time trying to explain that she had never had her brows waxed. Which was obvious).

We were ready. We were done. We presented her and reached for our coats.

"Not you, Lily," Meph restrained me.

"What do you mean, not me?" I protested. I'd done the most of anyone to get Raven ready, to hire Nathan, to try to get Vincent back. I wanted to be there for the showdown. I deserved to be there!

"You still look like yourself, Lily. They'll see the substitution with you standing right there," Desi explained gently.

No, no, this could not be happening. I was going to go. They were not about to keep me away.

"Give me one minute," I begged. "Just a minute. I've got a wig . . ."

"No, Lily. Not this time," Meph interrupted. "You've done brilliantly, you've served Satan well and I would expect that She will admire your efforts. And one of those efforts has to be staying away from the exchange. Desire is right—your presence could destroy the entire plan."

I pouted. I protested. And I gave up, or at least acted as if I accepted my defeat.

And as soon as they left I ran into the bathroom.

chapter
EIGHTEEN

It took all of ten minutes. Out of my four wigs I chose the dark brown page boy. It was good enough to pass in the dark.

I found the light blue running suit I'd bought in a fit of insanity last summer when I thought I could find prey jogging through the park. That had lasted for exactly one session. There were plenty of prey in clubs where I could wear pretty clothes and where the men were actually looking for women. Girls in sweats and sneakers didn't appeal so much, or maybe seemed too wholesome to go home on first acquaintance. In any case, I still had the outfit, white running shoes trimmed in a matching powder blue to go with the soft blue pants and zippered jacket. The clothes and the wig (with a matching blue cap pulled down over the bangs) made me entirely unrecognizable.

I didn't even try to use makeup and besides, I didn't have the time.

I nabbed a cab right in front of the building and then hesitated for a moment trying to remember exactly where the kidnappers had said to meet. Central Park is a big place—bigger than many small towns. There's Sheep Meadow, where concerts are held in the summer (it wasn't there) and the tennis courts (not there either) and the pond and the Met. I'd only seen the note for a minute and I had to reconstruct . . .

"Central Park. The Carousel."

The Carousel was at the south end of the park. In good weather I could walk there from Barneys to celebrate spring. It's an old-fashioned one, with horses trimmed in painted gilt and silver, an Edwardian fantasy, and it's popular with families and dating couples alike.

The cabdriver let me off at Fifth Avenue, and I walked quickly into the park. From afar, the Carousel looked shadowy and haunted; it offered a lot of hiding places. I'd never thought of that before, on the bright spring days when nannies scolded and I'd giggled with my girlfriends and we hung on to the fantastically painted poles and ponies. I would never see it the same way again.

The Carousel stood out from the trees that were still winter bare. In a month or two everything here would be obscured with foliage, but now it was still stark and barren, the trees just raw trunks emerging from the earth, with none of the wild ferns or cultivated plantings that made the park so inviting when the weather turned warm.

I peered into the darkness and studied the shadows, but I didn't see anyone, not the kidnappers, not Meph and Raven and Sybil either.

Where were they? Had I forgotten, or gotten it wrong? Were they over on the West Side near the Museum of Natural History? Were they hidden in the bushes where New York's teenagers go to lose their virginity and often their wallets under the hedges? It was still too cold for the kids to be huddled making out where no one might recognize them or pickpockets working the area looking for pants and purses that have been flung aside in the abandon of adolescent passion.

Fear warmed my belly. It had been a long time since I'd been afraid, really afraid. But I was still afraid of holy water, of attacks, of these Burning Men who knew our weaknesses and wanted to make us suffer. Even more, I was afraid of being wrong, of not finding them, of being thwarted. I was afraid that they'd left me and I would be left out of the action.

Might as well check out the scene before going anywhere else, I figured, and I made my way down the long flight of steps that hugged the wall. I was careful but my heart was pounding. Not just because of what I might or might not find, but because everyone knows that a woman should not be alone in Central Park this late at night. Central Park in the night belongs to the dealers, the teenagers and lovers, and the people who prey on them. And Central Park late at night has belonged, on a few infamous occasions, to serial killers.

I may be a demon and impervious to death, but I was also a New Yorker to the bone and I knew right down to the soles of my ridiculous white Nikes that I was entering the danger zone. I pushed my hands into the pockets of the warm-up jacket, and there found a hard metal tube. I clutched it in my palm, finding the nozzle area with my thumb. Pepper spray. I'd tucked it in the pocket of the suit when I'd used it for jogging, along with a whistle.

Great. I had a whistle and pepper spray against a gang of demon hunters who were armed with holy water that burned like napalm, and probably other things besides. Possibly blessed crosses and maybe even relics. I hadn't been close to a relic in over a hundred years.

And I was going to fight them with pepper spray? I was clearly an idiot.

Then I saw a flicker of movement, shadow in shadow, deep in the undergrowth. I heard something scuffling, something large. I held my breath and pressed myself against the cold damp stone wall.

The shadow moved again and it was large, human-sized. Though what kind of human? I wanted to crouch, to hide, only there was nowhere to go without drawing attention to myself. Very slowly I slid down to the steps, holding my breath. Please please please don't look this way, I thought. I held the pepper spray can and pulled my hand free of the pocket. Just in case.

"Miss, are you okay?"

I looked up and nearly screamed. I knew that face and . . . didn't he recognize me? If I could fool Nathan then I could certainly fool kidnappers.

"It's me, Nathan. Lily."

"Lily?"

I sat up a little straighter. He was bent over me, shielding me from the view of the Carousel. "What are you doing here?" I demanded.

"I should ask you the same thing," he hissed. "And you're obviously in some kind of disguise. So tell me why you're here instead of safe where I left you."

"I asked you first," I said, petulant.

He sighed and rolled his eyes. Which I could see quite clearly in the dark, the whites shining in the starlight. "This happens to be my job. You hired me, remember. So I'm out here to see if I can observe these kidnappers and maybe follow them back to their lair. You weren't going to do anything stupid?" He looked at me and groaned. "No, you're already in the middle of doing something stupid. Why couldn't you stay home? I'm a professional and we have procedures for these situations. You're an amateur and you don't belong here. Go home, Lily, and let the professional you're paying take care of this."

I shook my head stubbornly.

Well, he could have been worse. At least he hadn't said that I was incompetent, and it was true that I wasn't a professional. Who'd want this job anyway, slinking around in the middle of the night in the park in the cold? Bleh. But I still had too much at stake, and it was personal now.

So I told him in a whisper that hurt my throat about Meph and Raven and how they were planning to make the switch and then track Raven magically.

"I told you, I told all of you, not to do exactly this. We. Do. Not. Give. In. To. Kidnappers," he recited as if it were the Prime Directive or something.

"This isn't exactly your normal case," I pointed out. "So how much time do we have?"

"Enough time for you to get in a cab and get out of here before they're supposed to show," he said, pulling me up.

I jerked away. "I'm not going anywhere. I'm staying here. He's my doorman and Raven is wearing my face and my clothes—"

"I should have known that the clothes would come into it somehow," Nathan interjected.

I looked at him curiously. "Well, she looked totally stupid in that garbage she had on. No one would ever take her for me."

"You're going home," Nathan ordered me.

He seemed to have forgotten that I didn't take orders well. "No I'm not. I'm staying right here."

He probably would have argued longer but I saw more movement behind him. "Shhh," I warned him. "There's something back there."

"Get under cover and stay here," he said, dragging me a few feet over to where a tree drooped close to the wall. It wasn't much cover but it was better than nothing. Only I couldn't see anything. So I waited until he moved into a better position and followed him.

I had to say I admired him then. He slunk from view, he merged into the few shadows of barren trees more than I thought possible.

I moved over at least fifty feet closer to where I'd seen movement. Then, aware that I was a shining beacon of pastel in the night, and that neither Nathan nor Meph wanted me there, I picked a spot that might not have had as much cover as the one where Nathan had deposited me, but where at least I could see whatever was going on. I pressed myself into the trunk of the tree and dared only peek around the side.

I couldn't see Nathan at all. Maybe he really was that good at hiding, or maybe I just didn't know where to look. I didn't have time to try more carefully because a sudden movement and a crackle in the dry twigs caught my attention.

It was Meph and my friends. I could hear Desi stage-whispering, making comments about outfits that people should really not have worn. They were walking loudly and too carefully, their lovely Jimmy Choos and Louboutins not up to the terrain. Maybe Raven keeping her boots had not been such a bad idea after all.

From this distance in the night she looked so much

like me that even I wasn't sure that she wasn't. The fake fur Betsy Johnson shrug over the thin lace blouse was probably not all that warm, but she walked as if she were walking on the runway in Milan, not through Central Park at night to be handed over to our enemies. Meph escorted her, her hand on his elbow.

They stopped and stood near the entrance, where during the summer days a bored employee takes money and tickets and opens the gate when the Carousel stops and a new round of people get on. My attention was so fixed on them that at first I didn't even see the kidnappers approach. They were leading Vincent with a pillowcase over his head. Not even a plain white pillowcase, but one with the logo of the Mets. That was pretty low, I thought. Vincent was a Yankees fan.

They were inside the Carousel gate and came up slowly. Meph came forward to them and talked softly to the man who appeared to be the leader. Although I'd seen Craig Branford several times, in the dark and half obscured by the rest of the company, I couldn't be sure if it was him. I hoped it was him. I would hate to think there was another one leading another group of Burning Men, though I knew that was extremely unlikely.

Or maybe it was a lieutenant; maybe Branford himself didn't dare show up in person. Maybe he was afraid of being revealed, or maybe he didn't want this action traced to his organization. Which was nuts since that would be the first place we'd look. But still. These self-righteous idiots don't realize that there are some fairly intelligent residents in Hell and that some of us can figure out their idiot devices.

Finally they took the pillowcase off and showed Vincent's face, slack and blank-eyed, as if he had been drugged. Sybil ran forward as fast as anyone could manage in four-inch heels on spongy earth and tried to talk to him. He didn't appear to be tracking. She took his hands, which had been tied together, and tried to lead him forward. He seemed uncertain about how to make his legs work, and there was still a hand on his shoulder. I'm sure it wasn't entirely friendly.

Meph shoved Raven/me forward, and the man who could have been Branford (but might not have been) appeared to study her. Then one of his confederates threw the pillowcase over her head, the same Mets pillowcase that had covered Vincent.

My friends began to retreat slowly. Vincent stumbled but Sybil caught him. Despite the heels, Sybil was strong enough to support him as he tried to make his way through the dark and the bare dirt path.

I turned back to look at where the kidnappers took Raven. They tied her hands first and started to lead her deeper into the Carousel area. It was hard for her to walk with her hands tied and the pillowcase over her head.

I was suddenly afraid for her.

And I tried to remind myself that the fate of some ambitious little she-demon was none of my concern. She had volunteered and she stood to gain a good bit by the bargain, and she knew it. The girl had her eye on the main event, her own advancement, and had been perfectly willing to go through with this. And she was immortal, I reminded myself.

Didn't help. I was overcome with worry about what they would do with her.

Where could they be going, with her head covered like that? Someone would notice, certainly, and there were police around at night. In fact, I was surprised that none had come by while they had been talking.

They headed farther into the park, not toward the comfort of the avenue running above us. I followed into the dark foliage, trying not to think about the fact that I was alone at night and the park was full of muggers and murderers and rapists. So I could deliver a few, I reminded myself. I didn't dare pay attention to that, I couldn't afford to lose Raven and the bad guys.

Then they turned and the path meandered, but after a few twists we came out of the park onto Seventy-second Street, one of the major crosstown arteries. That had been quite a trek, and I was grateful to my disguise. At least the running shoes had made the long walk possible.

They waited for less than a minute until a cab came by and picked them up. Cabs are never that convenient. They must have set that up beforehand, or it was one of their confederates using a taxi as a getaway car. Which wasn't a bad idea if you don't want to get followed.

So I was alone in the park at night, deep in the middle of the danger, and not a cab in sight. Rage and frustration threatened to overcome me.

And I had better get home.

A man came out of the trees toward me. Oh no, not that too. I could not, just could *not* believe it. I could not endure being mugged on top of this horrible night.

"Didn't I tell you to go home?" The familiar voice was weary and annoyed.

"I don't have to do anything you tell me to do," I reminded him.

He sighed and stuffed his hands into his pockets. "You're right, you don't," he agreed, which shocked me straight off. "You never did, although I had hoped that you would take my advice since you're paying for it."

"You let them go, too," I accused him. "I couldn't follow them and you didn't manage to follow them and now we're both in the middle of this park and I want to get home. And I want to find Raven. I don't know why I'm so worried about what happens to that girl."

"I've got a company car here," he said softly. "I'll drive you home. And then we can figure out what to do."

"What do you mean, what to do?" I asked.

"Come on, let's get to the car. You've got to get some sleep if you're going to get to work in the morning."

The company car was only about two blocks away. It was a brand-new Mercedes in a dignified dark green. I slipped onto the leather upholstery and leaned back, relishing my rescue.

Oh, no, I told myself. I am not a damsel in distress and I do not need a man to rescue me. I could easily have waited for a cab. I could perfectly well have walked out myself and I didn't need Nathan Rhys Coleman at all, ever again.

So I could accept the ride in the assurance that I didn't need it. I could take care of myself, and if he wanted to help me because he was my employee, then that was reasonable.

It was a good thing I decided he was permitted to give me a lift because we had reached my building.

"Now tell me what you meant back in the park," I said as we sat in the car, idling and double-parked.

"What are you talking about?" he asked, all innocence.

"About what we're going to do. Because you lost them, right? You have no idea where they are."

He shook his head and his long black hair caressed his shoulders. "Yeah. Okay. I lost them. At least I didn't lose you."

Then I smiled, not nicely. "You lost them. But I can find them, I think."

It was his turn to be startled. "How can you find them? You were in the park, neither of us could follow that cab . . ."

"Why didn't you follow them?" I asked softly.

Nathan looked down, abashed. "I was too far from the company car. By the time I ran over there, the cab was gone. And once they left the park . . ." He shrugged, and his expression changed to discomfort, probably guilt.

I smiled, not to reassure him, but from my own feeling of power. "Don't worry about it. I can find her without you."

chapter
NINETEEN

"It's late," I said. "And it's been a really long night and I still have a few things to do if I'm going to find Raven." I started to get out of the car when he hit the master lock.

"First you're going to tell me how you're going to find her and then I'm going to tell you that you're crazy and let me handle this. I'm the professional."

A cab honked loudly behind us.

"I guess we'd better not discuss this in the car," I finally sighed, giving in to the inevitable. "Why don't we park and you can come up for a few minutes while I explain."

"Thank you," he said solemnly.

We drove around for ten minutes before he found the entrance to the nearest lot and parked, and then it took us that long to get back to my living room. My own safe, familiar living room. I could still smell the Chinese food that we had eaten hours ago, and it made me realize that I was famished. I went to the kitchen and dished out the leftovers. Maybe Chinese wasn't Nathan's preference, but that's what I had, and I needed sustenance for what I was about to attempt.

I wanted him here and I didn't want him here. I wanted

to take a bath and crawl into my nice clean Frette sheets and forget that any of this had happened. To pretend that I was a normal girl and that my biggest worries were my ex-boyfriend sitting in the living room and my maybe boyfriend in Aruba and Lawrence in the office. That would be a very nice illusion indeed.

Unfortunately, it would be very far from the truth.

And there was Nathan sitting on my sofa waiting for me to explain. I made him wait until I'd finished my entire plate.

"You're not going to like this," I muttered, trying to prepare both of us. "Okay, it works like this. It's magic. We dressed Raven up in my clothes. Nobody thought of it at the time, but I have a personal connection with my clothes, especially that lace top. I can't believe she didn't like it; it was my favorite for two years! Anyway, and especially because it was my favorite top, there is a definite connection. Call it a vibratory sympathy, if you will. The blouse Raven is wearing will be the strongest resonance because it touched me most recently and because giving it to her was imprinted with emotion. So there is a ritual, a way for me to enter the world of Yetzirah, of Formation, and find it. When I find the blouse I'll find Raven."

Nathan just looked confused. "What do you mean by Yetzi-whatever?"

"Short version, because we don't have time for the long one." I started out quickly with some of the basics that come up in Level Five of demonic training. "There are four levels, or types, of manifestation. There's Assayiah, the Absolute. That is the first emanation, the spiritual level of existence. Then there's Briah, which is the Creative World. Those two are the abstract levels of being and are the functional levels of On High. We live in Atziluth, the World of Manifestation. And Yetzirah is the World of Formation, where ideas are real objects and we can find them. This is where all the psychic stuff happens, where you get all the illusions and hallucinations and visions and dreams, too. It's all this malleable energy that becomes the pattern or form on which physical reality is based."

Nathan shook his head. "I'm lost," he admitted.

"It's okay. It's easier once you actually use the system." I tried to salve his ego. "You'll see what I mean. The thing is, in that world there is nothing like physical distance. Things are near or distant according to how closely they resonate for an individual. So something that is very sympathetic is easy to find and nearby. For example, my blouse. I wore that blouse for years so there is a strong sympathy built up, and if I concentrate on it in Yetzirah it will be close by and easy for me to find. This is where all the famous magical attacks and defenses and such happen, not that that's relevant to you."

He thought for a moment and set his plate down on my coffee table.

"You said 'should be able to' when you talked about this," he mused. "I take it that you mean you haven't actually done this before."

I winced. Truth was, I had very little idea of what I was doing. I had a lot of theory and some bits of ritual, but it had been over a century since I'd tried anything akin to ritual magic and I remembered vaguely that the results had been less than impressive.

Marten looked really good again. Strange to think that I would prefer to have Marten around when I had

Nathan sitting right here, but Marten would explain to me what tools we needed and would have at least two variations on appropriate invocations. Invocations are my weakest point in ritual—they all seem so over-the-top absurd.

Like this one, from the *Book of Sacred Magicks.* Which is a pretty decent text as these things go. *I invoke the Sacred Flame of the Universe and the Heart of our Order to be Guardians of this Sacred Space and watch over the portals of this Temple. Guide and teach me so that the Shekinah may shine through my magical mirror of the cosmos so that I may be initiated into the Secrets of the Heart of Creation.*

How lame is that? And that's not even one of the really awful ones, just one of the ones I could remember off the top of my head.

"I haven't done ritual in a while," I admitted. "But I've got a lot of theory and have done it in the past. So it's just a matter of looking up the appropriate bits. Most of it should be relatively straightforward."

"Hmmm." He leaned forward, thinking. Then he started to scribble on the back of the Jade Moon menu. I tried to read it—it was Akkadian, my very first language, but it was still hard to read upside down and over the combo lunch plates. "If you have some paper and a pen I could maybe give you something," he said tentatively.

I searched for a pen that wrote and a piece of paper that wasn't the back of an envelope or torn off a grocery list. Finally I remembered that I had some stationery stuffed into my jeans drawer and handed it over to him.

He thought again and wrote, and this time I could make out the cuneiform. Then he went on and translated, writing out a second version in English. It was a little stilted and not exactly the words I would have chosen, but really it was a pretty good job.

"I'm not sure if this is what you're looking for, but it's a Babylonian prayer I always liked. Seems like it would be appropriate."

"This is great! This is so much better than the stuff they gave us in class!" I jumped up and kissed him without a thought, and only realized and reconciled myself when he shrank from my touch.

Oh Nathan, poor dear Nathan, how I wish you would grow up and get a clue or six. But just then I was really pleased with the piece he'd come up with, not the least because it was one of my favorite prayers from childhood, one my mother taught me to recite before the household altar in the women's quarters long before I became a Priestess myself. It was charming.

I returned to my seat opposite Nathan, who stood as if to go. "I think I should let you do your magic on your own," he said stiffly.

But he didn't head immediately for the door. He waited and studied me.

"This works better with help," I said, trying not to sound too needy. In fact, I could manage well enough alone but I wanted him to stay.

"I'm not sure . . ." he equivocated.

"Would you mind helping me move the big chair before you go?" I asked, nonchalant. Never seem too eager; Eros was always trying to impress that upon me. I wondered if she'd be proud of me now.

He took off his jacket and then we rearranged the furniture. Then I grabbed a picture of me wearing the blouse before I spread a white cloth over the coffee table.

Nathan watched as I set out large pillar candles near the walls at the cardinal points: East, South, West and North. "I'm going to start real soon," I warned him. "So if you want to leave, now would be a good time. And if you're going to stay here and help me, take off your shoes and kick them by the door."

He took off his shoes, also his jacket and hung that in the closet. "What do you want me to do?" he offered.

I assigned him to light the candles and get my lovely little silver hand mirror from my dresser. I lit the charcoal and held it with my sugar tongs while it sputtered and spit. Finally it settled into actually burning properly and I added the incense to the brazier. Finding the Lost incense is lovely, mostly lavender with a hint of vanilla and some sweet balm. I felt calm as I lifted the brazier and walked the circle, sealing the space.

"This is to create a workspace where we can open a door into the Formative World," I explained. "Essentially, we are making a little Formative World right here."

"Like an embassy," Nathan said.

"Exactly," I agreed. "We're setting up this embassy in the Formative Overworld to look for my blouse. Which I should find because it's mine, it's imprinted with me all over it. Nobody else should be able to do this."

He nodded gravely, and then began to speak in sonorous but weirdly accented Akkadian. The fragrance grew heavy, the incense clouding the small space and obscuring my very ordinary living room with a scented haze.

"Now look into the mirror, and keep looking as we repeat the prayer," I instructed him. We both bent our heads and gazed into the depths of the mirror as we chanted in English.

The mirror was large enough that we could see both of us at the same time, framed in whorls of smoke and obscured points of light from the candles. The points of light glittered and the color changed from orange to yellow and red, and then into all the colors of the rainbow.

"Now," I murmured and took both his hands in mine. "Pay attention to the mirror, transfer your consciousness to the image you see in the mirror. And don't let go of my hands."

Slowly, the mist solidified around us and the image in the mirror showed more of my piled-up furniture. "Look around," I whispered.

We were in a different kind of existence. All around us was gray haze and distant sparkles, like pastel glitter under a veil. Bells sounded muted in the far distance.

As we looked, the glitter and the haze formed themselves into different images. People, animals, buildings, clothing, all at random and all pallid and colorless, formed and dissolved.

"Think of New York," I instructed, and between the two of us we saw the image of the New York skyline gain more depth and hold firm. It was still all made of smoke, but I whispered to him to pay attention to the details. I picked out the stately Art Deco lines of the Empire State Building and the Chrysler Building. I thought of Rockefeller Center, of the Plaza, of the Met and the Carousel and Barneys, and our New York coalesced and became almost solid.

"What would happen if we put in the Twin Towers?" Nathan asked.

"Then we would go back in time, and this would be New York before 9/11. Which we do not want to do."

"Just asking," he defended himself.

"Now," I told him, "now that we've got the city and the location clear, we have to think about my blouse. Form a clear image of it on Raven, with those clunky awful boots of hers. Look in the mirror and you'll see the picture of me wearing the blouse if you forget what it looks like."

"Oh," he said as he stared into the mirror, and I could understand his surprise. Because the photo, which had been lying near the mirror on the table, not reflected in it, floated as an image in the background.

An image of the blouse floated gauzily over the charcoal solid representation of New York. I concentrated on it, on the precise pattern of the lace, on the delicate pink of the ribbons, on the organza roses.

The etheric blouse rippled and filled out with a full bust and a tiny waist. Slowly an image of me in the blouse emerged like a tiny Barbie doll in a new outfit, auburn curls cascading down its/my back and a pair of good jeans showing off long legs and a round bottom. And Michael Kors boots.

No, wrong. The boots had to be changed to Raven's clompy old Docs with their creases and stains. I remembered her boots clearly, ugly and worn-down.

The boots changed, and in some subtle way the image of me/Raven shifted so that the body was just a touch less luscious, as if to reflect the fact that her real chest was fairly flat and whatever shape she had was borrowed from me via Meph's magic.

"Good," I whispered. "Now hold it. Just hold the image and wonder where it is."

This was the difficult part of the working, holding together the image of the city, Raven's face, and my question in my mind. Without any interference.

Whatever anyone says about magic, really it's all about concentration. At least in Yetzirah. The very stuff of that plane is infinitely malleable, shaped by the mental energy of someone who knew how to mold it and hold it in place.

But I couldn't think of all of that then. All I could do was hold the image of the little doll in my Betsey Johnson blouse over the representation of New York and wonder "where, where"—wonder with my whole being.

The image shivered and started to move. That is, she remained doll-like but floated eastward over the park, over the Upper East Side, over Barneys and down toward Midtown.

I waited for her to cross the river to Brooklyn, but she stayed on this side of the water and came to a standstill at Gramercy Park.

"Imagine Gramercy," I hissed.

I tried to remember every detail I could of the gated and locked one-block park and the elegant houses that ringed it. Residents of the buildings right around the park had keys to the park, which kept it safe and private.

We almost got the park but the buildings remained hazy and indistinct. The Raven doll floated over to one on what I was certain was the north side. I counted doorways but I was uncertain whether it was the fourth or fifth. Or maybe the sixth, I just couldn't make out any features clearly.

It was our images of Gramercy that built the model, and where we were uncertain the haze couldn't form. I studied the building where the doll landed carefully, hoping that some distinguishing characteristic would emerge. And, slowly, I noticed light on windows. Mullioned windows in a pseudo-Tudor with an arched doorway.

The images we were holding started to fade and I couldn't keep them coherent. The hazy etheric matter couldn't hold its shape without constant attention, and we had learned all we were likely to learn from the exercise.

Time to return. I was only barely aware of Nathan's hands in mine as I let my mind drift along with the smoky cloud, and I started to see the pastel sparkles of the beacon points, those cities and images that have been nourished so deeply that they have become real. New York and London, Paris and Rome, Tokyo and Beijing all existed here in extreme detail. Smaller places also were beacon points, but not all of the points were places. Emotional energy creates the landscape in the Formative World. Some focal points were images of deities, energized and lit in this place by thousands of years of worship or dread. Newer thought images achieved beacon status here—Elvis and the Beatles were particularly notable—though if they are forgotten in the material world the beacon will fade.

"Back through the mirror," I instructed, and both Nathan and I turned our concentration to our reflections.

Getting back was easier than getting there, which was good because I was tired. I was relieved when I turned and saw that we were sitting in my living room again, the coffee table between us, and the furniture shoved together in the far corner.

Nathan dropped my hands, looking like he wanted to bolt, but I told him that he had to wait. We had to finish the ritual and open the space back into the world again in the formal and prescribed manner. Otherwise entities like elemental beings could possibly leak through from Yetzirah, which was the origin of most hauntings and other psychic phenomena. This was drilled into every junior demon in second, third, fourth, fifth, ninth, and eleventh level. No demon doing magic would ever leave a ritual space until it was properly shut, something like cycling through an airlock, as far as I could figure it.

"We chant the prayer again, and this time we add our thanks to the deity in charge for permitting us access," I instructed Nathan. "And then we close down the circle."

Nathan chanted obediently, even adding a very nice thanks in Akkadian.

We dropped hands. I closed with a simple Ritual of the Banishing Pentagram, which was really too Upstairs-oriented for my general taste but it was easy and effective. And impressive, I have to admit. I was aware of Nathan's eyes on me, and I wanted this to look good. So I banished with the best of them, drawing elegant pentagrams in the air with a small knife, lunging as I broke through the protections and using sweeping dramatic movements in the finale. Then it was done, and I was shivering and exhausted.

chapter
TWENTY

Nathan slumped over the table. "You okay?" I asked, touching his shoulder gently.

"Tired," he murmured. "So tired. Can I pass out on your floor?"

I'd thought, from reading some of the relationship articles in the magazine, that letting your ex spend the night in your apartment was generally considered a bad move. But I didn't have much experience of exes and I knew this was no ploy on either of our parts.

Magic takes a lot of energy. It's hard physical work, even if we had been sitting down the whole time. No wonder demons use technology rather than magic whenever possible.

"Sure, crash," I said. "I'm going to grab a cab to Gramercy Park."

Nathan heaved himself up. "No. Tha's my job."

He was so exhausted that he was slurring his words. "You're not in any shape to move," I observed.

"You're not, either," he said.

And he was right. I could barely stand up. But I had an answer. "Coffee."

I dragged out the Braun espresso maker and filled it with my favorite strong Italian roast. I think I phased out for a minute or two while the coffee was brewing, then I poured it into mugs and added generous helpings of sugar.

We grabbed our coats to go back outside. I'd forgotten that I was still wearing that dreadful jogging suit and the wig. Well, no help for that now.

"Really, Lily, I'm feeling a lot better now," Nathan protested. "This is my job. You're not trained to do this, and you're exhausted."

I shook my head. "You're not all that trained either, from what I understand. Mostly you were hired to do research, not to play HRT. Besides, I'm immortal."

He looked hurt. I would have to ask one of my friends . . . maybe I shouldn't have said that? Maybe it hurt his fragile male ego to mention that he wasn't Indiana Jones. I totally do not get guys. Here was this perfectly elegant, smart, educated, sophisticated, and seriously hot man and he got all huffy if I happened to mention that he had spent most of his life learning to decipher ancient texts rather than in Quantico.

"Remember, Indiana Jones was an archaeologist in Ancient Near Eastern Studies," Nathan said. "I think seeing some of those movies when I was a kid inspired me to go into ancient history. It looked a lot more adventurous than other fields of scholarship."

Somehow I managed not to groan at his admission.

"Well then, between the two of us the bad guys don't have a chance. Indiana Jones and the Demon from Hell. Sounds like a movie title to me," I quipped.

Nathan grinned. "We'll have to find someone to play me. Harrison Ford is getting a bit old for all that action."

"Be careful," I warned him. "I could get sensitive about my age."

We rode the elevator and got into his car without a word. Even with all the extra-action caffeine, the movement of the car down sixty blocks lulled me to sleep, so I was surprised when the car stopped and Nathan announced that we'd arrived at Gramercy Park.

It was dark and cold, the last hour before sunrise when the temperature drops and even muggers stay in bed. After-hours clubs would be letting out and no one was in the breakfast places except the first early wait-staff, wiping down tables and setting up the ketchup and maple syrup bottles. The city was as silent as it ever gets in the change of shift between late late night and the crack of day.

We faced north and looked at the buildings. I counted and the fourth door in seemed attached to a mullioned window. Bingo. I hoped. I marched across the street.

"What do you think you're doing?" Nathan hissed behind me.

"I'm going to get Raven. That's what I said I was going to do," I hissed right back.

"Wait a minute," he said, and popped the trunk of the car. He pulled out an aluminum briefcase and sat in the backseat. I was interested enough to return to the car and ask him what was going on.

"Electronics," he said as he fiddled with some large, dangerous-looking black tube thing. He pointed it out the car window and I saw a distant dot of light on one of the glass mullions.

"What is that thing?" I asked, but he just smiled and adjusted several dials before he answered. "Laser eavesdropping. Top-of-the-line equipment. It can read and decipher sound waves against a pane of glass. Impressed now?"

Yeah, well. Okay, I was impressed. But I wasn't going to tell him that.

Only there was no sound coming from the unit. Nothing. He moved the dot up a story and suddenly we were hearing—something. A slap. A groan. A rough male voice said, "When's he gonna get here, bitch?"

Suddenly I was furious. I hate hate hate it when a man calls a woman a bitch. That is the cruelest, lowest, worst thing. Because any woman who isn't doing what a man wants gets called that and nothing, *nothing,* makes me want to deliver a man more.

Nathan grinned slowly and I wanted to slap him. How dare he smile when someone called *me* a bitch? And slapped *me*?

"Got 'em," he said. "Now we know which apartment they're in. Okay, a few more preparations . . . How were you going to get in there, anyway?" he asked with real curiosity.

I shrugged. "Magic. I can usually get through a lock if I really want to. And if worse comes to worse, I can up the pheromones so that any man there will be drawn against his will to open the door. How were you going to get in?"

He shrugged and pocketed a small velvet case. "Lock picks."

I let him lead the way. After all, he was the professional and I was paying his fee. Why should I do all the work?

He got through the security system of the building as quickly as I could have with a key, and faster than I might have managed with magic. Practice, I guess. I don't have any reason to break into places all that often.

"I do not want you in here," Nathan said as he slipped

into the building. "Go back to the car and sleep, okay? You're exhausted."

"I'm not going back to the car and you can't order me around like I'm some obedient little girl. I'm paying your fees, mister, and don't forget it. And I want to go along. I have a few things to offer and besides, you never would have found them if it hadn't been for me."

"Lily, you have proven that you are smart and strong and resourceful. But this is a dangerous situation and you're still an amateur. You could get hurt and I couldn't live with that. Please. Go back to the car."

"Forget it," I answered.

We heard a long, low scream followed by a sob.

"Go," I pushed him. In he went, with me right behind him.

We entered the most amazing apartment I'd ever seen in the entirety of New York. The door opened into a huge great room, two stories high with a vast wall of windows overlooking the park, interrupted only by a stone fireplace large enough to stand in. Thick Oriental rugs covered polished hardwood floors, which served to muffle our footsteps more effectively than any sneakers could have done.

Now that we were in, I could hear steady sobbing overhead. Raven, I was sure, and in terrible pain. I clenched up inside and wanted to run up the stairs to the gallery, but Nathan held my arm. He led the way, slow and deliberate, testing each step before he eased his weight forward. Fortunately, the steps were carpeted as heavily as the room and were solidly constructed. No squeaks gave us away as we ascended toward the crying.

At the top of the stairs we entered a long gallery that overlooked the great room. The décor was vaguely medieval, the walls were stone, and there were gargoyles mounted in arches on the gallery railing. Several doors, all shut, lined the room. The sound was coming from the room to the left behind a thick oak door.

Nathan crept forward slowly. I tried to follow him but I hit . . . something. It was like a wall, invisible and impenetrable. There was nothing there and yet I could not go one inch farther.

A magical barricade, then, something warded against demonkind. To keep rescue out? Or to keep Raven in?

Nathan must have noticed that I wasn't keeping up with him because he looked back at me. "Good," he whispered so softly that I could barely hear him, although his mouth was close enough to my ear that his lips tickled my earlobe. "Stay here. I'm glad you've got some sense. Go back to the car, okay?"

He didn't wait for me to answer, but put his hand under his jacket as if he were carrying a gun (he couldn't be carrying a real gun, right? He was hired for his research skills, not to shoot anyone). Just freaking great. Now I was going to have to rescue both of them instead of just myself.

And I wondered if he knew that Raven wouldn't be able to leave the demon triangle that restrained her, even if he could reach her. Probably not. Six weeks ago he thought magic was a product of CGI. He hadn't had time to learn enough to go up against actual demon catchers, let alone get any one of us out of a ritual working.

And he had the nerve to call me an amateur!

I was dead exhausted, but either the coffee or the danger had kicked in, and my brain was working fine. I was clear, focused, and strangely calm, as if there were all the time in the world.

Neither Raven nor I could cross the barriers set in the physical world, but that didn't mean that I couldn't get nondemonic help.

That's the problem with religious and ceremonial magicians both. They tend to be rigid about what must be done and how to do it. They're trained that way, I suppose, but it limits them. Magic can be very adaptable if you are able to work from the basic principles.

I wondered . . . The first thing any magician of any stripe does is cast a circle in each of the elemental kingdoms. But a demon is not held within the circle, as that would leave the practitioner vulnerable. A demon is held in a salt triangle outside of the circle. Salt is earth, and since earth is the most basic and dense of the elements its protection naturally carries through all the other kingdoms. But this particular demon triangle had to be permeable so that the torturers could have some access to Raven. In order to get in and out themselves they would need the barrier to be less solid.

A demon could not get through the triangle, but I could call on a nondemon, an elemental being. Elementals are etheric creatures. They can affect the physical world without having to obey its laws. If I could get one into the circle I could have it snatch Raven and return through Yetzirah, the World of Formation.

Fire is the sword that cuts through all obstacles, besides being my natural element as a succubus. So I would call a Salamander and send it to grab Raven.

I had no experience calling a Salamander. All elementals were notoriously unstable and unreliable but Salamanders were the worst of the lot, which made it more likely that it could permeate the barrier.

I also had no equipment.

Cancel that. I had a mirror (on my lipstick case) and I bet I could find a candle and a knife in the kitchen. I remembered my instructor in Advanced Seminar, her gravely demon voice low and husky, and her accent vaguely like Marlene Dietrich's, saying, "A true magician can do a ritual with a burning twig and a butter knife in the middle of Cathedral Square on a market day!" I was about to test that theory.

I went down the stairs as silently as I had ascended and found the kitchen tucked under the gallery hallway. It was a separate room with a door, which I closed behind me. The room was humongous. All in white tile and stainless steel, it looked more like an industrial kitchen than someplace featured in our sister home design magazine. No granite, no cherry cabinets, no homey crockery or food interrupted the pristine sweep of the stainless steel counters.

I found knives of all sizes and shapes, from cleavers to tiny paring knives, and selected one of the smaller Cuisinart chef's knives with a stainless steel handle. I chose it mostly because of the metal handle, because that seemed more swordlike to me and because, if I remembered my lessons correctly, the magician should touch the metal of the sword directly.

So, middle of the kitchen. I had the sword. A wooden spoon would do for a wand, and a small metal candy dish would stand in for a pentacle. I had my pick for the chalice, but decided against the Waterford. I chose the plain juice glass instead. I still needed a candle.

Okay. Time to improvise. Even though I was isolated

from the room upstairs, I could hear Raven's cries, and they chilled me. That sound more than the possibility of discovery kept me focused.

I took one of the high stools from the breakfast bar and dragged it over to the stove. The gas burner would work for fire, and the stool would hold the rest of the tools as an altar. I set out my mirror and the collection I had scrounged and set off to work.

I had no incense or brazier to walk the circle and seal the space, but I did have an atomizer of Estée Lauder's Beautiful that I'd gotten in one of their promotional packages. How it had ended up in the pocket of my blue fleece jacket I did not know or question. I just used it. I sprayed it as I walked a circle that, with a sweep of my arm, included the nearest two burners of the six burner Wolf stove.

I walked the circle with the sword, imagining blue flame to match the gas burning on the stove from the sharp tip. I saw it seal, a ring of electric neon blue that protected me and kept the magic concentrated.

I wished I knew a formal Fire invocation, but some kind of statement was necessary. "Element of Fire, I call upon you as your sister. Fire to fire I call, Salamander of the worlds, come to me as a friend and aid in this, my time of extreme need. Come, Salamander, come."

I repeated the last over and over, my mind utterly focused on nothing but my own desire for the elemental to appear. Yearning, needing, imploring, I built the emotions and let them ride the words as I spoke them.

Come, Salamander, come. I saw the words in raging red flames tinged with yellow; I imagined the creature itself brilliant and burning, called not by my words but by the force of my will and my power under Satan. My whole being was intent on only that, and if the entire 82nd Airborne had landed in that kitchen I wouldn't have noticed.

In my mind's eye I saw the Salamander. I felt its heat and violent energy. I felt its unshakable will within my own. This one picture filled my mind so completely that I could smell the flames and feel the heat blister my skin.

I gazed into the mirror and saw it reflected clearly back to me, every scale blazing, every talon sharp and flaming. Only its coal black eyes were dark and calm, unperturbed by the flames. The mirror became liquid and the Salamander poured through the glass and stood flaming on a stainless steel counter. The white ceiling blackened from the smoke.

"I hear your call, Sister," it said in a raspy, crackling voice. "What would you of me, and what do you offer?"

A bargain. Always a bargain.

"I want the young demon being held upstairs," I said. "Can you snatch her away from the place where they hold her confined?"

"And if I can, what will you give me?" the Salamander demanded.

I thought hard and fast. There are currencies in the world of magic, and one of the most desirable of those I have easily at hand. "I will give you a drop of my ichor," I said. "Which you can use for yourself or to trade, so long as it is never used against me or mine."

"One drop we will need for the working. I will have three drops when it is finished," the Salamander demanded.

"Done."

I used the blade of the chef's knife to cut the tip of my finger. One drop of ichor glistened on the edge. I held it out to the Salamander, who incorporated it with a delicate flick of its tongue. And in a blaze that was so bright my eyes ached, the Salamander left and transported through the element into the room upstairs. I rode inside of it, disguised, my inner self (that would be a soul in a human) being overlaid by the ferocity of Elemental Fire.

The Salamander took us to the upstairs room and I saw Raven chained to what appeared to be an altar, her belly slit open and bleeding. I screamed. I could see everything and I was there, but from the vantage of the Salamander I couldn't do anything to intervene.

A shocked voice roared out behind me. "What in hell are you doing here?"

I turned and there, in the middle of the working circle, dressed up in his gray silk robes with a pewter laman on his chest, stood Marten.

chapter
TWENTY-ONE

"Marten?" I squeaked, shocked. Ohmygoodness, was he one of the bad guys? Had he been one of the ones who was torturing Raven? I screamed inside my head. Outside the Salamander roared.

"Lily, get out of here. It is dangerous," he said.

"What are you doing?" I demanded.

"Trying to save Raven," he hissed, flickered, and disappeared.

And then, without warning, something flashed a brilliant red.

And I was in a beautifully appointed study, trapped inside a blazing red triangle. The Salamander had tricked me! It had dumped me in the physical reality, the actual room, and had itself fled.

I didn't have time to wonder why. Raven was nowhere in sight. But four mortal men, one of whom I recognized, were ringed around me. The one I recognized, Craig Branford, held a sword pointed at my throat.

"Speak, demon, I command you in the name of Heaven," he intoned.

"Buddy, I hate to break it to you, but I'm not the enemy of Heaven," I told him. "The Hierarchy goes all the way down. Satan still serves On High, though don't ask Her to admit that in polite company."

"It tries to beguile us, Leader," one of the others whimpered.

I sighed and sagged with more exhaustion than I had felt in a century. "I'm just telling the truth. It's not my fault if you're a bunch of half-educated halfwits. Where's Raven?"

Only they weren't going to tell me. They didn't know what had happened, and I'd bet three pairs of next season's Manolos that they hadn't even noticed the substitution. If substitution it was.

But I could find no trace of Raven. She had vanished from the triangle, a triangle specifically designed to hold a demon. She was gone, and I was trapped.

As I realized the depth of my situation, I wanted to cry, to scream with frustration. *This is what happens when you try to do something decent,* I thought.

Then Branford pierced the triangle with his sword and it burned. It never touched me but the intention in that blade piercing my prison (and protection) became a torment.

I was hurt and angry, and I admit I wasn't thinking very clearly. There was probably a better way; if I'd been a hostage negotiator for the FBI this could have gone down differently. But I'm not, I'm an accessories editor and a succubus. Diplomacy is not a job requirement.

So instead of trying to calm them down, I put my hand on the blade of the sword. And I shrieked with the pain of the intentions of the blade but I couldn't let it go.

Branford had violated the most important rule of confining demons. He had breached the barrier. Give any of us the slightest crack in that magical barricade and we will exploit it. And I did.

I held the sword and swung it around. Every movement rent the triangle further.

I screamed. Branford screamed. The door burst open and Nathan entered, yelling and swinging a fireplace poker.

Branford's companions fled, terrified, as I stepped out of the restraining triangle, which left me and Nathan to deal with Branford. Who, fortunately, was not about to let go of the sword. Yeah, he must have learned in Self-Righteous Fanatic School never to take his eyes off the demon.

Which would be good advice, but it didn't take into consideration the mortal team member who wasn't confined by magical barriers and who didn't conform to magical protocols. As Branford and I danced around with the sword between us, Nathan swept his legs with the fireplace poker and the man went down. His hands came off the sword and I had control over the weapon. Which, being a ritual item, wasn't at all sharp.

But Branford didn't know that, or didn't care. Or was more afraid of the magical properties than I understood, because when I held the point of the sword to his throat he lay very still. His eyes were steady and blazed with the absolute certainty of a raging idiot.

"God will save me," he said with perfect conviction. "You may destroy my body but you cannot have my soul in Hell."

"Don't worry, we don't want your kind," I said as Nathan started to duct tape his wrists behind his back.

Branford smiled thinly. "Of course not. You can't

have me. I belong to the Lord God wholly and entirely, and my being is dedicated to doing His work."

I shook my head and sighed. "I don't think so. You people are so . . . ignorant."

By then Nathan had gotten his ankles and came around front to tape his mouth shut. Thank goodness.

"What should we do with him?" Nathan asked.

I shook my head. "I don't know. Where's Raven?"

It was Nathan's turn to look confused. "I didn't see anyone but you and the men who were here. I thought you did some kind of magical snatch or substitution or something."

"No," I admitted.

But someone had. Someone had snatched Raven out of the triangle and substituted me. Something was going on, something that involved Meph and Marten and I didn't know what else. But the vast array of sky visible through the windows was starting to lighten, and I was tired beyond belief. Craig Branford would wait a day or two. We could stash him someplace later, but for now I was too tired to think.

"Do you have someplace you can take him?" I asked Nathan.

Nathan hesitated. "I think so. Probably."

"Then take him there and we'll figure it out later," I mumbled. "I've got to get some sleep. And I've got an editorial meeting tomorrow."

"I'll drive you home," Nathan offered, but I waved him off. "No, you take care of Branford. I'll take a cab."

I nodded off until the cabbie announced we were at my door and I stumbled out. Only to be greeted by Vincent, looking handsome and unharmed, who took me by the shoulders and delivered me upstairs.

Three hours of sleep and two extralarge espressos later I was pretending to keep my eyes open during the editorial meeting. Which was excessively quiet due to the fact that Lawrence was notably absent. We had gotten through a very civilized discussion of sculpted wedgies, the hot new trend in shoes for next spring. Over a year away, and I still wasn't into *this* spring's clothes.

I was aware that my mind was wandering, but I managed to come up with deadlines and photo shoot information when I had to give a report about my shawl feature.

That was it. No mention of Lawrence or his absence, or whether we would ever see him again. After the meeting ended I walked down the hall with Danielle.

"No Lawrence?" I asked.

She raised an eyebrow in that oh-so-French way. "I have heard nothing. No rumors, no gossip. Not about him."

"He could just have the flu, then." I sighed.

But when we got to my door, Danielle followed me into my office. Which was fine with me, but we both had work to do. If I could work. I had been thinking about collapsing on the sofa for a couple of hours since really I was not equipped to handle an all-nighter and be fresh and productive the next day. Danielle pulled up one of the chairs to my desk while I sat down and pretended to be awake.

"I have heard no rumors about Lawrence," she stared. "But, Lily, people are starting to talk about you. You have been out of the office a lot recently, and when you are here you look like you need to be someplace else. You are too tired during meetings and I think you are not keeping up with work. You have not contributed to the editorial meeting in weeks."

I froze. My hands curled around the edges of my desk and I sat stock-still. Fear, cold and solid like ice in my stomach, knotted my insides.

"Did someone ask you to speak to me?" I asked carefully.

Danielle shook her head. "I do not believe that there is much said, not yet. But I am your friend, Lily, and I do not want to see you in trouble. I want this to stop before anyone else pays attention. I am worried for you also, because something must be happening at home for you to be so tired all the time here. And you do not focus the way you used to."

"Do you think I'm in trouble?"

"No, no," Danielle attempted to reassure me. "But I can tell that something is wrong. And I thought before that this was something small and you would recover quickly. But it is getting worse and you are not better and I think that soon someone else will notice. Whatever is happening at home that keeps you up all night, this is no good thing. And if I can help you I will. Can you at least tell me what has happened?"

My friends all knew. But Danielle was my friend too, my only real mortal friend. My only friend who didn't know about the rest of my life, who took me as a mortal woman like herself, and that was important to me.

"There's this guy," I started, and Danielle nodded.

"I thought it was a man," she said. "You have not had so much romance in your life, I think. Who is this man?"

I gave her a very edited version of Nathan and Marten, leaving out all the magic, Hell, Mephistopheles, and the Treasury. It ended up sounding lame to me, but Danielle nodded sagely at points in my narrative. And at the end she sighed and shook her head.

"American women," she said. "I have lived here since I was twenty, but I still do not understand. Why do you not date both of them? Why must you choose? And even if you must choose, why must you choose now?"

"I can't date two guys," I protested, confused.

"Why not?" she countered. "You are only dating them, you have not known either for long, and you have no commitment to either of them. Your heart, yes, your heart is torn. But why? Because you believe you must give one up? So this Dutchman is in Aruba and that distance makes a problem, I agree. But this Nathan seems very young and undecided. He is in school, he is not in school, he is a scholar, he is a pretend detective. How can he commit to you if he cannot commit to even a plan of action for his life?"

"You think that's the problem?"

Danielle shook her head delicately, jangling the lovely chandelier earrings I recognized from our April issue. "I think that you are being quite silly not to see that it is the problem," she countered. "He clearly has feelings for you, but he runs. Why does any man run when he cares? Because he is a coward, because he is tied to another woman, or because he cannot make a decision. Because he cannot take a risk with his heart and his life."

"That's so romantic if he's actually afraid that he'll risk his heart for me," the words came out before I realized what I had said. And it was true, that was a very romantic view of life. As a succubus, I was anything but romantic.

"Ah, but there you are wrong," Danielle said almost as if she had been reading my mind. "It is merely realistic. Your Marten, it appears, is willing to take risks. He came up to New York without telling you to see you."

"That was business!"

She waved her hand. "If he did not wish to see you he would not have come. He used the business as an excuse. And he is, after all, Dutch. He cannot let you know that he was so rash. But that is exactly what you need, Lily. You have always been so sensible. I have seen it. You have always been so focused on your career, on your achievements. You only want to date men who will fit into a particular pattern and so you have not dated at all. So neither Marten nor Nathan fit into the mold of the proper boyfriend you had envisioned for yourself. Nathan is not employed enough, not serious enough, not committed enough. Marten doesn't live in New York. But both of them seem quite good for dating. Why not just date both of them and enjoy them?"

"You're probably right, Danielle," I admitted. "But I'm too tired to think about it now."

"No," she said. "You should not think about it at all. You should feel about it. What do you feel? What do you desire? That does not come from your head. You live in your head too much, Lily. Listen to your instinct."

I think I was almost awake. Danielle sounded like a self-improvement and motivational book come to life. It was terrifying; I hadn't known she'd had that in her.

I got up and hugged her, although Danielle was not normally the huggy kind. She was more of the air-kiss-on-both-cheeks kind. "Thank you, Danielle. That was what I needed to hear. Now—maybe now I can try to get some work done."

Danielle shook her head. "And what will you do about these men?"

"I don't know," I admitted. "I'm not sure yet but I do know that I've got to pay more attention to work right now. And . . . just talking to you I got this funny feeling that I'll figure it out."

She nodded gravely. There is something about a Frenchwoman in a Dior outfit who takes affairs of the heart as something profound and serious. "That is true. And sometimes the best way to discover what you think is not to think about it."

Then she turned and left me standing, slightly in shock. And in desperate need of more caffeine.

So I went down to the Starbucks in the lobby of the building to buy myself the biggest, most potent fix I could find and asked for a triple shot of espresso (along with vanilla syrup to make it a bit tastier) and returned to work. I worked hard and thought about nothing else for the first time in what seemed like weeks. I'd forgotten how good it felt to match the right accessories to different editors' needs. It was more magical than anything I'd done with ritual. Then I checked in with the writers for the feature articles and the photographers for the next two issues' Accents page.

Then it was time to go home. Most of the department had left and the hallways were silent. I realized that I hadn't seen Lawrence all day—not at meeting, and I hadn't heard his bellow down the hall.

I hoped it would stay that way.

Vincent was on duty when I arrived home with my

dinner in a drippy pizza box. He took it from me while I fumbled for my mailbox key, dropped the junk into the conveniently placed trash, and found the three keys that would let me in to my apartment. Only then did I think to inquire as to his well-being and state of health.

"I'm fine now," he said gravely. "Sybil has been wonderful. She took today off and we went to the Carnegie Deli for lunch because she believed that I needed chicken soup for a complete recovery. But we're fine now."

"Do you know what happened with Raven?" I pursued the subject.

Vincent shook his head. "Have you talked to Meph and Nathan about what happened when you were kidnapped?" I asked.

"Yes," Vincent said wearily. "And I don't want to talk about it anymore. You can ask Nathan or Mephistopheles if you want to know."

Then the elevator arrived and really, I was too tired and overwhelmed to pursue the matter. I stepped into the elevator and let the doors close on Vincent and on anything else that could interfere with a serious evening of Taking Care of Me.

I didn't check my e-mail or my voice mail. The only thing I turned on was the TiVo (where I'd recorded last week's episodes of my three favorite shows) and didn't even bother with heating up the pizza (though it was not as warm as I would like it and the cheese wasn't runny anymore). It was the most delicious pizza I'd tasted in ages, and the *Gilmore Girls* sparkled and I indulged in a hot bath in my deep clawfoot tub with a Black Pearl bath bomb. At which point I was so tired and so relaxed that getting out of the bath to get into bed was the hardest task I could manage.

I slept for eight beautiful, glorious hours and when I woke up it was morning and sunny and warm. Spring had finally come.

My joyful ignorance lasted through my first cup of coffee, through two fried eggs, two slices of bacon, and a cheese Danish. I hummed, I went through my closet looking for a proper spring outfit for the day, and it was only after I'd chosen the pin-striped pencil skirt with black tights and a shell pink Anna Sui silk blouse trimmed with black Venice lace accents that I turned on my e-mail.

Which was a mistake. Twenty new messages, and none of them were spam. From Meph, from Marten, from Nathan, from Sybil and Desi and Eros. From everyone except Satan Herself, thank goodness. E-mail from Satan is always really bad news.

Even then it was not too late. I could have turned off the computer and gone into the office and thought about beautiful clothes. There were probably new bags and scarves and belts to catalog and coordinate for different editors, there were interns to provide with gossip, and maybe Danielle would even have some shoes to hand off.

But I'm an idiot, so I opened the first one. And all of my resolve and good mood was immediately destroyed.

chapter
TWENTY-TWO

All the e-mails said the same thing, basically. Where had I hidden Raven? Had I kidnapped her when I crashed the Burning Men's circle? Didn't I know she was wearing a wire, in magical terms, so they could find her and the kidnappers? Why had I disrupted their carefully laid plan with my idiot amateur attempts at a rescue? The fact that no one had ever told me the plan was ludicrous.

Meph, at least, was restrained. Marten wanted to know how I'd done it, after he'd made a talisman tracer so that they could follow her and had it flown up specially to New York from Orangestad. Eros said that I should have trusted everyone else and I never believed that anyone else could take care of things. Sybil said I was a doll for trying so hard, but clearly I had been overtired. Desi asked where I thought Raven might be.

The truth was, I had no idea where Raven was.

But since everyone thought I'd messed up, why was it my job to try to save Raven?

And where in Hell was the girl, anyway?

I couldn't think. I couldn't focus. I managed to get to the office, and given how much I'd done the day before I could handle most of what I needed on autopilot.

Which was a very good thing because my brain was definitely elsewhere.

Where was I going to find Raven? And how? I didn't know if the shirt connection would work again. I wished I could call Marten in Aruba and ask him.

Maybe I could, I thought. I had his cell number somewhere, but I would have to wait until a decent hour. It was still early for a party animal.

Then the phone rang. I looked at the caller ID. Nathan.

How did he even know I was awake?

The phone did not stop ringing. Why didn't it roll over to voice mail already? And then voice mail picked up and there was silence. For two minutes. Until my cell phone started ringing.

There was no way around it, I was going to have to talk to someone sometime. I picked up the cell phone and answered brusquely.

"I found them!" Nathan said triumphantly even before I could ask what he was doing, calling me at eight in the morning.

"What do you mean?" I asked, wary.

"I mean I traced the owner of the apartment like I said I was going to. And I discovered that the title is in the name of one Steven Balducci. Ring any bells? And that's not the only property he owns."

The name was familiar. I thought for a moment. "Not that cop who dumped Desi because he's in with Branford?" That felt like years ago, but it had only been two months since Desi had met a very cute cop while we were all at brunch. And he'd dumped her in Brooklyn in the middle of their first date when Craig Branford told him she was Hellspawn.

A cop who owned an apartment that large right on Gramercy Park? That seemed a little odd. Unless it belonged to his famous, wealthy uncle. But I couldn't see how it fit.

And I couldn't be the one to ask. Not right now, not when Desi was furious with me. So I told Nathan to call Desi and see what she knew. She must have learned more about him on that date they had than she had told us. And she would have figured out if he was rich. Desi is good that way.

"And wait a minute," I said, cutting Nathan off before he could say good-bye. "Can you find out if he's a cop?"

"Why?" Nathan asked.

"Because there was a guy who dated Desi whose name was Steve Balducci but he was a cop. Or he said he was a cop. But cops don't live in apartments like that, so either it's a different guy or he isn't a cop."

"Or he is a cop for other reasons," Nathan sounded huffy and defensive. "He wouldn't be the first guy with some family money to join the force."

Right. And Nathan wasn't the only almost Ph.D. in Near Eastern History who was playing PI while he figured out what to do with his life.

"But still, can you find out?" I asked, suddenly interested. What if the guy had lied to Desi?

"I can find that out," Nathan said. "Do you want to have lunch today? We can go over what I've found and then figure out how to approach the others."

"I can't. I have to work. I'm already in trouble for all the time I've taken off and I have got to actually get things caught up. Because if we don't have an Accessories page in the July issue then I'm going to lose my job."

"Dinner? I can bring some takeout."

The guy was persistent, I had to give him that. "Okay, dinner," I agreed. "I want egg rolls and Crispy Chicken."

"How about Benny's?" he suggested. "I could really use a burrito."

"Hmmm, a burrito sounds good. I haven't been to Benny's in ages," I said, suddenly wondering if the last time I hit my favorite burrito place it had been when I'd run into Nathan. It brought back memories of how much fun he was during that dinner and how much we had in common.

"Get me a steak burrito with extra guac and cilantro," I reeled off my favorite without thinking. "And chips. Get extra chips and salsa and a side of guac. Or maybe two."

What can I say? I love guacamole and I'd only discovered it in the last twenty years.

"You're on," Nathan agreed and I could almost hear the smile in his voice.

For some reason his call put me in a better mood. Maybe because we were making some actual headway with this thing. Maybe because I didn't have to worry about dinner. Maybe because I was not going to think about this mess for the next eight hours. I was going to pay attention to doing my job. For once.

I had lunch with Danielle at the deli around the corner, where we indulged in fatty corned beef and French fries and chocolate shakes, the old-fashioned kind where they put the leftovers in a second cup and give you both.

One of the great benefits of the deli was that no one from *Trend* would go there.

"What's up?" I asked innocently as both of us scanned the room to make sure that none of the interns or graphics people had come down for chicken soup.

"I have not seen Lawrence for days," she said, shaking her head. "Do you think he has left *Trend*?"

"I can hope," I said fervently.

The waitress arrived with our food, a sandwich that could feed a small village in Africa, a pile of fries that could induce altitude sickness, and two gloriously thick chocolate milk shakes made with U-Bet syrup and tasting like nothing else on earth. For a full ten minutes we savored one of New York's great local cuisines, reveling in the crisp fries and the salty deli meat on real rye bread with a hard crust. We held the shakes for last, for dessert, for pure sinful indulgence.

I wondered idly as I ate whether Meph, foodie that he is, had ever had a chocolate shake made with U-Bet. He generally specializes in gluttony with gourmet food, the very finest restaurants with crisp tablecloths and silent waiters who refill the glasses just as they get within two swallows of empty.

"What are you fantasizing?" Danielle asked sharply, breaking into my reverie. "Is it about those men you are dating?"

I shook my head slowly and smiled. "No. I was wondering if my gourmet uncle had ever had a milk shake in his life. And if he hasn't, I should take him here sometime. He never goes to places like this."

"I didn't know you had family in New York."

I shrugged. "He doesn't live here, he just comes in on

business sometimes. So what do you think is up with Lawrence?" I distracted her easily.

"I do not know," Danielle admitted. "No one knows anything. This is very mysterious, is it not? Do you think we should try to discover what has become of him? Something terrible could have happened to him. He has no family here."

And then the demon part of me just exploded. "No," I told her. "We hate Lawrence, remember? And if he doesn't have anyone looking for him if he really is missing, then that's his fault. He hates Americans, he says so all the time. He trashed my office, remember that? And have I just become the finder of missing people? Is that my new job title?"

"What do you mean? Who else is missing?" she asked with some confusion.

"My doorman," I said hotly. "He was kidnapped, but now he's back."

Danielle rolled her eyes. "I did not know that you had to find your doorman. He is your . . . doorman. And who would kidnap a doorman? Surely he had no money. Unless—is he the member of a powerful family, incognito, posing as a doorman for some reason? Perhaps he is with the CIA and is staking out the place because there were threats of terrorists. Lily, do you have a terrorist living in your building? On the Upper East Side? That is insupportable."

That's what I love about Danielle. She can take a few facts and weave them into a story that would run John Grisham around the block. "Danielle, that sounds like a plot for an international thriller. Sounds like half the best-seller list."

I thought she would laugh or shake her head gravely.

Instead she went white. "I have told nobody! I keep it a secret and even my boyfriend, even my mother does not know. Lily, how do you know?"

"Know what?" I asked. "I mean, that's an amazing story you made up about my doorman. Who isn't from a powerful family and isn't in the CIA and isn't a terrorist. So I was just saying that you have a great imagination! You should write a novel."

"I have written novels," she admitted. "Six of them."

"You've written six novels?" I squealed. "Are they published? Why are you still a shoe editor?"

Danielle flapped her hands in what appeared to be despair. "They are published, yes, but the money is not so good. Not enough to live in New York, at least. And—where would I get new Manolos and Jimmy Choos and Christian Louboutins if I were not a shoe editor?" she asked very reasonably. "I could not afford to buy all of them retail." We both shuddered delicately. I could afford it and I still didn't like to contemplate the collateral stuck in the back of my closet.

"But tell me about these six books," I said, fascinated. "Do you write under your own name? What kind of books are they, and are there great shoes in them?"

"Of course there are great shoes, and beautiful clothes," Danielle said. "They are romantic thrillers, about CIA or sometimes the FBI, and mostly they are about American women on holiday in Paris who fall in love with wonderful Frenchmen, and then there is international intrigue with terrorists and crime families. You will not tell anyone? I don't write under my own name. I think everyone will laugh at me," she admitted.

"Why would anyone laugh at someone who has published six novels?" I asked. "I think we should go out sometime and celebrate your next book. You should be proud of them."

"But really it's not something I want people to know," she said modestly.

I just stared at her. The things you don't know about people. I had worked with her for four years; she'd been my best friend at work all that time and I'd had no idea.

"What else haven't you told me?" I asked, half joking. "Are you also an agent for Interpol, or maybe in line for the Russian throne?"

The waitress chose that moment to start clearing our dishes rather loudly. "Can I get you ladies anything else? Dessert? Coffee?" When we shook our heads, she slammed the check onto the table and stood over us as we fished for the money.

Danielle and I returned to the office chatting about nothing, pretending that nothing had been said and everything was normal.

Nothing was normal. I closed my office door and sat behind my desk but I couldn't even see the purses I'd lined up before lunch. I had intended to assign them for various shoots and I was even fairly certain of a few. I tagged those mechanically as I thought about Vincent and Raven and Marten and even Lawrence. Everything was a mess; nothing made sense. And yet I had this feeling that there was something much bigger going on, something that was just out of reach. It was like seeing something out of the corner of my eye, a flash of movement where I couldn't actually see the culprit.

My hands had worked while my brain had been involved in other things, and suddenly the bags were all gone, in various boxes, and I didn't even remember which I'd assigned to which article.

I wanted to call Desi. I wanted to talk to her about Steve. But more, I wanted to just talk to my friends again. I wanted them to tell me that it was okay and I was okay, and I could ask them about why this was all happening. Why had they kidnapped Vincent? Why had they wanted me? I had managed to shove those thoughts aside for a while but they kept intruding as I contemplated the new twists. I really needed to talk to one of my girlfriends, one who was a demon who knew about Hell and Vincent and the Burning Men. Much as Danielle was a real friend at work, there was too much else about my life she didn't know.

Then the phone rang, and it was Desi on the line.

"Lily?" she said hesitantly. "Look, I just talked to Nathan about Steve and he told me about the two of you trying to rescue Raven. That was really brave of you and I wish I'd been able to help. But what happened?"

"I did the whole ritual right, I know I did. I was in that room and she was gone. Just gone, like she'd been snatched magically. Through a salt triangle, too, which is how I got trapped," I told Desi.

There was some dead air on the phone before Desi continued. "When I heard about what you had done I was afraid for you. And I know that Eros and Meph were too. I think they were more angry that you had put yourself in danger than anything else. We were scared, Lily."

"I was scared too," I told her. "We need to get together, all four of us. And Meph too, at some point. But we've all got to work on this and make a plan, not just react to what the Burning Men do."

"Meet me at Public," she said. "After work. We'll all

meet at the bar and have a drink before it's time for strategy."

"Nathan is coming over with dinner," I said hesitantly. I didn't want her to think that Nathan was more important in the scheme of the universe than she was. But he was also the prior commitment.

She thought for a moment. "We probably want to know whatever Nathan's discovered," she said finally. I considered the options. "How about this? I call you when Nathan leaves. I don't think he'll be long, things are kind of uncomfortable between us. So I'll call and then you and Sybil and Eros can come over and we can have ice cream and plot."

Desi laughed, not the somber or forced laugh but one that was light and musical with pleasure. "A pajama party! We haven't had a pajama party in ages. I wonder if we could make s'mores?"

Yes. A pajama party. To remember that we were all stronger together than any of us was alone. And to also remember that we needed one another. Danielle was my friend, but she was mortal. We demon women have to stick together.

chapter
TWENTY-THREE

When I got off the phone I wondered how bad my apartment looked. I couldn't remember how I'd left it, if I'd cleared the dirty dishes off the coffee table, if I'd left a pile of laundry in the back hall, if I'd hung the towels up in the bathroom. I didn't worry so much about Nathan seeing it—he was my ex and my employee. More important, he's male and somehow men do not see dirt. Clutter, yes, they notice clutter, but they don't really track on dirt.

Women do. I knew I would want to at least vacuum before the women arrived, and time was going to be very tight.

I concentrated on work for the next three hours, and when I go into overdrive I can be very productive. I needed to be very productive because I was in for a long evening and I didn't know how late I would show up tomorrow.

No one makes provision in regular jobs for time off for magical emergencies. Women even have trouble getting time off to take care of sick children, let alone have severe metaphysical crises. And there was no way I could explain any of it at work. The only thing I could do was make sure that I was as prepared as possible.

In three hours I managed to sort and arrange accessories for every shoot on the schedule for the next two weeks. I was a whirlwind of efficiency, so I was able to hop a cab by six with enough work done that, should I need to, I could sleep tomorrow away on the office sofa and no one would notice.

So I managed to get home by six thirty and Vincent didn't start until seven. Roger, the doorman on the day shift, helped me with my portfolio, my bag and my mail. Which, I was glad to see, consisted only of junk mail and catalogs. Nothing in that stack could be sabotage from Branford and his coterie.

I stepped out of my olive stilettos as soon as I hit the door. Threw the purse and the portfolio on the coffee table and grabbed the vacuum out of the front hall closet. In ten minutes I'd managed to get the worst off the rug and the dust bunnies out from under the sofa. Given that my cleaning lady wasn't due until Thursday, the place was pretty presentable.

I had just stowed the vacuum, picked up my shoes, and wondered whether I should change out of my plaid Prada suit when the intercom rang. I told Roger that Nathan was welcome to come up, and he must have stepped directly onto the elevator because he rang my bell not a minute later.

I could smell the Benny's from behind the closed door, so I opened up to see him with a large bag of food in one hand and a bulging briefcase slung over his shoulder.

"Did you look?" he asked without even a greeting. "Did you know who it was? You live in this city, you should know that you never ever open the door without checking who's there."

"I pay for a building with a doorman for that very

reason," I chided him. "Besides, I could smell the burritos. It had to be you."

He shook his head as he unpacked the food. I got out plates and utensils while he set cartons on the bag, which he'd flattened over the wooden surface of my coffee table. I was pleased to see his care for my things. I hated it when people just threw food on the good teak without trivets. I liked that table.

He put a foil-wrapped burrito on one of my plates and handed it to me. I peeled off the aluminum cover to find a bit of comfort. I didn't really want to talk to Nathan and I wanted to talk to him too much. In spite of that, I ate my burrito in silence and then started in on the guac and chips.

"I have found out a few things," he started when he put his empty plate down. "First, you were right about checking on Balducci. He isn't a cop. I did some rather interesting Web searches on him and found out that he's connected to some, well, not precisely standard banks in the Caribbean. I also checked out your friend Marten. Did you ever even Google him?"

I shook my head. I knew I should have, but really, it was a vacation thing. And, of course, Meph had vouched for him.

"Well, I don't know what he told you he does," Nathan started and his voice had a bit of an edge.

"He told me he's an accountant," I answered. "And I know he's a magician. He got some kind of great deal out of Hell. And how did you know his name or what to search on anyway?"

Nathan shrugged. "Well, he didn't tell you the truth. He's with Interpol."

"What?" I think my neighbors two floors down heard

my shriek. "Are you sure? Maybe it's someone else; it could be someone else."

Nathan shook his head. "I checked. And there's a picture. He's Interpol. Okay, you couldn't have gotten that from Google. I had to use the firm's credentials to check international law enforcement sites. You can figure out what he's doing in this mess later. Back to Balducci. He does own the apartment, but the down payment was made by his uncle."

I shrugged. "That doesn't mean anything."

Nathan sat back in the easy chair and closed his eyes in something close to a wince. "I'm trying to explain something, Lily. Steve Balducci was not just Branford's pawn. I think Branford might be under the architect, whose wife is a leading contributor to some rather dubious conservative causes. So they're in it up to their necks."

"But that doesn't tell us where Raven is," I protested feebly. To cover my uneasiness I scraped the last morsel of guac out of the cup with my finger. I'd already demolished the chips.

"No, but it gives us some possibilities," Nathan said briskly. "I've got a list of other properties owned by the Balduccis: Steve, Franco, and Paola. There are two in Brooklyn and a townhouse in Hoboken. And two more apartments in Manhattan. So that's where we start."

"What about Branford?" I asked.

Nathan shook his head. "Nothing for Branford. I think he's small-time, being manipulated by Balducci and family, if you will."

And then my thoughts started to come together. It was like when I visualized what an editor wanted for a shoot, the whole thing coming together effortlessly in my mind. I opened my mouth and closed it again, because the rest of the story was none of Nathan's business.

No, this was the business of Hell. And Balducci. Maybe he was in charge and Branford was just their figurehead. Maybe the older people were the real organizers and Steve was just his uncle's gofer. That made more sense. There hadn't been any whiff of magic around Steve, nothing that smelled of demon. And I hadn't gotten close enough to the uncle and aunt to tell.

I was suddenly anxious to talk to Desi, to discover what she might know about the family of demon hunters in her very brief acquaintance.

And all the while I was aware of the clock running, of Raven lost somewhere, probably imprisoned, likely tortured. I hadn't liked the girl at first and feeling guilty over what she was possibly enduring didn't endear her to me further.

I couldn't get Raven out of my mind, in those awful boots and my cute Betsey Johnson top, on the rack or being branded with red-hot pokers. She would have to pay Admin a hideous amount to have her skin restored—unless Satan would take care of her as She had cared for me. Or maybe I should pay for her? That was dangerously close to altruism for a demon, but the girl was suffering in my place. It was the least I could do.

"So what do you think?" Nathan was asking. I realized I hadn't heard anything he'd said in the past two minutes, and he must have noticed. "I said, Lily, I think we should investigate this location. It's one of the Balducci-owned properties and was listed as the address of the Knight Defenders when we first discovered their activities. Branford is listed as renting an apartment there, but the entire building is owned by Aunt Paola. Do you want to bet that Branford isn't paying any rent?"

"Why didn't we go there in the first place?" I asked, irritated. We'd waited so long, Raven had suffered for hours because he hadn't told me about this lead immediately.

"I've had a listening station on the window," he told me. "Ever since we failed at the Gramercy Park location. And I haven't picked up anything to indicate that Raven is being held there. No screams, no torture, nothing. So it may be another false lead."

I leaned back in my chair and rubbed my eyes. The mascara smeared—it always smears—but I didn't care. "If you've had surveillance then let's not waste our time. I think we should take this real estate business to Meph immediately and see what he says."

"That's your great idea?" Nathan seemed wounded.

"I'm out of ideas," I admitted. "I used up my last one on tracking Raven in the first place, and I'm pretty sure it wouldn't work again. They would shield better now that they know we're using ritual."

"Aren't there ways to break that?" Nathan asked very unhelpfully.

"I'm calling in Meph. We need to consult with him and you need to give him all the information you've given me," I said decisively, as if I were in charge of the situation and not just another succubus dear to Satan's heart but not generally given executive powers.

And then I pulled out my Treo and hit speed dial (number seven) and Meph picked up on the second ring. By the time I hit End there was the scent of sulfur and a dapper, urbane Mephistopheles stepped out of the stinking yellow cloud.

"What happened to Raven? You botched the whole scheme," Meph shot at me like a drill sergeant in boot camp.

"I don't know," I pleaded. "You never told me about your plan. I was trying to rescue her, and then when I got into the triangle she disappeared. Just flat-out disappeared. I don't know how they got her or who made the exchange. I've already tried to rescue her once and I'm ready to try right now as soon as I change my shoes. But you have to know how to find her. You have to."

Meph softened only slightly at the sight of my distress. "We don't have time for this," he said gruffly. "Let's get started."

Nathan briefed Meph on all that we'd discussed, and Meph listened closely. "She could be anywhere," he said finally. "That snatch was magical, as if the entire procedure was to find you . . ."

"But why? Why me? I'm not any more use than any other of the Chosen," I demanded. This was all too much and I wanted it all to stop. How come things like this didn't happen to Eros?

"You're linked to her through the glamour," Meph said. "We need to trace where she was taken. The situation you describe, where she disappeared just as you arrived, had to be a trap. Set up in advance."

"But it didn't work—I got out and they all ran," I protested feebly.

Meph shook his head. "They weren't counting on the human coming along with you. They were prepared for a magical attack but they didn't prepare for a living person with a gun who couldn't be barred with their demon barricade. Raven could well not be on this continent. Even on this plane of existence. They could be one place and holding her in another. In fact, that is exactly what I would do if I had set up the trap. Which means that the men who were there are disposable. There is a larger conspiracy with branches elsewhere. Branford and his crew are pawns, foot soldiers. Not worth contemplating or following. We need to find Raven and let these peons go." He waved his hand in dismissal. "Maybe then they'll lead us to the demon who is tipping them off."

And suddenly I had an idea so stunningly simple (and ridiculous) that I shrieked. "Magic! Demon magic. Summoning," I yelped as if the idea had bitten me. "We need a real magician, Meph, a human who knows how to command demons. One who we can trust, who's on our side."

"I expect you're referring to Marten," the senior demon said dryly.

"He would do," I agreed. "But if you've got one closer, then let's go with convenience."

Mephistopheles shook his head. "None that I would trust, not on this side of the Atlantic."

"What's going on?" Nathan interrupted. "What is this great idea?"

"The thing is, I can't do it myself," I admitted. "I know a reasonable bit about ceremonial magic, but a demon cannot do a demon summoning. It takes a human to do that, and I think that was the original nature of the trap. They had Raven in a summoning and that's how she was snatched out of the triangle of salt. What we need is a human magician to summon her! It's all so obvious I don't know why we didn't think of it as soon as Vincent was taken."

"Because if we had immediately summoned Vincent back, we wouldn't have been able to set any tracers on this faction. I believe they are tied in with the demon who is undermining Hell and skimming from the Treasury, because of some information Azoked ran down in the Akashic. The way their records are obscured reeks of high demon tampering. Given that, it was more important that we got a tag on them than that we save any younger demon from some discomfort. Which is the major reason we wanted to use a substitute and not you, Lily." Meph's face grew just the tiniest bit tender. "Satan would not hear of you being used to tag the perps, as it were."

I blinked. I hadn't known, hadn't realized exactly how serious Meph was about tracking down whoever was after us.

"I still don't understand what you're talking about," Nathan said, and I thought I detected a creeping note of whine in his tone.

So before I explained I went to the kitchen and started another pot of coffee, my best Blue Mountain blend, hoping it would go a good way toward mollifying all the frayed tempers. Then I dug in the back of the cupboard and found a bag of Pepperidge Farm Tahoe cookies, which hadn't been high enough on Azoked's list of preferred snacks to merit annihilation.

The guys took their coffees and helped themselves to cookies with enthusiasm. Meph had already placed a call on his cell phone and had wandered out of the living room and into the back hall. I didn't have to guess who was being awakened in the middle of the night in Paradise.

"It goes like this," I started to tell Nathan. "There are particular rituals for magically summoning demons by humans who are willing to barter their souls. This is standard economy down below. The rituals are difficult and they take a lot of study and skill to pull off. But the important thing here is that a demon can't do it. We don't have souls to barter, so the summoning won't hold. Even a demon who was a top ceremonialist in life couldn't pull it off after joining the ranks. The soul is a crucial ingredient."

"Okay, I get it, one human magician with a soul," Nathan sounded like a petulant child. And he had sprawled over the sofa, taking up as much space as possible. Juvenile, I thought. But also vaguely appealing. He had been hurt by all of this, I saw, and he wanted to do something. He wanted me to admire him. I think that maybe he even wanted to save me. And he hated himself for wanting that. He still didn't get it, still couldn't cope with the demon/human divide between us.

"Yeah. A magician with a soul. With the right rituals and preparation and talent an excellent human magician can summon any demon from the Hierarchy. Who must show, by order of On High. It's one of the bedrock rules of how demons can interact with humanity. And how we must interact with magicians. And there is nothing, nothing whatsoever, that can interfere. So you get the right kind of magician with the right talents and all, and he or she can summon anyone in the Hierarchy. Anyone at all."

That got his attention. "Anyone? What about what you call them—ummm, Upstairs?"

I nodded. "It's called Enochian and it's the hardest form of magic to learn. But that's angelic summoning and that's not necessary here. Although, for your information, demons are in the ranks of angelic orders. Yeah, there's a divide, but we also serve On High, just so you know. This Satan versus God thing, took humans to think that one up."

But he wasn't really listening to that bit.

"So if they wanted you, why couldn't Branford have just summoned you?"

I heard Meph's voice change in the hallway. He was speaking very distinctly, as if to voice recognition software.

I decided to answer Nathan's question. There was obviously time. "Because the magician who does the summoning has got to be ready and willing to barter, to give up some of his or her soul. Those fanatics aren't."

"But your boyfriend Marten can."

"He's not my boyfriend," I protested. *Well, maybe,* I thought, but it wasn't any of Nathan's business. "But yeah, he's the right kind of magician."

"And I couldn't?" Nathan asked.

And here I saw the heart of the matter. Nathan was jealous. Nathan couldn't stand the idea that Marten, or anyone, could do something that he couldn't. Especially when that something concerned me.

I would have been gratified if I hadn't felt so confused and tired and beaten down. I had wanted Nathan. He was the one who had walked away—and now he was the one complaining.

"You couldn't on two counts." I decided to enlighten him. "First, ceremonial magic takes years of study and preparation. I just hope that Marten is in condition to do a ritual like this—it can take days of fasting before they even start. And there are a series of purification rituals that they have to perform before they can actually do the summoning. I guess one thing Meph needs to find out is whether Marten is in a state of ritual readiness, so to speak. If not, it could take a week or more for him to be fully prepared.

"The second reason is that you don't want a demon around. You've rejected me and you didn't even have to barter or summon me. You have to be willing—no, eager—to deal with Hell to do a summoning. You might think you can remain in control, but every serious ceremonialist knows that it's really a negotiation."

He got up from the sofa and turned away from me, gazing out the window into the deep night. "Intent is that important? You can tell?"

I sighed. "Intent is everything. Without trained, single-minded, focused intent there is no magic," I said, feeling like I was playing instructor in a fourth-level demons' initiatory class. I guessed that Raven and Vincent, being third-level, hadn't made it quite this far yet. Or maybe they had. I'd heard there had been some tweaks in the curriculum since I'd been trained.

"We're booked on the eight a.m. flight," Meph announced. I hadn't heard him come in and I started a bit.

"What?" Nathan stuttered, covering the question for me.

"The eight a.m. to Miami. Where we connect to Aruba. You do have your passport with you?" Meph cocked an eyebrow at Nathan.

"Wait a minute," I protested. "I can't go to Aruba again. I'll lose my job. And I presume Marten can do the ritual, but he doesn't need us."

"No," Meph said. "He doesn't. But he would like you there and Raven will need us once we pull her through. So will Marten very likely, though he didn't say anything about it. This isn't going to be easy on anyone."

Much as I wanted to see Marten again, this was too

much. I was dead exhausted to the bone and had my heart broken, I owed Satan on deliveries, and I didn't know who I was dating, or *if* I was dating. My skin was sallow and I looked drawn, and I really didn't want Marten to see me like that. On top of that, I'd already lost too many days at work. This was just too much.

Meph's phone rang. He answered, bowed his head, and handed it to me.

Satan was on the line.

chapter
TWENTY-FOUR

"Lily, dear," She purred. "Why don't you catch a cab right now? There'll be one waiting when you get downstairs. You can leave the men to finish up the details. Meph will pack for you—he's very good with clothes. You come down and meet me in the bar at the Pierre."

There is only one answer ever for Satan, and I gave it. "Yes, Satan. Thank you, Satan." Then I handed the phone back to Meph as if it were hot.

"Gotta run," I said. I was glad I hadn't changed from work. The Prada tweed suit in olive and raspberry would be perfect at the Pierre. My olive Manolos from two seasons ago lay in the three square feet that pretended to be an entry hall. I stepped into them and grabbed a coat and left.

The elevator had hit the second floor when I realized that neither Nathan nor Meph had keys and couldn't lock up. I panicked and then forced the terror back down. Vincent would be vigilant. And I was responding to Satan's summoning. Surely no harm would come to me, or my apartment, because I had obeyed immediately. So immediately that I hadn't even thought to give one of the guys the spare key.

Vincent had a taxi ready, motor running and door open, as soon as I hit the lobby. I dashed past the security desk and ducked into the cab. "Lock my apartment up when Meph leaves, okay?" I asked him. He nodded once, sharply.

There was no traffic and the lights were green all the way, and the cabbie drove like we were in his NASCAR fantasy life. Less than ten minutes after leaving my building I was in front of the elegant cream and gold façade of one of the most famous hotels in New York. John F. Kennedy had stayed here. Ambassadors and foreign dignitaries and prima ballerinas from Russia and French fashion designers had stayed here. I called the girls. I got Sybil's cell first. "Where are you?" she asked. "We're all at Eros's waiting."

"I'm on my way to meet Satan at the Pierre," I said.

"I guess you won't be on for a pajama party," Sybil surmised.

"I'm really sorry," I apologized. "Nathan showed up and then Meph and now Satan wants to meet with me and this thing is just getting out of hand. I don't know what's going on anymore."

"This whole party was about you, about you telling us what actually happened," Sybil protested. "But if Satan wants to see you personally, I guess we can take a rain check."

"Thank you," I said, relieved. "You guys are the best."

The lobby at the Pierre is vast, a study in ormolu and tapestry upholstery and painted ceilings that would not look out of place in a palace in Europe. The bar is based on the same period (Louis XIV), and the same royal abode (Versailles), but it is a study in silence, the deep, luscious silence that great wealth and attention to details (not to mention deep pile, hand-loomed French carpets) bring. The cream and gold was rich and soothing, and the rose and blue wall hangings and rugs merely made the space warm and attractive.

Satan sat on a Louis XIV-style chair upholstered in rose and gold, wearing a Lanvin dress in deep sea green. Her hair, so very dark, sparkled with gold and copper highlights brighter than the Tiffany diamonds in Her ears or on Her hands.

Satan is breathtakingly beautiful. She had been the most beautiful angel of the Host before She had been given Her current assignment by On High. Don't fall for that story of a rebellion in Heaven and Satan saying that She would rather rule in Hell—that's the human version. Good poetry, of course, but Milton and Dante would have made the laundry list sound like the Angelic Hosts. Trust me, the real incident of Satan's assignment was far more complex than any human author ever suspected.

Anyway, She had a glass of amber liquid in Her hand, from which She was sipping slowly. As I entered the room Her eyes found me and I came to Her and saw nothing else. No hotel bar that could serve as a movie set for Versailles, none of the very rich and very important guests who sat clustered in the corner or at the bar, nothing but Satan.

Her face was perfectly composed. She looked like a magazine shoot come to life. She smiled and patted the seat beside Her. I wanted to drop in obeisance as I would if we were at Court, but we were in the Pierre where such things might be frowned upon. So I sat and a waiter appeared with a cosmo as soon as I hit the cushion.

"I ordered for you," Satan said graciously. I wondered how She had thought of the cosmo—it wasn't a Satan kind of drink.

"Thank you, Satan," I said formally. For all the venue and the drinks, this was a formal interview.

Sometimes, for the record, Satan is my friend. We shop, we lunch, we take tea at Lady Mendel's, we sometimes go to the opera or a rock concert together. Sometimes She is a girlfriend. Sometimes She is more of the senior aunt, or beloved professor, more knowing and powerful but benevolent. In the mode of friend and mentor, Her Chosen call Her Martha.

She was not Martha now. I studied Her face, Her slender hands, Her elegantly crossed calves, for any sign of displeasure.

Then She smiled and I let go of the breath I had been holding.

"Oh, Lily, dear," She said, and patted the back of my hand. "I understand that you're concerned about your job and about Raven. And I think it's dear of you to have tried to rescue her yourself, with help from a human man who doesn't even practice magic. That was very brave and generous of you and I want you to know that I have noted it. I want you to go to Aruba. Since you have shown such kindness to this young demon, I would like you to become her mentor. She may one day be fit to join you as my Companion."

"She has awful taste in clothes," I mentioned, just so that Satan would understand that shopping with Raven wasn't going to be any fun.

Satan laughed and I relaxed. Making Her laugh is always a good sign, a hint of Martha in our Master.

"Well, then, perhaps you can teach her. But it is My personal wish that you go down to Aruba to be there when she is retrieved, and to act as her comforter. I trust Mephistopheles with everything in Hell, but really, he isn't the most supportive person for a young girl demon. She needs the nurturing of a woman, a succubus, a devoted daughter."

"Of course, Satan. Since it is Your wish, of course." Because no matter how much I wanted to keep my job, I knew I had to serve Satan first. Come to think of it, that would be a pretty good slogan for us Hellspawn— *Serve Satan First*. I could see it on bumper stickers, in .sig files, on the bottom line of the official engraved stationery.

"Good." She smiled again. "I wanted to be sure you understood. This is important to Me. This girl may have evidence of which of My demons is betraying Me, and I must know who it is. Some things are simply intolerable."

"To all of us, Satan," I said from the depths of my heart. "Our first priority is discovering the traitor, all of us."

"But you're in the center of it," She said, sipping what I assumed was a fifty-year-old single malt. "I am aware of all you have done, which is why I have not mentioned the lack of deliveries of late. I understand that you have been too busy with My other affairs, and I give you leave to pursue My interests even if it takes time from your primary occupation."

I think I blushed. I had been aware that I had been falling down on the deliveries, but I had been overwhelmed. I was grateful that She was, in essence, forgiving me.

"Thank you, Satan."

"But once this business is over, you will need to step

up production just a tiny bit. To make up and show your gratitude for My generosity."

"Of course, Satan." Because there is no other answer to Satan. Because, no matter how much She loves to eat at nice restaurants and shop, She is still the autocrat of Hell. I was lucky that She was willing to overlook the fact that I had been falling down on the soul deliveries. Lucky—and Her friend.

"I wanted to make this direct and personal," She continued. "And there is one more thing. Go to Aruba. Become Raven's mentor. Hire her as an intern at the magazine, maybe in the art department. She does have talent and will do an excellent job. And I will make sure that your job is there for you when you return. There will be no problem with your bosses."

"Thank you, Satan." That was as heartfelt a prayer as any I had ever uttered. I didn't care if I had to go to Aruba (hard job, that, when it was still cold and raining in New York and there was a hot guy I was dating waiting down there to see me as well) and mentor a sullen, suicidal she-demon. Satan Herself had guaranteed my job. And my life.

"May I ask a question, Master?" I asked softly.

She inclined Her head graciously. "You may."

"Why must we go to Aruba? Why can't we do the summoning here in New York?"

Satan raised one perfectly waxed eyebrow over Her glass. "That was Mephistopheles' decision," She replied. "He believes that Raven will be safer out of New York right after the ritual. Of course you will return immediately, but the fact that they won't be able to trace you to the city by magic should delay any trace they might make. I believe that Mephistopheles hopes that taking the ritual over water will also break some of the magical links."

I didn't point out that Manhattan is already an island. Satan knew that. If She and Meph felt that going well offshore would increase the safety of the working I was happy to agree.

"Now get back and go to sleep," She ordered me. "You have to be at the airport early. And I will be watching what happens in Aruba. I will be watching Raven and of course I am always watching over you. Now, out."

I rose and nodded deeply enough to indicate a bow before I left. I didn't even remember tasting my drink.

Vincent greeted me at my door. "Mephistopheles said that he will meet you in the first-class lounge inside security tomorrow morning. Both gentlemen have left. Do you need help with the bags?"

The apartment looked good when I arrived. Meph, or more likely one of his lower servants, had straightened the place out. The dishwasher had run; the bed was made and the towels fluffed and folded on the rail. In the bedroom, my medium-sized Louis Vuitton lay open and full of carefully folded garments.

Well, Satan had told Meph to pack for me and that he was better with women's clothes than I had ever dreamed. He had picked out all the turquoise beachwear I'd bought the month before when I'd gone down for vacation and even included two light silk dresses (one Versace and one Dolce & Gabbana) for going out, my favorite pair of Seven For All Mankind jeans, and one pair of black open-toe Christian Louboutins.

I wondered if Mephistopheles, second only to Satan, had been humiliated to be ordered to pack my bag. In any case, he had done a brilliant job. I checked the makeup case, made sure I had some bronzer and the summer tawny blush that I'd put away until the sun shone in New York again, and called it done.

I didn't bother with the TSA-approved locks. TSA works for us on the side. And I went to sleep until the alarm woke me, way too early.

chapter
TWENTY-FIVE

The Queen Wilhelmina Airport in Orangestad, Aruba, hadn't changed. The flights had been uneventful and we'd made our connections without any trouble. Airports and air transportation come under the jurisdiction of Hell, and we do our best to give our customers a foretaste of the afterlife. I've always tried not to look at people in airports. Some of them are damned souls, condemned to eternal flight delays, missed connections, and lukewarm airport pizza.

But for our own our system is a glory of efficiency and comfort. First-class lounges, automatic upgrades, and decent food and wine greet the aristocrats of Hell. And why not? Don't we own the place?

Marten met us in the brilliant sunshine that greeted us when we exited customs and the building. We were practically in downtown, not a far walk from the Royal Sonesta where we had reservations waiting.

Meph had gotten us a suite with a living room and three bedrooms, each with a Jacuzzi bath and Dom Pérignon in the mini fridge. The living room had sofas, a dining table, and a separate kitchen that was about the size of my entire apartment.

Nathan, Meph, and I took about an hour to shower, change out of travel clothes and settle in. Meph wasn't finished when I arrived in the living room of the suite to see Marten and Nathan studying each other warily, like two tigers sizing up a rival.

It was an interesting contrast. Nathan with his long black hair and winter-white skin looked almost like he came from a Russian fairy tale. His tight jeans and custom-made, white button-down shirt didn't quite go with that image, but it was hot in Aruba and his leather drover's coat would have melted him.

Marten, blond and tanned, appeared cool and comfortable in pale khaki linen slacks and designer flip-flops. He wore a black Armani tee that showed off rather spectacular muscular development and wouldn't have hidden a handgun had he been carrying one. Was he really an Interpol agent? Do Interpol agents carry guns? Even the accountants? There was no holster and that tee shirt left little to the imagination.

They were talking, so focused on each other that they hadn't noticed that I'd arrived.

"So, in your studies, did you find any references to demons and demon magic?" Marten asked. "We are told there were excellent texts, now lost, with full rituals of evocation and guarding. And the words of power, of course."

"Very few of the population were literate," Nathan countered. "Are you talking about the Temple rituals? We do have some records of those, at least of some of the chants."

Marten shook his head very slightly. "So much knowledge has been lost."

"Can't you call up a demon from then and get it to tell you everything?" Nathan asked, half challenging.

Marten sighed. "It is not so easy. To call a demon, to

create a real ritual call, is very difficult and time consuming. One wishes to have more to show for it than an ancient ritual."

"But you're ready now?" I asked, interrupting.

"Yes," Marten said. "I am ready."

"But I thought there were a lot of rituals and things you had to do before you could do a demon calling, or at least that's what it sounded like," Nathan probed.

"This is true," Marten agreed. "But since I have been working with Mephistopheles I have been keeping a level of preparation just in case of such a necessity."

"Okay, so you're not eating much, but celibacy?" I was truly amazed. Marten did not strike me as the type who could manage celibacy at all, let alone for any period longer than a day or two. The longer periods of fasting were manageable, I suppose, since mostly they mean no meat or sugar, any substance that keeps the magician anchored to the physical world. So he was being vegetarian for the time being—that was possible. Even reasonable. But celibacy? Marten?

"There are rituals where sex is central," Marten countered, staring right at me. "As a succubus, you are at the center of one of them, but there are many more."

"Yes, but not demon calling," Meph said as he entered. "That has always required a period of celibacy that lasts from a few days to a few years."

Meph looked amazing. He had not only showered and changed into jeans, but had changed his face and hair subtly so that he looked younger and more dynamic (and slightly less frightening) than he did in New York.

Marten shrugged. "I have said that I am ready. That should be sufficient."

"What happens if he isn't all, ummm, prepared?" Nathan asked me.

There was a lovely flower arrangement on the coffee table, huge orange and brilliant yellow tropical flowers that looked like exotic animals. I bent over to inhale their heady, overly sweet scent. "He could die," I said, keeping my voice light and casual. "He could be eaten by the demon he calls, he could be torn apart by enemies in the World of Formation, he could fail to rise through the planes and be trapped in the illusion."

"Which means?" Nathan was urging me on. I don't think it was so much an academic interest in magic as it was a hope that this other strong, virile, vigorous man who had a great deal of my attention would be undone. Suddenly I felt embarrassed by Nathan and had a tug of tenderness for Marten's maturity and compassion in handling my ex.

"Which means he would be locked in a lunatic asylum until Hell collected his soul," Mephistopheles commented dryly. "Marten has been doing magic for a while; he knows the risks."

"I thought we could work here instead of my place, if you do not mind," Marten continued, his face carefully bland. "The incense, you understand . . ."

And the possible destruction of property. I understood too well.

"So when do we get started?" I asked with forced cheer. I wanted this done, I wanted it over with, I hated the way Marten and Nathan seemed to be sniping for advantage. I didn't believe that Marten was an Interpol agent either. That was just more of Nathan trying to score against a rival.

"We can't do anything until after dark," Mephistopheles announced. "So we will go to dinner. I'm glad to say we were able to get a reservation at the best restaurant in town."

I hid my smile. Trust Meph!

And he wasn't joking. Bistro M used to be Chez Mathilde, always a favorite but now turned so elegantly modern that it would have gotten notice in New York. From the gravity fountain outside to the deep plushy seats in the bar, it was spare and modern but comfortable and even lush. In the dining room, framed flatscreens cycled through great works of classical art (heavy on the Dutch masters) in a blend of modern and postmodern that would make my head spin if I thought about it too hard. Someone should do that in New York and invite writers from *The New Yorker* to engage in some semiotic deconstruction. Which might be almost as delicious as the meal we were served.

So we ate. We ate extravagantly well. Crisp fried goat cheese with mango chutney and Asian duck salad, and an asparagus soup with hazelnuts to start. For a main course I chose the grouper because it came in a coconut sauce and Nathan had the same, Meph had the veal, and Marten had no choice at all—by the rules of high magic he was stuck with the vegetarian entrée. Which turned out to be a very tempting-looking wild mushroom risotto. He wasn't about to get any sympathy for a meal like that. A bottle of Pinot Grigio with some slight effervescence perfectly complemented my fish, though Marten didn't touch the wine.

The entire dinner had the air of being a last meal for the condemned. Still, it was not too shabby for being a ritual fast, and I had to admit that I found Marten's restraint really hot, all the more so for being underplayed.

Magicians are sexy. I always thought it was because I was a demon and there is something particularly delicious about the souls of those humans who spend so much of their lives studying and struggling to call—us. But it was more than that, I realized. Magicians talk a lot about discipline and focus, but I'd never seen it in quite such high relief. Marten the omnivore eating vegetarian dishes and avoiding alcohol without complaint was far more a turn-on than he was when he ordered what he liked and joined in imbibing the wine.

Though that was only the outward sign to confirm my knowledge that this very sexy man hadn't had sex in—I didn't know how long. But anything more than a few nights I thought would have required extreme willpower, beyond what I would have considered even reasonably possible. But he had done it, he must have in order to perform the ritual. He had not had sex—maybe since he had last seen me.

That thought was more delicious than our dessert.

Marten refrained from joining us in splitting a crème brûlée and a chocolate cake with a dark liquid center. He made do with a fruit cup, with a show of enthusiasm that made it appear this was his free choice and not a requirement. On top of the celibacy, that was so sexy that I wanted to rip his clothes off immediately.

Meph, as always, ordered the cheese plate.

It was dark by the time we finished and we walked the few blocks between the restaurant and the hotel even though I was wearing four-inch heels. Meph puffed on a cigar as we took the short stroll, and no one talked. We'd run out of chat and really no one wanted to discuss what Marten was about to do.

As we walked, Marten seemed to retreat into himself. He didn't look at me, didn't give the appreciative glances that I had come to expect from him. He didn't accept one of Meph's cigars, didn't respond to any of Nathan's remarks.

Finally we got to the suite and Nathan turned directly to Marten and asked, "Okay, what do we do?"

Marten told us to clear the living room, get the furniture out and make things open. He directed that we set up one of the side tables just to the north of center of the room, cover it and lay out his magical weapons. That seemed rather interesting since magicians usually do not like others touching their tools. On the other hand, Mephistopheles probably knows more about setting a ritual altar than any four ceremonialists put together.

"And what will you be doing?" I asked softly.

"My job," he answered.

But I knew what he was going to do. Demons have to know the basics of the rituals in which we can be summoned, if only to know if that magician has the right to call us and when we can break the hold. If a magician has not observed the correct fast, has indulged in any of the pleasures of the senses, or has not prepared every element of the ritual with full focus and intent, then he is fair game.

So I knew that tonight Marten would start with a bath in still water, infused with demon-specific herbs (in this case, I would expect vervain, nettles, maybe dragon's blood root and possibly belladonna or poppy or cacao leaves) and sealed with magical sigils. After the bath he would anoint himself with ritually prepared oil specific to the working and possibly the astrological conditions, and then dress in only a simple robe tied with a cord around the waist.

I thought of this as I heard the bath run and smelled incense. Nathan had done most of the heavy lifting and Meph had set up the altar. The long embroidered gold gauze cloth lay over shimmering white satin. These must have come in Marten's bag, probably wrapped around the long sword and the chalice that Meph had arranged. I found a bottle of Perrier in the mini fridge and poured it into the elaborate silver goblet covered with repoussé roses and lilies. I studied it for a moment; it was beautiful, and if I remembered my lessons correctly roses stood for desire and lilies for knowledge. A very small brazier held a charcoal already lit and turning slightly gray at the edges. With what must have been a demitasse spoon I scattered fragrant resins and herbs—myrrh, balm of Gilead, cedar—over the coal.

Meph set up another much smaller altar in the north. This one he covered with a white pillowcase, and on it he laid a book and another candle. This was the demon altar, where we hoped Raven would materialize.

At that point, Marten came in, fully prepared in his robe and insignia. And even though there was nothing designer about it, he cut a dashing figure. The robe itself was silk in a blue so dark that it looked black except where it rippled and caught a stray photon from the candles. The silk was very thin and clung enough to accentuate his athletic build. Around his waist was a dark silvery-black cord, and a pewter lamen hung around his neck. His hair, still damp from the bath, clung to his neck and the ends, which had started to dry, curled over his shoulders.

In a word, yum. Marten was quite a delicious specimen in street clothes. Robed and ritually intent (not to mention ritually pure), he was irresistible. What is sexier than this already very sexy man who has gone for weeks without any sex—just for me? Who has fasted? Who has concentrated his will? Devastating. No Hellspawn could resist him.

I think I was quivering with desire when I saw him clothed in the power of his will. Because the center of all ceremonial magic is the trained, focused will of the practitioner. I'm not even sure if he saw us—nothing could break his concentration.

"Can we watch?" Nathan asked.

Marten did not react at all. Perhaps he hadn't even heard the question.

"Not a good idea," Meph replied. "If an angry demon gets out of the triangle, she could tear you to pieces."

"But it's not supposed to be an angry demon. We're saving her," I said. Truth was, I wanted to see, too.

"Hmmm," Meph said. And then he whispered very softly and herded Nathan with me back into a corner of the dining room. The table acted as a barricade and I felt safe when Meph threw up a wall of energy between us and the ritual space Marten was creating. So even if the demon did get out (always a possibility) and breach Marten's defenses (which, given the way I was reacting to what he was creating would take a whole lot more power and training than someone studying in the Third Level could have achieved), it wouldn't be able to get to us. Or maybe would find refuge here behind this wall with the ever-protective and -powerful Mephistopheles.

Marten began with the Banishing Ritual of the Pentagram, the first thing every apprentice and wannabe magician masters (or attempts to master). Only performed by a true Ritualist, it was powerful and elegant. The chants vibrated and called the protective presences for each of the cardinal directions, sealing us from harm. The pentagrams blazed from his fingers in each quarter, the entire space quivered and became something different, something set apart.

Then Marten began to set up specifically to call a demon. He drew a triangle around the small altar with a fat piece of yellow chalk. Then he picked up the sword and drew the triangle again, etheric brilliant violet energy pouring from the sharp blade. He followed with the censor and the chalice in turn, binding the holding area not only with the four elements, but in all four Worlds of Creation as well.

Truth was, I was just a little bit impressed. He'd not only mediated the Worlds but created a reception for a demon that would be a prison as stout as Alcatraz. I shivered a bit, thinking of how it could contain me as easily as Raven or any other demon who might manifest itself.

Then Marten cast the circle of protection that almost touched but did not actually abut the triangle. The magician does that to protect himself in case the demon does break the bonds, when under most circumstances the first instinct of the demon would be to tear the magician into as many bits as a shredder in a casino. So the worker stays behind two barricades and never bridges the gap. Never never never. They are all taught that a cunning demon will play docile and wait until the magician invites him or her into his circle and then wreak havoc.

Protections completed, he raised the sword in salute and began a long summoning in that particularly bad, archaic Latin beloved of Hell. I never liked invocations and this one was particularly long and a bit over the top with the sycophancy. I had to work really hard not to giggle.

Nathan, beside me, was saucer-eyed. He had never seen actual magic before, not like this. He'd seen what we'd bollixed up in my apartment, but this was something different, and it was in a language I didn't think he could understand.

"What's he saying?" Nathan whispered so softly that I could barely catch his words.

"It's an invocation, and a really long one. Lots of flattery. They think that demons like a lot of flattery," I told him.

"You don't?" he asked, half teasing.

"Only when it's sincere," I replied. And I meant it.

But the restraint of the practitioner, oh the restraint—that smelled more enticing than thick steak sizzling on the grill in September, sweeter than two dozen roses, more irresistible than a private sale at Barneys. As he chanted the words of invocation it was not the silly statements that flooded my consciousness, but the desire behind them. A desire so deep, so powerful, that this ridiculously good-looking hunk had not had sex, had not even masturbated, for weeks. Just in anticipation of this moment. Of *me*.

Well, it felt like me. *Down, girl*. That was the point. The whole ritual was geared to create precisely this effect in any demon in the area, any demon who could hear the summoning. Which, supposedly, was pointed to only one demon in particular, but I was here in the background and I couldn't help it.

Nor could Meph. Glancing over I could see him quivering, his face taut with anticipation. He had to have known that it would hurt like this to watch. Meph wanted to throw himself at the magician, into his circle, into his prepared prison even, for the chance to touch and savor that yearning soul. And Meph is mostly straight.

Magic is made of the material of the soul. That they, the humans have, that we, the demons, desire to touch with all the aching agony of eternity. We serve On High, we serve forever, and yet we are always waiting outside. And here, offered before us, is the whiff, the taste of that which all Creation desires.

The center of the ritual is the Offering. Because Marten didn't do things halfway, he didn't stint. If he put something on the table it would be something of value, something that I would be insane to refuse.

Marten had stopped chanting. He raised a small knife and suddenly there was deep silence as if even Meph was afraid to breathe. *Oh no,* I thought. *He wouldn't.* But Marten would, that was what made him truly great. Truly a Master who could command. He was not a bully. In ritual he was the same as he was in the bedroom, a seducer, always promising (and giving) those things a girl/demon craves.

And yes, he gave like that in ritual, too. The thing above all things that the Hellspawn desire and adore, that we pursue and cherish among humankind, this he gave freely. He held the blade against the pumping blue veins of his wrist and then, in a single flashing movement, cut deeply. Not across, just a single deep nick. Dark blood welled up and he held his wrist over a second cup. This one was very small, a crystal cordial glass, simple and perfect. Drop by drop the crimson blood flowed into the glass.

chapter
TWENTY-SIX

Some magicians would have stopped with the traditional three drops. Others, more committed and adventurous, would have done three times three. Marten stood rock steady until the glass was full to the brim, no counting of drops, no careful blotting. No, Marten just poured out his own life stuff, still warm and shimmering with the vital energy of his own soul, and created one of the most generous, elegant, perfect offerings I had ever heard of from his kind in three thousand years.

Then he placed the tiny cordial glass on the flat blade of the sword and passed it to the smaller altar in the triangle. Only a blade could pass the bonds, and my breath caught in my throat as he manuevered the little glass onto the table without tipping it.

Once the sword was withdrawn, he sealed the penetration points with words and will. But there was still a weakness there. There was a patch, undetectable to newer demons like Raven, but visible to me. After the triangle was resealed Marten tucked his robe around his legs and sat down on a cushion before his altar.

"What's he doing?" Nathan asked.

"Now we wait for Raven to show. Given what he's just offered her, she'd be a complete idiot to ignore the invitation. Well, I think she'd actually be under compulsion to arrive. Even Meph and I can feel it, and we're not the targets."

"Why is he sitting like that?"

Hmmmm. It might have made a more elegant picture if he'd been kneeling, I thought, with his head just slightly bent. The thought made my toes curl.

Though, really, the cell phone would do just fine.

What was I thinking? Nathan was right here. Was I over him, had I forgotten him in the extreme inducement of ritual?

But I didn't have time to consider the problem any further because a dark roiling started in the middle of the triangle. Marten's walls held firm and I could see the neat, triangular construction of the trap.

The gray, smoky etheric matter coalesced and I saw Raven, still looking like me, still wearing my Betsey Johnson blouse and her own stupid boots. She was all in shades of gray.

As her form became stronger, more defined, I could make out the look of absolute panic on her face. "No, no," she whimpered so softly that I could barely make out the words. Raven was not alone. Squeezed into the triangular confinement, another demon was materializing. Someone large, someone who took up most of the space, leaving Raven pressed against the invisible barricade.

If only Marten had caught the head demon along with Raven in his net—but that would have been too easy. No, Raven had been overwhelmed and shunted aside for a male demon of incalculable beauty. He could have come off the cover of half a dozen romance novels, complete with the open white poet's shirt and tight black jeans.

I knew at once what he was. He was one of my embittered male counterparts. He was an incubus. He must have been one of Raven's tormentors, and had grabbed her to ride along when she was summoned.

Raven, poor girl, was crying and trying to put a brave face on things. "Send us back," she whimpered, trying to be strong.

And, much as I had not been thrilled with her choice of footwear, or her angsty arrogance, I was still moved to my nonexistent soul by what she had endured. Her face and arms were covered in bruises and smeared with dirt and blood. Her hair, which was still auburn and in long curls, had been matted with sweat and filth and the weak new ichor that stained my Betsey Johnson.

Her hands and wrists appeared to have taken the worst of it. Purple bracelets of bruises showed where the restraints had been too tight and that she'd fought against them, and her fingernails had been bitten or ripped down to the quick. Other wounds showed where she had fought and tried to defend herself against some kind of blade. Silver, I'd bet, because some of them were still oozing.

I was moved to pity, but there was no time for that. The incubus was clearly not Raven's friend and he was holding her with a large hand around her throat.

"What's that other demon?" Nathan asked.

"They sent him with her so that the magician can't bring her through," Mephistopheles said. "It's exactly what I would have done. Marten can't pull Raven in without the incubus, who is loyal to my enemy. He'll rip Marten and us to shreds if he's permitted."

Marten had gone dead white and his breathing was shallow. He could not break the seals and bring Raven out while keeping the incubus confined. And from the way the incubus smiled, I had no doubt he was looking forward to ripping Marten to shreds.

The incubus knew we were in a bad position. He smiled, a beautiful smile that would have been worth millions in a Colgate campaign, but so cruel it made me shiver.

"Well," the incubus said softly, in a voice that was low, musical and seductive. I wondered if human men saw me as I saw this creature, my counterpart. I remembered the incubi from long ago, before the great rift, but mostly I remembered the screaming, the politics, the boys who didn't want to play with the girls.

"Well," he said again. "I wonder what you will offer me, Magician. The blood was . . . irresistible. As it was meant to be. But there are only two beings here with souls and I think we need to bargain. And—I am sorry to say, High Magician, you are tasty and oh so pretty, and I would enjoy claiming your soul. But you have already parceled out too much of it for my liking. I prefer to take the whole of a mortal soul."

Marten remained stark still, keeping his eye on the demon.

The incubus's eyes shifted and pinned Nathan.

No. He couldn't have Nathan. The words formed not just in my head but through my whole body. He could not have Nathan. The guy might have made me miserable and even made me cry, couldn't handle Hell (okay, that's kind of a tall order, come to think of it) and had left me. But he also read to me in my own language and was smart and funny and had worked really hard for us when Vincent was kidnapped.

I glanced at Marten, sitting so very still and quiet.

Would I have reacted so strongly if the incubus had wanted him? Of course, Marten understood these things; he was an experienced practitioner who knew what he was doing and getting into.

None of that mattered. I wanted to protect Marten too. He looked so vulnerable and brave there in his circle, unmoving. I could see the fear in the tension around his eyes and the way his hands went rigid, but I'd spent a lot of time recently paying a lot of attention to Marten.

I was terrified for him. I was terrified for both of them.

In that moment I realized that I was crazy in love with them both. Which meant I had to figure out a way to save them both.

Well, the incubus said he wanted a bargain.

That was . . . something I do exceedingly well. I know and love bargains and always have. Had I not bargained on six continents (there really being nothing on Antarctica worth acquiring)? Driven down the prices of opals and emeralds, Turkish carpets, and a lease in the East Eighties? Best ever, I had managed just last season to talk another twenty percent off the redline price for a Derek Lam dress and two Versace blouses at the last seasonal sale at Barneys.

"Incubus, I have something that you might find appealing," I shouted across all the magically barricaded spaces.

"You? Succubus? Your kind are not friend to us," he replied scornfully. "And you have nothing to offer me."

I grinned. I think I must have looked that way at the Barneys spring sale. "Oh yes, I do. I have something very tasty indeed. Not my own, no, but a whole soul entire. And it is a victim that I cannot claim."

The incubus licked his lips. "One you cannot deliver and you would give it to me? That is . . . interesting."

I took a deep breath. I would have liked to come closer to him but I was penned in by Meph's magical barrier, to say nothing of Marten's circle. I had to make the point from where I stood.

"A human male, tall and well-favored," I began. "Of my acquaintance and knowledge. I would give him to you, his place of work and his home address, and, when I am able to return to my home, a sample of his hair or nail or other piece of his corporeal being for you to use to identify him."

"This one you could not conquer yourself? That would be a sweet victory," the incubus said.

I shrugged. "He is impervious to women, even succubi," I admitted. "But I will give you all you need for full access, and you rarely have the opportunity to deliver a man, I think. I am sure Satan would appreciate it."

"How will I know that you tell the truth and that you will be bound to the bargain?" he asked. "And what do you ask in return?"

"The little demon you hold. Give her to us, as it was she we summoned. Let her go, let her remain in the triangle as you depart. Give me your name and sigil and I will deliver everything you need to you within three days."

The incubus considered, long enough for me to get worried. "How do I know you will honor your word?" he asked finally.

"Mephistopheles is here, he will stand witness," I said, pointing, just in case Mr. Idunno had missed the second most powerful demon in Hell standing right beside me. "You know what Mephistopheles will do to me if I do not honor my bargain. I swear on his name, and on the name of Our Prince Satan."

I sensed a shift in the room but I was too intent on the incubus and the bargaining to pay attention. Every atom of my being was focused on making the incubus believe that I meant what I said. Which I did. A millionfold.

"I will bear witness," Mephistopheles said, and his voice vibrated with all the power of Hell behind him.

Still the silly incubus pondered.

We waited.

"I will give you three days. If I do not have all that I need, or if the soul of this mortal is not as desirable as you have claimed, then I shall claim the right of revenge upon the magician."

"Fair enough," I agreed solemnly. "It is agreed, and sealed with this magician's blood, which you have received in sacrifice. Now withdraw and leave the demon he has called to his bidding."

The incubus nodded his agreement. His Harlequin-cover hair fell over his shoulders and his warm eyes sparkled with desire. For a mortal soul.

He withdrew, slowly, fading into shades of gray that became less substantial until the etheric matter drifted apart.

We heaved a collective sigh.

Marten waited until there was silence. Slowly Raven sat up. She looked a mess, the bruises standing out purple against her paper-white skin.

"He is gone," Marten murmured to the beaten demon. "He is well and truly gone and will trouble you no more. We shall keep you safe. Take the offering, it will restore you."

Raven looked slightly wild-eyed, as if she couldn't believe that she had some respite from the pain. Marten repeated himself twice, three times. Me, I wouldn't have needed a second invitation, but Raven had no experience of this kind of thing. And she wouldn't know that there would be anything restorative in Marten's offering.

Slowly she raised the glass. "Do I drink it?" she whispered.

He nodded and she raised the small crystal glass to her lips. She seemed hesitant, which I could understand. Our kind do not necessarily drink blood. There are so many stories of vampires, of blood as the currency of magic, that a young and quite ordinary demon would be confused.

The blood is the life.

We of Hell use blood to seal a pact, to bind ourselves and others. We use it because it carries the recognition of the soul. Demons have no blood to give. We have ichor, a thing very like blood. A human could not tell the difference, though possibly a chemist in a crime lab might. But our ichor is red and viscous to the degree of human blood, salty and slightly metallic. What changes it, what it lacks, is the energizing existence of an independent soul.

Raven drank the offering and made a face. But the soul stuff within it started the healing and, as we watched, as she was trapped in the magical triangle, we could see it take effect. The bruises faded, her skin became clear and then started to glow subtly, her hair straightened out and fell dark against her shoulders. But now that hair was gleaming, healthy and strong and clean. Her nails healed before our eyes, and the ends of her fingers, and suddenly her hands re-formed and became smooth and whole and undamaged.

Her body changed. The magic stripped the glamour that made her resemble me and she appeared as herself, but a vigorous, vital self that had more energy, more presence, than she had had when she appeared for the first time at my apartment. She didn't even appear so skinny and drawn, but graceful and willowy. The same Raven, but Raven perfected, as she ought to have been, as perhaps she might have been before despair and fear had sapped her and led her to suicide and soul death.

She was still adolescent, and defiant. And she was still a demon. But I could see beyond that to the demon she could become if she survived and advanced and found favor. As she already had, since Satan had given her to me as a little sister of sorts.

I could even imagine liking her.

She got up, stretched, and showed off her navel piercing and the tattoos on her arms.

"I feel . . . fantastic," she said. Then she turned to Marten and smiled. "Thank you."

Marten smiled back, but not with quite so much innocence. "In return I will request a bargain," he said evenly.

"Oh?" Raven asked, immediately on guard. She probably hadn't gotten to even beginning bargains in the curriculum yet.

"First, of course, I will require that you do nothing to cause me, or my place and property, or my friends, any harm," he said, setting out the first condition in the prescribed pattern.

"Oh, sure," Raven agreed immediately. "I wouldn't have done anything anyway."

I heard Meph sigh next to me. She really did need to learn a lot before she could be sent off unsupervised.

Marten nodded. "Second, I will require that you come to me when I call, simply and without ceremony, and that you answer truthfully and fully any questions I will put to you."

"Okay, I don't like all the hokey stuff anyway," she said, again too easily. "I mean, the implements are nice but some of the wording of those chants is just a bit pretentious. Don't you think? Do you feel funny doing it?"

Marten raised an eyebrow. "You agreed to answer my questions. I did not agree to answer yours. But the truth is that no, I do not feel funny or hokey. The words and phrases and even entire segments are formulae that correspond to levels of Hell, types of demons, astrological conditions and—well, it takes years just to learn the basics. But no, I feel they are no more hokey than you might think singing a song was hokey."

"I think he just likes saying 'hokey,' " Nathan whispered into my ear.

It took all my concentration not to break out laughing. And suddenly my equilibrium was restored. I looked at Nathan again and saw why he was here, saw what I'd seen in him when I first met him at the end of the winter. He was attractive, beautiful even. At least as beautiful as Marten, though a different kind. The dark, brooding, scholarly kind, in fact, that I'd always found attractive.

But I'd recovered my memory of Nathan's sense of humor, his slightly offbeat, sardonic take on events. And I could see as he adapted to the ritual that he was able to break through his own prejudices and assumptions. I started to wonder if he could adjust, if he could learn to handle my life as a succubus.

Hope sprang unbidden to my heart, evil bad hope that made me want what I couldn't have. And that hope was tinged with something else—with a feeling that maybe I was being unfair to Marten in hoping for Nathan. Marten had proven himself to me over and over again, and even for Nathan I wasn't willing to give him up. Was I?

But Marten wasn't finished with his bargaining yet. "And further, you will agree to come to my aid, as I have come to yours. To do as I bid you and to aid those I have chosen to be my friends."

Raven cocked her head. "That's taking it a little far," she said warily. "What if I say no?"

Marten shrugged. "Then perhaps I will send you back from whence you came."

"Yeah, well, I'm not so sure about that." Raven smiled and so did I. Much better, given her lack of experience and Marten's long training. I was actually proud of her.

"You can take your chances, but vowing to aid me will help you in the end. You know that I work for your masters, that I am here at the bidding of Mephistopheles."

Raven bit her lip as she considered his response. Bargains in Hell are . . . legalistic. We're very careful about the letter of the law, about the precise language, about what we promise. Marten was giving her very little and asking a lot.

"Ask for something in return," I muttered, but Meph turned to me and shook his head. "No coaching. You know that, Lily. No coaching once they enter negotiation."

I could hear the tension in his voice, and I bet that he would dearly love to be coaching her. Oh, the things he would ask for—the things I would ask for! If I were in that triangle with him needing information from me, there were all kinds of things I would require.

She thought about it. "Well, if I agree to that then you have to promise that you won't ask me to do anything that Mephistopheles wouldn't approve of," she eventually suggested.

Meph and I smiled together. She was good, this kid. That was a perfect comeback, a request that Marten couldn't refuse as Mephistopheles' ally, but that protected Raven from any requirement that she might find at odds with her own preferences and loyalties.

Well done, I thought at her. And I resolved then and there to take her to brunch on Sunday. Raven was showing the kind of mettle my friends would like. No wonder Satan wanted her groomed.

Marten agreed to her condition. Reluctantly, I could tell, because no magician wants to give up anything, even a codicil he had no intention of ever using. But I could see the way he looked at her now, with a new respect. In fact, I felt some of the respect myself.

I turned to Meph. "Girl's got game," I said. He smiled and nodded.

I turned to Nathan and took his hand briefly and squeezed it. He turned to me and I saw a bit of haunted pain in his eyes.

Or maybe it was just overwork and exhaustion. In any case, he didn't pull away.

chapter
TWENTY-SEVEN

"It is agreed then," Marten intoned, and went over the points of their agreement. "To this I put my hand and seal." And he wrote it all down with a quill on parchment (magicians are very fond of parchment) and signed with a flourish (but no blood). "You give your word that you will emerge into this space in peace, and sign this agreement, and be as a friend to all gathered here?"

"Yeah, like I said," Raven sighed. "As long as it's written down the way we said."

Meph and I exchanged glances. I'm sure this is the way parents must feel when a child does a good job at a recital or in a soccer game.

"Of course," Marten said graciously. And then he raised the sword and cut an opening in the triangle that held Raven prisoner—and held her safe from her kidnappers as well. Then, very slowly and deliberately, he cut an opening into his own circle of protection.

Raven stepped inside delicately. If she were bent on his destruction this was the moment when she would have struck. She was inside his defenses now and had not yet signed the pact. She was, technically, a free agent. This is the peak of danger for the magician, the fraction of time when the demon can renege and tear him limb from limb.

But not Raven. No, for all her tattoos and scowls, for all her ugly shoes and nasty attitude, she was a perfect lady in the circle. She waited quietly in the North, the appointed region of the demon, and took the parchment with the agreement with dignity. She read it over carefully and slowly. Her Hell Latin was probably not up to full speed and I could see her lips moving as she sounded out words to herself. But she made it through, nodded, and took the quill that Marten offered her.

She affixed her signature to her very first Magical Contract as the representative of Hell. Then she put out her hand and Marten shook it, something that I had never seen or heard of in a magical ceremony and contract between Hell and human. Marten instructed her to remain just north of the main altar, and he began the ritual of dissolving the circle, banishing the quarters and removing all the barriers.

Except ours. Meph, who had constructed this final protection, had to dismantle it, which he did with a sweep of his hand. And then we were all in the same space together, the two-level sitting room of the hotel suite.

Exhausted, Nathan, Meph and I sank into the sofa together. Raven flopped onto a wing chair, one leg thrown over the arm, giggling. "Awesome. I don't even need a shower," she said between bouts of laughter. "And you have no idea, really none, how much I wanted just to take a bath and eat something and, well, just to stop hurting. That's what I wanted most of all; I just didn't want to hurt anymore. And now I feel fantastic."

"It was a very powerful gift, and an uncommonly generous one." Meph decided to use the teaching moment. "I'm not sure I've ever seen a ceremony where the magician offered so much of himself. You should feel wonderful, and you should honor the magician who gifted you so generously."

"Yeah, yeah," Raven said, twirling her hand. "I'll do what he says, and I'll answer any of your questions that I can. But there's this one problem." She sat up and clasped her hands earnestly, like an eager schoolgirl. "I didn't see anything useful. I don't think. I didn't hear anything that would identify them. They used really dorky fake names."

"What fake names?" Nathan asked.

"Stupid things," Raven said. "Lemme see. Percival and Lancelot. They were an old guy and a young guy. The young one was pretty hot, too, if you like the type."

"What type was that?" I asked.

She shrugged. "Not mine, that's for sure. Short dark hair, pushy, really cute ass though, and shoulders to there." She spread her hands wider than any human's shoulders could be.

"That's not a description we can use," Marten said wearily, one hand raking through his own hair. He looked tired, as if he were barely hanging in for the debriefing. "Please try to be more specific."

Raven sat quiet, trying to think.

"How about if I show you some pictures?" Nathan asked gently. He moved near Raven's side and opened his computer and began showing her pictures.

"No, not that one," she said, shaking her head. "Not him, either," to the next. The third was just a shake.

And then she became agitated. "Yeah, that one. He was there, I'm sure of it. And he wasn't one of the ones who was being an asshole, either. I mean, he didn't torture me or anything. The others were into it, you know? They were hurting me and they thought it was funny."

"But he didn't do that?" Nathan asked, his voice still low and warm.

"No, that one just came by a few times. He didn't talk to me at all, he only talked to the old guy, Lancelot. They called him 'Guardian.' "

"That's great," I chirped encouragement. "That's really useful."

Nathan just shot me a look to shut up and hit another key. Two more nos, and then one that got more reaction than any of the others. "Him, him, him," Raven said, turning away from the screen and wrapping her arms in front of her body. "That was the one with the cute butt like I was telling you. They called him Gawain. I told you the names were stupid."

Nathan motioned me over and it took only a moment to recognize the face. The photo wasn't very good and was grainy, but it was clearly Steve Balducci, who had picked up Desire and dumped her at the Brooklyn Museum when this all began. Who had known about Public and had managed to position himself so that one of us would find him appealing.

Gawain, huh? Raven was right, the Arthurian stuff really was a little moronic.

"Do you have any sketches of high demons?" Marten asked from across the room. Marten's voice was thin and exhausted. He lay draped across the chair like a limp ribbon, utterly spent, with a blanket wrapped around him.

While Nathan tried to pull up a few of the better-known faces of Hell, I called room service for tea and coffee and plates of tostis. We could all use tostis, little sealed melted cheese sandwiches that were particularly Dutch and warming and comforting.

"I don't think I saw any of those," Raven was commenting as Meph and Nathan consulted on the faces.

"That's fine, no surprise," Mephistopheles told the girl. "I don't think the higher demons would show themselves anyway. These idiots don't even realize that they're working for Hell. They think they're working for Upstairs, as if that were a completely different Administration." He shrugged elegantly. "Probably they forget that Satan was one of the greatest angels Upstairs before She took the job in Hell."

Meph, being utterly elegant and understated, didn't have to make the point to us that he had been an angel of high rank himself. And could probably look like one again if he wanted to.

"Let's call it a night," Meph said. "We're all tired, it was a very hard evening and we could all use some sleep. And some food. We've got at least tomorrow before we have to return and we can continue with the debriefing then."

Just on cue, room service rang the bell. Raven jumped but I got up and got the door. A young man in a starched uniform rolled in a cart with three large silver pots and two trays of small golden sandwiches, which he unloaded on the dining table. They must train the staff very well at the Royal Sonesta because the waiter's face did not change at all as he set aside the altar furniture, spread a damask cloth on the table and set it up for our snack.

"These have tomato," he said, gesturing to one tray, "and these others have ham. Have a pleasant meal."

We ate. I put together a plate for Marten, two sandwiches with ham and one with tomato and a large mug of hot tea. He was too drained to leave his chair but he perked up just a bit when I brought over the food.

"You're cold," I said. "Have something to eat, it'll ground you."

He nodded and dug in. I knew that much about ritualists, after they expend energy in ritual they are more than mortally tired and they get horribly cold. It's too easy for them to drift at that point and hurt themselves, too open and without reserves.

He didn't say a word until he had cleaned the plate and drained the mug. Then he closed his eyes for a moment. "Thank you," he said, looking me full in the face. His gaze was naked, undefended, which is dangerous around demons—but then he was used to us. And in that naked, vulnerable moment I saw something else in him, something beyond the magician and the expert lover. I saw just a touch of his soul in his eyes, tired and lonely and used hard, but still hanging on. A soul that was forfeit to Hell, that was destined to join us.

And there was a tenderness when he looked at me that was more than just desire, more than simple sex or even not so simple sex.

I'm a succubus and I can recognize the difference between lust and something more. This was definitely a something more, and it ambushed me.

He wrapped his fingers around my wrist. "I am so tired now, Lily, I am sorry. But you do not leave until after tomorrow, I think. Promise me some time tomorrow. Alone."

And for all my skill at bargaining and for all I know that one does not make promises to a magician, I promised. "Tomorrow. Right now you need to get some sleep. We should get you home."

Nathan volunteered to take Marten home in a taxi. The whole thing seemed odd to me but it left the demons all cozy together. When the humans were gone, I got up and hugged Raven. "You were magnificent!" I said. "You were amazing. And Satan has already asked me to mentor you."

"Thanks," she said and she smiled.

We put her on one of the sofa beds in the living area. I was too tired to even take a bath. I just climbed into bed and slept like the dead thing I was until well into the morning.

The next morning we all woke up late. Nathan emerged from his room in the suite, so obviously he'd made it back. Meph had ordered room service for us, a big hearty Dutch breakfast of cheese and ham and fruit and bread and coffee. Disgusting. I took a cup of the coffee and tried to ignore the rest of the mess.

Neither Meph nor Raven was anywhere to be found. As I sat in the farthest chair from the food sipping my French Roast, Nathan came and pulled over another chair. "Lily," he said.

I looked up expectantly but said nothing. I had no idea of what was coming, only a fluttering of hope. Hope that now that he had seen us, had worked with us together, he would be able to accept what I did. That he would be able to deal with me and with himself.

"Lily, I . . . spending time with you has been, has reminded me . . ." he began slowly. Nathan, scholar, almost a Ph.D., did not normally sound confused and confessing.

"Are you in love with Marten?" he asked abruptly.

"What?"

"I took him home last night," Nathan reminded me. "He was exhausted, yeah, but he talked. At least a little bit. And I think he's got a real thing for you. So I wanted to know, are you in love with him?"

Nathan is not used to the negotiations of Hell. He doesn't know quite how close we stay to the letter of an agreement. And I knew what he really wanted to know and what I needed to tell him. I pulled myself up just a bit and rested my warm cup on my knees and looked straight into his eyes. I knew that my face, innocent of makeup, revealed only the most sincere and heartfelt truth. "I'm in love with you," I said very softly. "I don't want to be, and it's really hard for me to work with you like this because I wish we were still together. But," I shrugged, "I am in love with you. Even though you dumped me. I'm trying to get better and get on with my life, and that's really hard when you're around like this."

He dropped his head so that the long dark hair fell forward, shielding him from view. "I wish I knew what to do, Lily," he said softly. "I want to be with you but then I see you with Meph and I see you as a demon and I'm so torn. If you were a woman, human, I would have no hesitation. I'm crazy in love with you but then I remember the other part and all I want to do is run away."

"What about right now?" I asked very softly. "Do you see a demon or a woman right now?"

Then his arms were around me and we were kissing, deeply and passionately and I wanted him with every cell in my body. With the whole entire soul I had signed to Satan three millennia ago. His mouth, the warm firmness of his body, the smell of his shampoo were all home.

He got up and took my hand and led me to his room. There were no words, nor any need for them. He slid his hands under my T-shirt and his palms were warm on my skin. Then he slipped it over my head and looked with appreciation at my body, my full breasts revealed in a baby blue bra.

He stood transfixed—but then how many men have seen a succubus unclothed and lived? His face strained with desire, and that wasn't the only thing straining, either. I smiled, wickedly, and stepped away from him before I unfastened the waistband on my jeans and slid them slowly down over my thighs. I took my time, stepping out of them, showing off my Italian lingerie. Which showed off the body underneath. In a long, languorous tease I turned my back and shook my curls so they brushed my lace panties, drawing attention to my posterior curves.

I reveled in my power over him.

"*Araamki,*" he whispered in Akkadian. I knew I wasn't supposed to understand.

It had been thousands of years since I had heard that phrase. "I love you," with the intimate intonation that reminded me of my mother and the Priest who had initiated me. Something that swept deeper than the succubus, that talked to the woman I had once been. And still was.

He held out his arms, open and empty. The desire in his eyes owed nothing to Hell and even his lust was something more complex, focused on me alone.

I went to him and he folded me into his embrace. I

lifted my face and kissed him, hard. Right then it was the only thing I wanted in the world. His mouth tasted of coffee and chocolate. I closed my eyes and lost myself in the textures of his tongue, his fingers on my shoulders and then my back and then tracing the curves of my hips.

Pressed against him I could feel his unmistakable desire, and for a moment the power rushed through me again. I owned his lust; I commanded his need.

His mouth moved down from my mouth to my throat. He licked the hollow in my clavicle before teasing out my ear from my hair and exploring it thoroughly with his tongue. He held me hard against him as he returned to my neck and my breasts. One thumb traced my nipples through the blue lace until I gasped. But he didn't remove the bra, merely increased the pressure just a bit, letting the uneven texture of the fabric stimulate me.

I must have whimpered because he said, "Shhhh," and lifted me up and carried me to the bed. His arms were like rock, like steel, like his hard cock wanting me without reserve. The only strain was his holding back, and I responded to the strength that I hadn't known he possessed.

I wanted him. I wanted his skin, I wanted him naked, I wanted to touch and taste and take from him. My nails scrabbled at his buttons, and then he grasped my wrists and held them at my sides as he knelt between my thighs, and I was pinioned on the mattress.

Completely at his mercy, I couldn't move. I gasped and realized that the immobility was exciting. "Please, please," I moaned.

His only reply was a throaty chuckle. He held me, his

hands like steel cuffs, his breath hot between my legs. I tried to wriggle, to position myself better, to get—more. Something more. The heat ran through me and only need and desire existed. Nothing else, not even thought interfered. I wanted him, I wanted his body, I wanted his soul. I wanted him forever and I wanted him Right Now.

"Be still," he commanded me.

Lust warred with pride through me. I was not to be commanded and yet—there he was, holding me down with one hand as the other carefully traced the pattern of lace over my mons. I tried to lift my hips and he stopped. "None of that," he crooned.

Oh whywhywhy wouldn't he touch me yet? Why wouldn't he remove those scraps of lace that I had thought so lovely when I bought them, and suddenly found so very annoying.

I lay still and he used one finger, far too lightly, over my panties. He'd turned his mouth to my nipples, first the left and then the right, sucking and breathing heat over my bra, and then he lifted my left breast out of the restraining garment.

I wanted to arch my back, to push my breast up to his mouth, to tear off his clothing and the last shreds of mine. I wanted *sex*. *Right. Now.*

Instead I lay without moving, waiting for him to torment me with pleasure as he flickered the tip of his tongue over my now bare left nipple. He barely brushed me with his lips, but arousal had made me even more sensitive than usual. I trembled with need as he waited, touching me far too gently. Finally he took the nipple into his mouth and played just a little with his teeth, just enough to make me pitch and moan.

"Still," he said, laying one hand on my stomach. The heat radiated out of his palm across my skin, somehow touching the center of desire in me although he was still too far away, teasing. And I was still in that dratted underwear.

Desperate, I lay back and commanded my muscles to remain soft and still, to sink into the mattress. He made a humming sound in the back of his throat and inserted one finger between the elastic and my quivering flesh. Without removing my lingerie, he pulled the panel aside against my leg and touched me as I had wanted him to for what felt like hours.

And when he touched me again I succumbed, pleasure knifing through me, cutting all control, all thought. Everything was gone and only need and desire and something else beyond both remained. I couldn't remain still any longer, no matter what the provocation.

Nor could Nathan. He ripped off his trousers as I grabbed at his shirt. We were both more than ready, overripe, and when he entered me the orgasm canceled out any conscious thought.

Gasping, desperate, he still waited. I could not be here alone. I needed him to be with me, to have his pleasure be as deep as what he had given me, our immortal union to be sealed in our mutual ecstasy.

"Will I live?" he asked. His rhythm did not change, his body pulsed with need and power held in check. But now I perceived the anger inside his lust. "Or do you deliver me as soon as I come?"

And I slapped him.

chapter
TWENTY-EIGHT

He released me and I picked up my clothes and ran out of the room. I didn't even think of Raven or Meph elsewhere in the suite. I went straight to the bathroom and ran the water in the shower as hot as it would go. I was still in thrall to the immense pleasure and desire he had given me, but I felt—broken.

I couldn't stop shaking and I couldn't stand to think about Nathan, who pounded on the bathroom door.

"Lily, Lily, please," he pleaded. "Come out here, talk to me. I didn't mean that."

"Yes you did," I said, but I wasn't sure the words could be heard over the water. I was sure I didn't want them to be.

"Lily, I'm sorry," he yelled. "Please, Lily, open the door. Talk to me."

But I couldn't. I couldn't bear to see him. I couldn't face how much I'd let myself be taken by him for the second time.

Fool me once, shame on you. Fool me twice, shame on me.

He didn't trust me, not even to let him survive. He was still afraid, too aware of the succubus in me, too afraid of his own humanity. Not arrogant enough in some ways, without the confidence in my feelings for him to know that I would never take his soul or his life.

"Lily?" I could hear his voice and I tried to let it fade into the background. I paid attention only to the pummeling water and the French-milled lavender soap and the shampoo that washed the smell of sex from my body without washing my memory clean.

I don't know when I stopped hearing him. I have no idea how long I stayed in that shower, just that my fingertips were all turned to prunes before I left. And then I thought only of the thick, thirsty towel around my body, smelling of good detergent and powdery fabric softener. Smelled all clean and safe like home, like the soap and the suite, everything from last night dispersed with sunlight and life.

"It's okay, you can come out now," I heard a young woman's voice. "He's gone."

I opened the door and Raven was standing there in her own form and her own clothes. She must have gone shopping with Meph, and there wasn't much to her taste in Orangestad. She held her arms wide and I collapsed into them.

"I told him to go and Meph told him too and he's gone. He'll be on the plane, but we can change the seating," she said, comfortingly. "Meph even said that he'll change the flights so that you don't have to see him. You should have something to eat and we'll get you dressed nicely. That will make you feel better. What did the jerk do?"

"He's not a jerk," I said, and sniffled. "No, maybe he is. He's a good guy who can't deal with me being a succubus. He's jealous. He doesn't trust me." Raven gave me a mango smoothie in a take-out cup. It was cold and sweet and almost as soothing as ice cream.

"That sucks," Raven commiserated. "But if he's acting like an asshat because he's just lame, well—you're too cool for a lame-ass, Lily. You do know that."

"Yeah. Thanks." I could almost smile at her choice of words. We'd have to clean up her language; Satan doesn't like thoughtless profanity.

"Smoothie good?" she asked kindly as I finished it. I nodded.

"Okay, clothes," she suggested. "Meph is coming back soon and didn't Marten want you to stop by before you leave? I mean, wow, I so envy you. I wish he wanted to see me. You'll have to tell me about his place and everything, okay? Are you actually dating him, or is it just, ummm, a thing?"

Well, after that ritual last night, no wonder the poor girl had a crush on him. Hot magician and all that blood, saving her, I couldn't fault her.

So—was I actually in love with him? I didn't know . . . no, I knew. I knew last night when I was afraid for him in the ritual.

"We used to be dating. We're not anymore," I said as Raven pulled clothes out of my drawers and draped them over every available surface. "These are okay," she pronounced a pile with my Seven jeans, my Rick Owens skirt, the D&G camisole and my Armani Exchange sweater. "That other stuff, I don't think so." Given that she'd consigned the Prada suit, the Anna Sui top and the Michael Kors pants to purgatory, I had to laugh. The girl had an awful lot to learn about clothes.

Laughing felt good. The smoothie was gone and Marten was waiting. To please Raven, I put on the jeans and the green camisole. She made a face at the cute green Jimmy Choo sandals that made the outfit. I made her come and watch me put on makeup, and we experimented with her a little bit too, though my foundation was all wrong for her skin.

"Blush? Yuck. I don't want more color in my face," Raven protested as I tried to warm up her cheeks.

"You're dead," I reminded her. "You don't want everyone to know you're dead. A little color helps."

She pulled a face and made me laugh again. "When I was alive I worked so hard to make myself look dead, and now that I'm really dead and have this perfectly dead white skin, you're saying I need color. I can't win."

Still, she did like the effect of the gray eye shadow and good mascara. And it was fun. I hadn't done this with my girlfriends since—not since we'd done the makeover on Sybil. That had been fun for her in Aruba, but she'd gone back to her sweet pastel palette when she returned to New York.

"This is like when I was in middle school and my friends and I would buy all this Wet N' Wild makeup at the drugstore and play with it," Raven said.

"I think you're going to have fun with us in New York," I said. "When we get back, with my friends and all. We'll go out to clubs and restaurants and shopping. And you've got to take your advanced exams as soon as possible because Satan's Companions should have high rank and set an example. It'll be great," I promised her.

Then I was all dressed and made up and my eyes weren't red, or at least weren't red enough to matter. I looked good. My heart might be breaking but Marten would still find me beautiful.

And thinking of Marten made me feel just a little better, a little lighter. The warm flush of emotion that I had experienced when I was afraid for him in the ritual washed over me again. Maybe it was time I admitted that if Nathan hadn't been in the picture I would have known I was head over heels in love with Marten for a while. Probably since his last trip, though the ritual had clinched it.

I did love Nathan. I thought. He hadn't treated me well but . . . he was hurting and scared and didn't know what to do. And I was certain that he was behaving badly because he did love me. Otherwise he would have just walked away. Otherwise there wouldn't be that electricity between us every time we looked at each other. Otherwise . . .

Otherwise, Marten was waiting for me. Marten who understood about demons and didn't care that I was a succubus. Marten who could talk about the politics of Hell and knew what we were trying to trace down and why it was important. Marten wasn't afraid of me—in bed or out.

Marten had been clear that I wasn't just a fling for him, either. He might like the fact that I was a succubus, but if I were being honest I had to recognize that he truly cared for me just as me.

He didn't live terribly far from Margit, my succubus friend (who was currently shopping in Paris), in an elegant section of the city with sprawling houses that looked like pastel bungalows from the outside. Marten's was painted a frighteningly cheerful blue with pink flowers climbing over the front of it. I rang the bell and Marten came to the door.

I couldn't help but look around, drink in his personal space. So very different from Nathan's trendy Brooklyn loft, this was a small, warm, cozy house. The Dutch like cozy. They have a special word for it, *hezellig*, and that applied perfectly to Marten's house. The floors were richly golden wide plank wood polished to a high sheen and matching gold-toned furniture upholstered in tan and café au lait leather. Inside the walls were a softer blue that set off the warm golds. The colors reminded me of the beach, sun and sand and water. Wide windows let in the brilliant tropical sunlight, making everything even more wholesome and cheerful.

Marten, with his casually cut blond hair that fell over the collar of his Caribbean blue cotton shirt with the sleeves rolled up, looked perfectly of a piece with the living room. Today he really was the Armani ad surfer boy: toothpaste smile, light bronze skin, expensive leather sandals on his feet.

For the first time I felt like I was seeing him just as he was, without the magician or the Eurotrash boy toy. He was more relaxed. Maybe that was because he was at home, or maybe because I'd seen him in ritual and now he and I had a history. He'd been in my apartment, in my life, and he was showing me his.

"Welcome," he said, and it sounded almost formal, almost like one of the old greetings of Hell. Stepping over the threshold felt like a kind of ritual. I had the impression that Marten didn't invite many people over.

"Would you like something to drink? Some coffee, perhaps? I have some made."

I smiled and accepted. He disappeared for a moment into the kitchen and came out with two blue mugs that matched the room. Sugar and milk in cheerful crockery were already on the table. He had set out a plate of little pastries, tiny flaky tarts with bits of pineapple and mango decorating the tops. Another plate held cheese and a knife, creamy gold Gouda and dill Havarti.

I thanked him and sat down on the sofa, which was comfortable and lush, and fixed my coffee. He seemed strangely shy almost, as if my being in his home had changed something between us.

"How are you feeling?" I asked. "You were in pretty rough shape last night."

"Quite recovered," he said, smiling.

"We did pretty well back there," I said. "I have to admit, what you did to get Raven back, I'm really impressed."

"I'm impressed by the way you bargained with the incubus," he said and smiled at me. "But I'm concerned about the fact that he showed up in the first place. We thought these were not the type to summon demons and here it appeared this one was working for them. Or with them."

"Could you have gotten the incubus with the ritual by accident? Does he have to be connected to the people who held Raven?" I asked. "Meph says he must have been sent by the demon who is running that group. To make sure that you couldn't pull her through without being destroyed. I guess whoever it was didn't know you couldn't summon Raven yourself, and so they didn't think there would be anyone else around. It's a good thing that Satan insisted that we come, even though I didn't think we were needed."

He got up and went into another room, returning with a thick book. He sat close to me on the sofa, close enough that the distance should dissolve entirely. Why were we bothering with coffee and stilted conversation when all I wanted was to be lost in his eyes?

He balanced the book held between us. It was covered in ancient leather, dark and worn around the edges. Once it had been stamped with gold writing, but only a few flecks of the foil remained.

"It's a grimoire, a real one. I have to explain something to you. I had not told you everything before. Yes, I am an accountant, but I'm a forensic accountant and I work for Interpol, mostly investigating money laundering. I was on a team that was following a money trail and broke a child-trafficking ring. I got into the library before anyone else in the team, maybe because they figured that was the right place for the accountant." He smiled at this and shook his head. "Anyway, the library was full of ancient magical texts, things that anyone trained in ritual would have given years of soul to own. All there."

"You took them?"

He shrugged. "None of my colleagues would have understood their value. And—I understood not only what was in them, but why the ring had managed to escape for so long. In fact, I was able to use the notes and diaries to trace the criminals to where they had hidden."

"I thought you'd caught them?" I was intrigued in spite of myself. If he could track down international child traffickers he could probably find our kidnappers and whoever was stealing from Hell. Considered objectively, Marten was one very impressive guy.

"We found more," he said. "There are always more with that kind of evil. Does this matter to you?"

"Of course it matters," I said. Everything he did mattered. But on top of being a ritual magician he captured criminals—and here I thought the days of white knights were long gone. "But if tracking down missing money and disappearing money is what you do, then you're much more what Marduk needs than I ever thought. It's all just so . . ."

"Efficient," Marten finished the sentence. "Mephistopheles likes the way this plan is coming together. Now all I need to do is actually sit down with Marduk's records. Which should have been downloaded to my machine while we were otherwise occupied."

"You haven't looked at them yet?"

He shook his head. "There will be time when you are not here, in my living room. I want you to stay, Lily. I know you cannot, that you have a life in New York that you cannot leave. But I wish that you could."

I didn't want to leave. Marten was staying here and I was getting on a plane to New York and I had no idea of when I would see him again. I had to know that I wasn't losing him, that we would work out . . . something. I couldn't imagine my life without Marten. I kissed him and it was as if he had been waiting for me all along. He held me so hard that it felt he was holding me safe from all the hurt and harm strewn around us.

I was in love with two men. One was afraid of what I was and fell apart when he thought about it, and the other one lived thousands of miles away.

For a moment I thought about it. Then all my attention was on Marten's lips and hands, the smell of his hair, the warmth of his skin and the strength of the muscle underneath.

We took our time. All I could think of was how he tasted of pineapple and sunshine and French Roast, black. He kissed my hair and I ruffled his, reveling in the softness. So little about Marten was soft . . .

He picked me up as if I weighed nothing. I could feel

no strain in his arms as he carried me across the living room and down a short hallway to his bed. The sheets smelled of sunshine and clean, the Caribbean light penetrating the gauze curtains and the scent of tropical flowers wafting in from the garden encroaching on the wall. I reached up to unbutton his shirt, but he shook his head. "No, let me . . ."

And he kissed every inch of my exposed arms and shoulders before he lifted the green silk cami over my head. No second agenda intruded. He didn't care that I was a succubus, or that he was a magician or that we lived thousands of miles apart. I didn't care either.

I wanted to tell him that I understood, but as soon as I tried to talk he lay a finger over my lips. "Shhhh," he said, and kissed me again. "Poor Lily. Everyone sees you for what you can do for them, for your beauty, for your demon irresistibility. Shhhhh. I want to show you that I love you for you, because you are smart and brave and so loyal to your friends, and I admire that."

I wanted Marten. I didn't want him to be Nathan. I wanted him to be Marten, the magician, the accountant, the surfer dude, the kind of guy who lives in Paradise. I wanted him to be exactly who he was, and I was a little awed and a little thrilled that he loved me.

Marten loved me.

He had removed his clothes. I wanted to trace the hollows in his hips, the delicate molding that defined his developed chest and arms, the deep curve of the deltoid meeting the bicep, changing topography as he moved over the sheets. He made no attempt to hide himself and his arousal was almost painfully evident, but his whole attention was only for me.

"Marten, please," I pleaded. Me, who never asked,

who never had to ask. He smiled lazily and stroked my belly and licked my belly button, which made me squirm and beg even more noisily. My fingers tore into his honey hair, trying to push him down to pay attention where he ought, where I needed him. Every second was eternity, every eternity doubled my desire.

He was beautiful and I wanted him, I wanted him right now. I wanted his fingers and his mouth and his cock. I wanted everything all at once, so badly that I couldn't even ask any more. I could only writhe and pant and moan.

Finally his hand brushed between my legs, far too gently, and found me slick. When he touched me again he wasn't too gentle and I screamed with relief and mounting desire.

"Now," I ordered him. "I want you hard now, now, now!"

He knew how to obey as well as command. He gave me his body as he slid into me, a gift without any thought of return. I had never appreciated just how large he was; now I reveled in how completely he filled me. And then I started coming and didn't stop, didn't stop for how long, until I felt truly, thoroughly satisfied, his huge cock hammering faster and faster until there was only overwhelming pleasure with no respite.

Only as the waves of desire started to build again did I realize that he had kept up the rhythm and his face was red with effort. "You may come now," I said, delighted with the notion of giving him permission, more delighted that he had waited, had served me so completely and still held off his own satisfaction. And even that was mine.

Then he gave himself over to the demands of his body,

and mine, with a focused passion that reminded me that he had remained celibate since he had left New York. His orgasm held nothing back and I felt complete and powerful again, fully satisfied and fulfilled in his abandonment.

Afterward he cradled me in his arms and wouldn't let me go. His skin smelled of sunshine and sweat, clean and simple.

I could have stayed all afternoon and all night. I could have missed my flight, missed New York entirely, if Meph hadn't called just then. The jangle of Marten's mobile interrupted our reverie. I didn't hear what Meph had to say, but after he hung up Marten told me that Meph had reminded him that I only had a few hours until I left. And that we should remember that we still had to check in and pass security.

Maybe I should have taken a shower, but I wanted the smell of him on my skin. I wanted to think about these moments all the way back to New York, think about my wonderful island lover who was, now, truly my love.

My boyfriend, I thought. Only the word boyfriend seemed too small to cover what I felt.

"What are we going to do?" I asked softly after I had dressed. My hair was messy and I hadn't touched the makeup that must have been smeared during sex.

"Something," Marten said softly. "I will not let you go, Lily. I will not let you slip out of my life into New York and never see you again."

"Promise," I said as he pulled me in to his chest. "Promise that you'll see me soon, that you'll come to New York."

"Or you'll come back here," he added. "Or we can meet on another island, not so far for you. I often have to work in St. Maarten or St. Kitts or any one of a thousand places. But you will come down and I will see you, if you will promise me too."

"I promise," I said solemnly, and he kissed me to seal our bargain.

I got on the plane brokenhearted and elated at the same time. Marten loved me. Really truly loved me. I spent the entire flight home thinking about this new relationship. When we changed planes in Miami I pulled out my Treo and found that Marten had already sent me a text message. Just a quick "I love you" that made me warm and glowy all over.

It wasn't until I had made it back to my own apartment that I remembered that I hadn't seen any trace of Nathan at the airport.

chapter
TWENTY-NINE

The next morning at the office Danielle greeted me with a large latte and a lemon scone. "He's back. We don't know where he was, he isn't talking, but he's back."

I was so confused that I had to ask "Who?" Which he? Nathan? Marten?

"Lawrence, of course," she said as if I had lost my mind. "Lawrence came back yesterday and he's been locked in his office and we're expecting an explosion any minute now. And you. You look wonderful." She stepped back and regarded me critically.

"That outfit is new," she said after appraisal. "I don't recognize it. Who?"

"Derek Lam," I said proudly. She nodded with admiration. Lam is a young designer, very likely one of the next generation of greats, who has been getting a lot more than just buzz in New York fashion circles.

"The outfit is wonderful," she conceded. "But there's something else, I think. I think you are in love, Lily. I think you are happy! You must tell me all about him. This is not that beautiful boy from Yale, is it? I thought he broke your heart."

"He did," I admitted. "And he did it again. And I met a wonderful Dutch guy who is elegant and smart and treats me wonderfully well. And he reads our maga-zine."

Danielle nodded sagely. "A Frenchwoman can always tell," she pronounced. "I want to hear everything, all about him. Even if he is Dutch. Aren't they, well, bor-ing? Stodgy?"

I laughed. "No. Wait until I tell you about him . . ."

But she held up her hand. "I am anxious to hear every detail, but first we must think about Lawrence."

Lawrence. Right. I thought I'd taken care of him! But the incubus was supposed to come in three days. Which now meant tomorrow, I thought. I couldn't exactly tell Danielle, but I could certainly hint at something. And I had to find something that had been part of him to give the incubus to hunt him down.

"Danielle, did you bring that latte for me? Isn't it get-ting cold? Why don't you sit down while I tell you. Be-sides, I want that scone. I'm hungry. I forgot breakfast."

"You often forget breakfast," she agreed. "I think you do not keep any food in your apartment. One needs a good breakfast to think and function. Coffee alone is not enough."

We could have an argument about that, but I wasn't in the mood. My plans for Lawrence were too exciting, and in the press of changes over the past forty-eight hours I'd forgotten them. "I think I might have come up with a solution for Lawrence. I met someone who is in-terested. I am going to introduce them."

Danielle sighed and shook her head. "Anyone reason-able will not want to date Lawrence. You must dislike this person very much to introduce him. And there is no reason to believe that finding someone to date will make Lawrence less crazy."

I think I smirked. "Let's just see how this goes. I think this person I have in mind is even more evil than Lawrence. In fact, I think Lawrence will be out of his league here. So—are there any new shoes I need to know about?"

Of course there were shoes I needed to know about. Sandals from Christian Louboutin and Jimmy Choo, and the first hints of fall boots from Dior and Versace. After she left, having shown me several choice examples, I found three delivery boxes from D&G, Fendi and Coach full of wallets and headbands (very big this year) and belts.

The Coach wallets were especially engaging, bright summer colors that would be easy to find in a purse. Hmmmm, that was a good note for the Accessories page, especially now that purses had gotten so large.

And because I was engaged with an entirely different world the time passed quickly and pleasantly. So when the phone rang and Desi told me that it was after six and wasn't I going to meet them for drinks, I was shocked. I told her I'd be right over. No one had told me that we were getting together tonight. It was a good thing that Aruba wasn't a bad change of time zone.

It was so good to see my friends again. It had been only a few days, but so much had happened. "I already ordered the lavender martini for you," Desi said, pushing over a suspiciously pale drink. "It has blueberries and we thought you might need the antioxidants."

"So, we're dying to hear all about it," Sybil launched right in. "Did you get Raven? What happened with Nathan? Did you see Marten? Did you defeat the Burning Men?"

"Did you identify the Burning Men?" Eros asked.

"We got Raven," I said, and told them about the ritual and the incubus and siccing him on Lawrence. Panic hit for a moment, and then I reminded myself that there would have to be something around the office.

In fact, his white shirt shoot should be done and I needed to collect the belts. That would give me plenty of opportunity to pick up something unobtrusive. Even the belts that he had touched would do in a pinch, his aura would be all over them, but I would like something better than that.

"Earth to Lily," Desi said. "So you're talking to an incubus now and handing over prey? That's a change of policy, isn't it?"

"I never had a problem with the incubi," I said. "It was a political division over a thousand years old, and honestly I think it's stupid. I would way rather that we all worked together. One happy island, you know."

"Aruba is clearly getting to you," Eros observed. "So I suspect you'll be going back there. To visit someone?"

I shrugged. "Well, he might be coming up here too. After all, it is going to get warm at some point and there are things you can't do in Aruba."

"Like shop," Desi came in on cue. "He has to go somewhere to shop. The man does know how to dress."

"What about you?" I asked, immediately contrite. "What happened when I was away? Is Vincent okay?" The last I asked directly to Sybil. "What happened?"

Sybil blushed. She has that delicate peaches-and-cream complexion that shows every emotion and her embarrassment was a shade that a makeup artist would sell her soul to Satan to reproduce. "He talked to Nathan and Meph about what happened when he was kidnapped. He's okay; they didn't torture him at least.

And Nathan played him some voice recordings and he could identify several of the voices, so we know for sure that Steve Balducci was one of them. Vincent also thinks that this operation was intended to make us and Meph and Operations look incompetent."

"I thought they were trying to target Lily as one of Satan's Chosen," Eros said.

Sybil nodded emphatically. "They wanted Lily in particular because of her friendship with Meph. If Meph's friends in Hell aren't safe, then he appears weak and powerless."

"So they're sure that this is a move against Mephistopheles as Satan's second in command," Desi added.

Sybil nodded. "This plot is a lot more complex than we had thought. Someone is attacking Meph and his allies from several directions at once, and Satan doesn't know about it."

"That's been our work on the investigation while you've been running off to pretty boys in Paradise," Eros added, smiling indulgently. "I've pulled a few strings to get Security interested. We had Vincent describe everything he remembered about the kidnapping, and what we think is that it took a ceremonial magician with experience with demons to control him. I'm fairly certain that he was confined in a magic triangle and placed under obligation not to harm any of his captors. Did you ask that magician of yours anything else? You should. He's the only magician we know of who could do that."

"No," I protested. "Marten is on our side. He's been working with Meph for years. He wouldn't hurt us. Or me."

"But he might know who could," Desi suggested.

"There can't be all that many magicians in the world who can actually summon a demon with that power, so he may at least have heard a few names."

"Des, you're brilliant! Why didn't I think of that?" I jumped up to hug her and nearly spilled my blueberry drink.

"What happened to Nathan?" Sybil asked plaintively. "Didn't you go down with him? We thought that you two would get back together, that once he saw how you took care of your friends, how smart and hardworking and dedicated you were, he would change his mind."

Suddenly the world reeled around me. "You set this up to get me back with Nathan?" I couldn't believe it.

"Oh no," Eros exclaimed emphatically. "But it did occur to us when we thought about hiring a PI. He may be the only PI we know, but it's not like we couldn't use the phone book or get a recommendation off the Web."

"And even then," Desi jumped on Eros's words, "even then we didn't think of Nathan because we were trying to get you back together. At least I didn't. I just thought it would be easier because he already knew we were demons. I didn't want to have to explain that all to someone who might be skeptical, especially since it was an emergency."

That made sense. I really would not want to have to explain what had happened to someone else. Plots against Mephistopheles and Satan? Embezzling from the Treasury of Hell? Kidnapping?

No, the girls were right, we couldn't have hired anyone else.

So I told them what had happened in Aruba. How Nathan and I almost got back together and he lost it again and hurt me. Possibly more than the first time.

"Of course," Sybil said, patting my arm. "The first time it wasn't personal. He just couldn't handle all those revelations all at once. But to be so horrible and hurt you like that? I think he should die. Really, you should have delivered him," she pronounced.

"I couldn't," I admitted.

"Because you're still in love with him," Eros sighed. "He's a weak creep who used you and treated you badly. You should have handed him over to Martha. She could use him. He's pretty. He could be a houseboy. He doesn't deserve you, let alone you defending him like that."

"I couldn't deliver him," I said again. "He didn't come. That's the way it works. I have to get him to come before I can take his soul."

"Of course," Desi said softly. "I just wish you could have delivered him because of the way he treated you. That's all. I don't know how you manage with all those succubus rules. They would drive me crazy."

I smiled weakly. "You get used to it. Though the younger demons aren't choosing to be succubi and incubi the way they used to. They like the less structured specialties."

"The young have always been lazy," Eros said. And she was right. Of course, everybody else was lazy too.

"Speaking of the young, what would you say if I brought Raven to brunch?" I asked, suddenly remembering. "She's really presentable and smart. Her sense of style is awful, but I think we can teach her better. I think she'd fit in with us. She was great in Aruba. We started to teach her to bargain, but she hasn't gotten that far in her coursework."

That took some consideration. It's always special when it's just the four of us. Even when Martha joins us, which is always a special treat, the dynamics change. But I felt that Raven really fit with us. And once upon a time we had been three, before we'd invited Sybil into our circle.

"How about we meet her before?" Eros suggested. "You can all come over and we can make s'mores again. It's been ages and I'd like to use the fireplace again before the end of the season. We could do that Thursday night, hang out, eat chocolate, and meet Raven."

"Oh, that's even better! We won't have to worry about her silly clothes in public; it'll take a while to groom her to where she can go out to nice places. And it'll be more relaxed. Thank you!" Eros always comes up with the best plans.

When I got home there was a reminder e-mail from the incubus, who signed himself Roman. Though whether that was an actual name or where he was from eluded me. Anyway, I was pleased to see that he had figured out how to use Eudora.

Which was my only quiet evening at home for a while, given that we'd just made plans for Thursday. Still, I had promised and this was the three-day limit. I thought about where to meet him. I didn't really want an incubus in my apartment, but I didn't know where else I should suggest.

And then I smiled slowly. In the office, of course. Lawrence might be there and we could effect an actual introduction. I could say that Roman was a model—he certainly looked good enough.

Feeling very satisfied with the incubus, the plan, and the quiet of my own apartment, I treated myself to a long bubble bath and a dinner of Pad Thai delivered from the really great place three blocks away. And a pint of Ben & Jerry's. Chocolate Brownie or Chunky Monkey was the biggest decision I wanted to make, and I pondered it far longer than made sense even to me. And then I bought Phish Food.

After that indulgence, I slept excellently well and got up in the morning feeling refreshed and ready to go. Alert and energetic enough that I started to worry about the fact I hadn't made a delivery in a while. It had all been on Satan's business, of course, but still—I wouldn't be surprised if She were a little disappointed in me.

I needed to hunt. Boyfriends are all very well and good, but I was still a succubus and I needed to deliver a soul or three.

Funny, I'd never really thought that I liked hunting. I don't. I'd rather never have to. But there was something in the nature of my calling that made me feel somehow unfulfilled when I hadn't handed a soul over to Hell in too long. Maybe it was feeling beautiful or desired, and some of it was anger and revenge, too. I missed the hard, clean feeling of the kill, knowing that I'd eliminated one of the bad guys. Knowing that some prime jerk had been sent to his just reward, that he wouldn't harass or insult or offend another woman ever again. Even in the modern world some people deserve punishment. And I hand it out.

I didn't know if I'd have time to hunt after work. Possibly. I didn't think I had anything on the calendar, though really I could use a quiet evening in. Okay, a short one, then. Later.

I dressed for work quickly. D&G cuffed trousers with a tweed jacket, very restrained and conservative after yesterday's Derek Lam. I pulled my hair back severely and surveyed the effect. I looked as powerful as anyone five foot three could look, perfect for any executive boardroom.

First order of the day was finding something for the incubus, who was due in my office at four. I looked around and thought and I couldn't find anything that would do. I remembered about getting the belts back from Lawrence and then I thought of something else, something even better.

I marched down to the Starbucks on the ground floor and got both of us the special for the month, cinnamon dolce. It was hard not to polish it off on the way back upstairs. The cinnamon smell permeated the elevator and by the time I got out on the forty-third floor I was salivating. Wait, wait, I told myself, and went straight to Lawrence's office.

I knocked. "I'm busy! Don't bother me," he yelled. The door was ajar, so I nudged it gently open with my foot. "I got you one of those new cinnamon drinks," I announced loudly, giving him a minute just in case he had been doing something that I didn't want to walk in on. "I thought you might have some advice since I'm putting together the bags and jewelry for your Dazzling Dresses shoot."

"Oh, sure, come on in," he said.

White shirts and jeans had been thrown over his easy chair and piled on the floor. Wardrobe was going to be angry, but there wasn't much they could do except launder the pieces and send them back to the designers from whom they'd been borrowed. His worktable was cluttered with sketches and cuttings from sources I didn't recognize. A red paisley and something with brown and aqua had gotten mixed into the white shirts. I hoped the samples were colorfast.

I handed him his cinnamon dolce since there wasn't any place to put it on his desk, and started to drink mine. And oh, it was just as good as I had hoped, all cinnamon and caramel and apple with a nice jolt of coffee. Yum. I hoped it would soften him a little bit.

"So I had a few ideas," I said brightly.

He glowered, despite his coffee. "I don't need your ideas. If you can give me exactly what I need without disturbing me, that is all I want from you. The less I see of you secondary editors, the better. I don't know why we have to pretend that you have anything to offer besides support. Our magazine is about fashion. Not shoes or bags or makeup. Fashion."

"Oh," I said. "Well, I had this model booked as the escort for one of my shoots and I thought you might be able to use him."

"Why?" he asked, suspicious. "It isn't Chad, is it? He's a useless prima donna and pouts all the time. He won't do a decent job of showing off a woman. I don't want him."

"No, not Chad. I don't work with Chad." None of us worked with him after he threw a tantrum doing an ad series for Calvin Klein fragrances. "It's someone new but really good, I think. His name's Roman."

Lawrence rolled his eyes. "What a ridiculous made-up name. Nobody's named Roman."

I shrugged. "It's not the name you're hiring," I said. "Well, whatever. He's a big fan of yours and asked me to introduce him, so I'm asking. He's going to be in the office at four this afternoon. Do you want me to bring him by?"

Lawrence made a big show out of consulting his calendar. Enough of a show that I switched our Starbucks cups without his ever noticing. "Four, you said? Okay, bring him here at four fifteen. I should be finished with my three o'clock by then."

"Okay," I chirped, far too brightly. Then I picked up his cup as if it were my own and walked out.

When I got back to my own office I emptied the rest of the drink into my ceramic mug. The stuff was too tasty to waste. I set the cup on my windowsill next to the pachysandra, as if it were there to water the plant that threatened to take over the next three floors.

I actually managed to do productive work for the next six hours. Lunch came on the trolley and then it was four and there was a knock at the door.

Roman had arrived, looking exactly the way I remembered him. Yes, he could certainly pass as a model, except for the suspicious scowl on his face. Though the scowl might work for Calvin Klein and they'd just fired Chad . . .

I handed over the Starbucks cup. "He drank from that, there should still be residue," I said. "And, even better, I have an appointment to introduce you in fifteen minutes."

"Why are you doing this?" he asked. "We are not allies."

"Well, we should be," I said. "I am sick of this stupidity, succubi and incubi at odds with each other. The argument is over a thousand years old. Were you even in the ranks during the split?"

He shook his head. I had thought as much.

"Well, I was, and it was stupid. Honestly, I think Hell

lost and since I'm loyal to Satan I think She is better served by having us all cooperate."

"Are you saying that I'm not loyal? Or that the incubi are fomenting rebellion?"

Eeeeck, what era had he come from? And why hadn't Admin updated his vocabulary? If he couldn't pull off modern American, Lawrence was going to figure this out before Roman could destroy him. Because I didn't want Lawrence just delivered, I wanted him utterly and completely in thrall, beholden to Hell.

And subservient to me.

"I'm just saying that I think we'd do a better job working together. We're not the enemy, we're on the same side. And I'm here to prove it. This is a good lead, this guy belongs in the Legions of Hell, and you're going to get the credit. So come on, we've got ten minutes to get down the hall."

The look on Lawrence's face when I introduced Roman was even more satisfying than I had hoped. One look at the incubus and he was smitten. Totally, completely, utterly in major crush mode. And Roman played it to the hilt, too. I'd never seen a man (or male demon) flutter his eyelashes quite so coyly, smile with just that right degree of shy, project a perfect blend of desire and reticence—perfect for Lawrence, that was.

"Thank you, Lily, were you and Roman finished with your discussion? Because I wouldn't want to keep you from your work," Lawrence said, dripping false respect. "None of us could manage without Lily's brilliant recommendations," he said as an aside to Roman, as if I weren't there. I wanted to hit Lawrence on the head, or at least roll my eyes at the incubus, but I knew better.

"We were done," I said. "I'll see you later." And with that I left my colleague with a demon of Hell bent upon his destruction.

Revenge, as they say, is sweet. I was flying with the success of my plan. While I wanted Lawrence to get his, I also wanted to build a bridge with the incubi. We were more alike than different and we had more reason to band together than remain at odds. I hadn't been exaggerating; I really did think that we weren't doing Satan any good by pursuing this very old and very ridiculous split.

Feeling good and powerful, and brimming with love and loyalty to Satan, I decided to hunt. No waiting for clubs to open, no getting dressed up for the evening. Right here and now I decided that I would claim a soul for Hell. As a kind of thank-you to Satan for how well everything was working out.

chapter
THIRTY

I felt strong and good and—it was time to go hunting. I wouldn't get any credit for Lawrence's delivery and I was way behind in my usual schedule. But the idea of going to a club or something at the Met didn't appeal. Instead, I dressed in jeans and took a taxi to SoHo, where I wandered around the Prada store and Barneys and mostly thought about Marten.

I wondered what he was doing, if he was at his computer poring over columns of numbers from Marduk. Or whether he was trying to trace tax evaders for smuggling drugs.

But the Apple store was all lit up and it had been a while since I'd delivered a geek . . . hmmmm. Many geeks are fine and upright people, maybe a bit socially clueless but otherwise decent enough. A few though, some very few, assume that any woman who dresses decently and wears makeup must be a complete moron. I was wearing makeup. This was too easy.

I walked in to see the preview of the new iPhone. Mobbed by all manner of technosnobs, I found myself thinking more about the phone than about the prey around me. Music and everything my Treo did with the touch pad—I had to love it. I wondered whether I should get one for Marten, too.

I got into the line to preorder when one of the unappealing geeks used his oversized belly to cut in front of me. His beard was flecked with crumbs and his hair looked like it hadn't been washed in days. He wore a Linux tee shirt in a 3X at least and stared at me as if he couldn't believe I was real.

Okay, if he behaved better I might search elsewhere. I detest line jumpers, but there are worse offenses.

"You getting one of those for your boyfriend?" he asked, sealing his fate.

I smiled. "No, I don't have a boyfriend," I said, and looked away.

He shrugged. "It'll be easy to use, though. You want easy to use."

I looked into his face, widened my eyes, and took on a breathless expression. "You could explain to me how it works, couldn't you? Maybe when we get through this line? I would really like that. This one is so hard," I said, holding my Treo and flashing my manicure.

"Sure," he answered. "I can do that. At least you know enough to go with a decent product."

I wanted to strangle him, but I reminded myself that better was coming. So I endured the line, the coffee (where he talked my ear off explaining the basics of binary) and his absolute inability to understand why I was taking him home with me. To help me sync my Treo with my computer was the fiction and we both knew that was akin to inviting him up to see my nonexistent etchings.

At least he was fast once I got him upstairs. Probably hadn't had sex in years. He came and he went, like all the others. And much as I disliked the act, I felt relieved and moral, glad that I had done my duty to Satan.

Now that I didn't have to run around after magicians

and kidnapped demons I would have more time and energy to do my actual job.

I wasn't even too tired after cleaning up the ashes. I took a good shower, changed the sheets, and then wrapped a towel around my hair and snuggled into my big bathrobe and turned on my computer.

Sometimes it is a mistake to look at e-mail. Sometimes it isn't. I had a message from Marten, which turned out to be a lovely, caring inquiry about how I was doing back in New York and to let me know that he hoped to visit again soon. That made me smile, and with the smile still on my face I opened the next message in the queue. Which was from Mephistopheles and written as a formal summons. This was not my friend and quasi-uncle writing, this was the First Lieutenant of Hell, and he required my presence at a meeting with Marduk on Thursday night.

Thursday! That was the day I was taking Raven by to meet the girls. Pj's and s'mores and girlie drinks. Much as I adore Meph, I hadn't had a real girls' night in ages. I'd been missing it. For all I'd been doing with him, I hadn't had time for a single mani-pedi, sitting on the massage chair and gabbing while my feet got buffed and polished.

For a moment I considered just saying that I had a prior engagement. But the only prior engagement that carried any weight with Meph would be with Satan Herself. No way around it, I had to reschedule with my buds. I sent out the e-mails and told Raven particularly that we would go out on Saturday and get our nails done. I doubted that she had ever taken care of her nails and it would be a treat for her as well as an introduction to decent grooming. I had to send everyone an e-mail and try to reschedule with that sinking feeling that things weren't going to work. The only thing that saved me was knowing that they all knew that I had no choice. Hell is not a democracy. We're a top-down organization, and when the second in command requires your presence, you are present. The end.

But I hate hate hate having to bail on my friends.

Then, knowing there was no way out of it, I looked back at Meph's e-mail to see where the meeting was taking place. He could not make me leave New York again, not when I had just returned.

The meeting was not in New York. It was not on Earth at all. It was in Hell. Specifically, it was in the Treasury Conference Room.

The week flew by in a blur. All I could think about was the meeting. I wondered if Marten would be there, I wondered if he had found who was stealing from Satan, and I wondered what to wear. The latter was the easiest since that was entirely under my control. On Wednesday I got an e-mail from Marten saying that he was going to be at the meeting and would I like to have dinner with him afterward.

Which I found odd, but then I remembered that the meeting was in Hell. He could use Hell as an entrance and exit point to any place in the world. It wasn't easy and it took a whole lot more energy than to simply buy a plane ticket, but I figured that Meph would be spotting some of the energy. Which made this something of a subsidized trip.

I would have said yes even if he hadn't suggested Per Se, the hottest foodie mecca in the city. Only a little trendy, the place catered more to gourmets than the glitterati. Meph had blogged about them at least three times, raving over some exquisite dish or stunning preparation in each review. I was interested to try the place, though it wasn't as popular in my crowd. But then, I'm not a proper gourmet. I adore food, but I want more than just exquisite flavor. I want fun people and buzz and a parade of elegant outfits to liven up the atmosphere.

Still, I was impressed that Marten suggested it and I wanted to go. And I wanted to be with Marten, even if we were only going to Ray's Pizza. Truth to tell, I hadn't stopped thinking about him since I'd gotten to the airport in Aruba. If we could use magical transportation between destinations this might even be workable. I was so full of hope and anticipation that I couldn't concentrate on anything. I spent most of the day staring at the wall wondering what Marten would wear and where he was staying. My biggest decision was that it was truly time for him to come to my apartment. No more hotels—that was crazy. I even called my cleaning lady to see if she could fit in an extra visit before Thursday.

The next day I felt effervescent, fizzing with anticipation and dread. For all I wanted to see Marten I was worried about why Meph wanted me at the meeting. I was so distracted that I hadn't noticed that the office was unnaturally quiet on Thursday. I had holed up in my office going over proof sheets for the July Accessories page (totes and sun hats) and ignoring my phone. With the thick walls I was protected from the world and I wanted it that way, so if I happened to drift off into a daydream nobody would notice.

I didn't even notice Lawrence in the elevator when I got on after a coffee run. There I was trapped in an elevator with the scourge of the magazine, with two grande lattes and a cardboard tray full of pastry.

"Nice to see you, Lily. Isn't it a lovely day?"

The lattes did not fall at my feet, but it was a close call. "Uh, yes, Lawrence, it is. Did you have a nice weekend?"

His lip curled and he squinted strangely. "The best weekend in ages," he said, and suddenly I realized that the unfamiliar expression was an attempt at a smile. "I never did thank you for introducing me to Roman. And . . . thank you, Lily. We both thank you. And we were thinking of having you in to dinner sometime in the next few weeks. Roman loves to cook for company. He is so talented. He cooks, he reads, he has a classical education."

"I'm so glad you're both happy," I said, utterly astounded. I would have thought that Roman would have delivered him immediately and had done with it. Apparently not.

"Yes, thank you," Lawrence said again. "And, Lily, could I talk to you privately for a minute?"

I nodded and the elevator doors opened. "Your office?" I asked. I didn't want to return to mine with him. He nodded and I followed him down the hall.

His office was marginally more organized than when I had been in earlier with the Starbucks to collect a sample. He gestured to the sofa, which had been cleared of jeans, and we sat.

"Look, Lily, I'm terribly sorry about your office. More than I can say. I don't know if you'll accept this or not, but I wasn't truly myself then."

"Oh?" I was completely confused. This Lawrence talking to me seemed stable and sincere. This man was nothing like the raging psychodrama on legs I'd worked with for nearly two months.

He shook his head and smiled wryly. "I'll ask you to keep this quiet, please." He hesitated and stared at his hands before he drew a breath and continued. "Roman explained what you are, so I must believe that you won't find what I am going to say to be the product of an overwrought imagination. Though I myself still find it unbelievable, even when we confronted the situation and have mostly resolved it."

I was shocked into silence. "You know what I am?" I managed to squeak.

"I know about the Hellspawn, that you are a succubus and Roman is an incubus. I'm considering my own options for the future," he said, very matter-of-fact. "Most likely I'll want to ask your advice further later on. But I wanted you to know. And I did want to apologize. I have more to thank you for than you realize. You see, I knew I was behaving horribly. I never had such a temper in my life, but as soon as I started at Trend something came over me, as if I were under a compulsion. You cannot imagine what it was like, seeing myself behave like some bad stereotype. When those tempers came over me, it was like I was locked inside my own head watching as something completely alien came over me. It was Roman who unraveled it. It appears that I was under a geas, a magical attack of some sort. Which Roman broke in a ritual last weekend. I feel . . . like myself again. It's like waking up from a bad dream, where I was locked in my own body and saw what I was doing but was unable to get out."

I nodded. "Geases can be bad," I said softly. "But who did it, and why? Do you know?"

"I have some ideas," Lawrence said. "Roman said he would help me track it down, but he did say that it was done very well. And it is not entirely broken. There are still threads that linger. I was hoping you might help us.

He said the magic definitely had a British flavor, and he wondered if I were being used against someone or something in New York."

I thought for a few minutes. "That's possible. Although it seems rather odd if you don't have any connections to the magical world. You're not, by chance, a practicing ceremonialist or the member of one of the Magickal Orders?"

He grinned and rolled his eyes. "If you'd told me such a thing existed before I had this experience, I would have thought you were irrational at best. I wouldn't want to say what I would think at worst."

Seeing Lawrence like this, I got the feeling that I was actually seeing him for the first time. A bad geas is usually placed by a malevolent magician, although Hellspawn are capable of making this magic. I wondered whether it was tied in with the Burning Men and the Treasury and everything else that was going wrong. I knew the notion was ridiculous. Just because there were traitor demons and Burning Men did not necessarily follow that every act of magic in the Western world was linked to me. Lawrence had probably angered a magician, and it probably was anger since that was the emotion that he displayed when the geas took over.

"Yes, I'll help you," I agreed. I didn't expect there to be any connection to my own problems, but knowing the origin of Lawrence's geas would set my mind at ease. If nothing else, helping Roman might start a dialogue between incubi and succubi, something that was long overdue.

I thought it was possible that whatever had been done to Lawrence was part of this much larger pattern that I was somehow mixed up in. I couldn't see how it came together clearly; there was some heavy-duty ritual magic going on, not just among the Hellspawn but among the humans too. Between the magical trap that had caught Raven and Lawrence's geas, there had to be at least one top-drawer ritual magician out there who was not Marten. Was this person independent, or working directly for Meph's nemesis?

I wondered whether Marten would know who it might be. After all, there couldn't be all that many elite magicians running around the world. Like Satan's Companions, they probably all knew each other, or at least knew *of* each other. And I liked any plan that meant I had to talk to Marten.

Instead of going directly to my own office I knocked on Danielle's door. The second latte had been for her anyway. At her soft "Entrée" I entered her domain and set the Starbucks on her antique Art Deco desk. "Lily," she said, "you look like you have seen a ghost."

"I have. I ran into Lawrence on the elevator and he was, well, he was pleasant to me. He smiled."

Danielle nodded sagely. "I think he is in love. He has been civil to everyone, even the interns, all week. He has not had a single tantrum. He was whistling yesterday. And he has left the office before six every night."

"Why didn't I notice?" I asked, curious that she had been so aware while I hadn't paid any attention.

"Because you are also in love," she answered matter-of-factly. "You are in love with two men, I think, and you are too American to simply accept the fact."

I thought about it for a minute, but the whole notion made my head hurt. So I tried to drink my coffee instead, but it was too hot. "Do you have a bag that will go with these shoes?" she asked, and we started in on work.

By the time Danielle and I finished, it was time for me to go home and take a long shower before heading off to Hell. I tried on six different outfits before I was able to settle on something conservative enough for Marduk and sexy enough for Marten all in the same meeting. Thank Satan for Gwen Stefani, though she doesn't belong to us. Yet.

Going to Hell is not as easy as it sounds. I had to activate the mirror in the old fashioned way, starting with the sulfur incense and candles and charging it with a smear of ichor (being careful not to drip on the dress). Then I had to draw the sigils in the correct order accompanied by chants that, while not quite so silly as the ceremonial invocations, were certainly a little over the top for the twenty-first century.

The familiar scent of sulfur engulfed me and the sickly yellow haze blotted out everything else. Something lurched, shifted, and the haze glittered. My stomach coiled up in a knot and I wondered why, with so many geniuses in our Legion, there was not a better transportation system. At least I'd avoided the humiliating handbasket that lower demons had to use for their first fifty years (unless released by Satan or Meph).

The bilious cloud cleared and I was in a hallway in what I expected was the Treasury. An Oriental carpet ran down the hall, which was richly paneled and hung with portraits of Marduk, Meph, Beliel, Al Capone, Ken Lay and other notables of the Underworld most famed for their fiduciary contributions. Sybil belonged on this wall, only she preferred to recruit souls instead of managing assets.

A short, round demon with skin like an orange peel bowed before me. "If you please, Lady, I am sent to bring you to the conference room."

"Why didn't I transport there directly?" I was curious. I have rarely seen a hallway or waiting room in Hell. Satan's Chosen are admitted as first priority.

"I am sorry, Lady," the little demon sniveled. "All of our conference rooms and offices are no-transport zones, enforced by Security, so that no one can get into the Treasury. It is a precautionary measure. I hope you can understand and will not hold our department responsible for your discomfort."

I shrugged. "No discomfort, really. Lead on."

My guide sighed with relief that I would not torture him for making me walk all of fifteen feet down the hall and through an ornately carved walnut door. He remained on the outside, not being of sufficient rank to be admitted, while I sailed past.

The conference room looked more like a Victorian men's club than a meeting room for the Fortune 500. Overstuffed leather sofas with plump round arms faced each other, each with a low table for holding papers and drinks set discreetly angled to the sides. A silk Qom carpet in cream, gold, and red looked so soft that I longed to slip off my shoes and run my feet over knotwork fine enough for a dressmaker's fabric. But with Marduk already enthroned in an oversized wing chair and Mephistopheles in the corner studying a pile of printout, I remained primly shod. The Librarian in the flowing pale blue robes of the Akashic who sat at Marduk's left was not Azoked, which relieved me greatly. This Librarian was not a Bastform but a demon of the fey, frighteningly beautiful and androgynous, with a steady stare.

First I walked over and made obeisance to Marduk. Not the full prostration that a mortal would give a god, naturally, but a discernible curtsey and a murmur of greeting in our shared mother tongue. I didn't look at the Librarian, but from the corner of my eye I noted that he (or she?) appeared to be following.

"Lilith, first of the lilitu, I greet you and welcome you to our council," Marduk said formally. "Please be seated among us." Some people might consider this stiff and overly proper, but Marduk was, in fact, granting me rank in the meeting. I was not simply an observer and a friendly party, but a full participant and a representative of demons (lilitu merely being the Babylonian word for succubus). I took a corner of a couch. Immediately a report and a steaming cup of cinnamon latte appeared on my side table, the former bound in leather with a gilt title, the latter in Royal Doulton with a sterling four o'clock spoon.

When I picked up the report a matching Royal Doulton plate loaded with lemon scones, melty oversized chocolate chip cookies, a slice of tarte Tatin and a wedge of St. André cheese appeared. The chef was clearly following the new dictates of multiculturalism, or at least pan-European unity.

The report bore Marten's name and that was the only word on it I understood. I wished that Sybil were here; she would be able to explain the long columns of figures, income sources and streams, percentages of equities, and the breakdown of expenses. To me it looked like the pile of material I paid her to decipher so I didn't have to.

I was so distracted by trying to make out the gist of the report that I missed the near silent opening of the door and footfalls on the luxurious carpet. "Marduk,"

Marten said as he entered, and he bowed precisely in the Japanese manner. Marduk nodded and waved a hand, indicating me, but Marten sat alone directly across from the head of the Treasury. For the first time I really did believe that he was an accountant. He wore a plain gray suit with a dark blue shirt and pale blue tie. In the United States it would be cutting fashion, but for a European it was conservative banker drag at its dullest.

He looked amazingly cute as an accountant, too, as well as solid. I liked that. It was hard for me to pay attention to the meeting while thinking about the delicious privacy we would have as soon as this was over.

I tried to give Marten a subtle smile of support, but the door opened again and the fifth member of the council arrived. Beliel. Of all the demons of Hell, Beliel was one I had not expected to be here. He had never been involved in the dull details of finance and I wondered at his presence. As usual, he wore a variation of a hussar's uniform, all in black with a high collar and deep bronze braiding with pants so tight they looked painted on and knee boots polished so brightly they would do for ritual mirrors.

Tension flowed between Marduk and Beliel. Marduk would not rise, Beliel would not come forward and greet him. Neither would acknowledge the other first. In Hell they were equals, but Beliel had never been a god and this was Marduk's territory. Challenge shimmered in the air like a magical sigil ready to explode.

Mephistopheles turned around just then and took a seat. "Now that we're all here, we can begin," he said, taking the precedence of his rank over both the senior demons.

"It is generous of Beliel to honor us with his presence," Marduk said, "but I do not understand why he is involved in what is an internal matter of the Treasury."

Beliel sat and picked up his coffee cup, added cream, and drank before he spoke. "It is an internal matter that concerns Security. If there is some breach in the Treasury it is our proper province to investigate and aid in any measures to safeguard our Master's Treasury."

"Perhaps we should start with a quick overview of the findings," Mephistopheles interjected, reducing the tension. "I don't think that either Beliel or Lily has had a chance to go over the report. Marten, perhaps you could sum up briefly so that we're all up to speed here."

Marten cleared his throat and took a pair of narrow German glasses out of his breast pocket to read over the figures. "Gentlemen, Lily," he started, nodded at me, "the evidence is that there has been some very subtle embezzlement that has gone on for at least two years here. The figures are hidden in the operating expenses, but done very well. Someone who was not familiar with this form of deception would not notice it, so there is no fault to any of the Treasury clerks who were simply following their normal routines. It would take a forensic accountant to track down the trail here."

"So someone cooked the books," Beliel said. "Who?"

Marten shook his head. "There are a number of possible candidates," he said slowly. "I wouldn't want to implicate someone who is innocent because they had the opportunity and the knowledge to do this."

"That would include you, would it not?" Beliel asked, arching an eyebrow.

"No, that would not include me," Marten answered quietly. "I did not have access to the Treasury at all, let alone the accounting programs, until Mephistopheles called me in. And I would be too easy to trace in the Akashic, had I done so." Here he nodded to the Librarian, who stirred coffee with great deliberation.

"Is that true, Alwynd? Would you be able to trace that misuse if a mortal were involved?" Marduk attempted to redirect the questioning.

The Librarian drank the coffee and set down the cup before making a reply. "Indeed," he said, and the voice was distinctly male. "If any mortal creature with a soul were involved in the theft, it would be clearly indicated in the *Records*. I have searched thoroughly, through time as well as worlds, and there is no indication of any mortal involvement. I have set my seal to the statement appended to this report."

"I haven't seen the report," Beliel snapped. "What is your conclusion?"

The Librarian appeared pained. "As I just said, no mortal was involved. This embezzlement is entirely within the Hierarchy. My role was to search for any indication at all, not only of mortal guilt but of knowledge. If a souled entity even knew about the plot and thought of it at any time, that thought would be recorded in the *Akashic*. No such record exists."

"So it had to be a demon?" Marduk asked.

"Or an angel," Alwynd corrected him gently. "But more likely a demon."

"And some of us are both," Mephistopheles acknowledged dryly. Satan's lieutenant nodded graciously at Marten. "Please continue with your conclusions."

"The culprit was clearly part of a larger conspiracy," Marten resumed. "That is indicated both by the amounts and the time in which they were taken. This individual is adept at accounting, and has access to Treasury records."

"So it is someone in the Treasury," Beliel mused. "Possibly rather high up."

Marten shook his head. "Begging your indulgence, I believe not. Someone involved in this kind of deception does not want attention. This kind of ongoing siphoning of funds is best accomplished by a fairly low-level functionary infiltrated into an organization. Not invariably, of course, but that is the general pattern." His face was pale and I wondered if he were worried about rebuking a demon of Beliel's rank.

"So all we know is that someone with access is doing this?" Beliel sneered. "An inside job?"

Marten swallowed and his eyes were tense. "Yes. But if you note the report, I have all the dates of the transactions and where they occur in the books. So it will most likely be someone who was present on these dates."

"I see. Very helpful," Beliel sounded unimpressed.

"It is," Meph said softly. "We can narrow down the possibilities to a handful here and get to the bottom of this now."

Marduk said nothing. He sat like his statue in stone in the Temple of the Kings, his face was the same color gray.

"Finding the low-level clerk responsible will not give us the demon who gave the orders," Beliel announced. "It is still the responsibility of the Head of Department to rectify the situation and make restitution or answer for the wrongdoing."

"And I am in the process of rectifying the situation," Marduk announced.

But Beliel shook his head and raised a gloved hand.

"Too little too late. As the Head of Security, I arrest you for embezzlement."

Three oversized demons in gray and black uniforms with high collars and tight pants that showed off their powerful thighs marched into the conference room and surrounded Marduk. One grabbed the ancient god's hands, but Marduk shook them off and rose. "You have the wrong demon, Beliel," Marduk said. "But I will come quietly. For now." And he marched out, trailing the Security goons behind him as if they were an indifferent honor guard.

Which left Marten, Meph, and me. And the Librarian, who rose gracefully and bowed in Mephistopheles' direction. "If I can be of further assistance, do let me know," he said. "But I believe my presence here no longer serves any purpose, and work awaits."

"I have a question," I said. "About several mortals—Craig Branford and Steven Balducci, in particular, and a group called the Knight Defenders. Did you run across them while you were looking for information on the Treasury?"

The Librarian gave me a thoughtful look and steepled his fingers. "Interesting. Those names are not unfamiliar. I can't tell you offhand what the relationship is, but I can look into it further if you'd like."

"Thank you, but I believe one of your colleagues already has an assignment to do that. I just don't think she was looking for any connection with the Treasury. I'll let her know."

"If I can be of any other assistance?" the Librarian asked. "Otherwise I should return to my research."

Meph nodded and waved his hand, and the Librarian disappeared without even the scent of sulfur in the air.

*   *   *

"If they were human, I would suspect Beliel," Marten volunteered. "Setting Marduk up, ready to attack him immediately, instead of getting to the bottom of the problem."

"I think it is beyond suspicion," Mephistopheles said softly. "Beliel just showed his hand. He's obviously been setting up Marduk for years, angling for exactly this moment."

"But why would he challenge you?" I asked Meph.

"Maybe he doesn't plan to challenge Mephistopheles," Marten said softly. "Maybe he only wants to eliminate the competition at his own level. Marduk was his major rival. Baal-Beryth is the Master of Ritual and Pacts, but he isn't interested in the politics of Hell. He wouldn't care if he was ranked under Beliel so long as he retained control over all ritual matters. Everyone knows that Moloch isn't a real power, he's only accepted as a courtesy because Satan is so delighted with his airlines. So if Beliel can eliminate Marduk, he's in a position just under Mephistopheles."

"But he is anyway, so I don't see where he has anything to gain," I mused, not certain where things were going, but filled with icy terror. If Beliel was responsible for all our problems, then where would that leave Eros? How could I face her, let alone tell her what her friend? mentor? lover? had done.

"Marten, does my department have all the detailed information?" Mephistopheles interrupted my speculation.

"Of course."

Meph sighed slightly. "Then I will begin to run the analyses. I've got enough demon power to narrow the list in a few hours if we get on it immediately. And I need to get there before Beliel does. So—I hear the two of you have a reservation at Per Se? Please do blog it for me. I've been meaning to go there for ages but things are a little too volatile right now."

Somehow he went from being the second most powerful demon in Hell to an overworked CEO trying to save the company before the shareholders found out something bad and dumped stock. (Come to think of it, I must have been listening to Sybil if I could think of a metaphor like that.)

Then, with no effort at all, we were standing outside the restaurant. It was still chilly, though whether that was the weather or the situation was unclear. We walked in and our table was ready immediately. The food looked amazing, and if Marten hadn't suggested that we share everything I would have had an impossible time choosing. As it was, I had only a slightly impossible time before settling on the pompano.

I was just happy being in Marten's company again. I had missed him horribly since I'd left Aruba, and now being with him I was more aware than ever just how badly I'd fallen for the guy.

"So do you really think that Beliel is setting up Marduk?" I asked when the waiter disappeared, mostly to make conversation. "And why was I invited?"

"I expect that you were invited because Marduk likes you," Marten said. "He certainly didn't expect what happened there. I'm not sure he expected Beliel at all. But Lily, I did not invite you to dinner to discuss the politics of Hell.

"I want to talk about us."

I don't have much experience with relationships, but one thing I had learned from listening to my girlfriends

and reading *Trend* was that men do not initiate relationship talks. They do not like talking about their feelings,
and they especially do not discuss anything so early.
Especially a guy like Marten, who mainly picked up
tourists for quick flings that would end in four to seven
days when she got on her plane (or cruise ship) and disappeared. No, Marten was definitely what Sybil would
call commitment phobic.

"So I have thought about this since I watched your
plane leave," Marten said. "I know it's difficult and
there are issues we would have to work out, but if you
are willing I do not see them as insurmountable."

"No, they aren't," I agreed easily enough. He'd made
it clear that he was interested in a real relationship. That
thought made me feel warmer and happier than I would
have imagined. Not that I had any illusions that Marten
was real boyfriend material. He didn't do relationships
any more than I did.

Yes, of course I wanted to date Marten. Even if he did
live in Aruba and distance would be a difficulty. We had
airplanes. We had MagicMirror.

"So you are saying yes?" He looked happy and a little
dazed.

"Of course," I enthused.

Then he pulled out a jewelry box and I realized what
I might have missed. A box. A ring.

And then the words, "Lily, will you marry me?"

I almost fainted when he opened the box to reveal a
Cartier setting, a two-carat diamond set in a glittering
pavé band.

chapter
THIRTY-ONE

Marten was asking me to marry him. Which would mean becoming mortal. I was dazed, utterly shocked. This was the last thing I had expected.

Mortal. Me. If I were mortal Nathan would want me back. He would be the boyfriend I'd always wanted. If I married Marten. I could be the woman Nathan wanted if I married him, too, but he wasn't asking.

My head was swimming and I felt like I was going to choke. My stomach clenched although the entrées we had just been served looked gloriously enticing. I didn't know what to say, what to do. I wanted to talk to my girlfriends. Who else would understand?

"You know, if I marry you I could become mortal," I told him. "It's in my contract with Satan. I could reclaim my soul."

Marten went dead white. "I love you as you are, Lily. I do not wish you to change."

My food was cooling in front of me, but I couldn't force myself to take even a forkful. Meph was going to be very disappointed.

"You want me as a succubus?" I asked, incredulous. "That means I'm going to keep having sex with a lot of men. And I won't age or be able to have children." From what Sybil had told me, these were all things that would upset a mortal man. Well, maybe not the never aging thing.

But Marten shook his head. "I am not interested in monogamy, Lily. Perhaps I have not made this clear. I do not plan to be monogamous and I do not expect you to be either. These are some of the things that we would need to work out. Also, my own life span is much longer than mortal now and I have very little soul left. If you were to become mortal, I would lose you in sixty or seventy years perhaps? And I have at least six hundred on my current contracts.

"Unless I reclaim my soul, I have a long time left as a magician, and after that I will become a demon. A very highly placed demon, I might add, worthy of one of Satan's Chosen. Already I am the right hand of Mephistopheles, and I intend to stay there. I propose a marriage of powers of Hell, not a union between simple mortals. Not a little house and children and vacations to the beach. I am talking about something much more."

"And much less," I said, disappointed to the bottom of the soul I had bargained away.

"No, not less," Marten said. He reached across the table and touched my hand. I wanted to pull away, angry that he wanted me only as a demon accomplice. But he held my fingers and stroked my wrist. "I love you. I love who you are, Lilith the succubus, the magazine editor, the New Yorker. I would not ask you to be any less or different than you are. And I would not wish to be any different than I am. But I do want you always, in my life."

It was too much, too soon, and yet I couldn't say no. The thought of that was devastating, far more than I would have imagined.

But what to do? What to say? Sybil would say to marry him and sort it out later. Come to think of it, Desi might say the same. Eros would point out that he was not only amazing in bed, but wasn't about to limit my other lovers. They would all tell me to say yes.

I hadn't touched a bite of my dinner. The waiter came, cleared the plates and brought something delicate and chocolaty for dessert. I was entirely unable to eat.

"I want to say yes," I started carefully. "I've been falling in love with you, but this is a little overwhelming. I mean, marriage? We've only known each other for six weeks and I didn't even know that you weren't interested in a more traditional marriage. I think we need to get to know each other a little better before we make this commitment."

"Then say yes," he said. "It can be provisional. You are right, we have not known each other long, and there are other issues as well. Like the fact that you are not about to leave New York and I must stay in Aruba, at least for the current time. And honestly, I like Aruba and my life there and I have no desire to leave Paradise. We will have to make some decisions. I have no interest in traditional marriage in any case; as I said, I have no interest in monogamy. Or children. But, Lily, I have never met a woman before that I have wanted to be with for more than a month or so. I have never felt the way I feel about you. And I want to know that you will be there to try to work things out between us."

This was not possible, and yet it was happening. The words were out of my mouth before I could think about them. "Yes, then. Provisionally. With negotiations to follow. But I certainly commit to the negotiation process. Yes!"

I felt giddy and scared and suddenly there was champagne, which I barely tasted as I gulped it. Although I'd hardly touched a bite of the food, I was not even the tiniest bit tipsy.

Marten slipped the diamond on my finger. How had he known I wore a size four ring? It sparkled so brilliantly that I could barely tear my eyes away. Our waiter and his two assistants brought over a serving of truffles with Congratulations written in caramel sauce across the plate. I heard faint applause and suddenly realized that the other diners had become aware of what was going on.

I was—engaged. Oh my goodness, I was engaged to be married, with a big fat diamond on my left hand. I was so overwhelmed that I was numb. And I really wanted to talk to my girlfriends and know that they thought I hadn't done something completely idiotic.

I didn't get to see the girls until brunch. I wanted to call Sybil and tell her about Beliel, but I was terrified to. What would happen with Eros? How could we tell her? And Beliel was smart and careful—I was certain he hadn't left any traces of his involvement with the Burning Men or the kidnapping. If he had been behind it. I really didn't have any proof. The fact that Beliel had arrested Marduk did not make him immediately responsible for the other events, which Eros would point out to me immediately.

I didn't have any hard evidence but the coincidences were overwhelming. I felt like a Ping-Pong ball, going back and forth between my terror and confusion about Beliel and Meph and my terror and elation about my engagement. My provisional engagement, that is.

Danielle noticed the ring as soon as I stepped off the elevator on Friday. She dragged me into her office, wanting all the details, and wouldn't even let me drink my coffee while it was still hot.

"But this is perfection, Lily," she announced when I finally paused for a sip. "He does not require you to be exclusive, so you might continue to hope for Nathan as well. Although Nathan does not seem the type to be amenable to such a civilized agreement. You will have to see."

I shrugged. "Nathan and I aren't dating. That was his choice."

I felt oddly distant from Nathan, as if he had been someone I'd known in a dream. If I thought too much I would probably become upset, but here on my hand was the proof that Marten (sophisticated, smart, hunky Marten) loved me. Yeah, we had a lot to work out, but that wasn't the issue just yet. Right now it was enough to know that someone loved me enough to ask.

After three thousand years, I wasn't quite sure I believed it, that I wouldn't wake up and discover that I'd dreamed the dinner at Per Se.

Maybe I'd dreamed the meeting, too.

I didn't get much work done. Every time I tried to pay attention to the needs of a future article, the sparkle on my hand distracted me. It was beautiful.

On Saturday morning I called Sybil. Thinking about Beliel and wondering whether he was actually responsible for the attacks had kept me up all the night before and I had to talk to one of my friends.

"Vincent is here," Sybil said. "I was taking him to Barneys. But if it's urgent we can meet for lunch at 212."

212 was a nice Art Deco place in the East Sixties, very convenient to her destination.

"Can we be private?" I asked. "I mean, I know you have a date so I shouldn't ask, but this is Hell politics and—"

"Of course," Sybil agreed. "Shall we say one?"

At one o'clock I was waiting at one of the small tables while Sybil gave Vincent a peck on the cheek before she rushed inside. The brunch menu was not as varied as Public's, though the bar boasted one of the best vodka collections in New York. But when I saw the salad with caramelized pear, fennel, and pistachios I didn't care what else was available. I was so wound up I wasn't sure I would be able to eat at all. Dinner last night had been a couple of crackers and a few indifferent spoonfuls of ice cream.

"Oh my goodness," Sybil exclaimed before I could say anything. She picked up my hand, admired my ring, and hugged me across the table. "Why aren't the others here? This is the best news! Or did you want to talk to me because I've been married before? And—you're going to think I'm crazy, Lily, but, umm, which one is it?"

I shook my head. "Marten, Syb, and we're still provisional. And that's not why I wanted to talk to you. It's about something else. About Beliel."

Sybil sat back down in her seat and placed her napkin on her lap. "Beliel? Wouldn't Eros be the person to talk to about him?"

I shook my head sadly as our drinks arrived, vodka and cranberry for me and something lavender-infused for Sybil. I took several sips, hoping the alcohol would steady me. "I was at a meeting with Meph and Marduk on Thursday," I started. "And Beliel was there—and, Sybil,

he had Marduk arrested. Because someone has been embezzling from the Treasury. But there's no evidence at all
that Marduk is responsible."

Sybil shook her head. "He's the head of the department, so in the end he *is* responsible," she said softly.

"I know," I agreed. The drink made this only marginally easier. "But arresting him is not the right tactic, not
if you really want to get to the demon who is doing it. It
looked to me like Beliel jumped a little too eagerly to
blame Marduk. Meph thinks he might be the one who is
orchestrating things, so that he can set up Marduk. So
we're pawns in his power grab, is what it looks like."

Sybil finished her drink and called for another. Our
food arrived, and she tasted her Eggs Norwegian with
smoked salmon and hollandaise before she answered. "I
think now you're the one jumping the gun," she said
after she swallowed. "Beliel is Eros's friend, and she may
know more. But if you want my advice, you should trust
Eros before you trust any of the men. If Eros says that
Beliel is clean, you should listen to her."

I nodded because I couldn't trust myself to speak.
Sybil's advice was politic, but she hadn't been there. She
hadn't seen Beliel arrest Marduk, she hadn't seen Marduk's terror when he admitted that he knew there was
money missing. I was sure I was right, and Meph and
Marten agreed with me. But Sybil was right about one
thing. I couldn't confront Eros about Beliel yet.

Sunday I stood outside Public and paced while I
waited for my friends to arrive. I struggled with the decision of whether to tell them all about Beliel and confront them, or try to find more compelling evidence. I
remembered that I had blown things with Nathan by

speaking too soon. I'm not good at keeping silent, especially where my friends are concerned, but as I stood outside in the last chill of March I decided that this time I would wait.

Eros arrived and lifted an eyebrow at seeing me there before her. "Let's get our name on the list," she said as soon as she saw me. "If you are already here, the others will come before we can be seated."

She sailed past me up to the hostess desk and lied breezily that our party was all here and ready. Whereupon the hostess armed herself with four menus and said that she could seat us immediately. Eros was so stunned that she couldn't speak or move. I think I gasped. Public is one of the most popular brunch places on the island of Manhattan. As I struggled for something to say, Desi and Sybil came through the door. Eros waved them over and we followed the hostess to a table near the back.

"This is a miracle," Desi said as we got settled and draped coats over the back of our chairs.

I waited until everyone was seated before I pulled off my gloves. "I have an announcement," I said, but I'm not sure if the girls even heard me. Their eyes were riveted to my left hand.

"She's engaged," Sybil squealed as if she hadn't known for a whole day already, and then she rushed around the table to throw her arms around me and kiss me on the cheek. "Oh, you'll have to let me help with the wedding planning. When is it going to be?"

"Which one?" Eros asked, studying me. "Nathan or Marten? And what will you do about the other one?"

The waiter arrived then and we ordered, food and mimosas because we had to have something bubbly to toast my engagement.

"It's only a provisional engagement," I said. "I really need to talk to you about it, too. I mean, I think I want to marry him but there are complications."

"Which one?" Desi echoed Eros's question.

"Marten," I said. "Nathan and I are not dating. Really truly we are not. We almost got back together in Aruba but in the end it was worse than when we arrived. And, I need your advice. Because Marten doesn't want to be monogamous. He hasn't said more than that about it, so I don't really quite know what he means."

"Are you leaving New York?" Sybil asked, her face white.

I shook my head. "That's another thing to work out. I'm not leaving New York. And I don't think he's leaving Aruba, either. So there's a lot to discuss and I'm not sure if it will work out. Which is why I'm not sure if it's real enough, if I should think of myself as truly engaged. Or if it's just the beginning of questions that won't ever get answered. What do you think? Should I have done it? Should I back off?"

"Do you want to marry him?" Desi asked slowly.

I thought about it for a moment. Frankly, I thought about it longer than I had when I'd accepted him on Thursday night. "I think so. I don't want to leave New York, though, and he knows that."

"I would be desolated if you left New York," Desi said.

"How do you feel about not being monogamous? Didn't that make you upset, that he isn't going to stop sleeping with other women?" Trust Sybil to ask the most naïve question.

"Can you be engaged and not be monogamous and

not live in the same place? Does that count? Is that what I've been waiting for all these years?"

Sybil shook her head. "You should hold out for someone who is willing to give up everyone else for you, who is willing to do whatever it takes to be with you."

Eros shook her head. "Monogamy hurts more relationships than it helps. Why shouldn't Lily have as many lovers as she chooses and continue to hunt? Nathan is a hidebound idiot who isn't willing to give up his stupid ideas of the universe. Face it, Lily, he's not worth your time or your bother. While this one, this one is almost one of us. He won't limit you, he'll complement you. And isn't that the whole idea of marriage? I think this is perfect!"

"You have never been married," Sybil said.

Eros arched an eyebrow. "I've never wanted to get married," she replied. "Domesticity is not exactly high on my list of desires. And I'd get bored with the same sex partner after a few weeks, even if I could have whomever else I wanted as well. Don't you ever get tired of sleeping with the same person all the time?"

"Not if I love him," Sybil replied. "I never got tired of sex with my husbands, and I was always faithful to them, too."

"Were they always faithful to you?" Eros asked.

"I don't know," Sybil said airily. "I was always too wise to ask."

The waiter arrived with plates of stuffed French toast, pancakes, omelets, bacon and sausage, and waffles loaded with strawberries and whipped cream. I was grateful that the food distracted everyone. I felt torn—completely wrapped up in the discussion of my engagement—but also aware that I was holding out vital information from my best buds. Every time I looked at Eros I wondered if she had any idea what Beliel had done to Meph, to Hell, and to us.

The waiter came back with our mimosas and I ordered a second round as soon as the first hit the table. Even if no one else wanted them, I was going to need the drinks. I needed my girlfriends, not only to support me but to counsel me and reassure me that I was really doing the best thing. And to keep me focused on the engagement so I didn't have to consider the problem of Beliel and Marduk, and Mephistopheles.

"Okay, so what do you think I should do?" I asked.

"Do you love him?" Desi asked. "Do you want to marry him?"

"I am in love with him. I don't know about the marriage part because that has to do with what you think about marriage. And it's changed a lot since I was a girl. For a long time I thought I wanted to get married to get out of the succubus business, but that's a bad reason to get married, isn't it?"

"That would be a horrible reason to get married," Sybil agreed with me. "Is that why you're doing it?"

"Well, the strange thing is, he wants me to stay a succubus," I admitted.

For the first time I can remember, well, at least in this decade, all of my girlfriends were stark silent.

"He wants you to do what?" Desi said incredulously.

"He wants me to stay a succubus. He's a ceremonial magician," I explained. "And he's already sold most of his soul to Hell, so he's got something like six hundred years on his contracts to live as a human. After that he'll be a demon. He said he doesn't want me to become mortal and die, he wants me immortal."

"That's so romantic," Desi sighed.

I drank some of my mimosa and considered. Desi could be right, it could certainly be romantic. And there wasn't anything wrong with him wanting me to live forever. "The thing that I don't know is whether he wants me for me, or if he wants me to stay a demon because he wants to marry one of Satan's Chosen. You have to admit, that does have its appeal."

"Especially to a ceremonial magician," Eros completed the thought. Trust Eros to see the nasty possibilities. (So why was she so blind to Beliel's bad side?)

"But you already said yes, didn't you?" Sybil asked.

I nodded since my mouth was full of banana stuffed French toast. Somehow eating crisp French toast soaked in maple syrup made the whole situation a little more bearable. Anything is easier to face when polishing off a plate of luxury brunch food and a third mimosa.

"So it's done," Sybil said. "You've agreed. You're wearing the ring. So now is not the time to be second-guessing his motives." She shot me a look that said her last statement covered the other problem besides my possible marriage.

I shook my head and swallowed hard. "We're just provisionally engaged," I argued. "It wasn't an absolute yes, it was a maybe yes. But if I'd said no, that would have been the end of any possibility and I don't want that. What would you have done?"

"I would have said yes," Desi announced. "Marten is dreamy and I think it's sweet that he wants you the way you are. Not like Nathan who wants you to be someone you're not. My next move is to plan your engagement party. I'm thinking of tea at Lady Mendel's. How does that sound?"

chapter
THIRTY-TWO

And Desi did plan the engagement party. I said no to Lady Mendel's, so she had it in her apartment with the best of Hell in attendance. I bought a very edgy Gwen Stefani dress and boots. The party was at the end of April because Marten couldn't get back into town before then, and he was more pleased than I was that Des was giving a party and that Meph and Beliel and Hatuman and Martha Herself had all RSVP'd in the affirmative.

I hadn't wanted to invite Beliel, but Meph insisted. "Positioning," he said curtly when I insisted I didn't want the Head of Security there. "Besides, if you exclude him he'll know we're on to him, and we have to avoid that."

Of course Marten was pleased with the guest list. Even if we broke up in the next week, he would have been personally introduced to Satan. Mephistopheles had already taken an interest in him, and would now take more. But strangely, when I talked to Marten (on Skype, so totally love Skype), I honestly believed that he was excited about the acknowledgment and not scheming for his own advancement.

When I was around my friends I was the Bride-to-Be. My friends all fussed over me. The morning of the party,

Sybil took me to Bliss for the Works—a hot-stone massage, oxygen facial, and mani-pedi before we hit Matsu for lunch. Marten had come in the night before and we had had an, ummmm, lovely evening. I think that's what you call loads of hot sex with your fiancé. I didn't know what he was doing this morning, but Sybil assured me that Meph and Vincent had some plans that might have involved some kind of male-bonding sports event.

"Really, it's going to be wonderful." Sybil sighed as she inspected my new dress and shoes. "I wish I could wear this. And I'm hoping that a demon engagement will give Vincent some ideas."

I was so appalled I nearly dropped my piece of California roll. "You haven't been dating all that long," I reminded her.

She shrugged. "You have been dating Marten for less," she observed. "Anyway, it's too early for Vincent to think about anything, and I wouldn't consider him until he passed his Level Six exams. Which he is likely to in a year at this rate. And with Meph behind him, you know he's doing well. So—I would like him to have the idea planted for when the time is right."

She dropped me back at my place, which seemed strangely quiet with Marten out with the guys and his luggage in my bedroom. I read MagicMirror, where my party was definitely The Event of the week. Demons chatted about what they were going to wear and how much they envied The Happy Couple. That would be us.

I should be happier about this, I thought. I was finally getting married. I didn't have to give anything up. I loved Marten and he wasn't even asking me to give up other guys. It was time to get dressed and I dutifully poured myself into the shower. If everything was so wonderful, why was I so confused?

The new dress hugged my curves and played up my tiny waist and mass of hair. Marten showed up after I had finished dressing and stood quietly, inspecting me. Then he shook his head. "You will forgive me if I say I am sorry we have to go to this party," he said. "Because really, I would like nothing better than to tear that dress off and for us to spend the evening here in your bed."

He sounded so sincere that I was ready to agree to his suggestion. More hot sex with Marten would take my mind off Beliel and Marduk, and if we missed our own party, well, we'd be the porn stars of the century in Hell. And Hell has a good selection of porn stars. So I smiled and told him that I would love to stay in with him, but Desi would kill me if we didn't show up on time and adequately dressed.

Desi's apartment is done in shades of tan and chocolate and cream with a few touches of turquoise silk. The sofas are leather and clubby, the love seat is silk and ladylike, and she'd hung two Mary Cassatt portraits, an Edward Hopper lighthouse, and a single stunning Modigliani that dominated the space. It was elegant and expensive, understated and tasteful without being bland. A traditional Murano chandelier in turquoise and gold hung over the dining table where the caterers had laid out chafing dishes full of rijsttafel in honor of Marten's Dutch heritage, lamb in pomegranate sauce, and spicy Moroccan eggplant in honor of mine. A man in full whites with a toque stood at a carving station armed with a giant fork and larger knife to deliver slices of roast beef, lamb or pork roast, or all three, to a guest's gold-ringed plate. Other servers circulated discreetly with trays of scallops and shrimp wrapped in bacon and asparagus wrapped in mustard-flavored pastry.

Meph and Moloch stood together near a window that overlooked Lexington Avenue and sipped what appeared to be martinis while Beliel looked daggers at them from the dining room door. Martha sat enthroned on a club chair surrounded by sycophants, her elegance unruffled by their presence. Among them were Lawrence Carroll and Roman. I thought it was brilliant of Desi to invite them and even better for them to accept. And Lawrence was every inch the sophisticated gentleman. Not a trace of drama queen remained.

Desi stood up and clinked a knife against her glass. "I think everyone's here," she said loudly. Her words slurred just the tiniest bit and I wondered how many cosmos she had managed to consume while supervising the kitchen staff. "So I want to take this moment to say that I've known Lily for six hundred years, and I'm glad that a magician like Marten had the good sense to appreciate what an amazing woman she is. And I hope they have the very best marriage in Hell."

I raised my glass to her. "And with friends like all of you, I don't see how we can have anything but," I said loudly to enthusiastic applause. Lawrence actually beamed at me and squeezed Roman's hand. Danielle came up on the arm of a gentleman who looked like he was barely out of high school and congratulated both of us soundly, including kissing Marten at least four times. Eros slid over to Beliel, who still glowered in the doorway, but projected less hostility when the demigoddess brought him a fresh drink.

And me, I enjoyed the party. Marten attended me but

didn't hover and Meph told me that he approved. He wouldn't let me marry just anyone, but he thought Marten would do right by me and asked if he could give me away at the wedding.

I don't really believe in the whole custom of giving away the bride so I told him that I would rather have him officiate, which made him look pleased.

I had been paying so much attention to Meph that I hadn't noticed someone else come in. I went over to rejoin Marten to find him talking to—Nathan Coleman.

Why had Desi invited him?

My stomach lurched at the sight of him. I still wanted him at the same time I was still furious at him for the way he treated me in Aruba. "Hello, Nathan," I said, and kept my tone cold enough to freeze oxygen. I did not hold out my hand.

"Lily, I wanted to congratulate you and Marten," Nathan said, and he looked miserable. "He's a great guy, I know you'll be happy." He sounded as if he were reading the notice of his own execution. And I was angry enough that I wanted him miserable. The satisfaction of his despair was not enough to make up for mine.

"So you two seem to be thick as thieves," I said, trying very hard to sound perky.

"Marten was explaining nonmonogamy to me," Nathan admitted. "And about immortal marriage in Hell."

"I could have become mortal," I reminded him. "Satan has granted me the option of leaving Hell and regaining my soul, if a man falls in love with me enough to marry me."

"But you're not?" Nathan asked.

Marten came up with a fresh drink for me and answered him. "I did not want my wife to die," he said simply. "I plan on a very long immortality myself and wish only for Lily to share it for always, not for the few decades humans have."

"Well," Nathan said, looking uncomfortable. "I wish you both the best. I just wanted to stop by and congratulate you." He gave me a look of such despair that I almost felt vindicated. Then he shook Marten's hand and left.

I hoped I never saw him again.

Afterword

Spring had finally, actually arrived in the city. Pale green haze dusted the branches of the trees in Central Park, the winter coats and boots had given way to strappy sandals and jackets, and a few brave pretzel vendors were advertising Italian ices from their carts. Spring, and who would have guessed just a month ago that I would be engaged, with a big sparkly diamond on my left hand and a demon-in-training trailing after me through the SoHo shops.

Raven had practically cleaned out Betsey Johnson. I was thrilled she had chosen to wear the plaid skirt and short sweater jacket that had been the more conservative choices in her four-figure splurge. She looked perfectly respectable, not quite Junior League but not Needle Park anymore either.

"Done? Ready for something to eat?" I asked as we divided the parcels between us. The shopping trip was over for the moment because we couldn't have carried another bag. I would have had it all delivered, but Raven insisted on taking them all with us.

"Okay," Raven agreed almost cheerfully. "I know this place—"

"No," I immediately broke in. "We're going to Balthazar. It's right around the corner. They have fennel ravioli to die for."

"I've never had fennel ravioli. Sounds good," my new little protégée chirped agreeably. Ever since I'd taken her out of Barneys to the Steve Madden shop she'd been almost frighteningly cheerful. Maybe we'd spoken too soon when we considered her future specialty in despair.

We entered the bistro and I spotted our table right away. Tucked into a private corner with red leather banquettes on two sides, Martha and Eros and Desi sat studying the menu. Satan was totally Martha today, taking a break for lunch with the ladies, all for Herself, and I was glad that She could manage a breather.

"I approve of the outfit," the Prince of Hell said graciously to her newest minion.

Raven blushed and looked at her new Steve Madden pumps. "It was really nice of you to have Lily take me shopping. Thank you," she said. Who would have thought that belligerent punk girl had manners hidden under her bad makeup and cheap jeans?

Martha beamed at the girl. "Our pleasure. Only your very first taste of vanity, I suppose, but it's always best to start slowly. Vanity is such a lovely sin."

"Well, it's so popular right now," Desi piped up.

"Just because a sin is popular doesn't mean it's not great. I mean, it's not like gluttony or something," Eros said. Martha smiled indulgently and shook Her head.

And then Sybil returned from the ladies' and we ordered. Martha insisted on a magnum of champagne and toasted my engagement yet again. "Such a fine magician," She said, nodding in approval. "I am so very glad that you're with someone who appreciates your best qualities." Her voice was silken, but I understood what she meant. She had not wanted to part with me, and was glad that my possible marriage would not invoke my get-out-of-Hell clause.

Raven was the center of attention and so I was free to look at Eros and wonder about her relationship with Beliel. This wasn't over, I thought glumly. It was only beginning. I was going to have to find some evidence to prove to Eros that she had to break with Beliel, that he was the author of all our troubles. But this afternoon was about Raven.

"I'm just really honored that you're all here in person," Raven sighed, even though she'd been introduced to everyone. "I mean, here I am with Satan's Chosen. With Herself present. I'm just—wow."

We were going to have to work on her vocabulary.

Martha smiled benevolently. "Well, dears, there is nothing so pleasant as the company of girlfriends. No one else is as dear to Me. And so, if you all agree, I think we can add one more to our company."

Sybil smiled and Desi patted Raven's hand.

And Martha handed Raven a small box in glossy Tiffany blue. Raven gasped.

"Well, open it," Eros told her.

And there, nestled in cotton, was a tiny gold trident pin. The same trident that made up the jeweled pendants Sybil and Eros and Desi and I wore, that all of Satan's Chosen were permitted to display as the mark of Her favor. Not the necklace of one of the Chosen, not yet, but it did identify her as a demon who Satan had personally acknowledged.

"I . . . wow . . . thank you. Wow," Raven stammered. Well, I could understand her loss for words. Demons had schemed for millennia for that token of appreciation, and here she was not yet a year dead and presented with her own trident.

"Well, what are you waiting for? Put it on," Eros directed her.

But Raven was overwhelmed, so Desi did the honors.

"And remember, no one is more important than your girlfriends. Ever," Satan said.

Raven's eyes shone as she looked at each of us. "Yeah," she breathed. "Girlfriends are the best."